HEROES OF OLYMPUS

THE MARK OF ATHENA

RICK RIORDAN

PUFFIN

PUFFIN BOOKS

UK | USA | Canada | Ireland | Australia
India | New Zealand | South Africa

Puffin Books is part of the Penguin Random House group of companies
whose addresses can be found at global.penguinrandomhouse.com.

www.penguin.co.uk   www.puffin.co.uk   www.ladybird.co.uk

First published in the USA by Disney·Hyperion Books, an imprint of Disney Book Group, 2012
Published simultaneously in Great Britain in Puffin Books 2012
This edition published 2017
001

Printed in Great Britain by Clays Ltd, St Ives plc
A CIP catalogue record for this book is available from the British Library

ISBN: 978-0-241-33554-3

All correspondence to:
Puffin Books, Penguin Random House Children's
80 Strand, London WC2R 0RL

To Speedy –
strays and wanderers are often sent by the gods

ANNABETH

UNTIL SHE MET THE EXPLODING STATUE, Annabeth thought she was prepared for anything.

She'd paced the deck of their flying warship, the *Argo II*, checking and double-checking the ballistae to make sure they were locked down. She'd confirmed that the white 'We come in peace' flag was flying from the mast. She'd reviewed the plan with the rest of the crew – and the backup plan, and the backup plan for the backup plan.

Most importantly, she'd pulled aside their war-crazed chaperone, Coach Gleeson Hedge, and encouraged him to take the morning off in his cabin and watch reruns of mixed martial arts championships. The last thing they needed as they flew a magical Greek trireme into a potentially hostile Roman camp was a middle-aged satyr in gym clothes waving a club and yelling, 'Die!'

Everything seemed to be in order. Even that mysterious

chill she'd been feeling since the ship launched had dissipated, at least for now.

The warship descended through the clouds, but Annabeth couldn't stop second-guessing herself. What if this was a bad idea? What if the Romans panicked and attacked them on sight?

The *Argo II* definitely did not look friendly. Two hundred feet long, with a bronze-plated hull, mounted repeating crossbows fore and aft, a flaming metal dragon for a figurehead and two rotating ballistae amidships that could fire explosive bolts powerful enough to blast through concrete . . . well, it wasn't the most appropriate ride for a meet-and-greet with the neighbours.

Annabeth had tried to give the Romans a heads-up. She'd asked Leo to send one of his special inventions – a holographic scroll – to alert their friends inside the camp. Hopefully the message had got through. Leo had wanted to paint a giant message on the bottom of the hull – *WASSUP?* with a smiley face – but Annabeth vetoed the idea. She wasn't sure the Romans had a sense of humour.

Too late to turn back now.

The clouds broke around their hull, revealing the gold-and-green carpet of the Oakland Hills below them. Annabeth gripped one of the bronze shields that lined the starboard rail.

Her three crewmates took their places.

On the stern quarterdeck, Leo rushed around like a madman, checking his gauges and wrestling levers. Most helmsmen would've been satisfied with a pilot's wheel or a tiller. Leo had also installed a keyboard, monitor, aviation controls from a Learjet, a dubstep soundboard and motion-control sensors from a Nintendo Wii. He could turn the ship by pulling on the throttle, fire weapons by sampling an album or raise sails by shaking his Wii controllers really fast. Even by demigod standards, Leo was seriously ADHD.

Piper paced back and forth between the mainmast and the ballistae, practising her lines.

'Lower your weapons,' she murmured. 'We just want to talk.'

Her charmspeak was so powerful that the words flowed over Annabeth, filling her with the desire to drop her dagger and have a nice long chat.

For a child of Aphrodite, Piper tried hard to play down her beauty. Today she was dressed in tattered jeans, worn-out trainers and a white tank top with pink Hello Kitty designs. (Maybe as a joke, though Annabeth could never be sure with Piper.) Her choppy brown hair was braided down the right side with an eagle's feather.

Then there was Piper's boyfriend – Jason. He stood at the bow on the raised crossbow platform, where the Romans could easily spot him. His knuckles were white on the hilt of his golden sword. Otherwise he looked calm for a guy who was making himself a target. Over his jeans and orange Camp Half-Blood T-shirt, he'd donned a toga and a purple cloak – symbols of his old rank as praetor. With his wind-ruffled blond hair and his icy blue eyes, he looked ruggedly handsome and in control – just like a son of Jupiter should.

He'd grown up at Camp Jupiter, so hopefully his familiar face would make the Romans hesitant to blow the ship out of the sky.

Annabeth tried to hide it, but she still didn't completely trust the guy. He acted too perfectly – always following the rules, always doing the honourable thing. He even *looked* too perfect. In the back of her mind, she had a nagging thought: What if this is a trick and he betrays us? What if we sail into Camp Jupiter, and he says, *Hey, Romans! Check out these prisoners and this cool ship I brought you!*

Annabeth doubted that would happen. Still, she couldn't look at him without getting a bitter taste in her mouth. He'd been part of Hera's forced 'exchange programme' to introduce the two camps. Her Most Annoying Majesty, Queen of Olympus, had convinced the other gods that their two sets of children – Roman and Greek – had to combine forces to save the world from the evil goddess Gaia, who was awakening from the earth, and her horrible children, the giants.

Without warning, Hera had plucked up Percy Jackson, Annabeth's boyfriend, wiped his memory and sent him to the Roman camp. In exchange, the Greeks had got Jason. None of that was Jason's fault, but every time Annabeth saw him she remembered how much she missed Percy.

Percy . . . who was somewhere below them right now.

Oh, gods. Panic welled up inside her. She forced it down. She couldn't afford to get overwhelmed.

I'm a child of Athena, she told herself. *I have to stick to my plan and not get distracted.*

She felt it again – that familiar shiver, as if a psychotic

snowman had crept up behind her and was breathing down her neck. She turned, but no one was there.

Must be her nerves. Even in a world of gods and monsters, Annabeth couldn't believe a new warship would be haunted. The *Argo II* was well protected. The Celestial bronze shields along the rail were enchanted to ward off monsters, and their onboard satyr, Coach Hedge, would have sniffed out any intruders.

Annabeth wished she could pray to her mother for guidance, but that wasn't possible now. Not after last month, when she'd had that horrible encounter with her mom and got the worst present of her life . . .

The cold pressed closer. She thought she heard a faint voice in the wind, laughing. Every muscle in her body tensed. Something was about to go terribly wrong.

She almost ordered Leo to reverse. Then, in the valley below, horns sounded. The Romans had spotted them.

Annabeth thought she knew what to expect. Jason had described Camp Jupiter to her in great detail. Still, she had trouble believing her eyes. Ringed by the Oakland Hills, the valley was at least twice the size of Camp Half-Blood. A small river snaked around one side and curled towards the centre like a capital letter *G*, emptying into a sparkling blue lake.

Directly below the ship, nestled at the edge of the lake, the city of New Rome gleamed in the sunlight. She recognized landmarks Jason had told her about – the hippodrome, the coliseum, the temples and parks, the neighbourhood of Seven Hills with its winding streets, colourful villas and flowering gardens.

She saw evidence of the Romans' recent battle with an army of monsters. The dome was cracked open on a building she guessed was the Senate House. The forum's broad plaza was pitted with craters. Some fountains and statues were in ruins.

Dozens of kids in togas were streaming out of the Senate House to get a better view of the *Argo II*. More Romans emerged from the shops and cafés, gawking and pointing as the ship descended.

About half a mile to the west, where the horns were blowing, a Roman fort stood on a hill. It looked just like the illustrations Annabeth had seen in military history books – with a defensive trench lined with spikes, high walls and watchtowers armed with scorpion ballistae. Inside, perfect rows of white barracks lined the main road – the Via Principalis.

A column of demigods emerged from the gates, their armour and spears glinting as they hurried towards the city. In the midst of their ranks was an actual war elephant.

Annabeth wanted to land the *Argo II* before those troops arrived, but the ground was still several hundred feet below. She scanned the crowd, hoping to catch a glimpse of Percy.

Then something behind her went *BOOM!*

The explosion almost knocked her overboard. She whirled and found herself eye to eye with an angry statue.

'Unacceptable!' he shrieked.

Apparently he had exploded into existence, right there on the deck. Sulphurous yellow smoke rolled off his shoulders.

Cinders popped around his curly hair. From the waist down, he was nothing but a square marble pedestal. From the waist up, he was a muscular human figure in a carved toga.

'I will *not* have weapons inside the Pomerian Line!' he announced in a fussy teacher voice. 'I *certainly* will not have Greeks!'

Jason shot Annabeth a look that said, *I've got this.*

'Terminus,' he said. 'It's me. Jason Grace.'

'Oh, I remember *you*, Jason!' Terminus grumbled. 'I thought you had better sense than to consort with the enemies of Rome!'

'But they're not enemies –'

'That's right,' Piper jumped in. 'We just want to talk. If we could –'

'Ha!' snapped the statue. 'Don't try that charmspeak on *me*, young lady. And put down that dagger before I slap it out of your hands!'

Piper glanced at her bronze dagger, which she'd apparently forgotten she was holding. 'Um . . . okay. But how would you slap it? You don't have any arms.'

'Impertinence!' There was a sharp *POP* and a flash of yellow. Piper yelped and dropped the dagger, which was now smoking and sparking.

'Lucky for you I've just been through a battle,' Terminus announced. 'If I were at full strength, I would've blasted this flying monstrosity out of the sky already!'

'Hold up.' Leo stepped forward, wagging his Wii controller. 'Did you just call my ship a monstrosity? I *know* you didn't do that.'

The idea that Leo might attack the statue with his gaming device was enough to snap Annabeth out of her shock.

'Let's all calm down.' She raised her hands to show she had no weapons. 'I take it you're Terminus, the god of boundaries. Jason told me you protect the city of New Rome, right? I'm Annabeth Chase, daughter of –'

'Oh, I know who *you* are!' The statue glared at her with its blank white eyes. 'A child of *Athena*, Minerva's Greek form. Scandalous! You Greeks have no sense of decency. We Romans know the proper place for *that* goddess.'

Annabeth clenched her jaw. This statue wasn't making it easy to be diplomatic. 'What exactly do you mean, *that* goddess? And what's so scandalous about –'

'Right!' Jason interrupted. 'Anyway, Terminus, we're here on a mission of peace. We'd love permission to land so we can –'

'Impossible!' the god squeaked. 'Lay down your weapons and surrender! Leave my city immediately!'

'Which is it?' Leo asked. 'Surrender or leave?'

'Both!' Terminus said. 'Surrender, then leave. I am slapping your face for asking such a stupid question, you ridiculous boy! Do you feel that?'

'Wow.' Leo studied Terminus with professional interest. 'You're wound up pretty tight. You got any gears in there that need loosening? I could take a look.'

He exchanged the Wii controller for a screwdriver from his magic tool belt and tapped the statue's pedestal.

'Stop that!' Terminus insisted. Another small explosion

made Leo drop his screwdriver. 'Weapons are *not* allowed on Roman soil inside the Pomerian Line.'

'The what?' Piper asked.

'City limits,' Jason translated.

'And this entire ship is a weapon!' Terminus said. 'You *cannot* land!'

Down in the valley, the legion reinforcements were halfway to the city. The crowd in the forum was over a hundred strong now. Annabeth scanned the faces and . . . oh, gods. She saw him. He was walking towards the ship with his arms around two other kids like they were best buddies – a stout boy with a black buzz cut and a girl wearing a Roman cavalry helmet. Percy looked so at ease, so happy. He wore a purple cape just like Jason's – the mark of a praetor.

Annabeth's heart did a gymnastics routine.

'Leo, stop the ship,' she ordered.

'What?'

'You heard me. Keep us right where we are.'

Leo pulled out his controller and yanked it upward. All ninety oars froze in place. The ship stopped sinking.

'Terminus,' Annabeth said, 'there's no rule against hovering *over* New Rome, is there?'

The statue frowned. 'Well, no . . .'

'We can keep the ship aloft,' Annabeth said. 'We'll use a rope ladder to reach the forum. That way, the ship won't be on Roman soil. Not technically.'

The statue seemed to ponder this. Annabeth wondered if he was scratching his chin with imaginary hands.

'I like technicalities,' he admitted. 'Still . . .'

'All our weapons will stay aboard the ship,' Annabeth promised. 'I assume the Romans – even those reinforcements marching towards us – will also have to honour your rules inside the Pomerian Line if you tell them to?'

'Of course!' Terminus said. 'Do I look like I tolerate rule breakers?'

'Uh, Annabeth . . .' Leo said. 'You sure this is a good idea?'

She closed her fists to keep them from shaking. That cold feeling was still there. It floated just behind her and, now that Terminus was no longer shouting and causing explosions, she thought she could hear the presence laughing, as if it were delighted by the bad choices she was making.

But Percy was down there . . . He was so close. She *had* to reach him.

'It'll be fine,' she said. 'No one will be armed. We can talk in peace. Terminus will make sure each side obeys the rules.' She looked at the marble statue. 'Do we have an agreement?'

Terminus sniffed. 'I suppose. For now. You may climb down your ladder to New Rome, daughter of Athena. *Please* try not to destroy my town.'

ANNABETH

A SEA OF HASTILY ASSEMBLED DEMIGODS parted for Annabeth as she walked through the forum. Some looked tense, some nervous. Some were bandaged from their recent battle with the giants, but no one was armed. No one attacked.

Entire families had gathered to see the newcomers. Annabeth saw couples with babies, toddlers clinging to their parents' legs, even some elderly folks in a combination of Roman robes and modern clothes. Were all of them demigods? Annabeth suspected so, though she'd never seen a place like this. At Camp Half-Blood, most demigods were teens. If they survived long enough to graduate from high school, they either stayed on as counsellors or left to start lives as best they could in the mortal world. Here, it was an entire multigenerational community.

At the far end of the crowd, Annabeth spotted Tyson the Cyclops and Percy's hellhound, Mrs O'Leary – who had been the first scouting party from Camp Half-Blood to reach

Camp Jupiter. They looked to be in good spirits. Tyson waved and grinned. He was wearing an SPQR banner like a giant bib.

Some part of Annabeth's mind registered how beautiful the city was – the smells from the bakeries, the gurgling fountains, the flowers blooming in the gardens. And the architecture . . . gods, the architecture – gilded marble columns, dazzling mosaics, monumental arches and terraced villas.

In front of her, the demigods made way for a girl in full Roman armour and a purple cape. Dark hair tumbled across her shoulders. Her eyes were as black as obsidian.

Reyna.

Jason had described her well. Even without that, Annabeth would have singled her out as the leader. Medals decorated her armour. She carried herself with such confidence the other demigods backed away and averted their gaze.

Annabeth recognized something else in her face, too – in the hard set of her mouth and the deliberate way she raised her chin like she was ready to accept any challenge. Reyna was forcing a look of courage, while holding back a mixture of hopefulness and worry and fear that she couldn't show in public.

Annabeth knew that expression. She saw it every time she looked in a mirror.

The two girls considered each other. Annabeth's friends fanned out on either side. The Romans murmured Jason's name, staring at him in awe.

Then someone else appeared from the crowd, and Annabeth's vision tunnelled.

Percy smiled at her – that sarcastic, troublemaker smile that had annoyed her for years but eventually had become endearing. His sea-green eyes were as gorgeous as she remembered. His dark hair was swept to one side, like he'd just come from a walk on the beach. He looked even better than he had six months ago – more tanned and taller, leaner and more muscular.

Annabeth was too stunned to move. She felt that if she got any closer to him all the molecules in her body might combust. She'd secretly had a crush on him since they were twelve years old. Last summer, she'd fallen for him hard. They'd been a happy couple for four months – and then he'd disappeared.

During their separation, something had happened to Annabeth's feelings. They'd grown painfully intense – like she'd been forced to withdraw from a life-saving medication. Now she wasn't sure which was more excruciating – living with that horrible absence, or being with him again.

The praetor Reyna straightened. With apparent reluctance, she turned towards Jason.

'Jason Grace, my former colleague . . .' She spoke the word *colleague* like it was a dangerous thing. 'I welcome you home. And these, your friends –'

Annabeth didn't mean to, but she surged forward. Percy rushed towards her at the same time. The crowd tensed. Some reached for swords that weren't there.

Percy threw his arms around her. They kissed, and for a moment nothing else mattered. An asteroid could have hit the planet and wiped out all life, and Annabeth wouldn't have cared.

Percy smelled of ocean air. His lips were salty.

Seaweed Brain, she thought giddily.

Percy pulled away and studied her face. 'Gods, I never thought –'

Annabeth grabbed his wrist and flipped him over her shoulder. He slammed into the paving stones. Romans cried out. Some surged forward, but Reyna shouted, 'Hold! Stand down!'

Annabeth put her knee on Percy's chest. She pushed her forearm against his throat. She didn't care what the Romans thought. A white-hot lump of anger expanded in her chest – a tumour of worry and bitterness that she'd been carrying around since last autumn.

'If you *ever* leave me again,' she said, her eyes stinging, 'I swear to all the gods –'

Percy had the nerve to laugh. Suddenly the lump of heated emotions melted inside Annabeth.

'Consider me warned,' Percy said. 'I missed you, too.'

Annabeth rose and helped him to his feet. She wanted to kiss him again *so* badly, but she managed to restrain herself.

Jason cleared his throat. 'So, yeah . . . It's good to be back.'

He introduced Reyna to Piper, who looked a little miffed that she hadn't got to say the lines she'd been practising, then to Leo, who grinned and flashed a peace sign.

'And this is Annabeth,' Jason said. 'Uh, normally she doesn't judo-flip people.'

Reyna's eyes sparkled. 'You sure you're not a Roman, Annabeth? Or an Amazon?'

Annabeth didn't know if that was a compliment, but she

held out her hand. 'I only attack my boyfriend like that,' she promised. 'Pleased to meet you.'

Reyna clasped her hand firmly. 'It seems we have a lot to discuss. Centurions!'

A few of the Roman campers hustled forward – apparently the senior officers. Two kids appeared at Percy's side, the same ones Annabeth had seen him chumming around with earlier. The burly Asian guy with the buzz cut was about fifteen. He was cute in a sort of oversized-cuddly-panda-bear way. The girl was younger, maybe thirteen, with amber eyes and chocolate skin and long curly hair. Her cavalry helmet was tucked under her arm.

Annabeth could tell from their body language that they felt close to Percy. They stood next to him protectively, like they'd already shared many adventures. She fought down a twinge of jealousy. Was it possible Percy and this girl . . . no. The chemistry between the three of them wasn't like that. Annabeth had spent her whole life learning to read people. It was a survival skill. If she had to guess, she'd say the big Asian guy was the girl's boyfriend, though she suspected they hadn't been together long.

There was one thing she didn't understand: what was the girl staring at? She kept frowning in Piper and Leo's direction, like she recognized one of them and the memory was painful.

Meanwhile, Reyna was giving orders to her officers. '. . . tell the legion to stand down. Dakota, alert the spirits in the kitchen. Tell them to prepare a welcome feast. And, Octavian –'

'You're letting these intruders into the *camp*?' A tall guy with stringy blond hair elbowed his way forward. 'Reyna, the security risks —'

'We're not taking them to the camp, Octavian.' Reyna flashed him a stern look. 'We'll eat here, in the forum.'

'Oh, *much* better,' Octavian grumbled. He seemed to be the only one who didn't defer to Reyna as his superior, despite the fact that he was scrawny and pale and for some reason had three teddy bears hanging from his belt. 'You want us to relax in the shadow of their warship.'

'These are our guests.' Reyna clipped off every word. 'We will welcome them, and we will talk to them. As augur, you should burn an offering to thank the gods for bringing Jason back to us safely.'

'Good idea,' Percy put in. 'Go burn your bears, Octavian.'

Reyna looked like she was trying not to smile. 'You have my orders. Go.'

The officers dispersed. Octavian shot Percy a look of absolute loathing. Then he gave Annabeth a suspicious once-over and stalked away.

Percy slipped his hand into Annabeth's. 'Don't worry about Octavian,' he said. 'Most of the Romans are good people — like Frank and Hazel here, and Reyna. We'll be fine.'

Annabeth felt as if someone had draped a cold washcloth across her neck. She heard that whispering laughter again, as if the presence had followed her from the ship.

She looked up at the *Argo II*. Its massive bronze hull glittered in the sunlight. Part of her wanted to kidnap Percy right now, climb on board and get out of here while they still could.

She couldn't shake the feeling that something was about to go terribly wrong. And there was no way she would ever risk losing Percy again.

'We'll be fine,' she repeated, trying to believe it.

'Excellent,' Reyna said. She turned to Jason, and Annabeth thought there was a hungry sort of gleam in her eyes. 'Let's talk, and we can have a proper reunion.'

ANNABETH

ANNABETH WISHED SHE HAD AN APPETITE, because the Romans knew how to eat.

Sets of couches and low tables were carted into the forum until it resembled a furniture showroom. Romans lounged in groups of ten or twenty, talking and laughing while wind spirits – *aurae* – swirled overhead, bringing an endless assortment of pizzas, sandwiches, chips, cold drinks and fresh-baked cookies. Drifting through the crowd were purple ghosts – Lares – in togas and legionnaire armour. Around the edges of the feast, satyrs (no, *fauns*, Annabeth thought) trotted from table to table, panhandling for food and spare change. In the nearby fields, the war elephant frolicked with Mrs O'Leary, and children played tag around the statues of Terminus that lined the city limits.

The whole scene was so familiar yet so completely alien that it gave Annabeth vertigo.

All she wanted to do was be with Percy – preferably alone. She knew she would have to wait. If their quest was going to succeed, they needed these Romans, which meant getting to know them and building some goodwill.

Reyna and a few of her officers (including the blond kid Octavian, freshly back from burning a teddy bear for the gods) sat with Annabeth and her crew. Percy joined them with his two new friends, Frank and Hazel.

As a tornado of food platters settled onto the table, Percy leaned over and whispered, 'I want to show you around New Rome. Just you and me. The place is incredible.'

Annabeth should've felt thrilled. *Just you and me* was exactly what she wanted. Instead, resentment swelled in her throat. How could Percy talk so enthusiastically about this place? What about Camp Half-Blood – *their* camp, *their* home?

She tried not to stare at the new marks on Percy's forearm – an SPQR tattoo like Jason's. At Camp Half-Blood, demigods got bead necklaces to commemorate years of training. Here, the Romans burned a tattoo into your flesh, as if to say: *You belong to us. Permanently.*

She swallowed back some biting comments. 'Okay. Sure.'

'I've been thinking,' he said nervously. 'I had this idea –'

He stopped as Reyna called a toast to friendship.

After introductions all around, the Romans and Annabeth's crew began exchanging stories. Jason explained how he'd arrived at Camp Half-Blood without his memory, and how he'd gone on a quest with Piper and Leo to rescue the goddess

Hera (or Juno, take your pick – she was equally annoying in Greek or Roman) from imprisonment at the Wolf House in northern California.

'Impossible!' Octavian broke in. 'That's our most sacred place. If the giants had imprisoned a goddess there –'

'They would've destroyed her,' Piper said. 'And blamed it on the Greeks, and started a war between the camps. Now, be quiet and let Jason finish.'

Octavian opened his mouth, but no sound came out. Annabeth really loved Piper's charmspeak. She noticed Reyna looking back and forth between Jason and Piper, her brow creased, as if just beginning to realize the two of them were a couple.

'So,' Jason continued, 'that's how we found out about the earth goddess Gaia. She's still half asleep, but she's the one freeing the monsters from Tartarus and raising the giants. Porphyrion, the big leader dude we fought at the Wolf House: he said he was retreating to the ancient lands – Greece itself. He plans on awakening Gaia and destroying the gods by . . . what did he call it? *Pulling up their roots.*'

Percy nodded thoughtfully. 'Gaia's been busy over here, too. We had our own encounter with Queen Dirt Face.'

Percy recounted his side of the story. He talked about waking up at the Wolf House with no memories except for one name – *Annabeth.*

When she heard that, Annabeth had to try hard not to cry. Percy told them how he'd travelled to Alaska with Frank and Hazel – how they'd defeated the giant Alcyoneus, freed the death god Thanatos and returned with the lost golden eagle standard of the Roman camp to repel an attack by the giants' army.

When Percy had finished, Jason whistled appreciatively. 'No wonder they made you praetor.'

Octavian snorted. 'Which means we now have *three* praetors! The rules clearly state we can only have two!'

'On the bright side,' Percy said, 'both Jason *and* I outrank you, Octavian. So we can *both* tell you to shut up.'

Octavian turned as purple as a Roman T-shirt. Jason gave Percy a fist bump.

Even Reyna managed a smile, though her eyes were stormy.

'We'll have to figure out the extra praetor problem later,' she said. 'Right now we have more serious issues to deal with.'

'I'll step aside for Jason,' Percy said easily. 'It's no biggie.'

'No *biggie*?' Octavian choked. 'The praetorship of Rome is *no biggie*?'

Percy ignored him and turned to Jason. 'You're Thalia Grace's brother, huh? Wow. You guys look nothing alike.'

'Yeah, I noticed,' Jason said. 'Anyway, thanks for helping my camp while I was gone. You did an awesome job.'

'Back at you,' Percy said.

Annabeth kicked his shin. She hated to interrupt a budding bromance, but Reyna was right: they had serious things to discuss. 'We should talk about the Great Prophecy. It sounds like the Romans are aware of it, too?'

Reyna nodded. 'We call it the Prophecy of Seven. Octavian, you have it committed to memory?'

'Of course,' he said. 'But, Reyna –'

'Recite it, please. In English, not Latin.'

Octavian sighed. '*Seven half-bloods shall answer the call. To storm or fire the world must fall –*'

'*An oath to keep with a final breath,*' Annabeth continued. '*And foes bear arms to the Doors of Death.*'

Everyone stared at her – except for Leo, who had constructed a pinwheel out of aluminum foil taco wrappers and was sticking it into passing wind spirits.

Annabeth wasn't sure why she had blurted out the lines of the prophecy. She'd just felt compelled.

The big kid, Frank, sat forward, staring at her in fascination, as if she'd grown a third eye. 'Is it true you're a child of Min– I mean, Athena?'

'Yes,' she said, suddenly feeling defensive. 'Why is that such a surprise?'

Octavian scoffed. 'If you're truly a child of the *wisdom* goddess –'

'Enough,' Reyna snapped. 'Annabeth is what she says. She's here in peace. Besides . . .' She gave Annabeth a look of grudging respect. 'Percy has spoken highly of you.'

The undertones in Reyna's voice took Annabeth a moment to decipher. Percy looked down, suddenly interested in his cheeseburger.

Annabeth's face felt hot. Oh, gods . . . Reyna had tried to make a move on Percy. That explained the tinge of bitterness, maybe even envy in her words. Percy had turned her down for Annabeth.

At that moment, Annabeth forgave her ridiculous boyfriend for everything he'd ever done wrong. She wanted to throw her arms around him, but she commanded herself to stay cool.

'Uh, thanks,' she told Reyna. 'At any rate, some of the prophecy is becoming clear. Foes bearing arms to the Doors of Death . . . that means Romans and Greeks. We have to combine forces to find those doors.'

Hazel, the girl with the cavalry helmet and the long curly hair, picked up something next to her plate. It looked like a large ruby, but, before Annabeth could be sure, Hazel slipped it into the pocket of her denim shirt.

'My brother, Nico, went looking for the doors,' she said.

'Wait,' Annabeth said. 'Nico di Angelo? He's your brother?'

Hazel nodded as if this were obvious. A dozen more questions crowded into Annabeth's head, but it was already spinning like Leo's pinwheel. She decided to let the matter go. 'Okay. You were saying?'

'He disappeared.' Hazel moistened her lips. 'I'm afraid . . . I'm not sure, but I think something's happened to him.'

'We'll look for him,' Percy promised. 'We have to find the Doors of Death anyway. Thanatos told us we'd find both answers in Rome – like, the *original* Rome. That's on the way to Greece, right?'

'Thanatos told you this?' Annabeth tried to wrap her mind around *that* idea. 'The death god?'

She'd met many gods. She'd even been to the Underworld, but Percy's story about freeing the incarnation of death itself really creeped her out.

Percy took a bite of his burger. 'Now that Death is free,

monsters will disintegrate and return to Tartarus again like they used to. But as long as the Doors of Death are open they'll just keep coming back.'

Piper twisted the feather in her hair. 'Like water leaking through a dam,' she suggested.

'Yeah.' Percy smiled. 'We've got a dam hole.'

'What?' Piper asked.

'Nothing,' he said. 'Inside joke. The point is we'll have to find the doors and close them before we can head to Greece. It's the only way we'll stand a chance of defeating the giants and making sure they *stay* defeated.'

Reyna plucked an apple from a passing fruit tray. She turned it in her fingers, studying the dark red surface. 'You propose an expedition to Greece in your warship. You do realize that the ancient lands – and the Mare Nostrum – are dangerous?'

'Mary who?' Leo asked.

'Mare Nostrum,' Jason explained. '*Our Sea*. It's what the Ancient Romans called the Mediterranean.'

Reyna nodded. 'The territory that was once the Roman Empire is not only the birthplace of the gods. It's also the ancestral home of the monsters, Titans and giants . . . and worse things. As dangerous as travel is for demigods here in America, *there* it would be ten times worse.'

'You said Alaska would be bad,' Percy reminded her. 'We survived that.'

Reyna shook her head. Her fingernails cut little crescents into the apple as she turned it. 'Percy, travelling in the Mediterranean is a different level of danger altogether. It's been off limits to Roman demigods for centuries. No hero in his right mind would go there.'

'Then we're good!' Leo grinned over the top of his pinwheel. 'Because we're all crazy, right? Besides, the *Argo II* is a top-of-the-line warship. She'll get us through.'

'We'll have to hurry,' Jason added. 'I don't know exactly what the giants are planning, but Gaia is growing more conscious all the time. She's invading dreams, appearing in weird places, summoning more and more powerful monsters. We have to stop the giants before they can wake her up fully.'

Annabeth shuddered. She'd had her own share of nightmares lately.

'*Seven half-bloods must answer the call,*' she said. 'It needs to be a mix from both our camps. Jason, Piper, Leo and me. That's four.'

'And me,' Percy said. 'Along with Hazel and Frank. That's seven.'

'What?' Octavian shot to his feet. 'We're just supposed to *accept* that? Without a vote in the senate? Without a proper debate? Without –'

'Percy!' Tyson the Cyclops bounded towards them with Mrs O'Leary at his heels. On the hellhound's back sat the skinniest harpy Annabeth had ever seen – a sickly looking girl with stringy red hair, a sackcloth dress and red-feathered wings.

Annabeth didn't know where the harpy had come from, but her heart warmed to see Tyson in his tattered flannel and denim with the backwards SPQR banner across his chest. She'd had some pretty bad experiences with Cyclopes, but

Tyson was a sweetheart. He was also Percy's half brother (long story), which made him almost like family.

Tyson stopped by their couch and wrung his meaty hands. His big brown eye was full of concern. 'Ella is scared,' he said.

'N-n-no more boats,' the harpy muttered to herself, picking furiously at her feathers. '*Titanic, Lusitania, Pax* . . . boats are not for harpies.'

Leo squinted. He looked at Hazel, who was seated next to him. 'Did that chicken girl just compare *my* ship to the *Titanic?*'

'She's not a chicken.' Hazel averted her eyes, as if Leo made her nervous. 'Ella's a harpy. She's just a little . . . high-strung.'

'Ella is pretty,' Tyson said. 'And scared. We need to take her away, but she will not go on the ship.'

'No ships,' Ella repeated. She looked straight at Annabeth. 'Bad luck. There she is. *Wisdom's daughter walks alone* –'

'Ella!' Frank stood suddenly. 'Maybe it's not the best time –'

'*The Mark of Athena burns through Rome,*' Ella continued, cupping her hands over her ears and raising her voice. '*Twins snuff out the angel's breath, Who holds the key to endless death. Giants' bane stands gold and pale, Won through pain from a woven jail.*'

The effect was like someone dropping a flash grenade on the table. Everyone stared at the harpy. No one spoke. Annabeth's heart was pounding. *The Mark of Athena* . . . She resisted the urge to check her pocket, but she could feel the silver coin growing warmer – the cursed gift from her mother. *Follow the Mark of Athena. Avenge me.*

Around them, the sounds of the feast continued, but muted and distant, as if their little cluster of couches had slipped into a quieter dimension.

Percy was the first to recover. He stood and took Tyson's arm.

'I know!' he said with feigned enthusiasm. 'How about you take Ella to get some fresh air? You and Mrs O'Leary –'

'Hold on.' Octavian gripped one of his teddy bears, strangling it with shaking hands. His eyes fixed on Ella. 'What was that she said? It sounded like –'

'Ella reads a lot,' Frank blurted out. 'We found her at a library.'

'Yes!' Hazel said. 'Probably just something she read in a book.'

'Books,' Ella muttered helpfully. 'Ella likes books.'

Now that she'd said her piece, the harpy seemed more relaxed. She sat cross-legged on Mrs O'Leary's back, preening her wings.

Annabeth gave Percy a curious glance. Obviously, he and Frank and Hazel were hiding something. Just as obviously, Ella had recited a prophecy – a prophecy that concerned *her*.

Percy's expression said, *Help*.

'That was a prophecy,' Octavian insisted. 'It sounded like a prophecy.'

No one answered.

Annabeth wasn't exactly sure what was going on, but she understood that Percy was on the verge of big trouble.

She forced a laugh. 'Really, Octavian? Maybe harpies are different here, on the Roman side. Ours have just enough intelligence to clean cabins and cook lunches. Do yours usually foretell the future? Do you consult them for your auguries?'

Her words had the intended effect. The Roman officers laughed nervously. Some sized up Ella, then looked at Octavian and snorted. The idea of a chicken lady issuing prophecies was apparently just as ridiculous to Romans as it was to Greeks.

'I, uh . . .' Octavian dropped his teddy bear. 'No, but –'

'She's just spouting lines from some book,' Annabeth said, 'like Hazel suggested. Besides, we already have a *real* prophecy to worry about.'

She turned to Tyson. 'Percy's right. Why don't you take Ella and Mrs O'Leary and shadow-travel somewhere for a while. Is Ella okay with that?'

'"Large dogs are good,"' Ella said. '*Old Yeller*, 1957, screenplay by Fred Gipson and William Tunberg.'

Annabeth wasn't sure how to take that answer, but Percy smiled like the problem was solved.

'Great!' Percy said. 'We'll Iris-message you guys when we're done and catch up with you later.'

The Romans looked at Reyna, waiting for her ruling. Annabeth held her breath.

Reyna had an excellent poker face. She studied Ella, but Annabeth couldn't guess what she was thinking.

'Fine,' the praetor said at last. 'Go.'

'Yay!' Tyson went around the couches and gave everyone a big hug – even Octavian, who didn't look happy about it. Then he climbed on Mrs O'Leary's back with Ella, and the hellhound bounded out of the forum. They dived straight into a shadow on the Senate House wall and disappeared.

'Well.' Reyna set down her uneaten apple. 'Octavian is right about one thing. We must gain the senate's approval before we let any of our legionnaires go on a quest – especially one as dangerous as you're suggesting.'

'This whole thing smells of treachery,' Octavian grumbled. 'That trireme is not a ship of peace!'

'Come aboard, man,' Leo offered. 'I'll give you a tour. You can steer the boat, and if you're really good I'll give you a little paper captain's hat to wear.'

Octavian's nostrils flared. 'How dare you –'

'It's a good idea,' Reyna said. 'Octavian, go with him. See the ship. We'll convene a senate meeting in one hour.'

'But . . .' Octavian stopped. Apparently he could tell from Reyna's expression that further arguing would not be good for his health. 'Fine.'

Leo got up. He turned to Annabeth, and his smile changed. It happened so quickly Annabeth thought she'd imagined it, but just for a moment someone else seemed to be standing in Leo's place, smiling coldly with a cruel light in his eyes. Then Annabeth blinked, and Leo was just regular old Leo again, with his usual impish grin.

'Back soon,' he promised. 'This is gonna be epic.'

A horrible chill settled over her. As Leo and Octavian headed for the rope ladder, she thought about calling them back – but how could she explain that? Tell everyone she was going crazy, seeing things and feeling cold?

The wind spirits began clearing the plates.

'Uh, Reyna,' Jason said, 'if you don't mind, I'd like to show Piper around before the senate meeting. She's never seen New Rome.'

Reyna's expression hardened.

Annabeth wondered how Jason could be so dense. Was it possible he really didn't understand how much Reyna liked him? It was obvious enough to Annabeth. Asking to show his new girlfriend around Reyna's city was rubbing salt in a wound.

'Of course,' Reyna said coldly.

Percy took Annabeth's hand. 'Yeah, me, too. I'd like to show Annabeth –'

'No,' Reyna snapped.

Percy knitted his eyebrows. 'Sorry?'

'I'd like a few words with Annabeth,' Reyna said. 'Alone. If you don't mind, my fellow praetor.'

Her tone made it clear she wasn't really asking permission.

The chill spread down Annabeth's back. She wondered what Reyna was up to. Maybe the praetor didn't like the idea of *two* guys who had rejected her giving their girlfriends tours of her city. Or maybe there was something she wanted to say in private. Either way, Annabeth was reluctant to be alone and unarmed with the Roman leader.

'Come, daughter of Athena.' Reyna rose from her couch. 'Walk with me.'

ANNABETH

ANNABETH WANTED TO HATE NEW ROME. But as an aspiring architect she couldn't help admiring the terraced gardens, the fountains and temples, the winding cobblestone streets and gleaming white villas. After the Titan War last summer, she'd got her dream job of redesigning the palaces of Mount Olympus. Now, walking through this miniature city, she kept thinking, *I should have made a dome like that. I love the way those columns lead into that courtyard.* Whoever designed New Rome had clearly poured a lot of time and love into the project.

'We have the best architects and builders in the world,' Reyna said, as if reading her thoughts. 'Rome always did, in the ancient times. Many demigods stay on to live here after their time in the legion. They go to our university. They settle down to raise families. Percy seemed interested in this fact.'

Annabeth wondered what *that* meant. She must have

scowled more fiercely than she realized, because Reyna laughed.

'You're a warrior, all right,' the praetor said. 'You've got fire in your eyes.'

'Sorry.' Annabeth tried to tone down the glare.

'Don't be. I'm the daughter of Bellona.'

'Roman goddess of war?'

Reyna nodded. She turned and whistled like she was hailing a cab. A moment later, two metal dogs raced towards them – automaton greyhounds, one silver and one gold. They brushed against Reyna's legs and regarded Annabeth with glistening ruby eyes.

'My pets,' Reyna explained. 'Aurum and Argentum. You don't mind if they walk with us?'

Again, Annabeth got the feeling it wasn't really a request. She noted that the greyhounds had teeth like steel arrowheads. Maybe weapons weren't allowed inside the city, but Reyna's pets could still tear Annabeth to pieces if they chose.

Reyna led her to an outdoor café, where the waiter clearly knew her. He smiled and handed her a takeaway cup, then offered one to Annabeth.

'Would you like some?' Reyna asked. 'They make wonderful hot chocolate. Not really a Roman drink –'

'But chocolate is universal,' Annabeth said.

'Exactly.'

It was a warm June afternoon, but Annabeth accepted the cup with thanks. The two of them walked on, Reyna's gold and silver dogs roaming nearby.

'In our camp,' Reyna said, 'Athena is Minerva. Are you familiar with how her Roman form is different?'

Annabeth hadn't really considered it before. She remembered the way Terminus had called Athena *that* goddess, as if she were scandalous. Octavian had acted like Annabeth's very existence was an insult.

'I take it Minerva isn't . . . uh, quite as respected here?'

Reyna blew steam from her cup. 'We *respect* Minerva. She's the goddess of crafts and wisdom . . . but she isn't really a goddess of war. Not for Romans. She's also a maiden goddess, like Diana . . . the one you call Artemis. You won't find any children of Minerva here. The idea that Minerva would *have* children – frankly, it's a little shocking to us.'

'Oh.' Annabeth felt her face flush. She didn't want to get into the details of Athena's children – how they were born straight from the mind of the goddess, just as Athena herself had sprung from the head of Zeus. Talking about that always made Annabeth feel self-conscious, like she was some sort of freak. People usually asked her whether or not she had a belly button, since she had been born magically. *Of course* she had a belly button. She couldn't explain how. She didn't really want to know.

'I understand that you Greeks don't see things the same way,' Reyna continued. 'But Romans take vows of maidenhood very seriously. The Vestal Virgins, for instance . . . if they broke their vows and fell in love with anyone, they would be buried alive. So the idea that a maiden goddess would have children –'

'Got it.' Annabeth's hot chocolate suddenly tasted like dust. No wonder the Romans had been giving her strange looks. 'I'm not supposed to exist. And even if your camp *had* children of Minerva –'

'They wouldn't be like you,' Reyna said. 'They might be craftsmen, artists, maybe advisers, but not warriors. Not leaders of dangerous quests.'

Annabeth started to object that she wasn't the leader of the quest. Not officially. But she wondered if her friends on the *Argo II* would agree. The past few days, they had been looking to her for orders – even Jason, who could have pulled rank as the son of Jupiter, and Coach Hedge, who didn't take orders from anyone.

'There's more.' Reyna snapped her fingers, and her golden dog, Aurum, trotted over. The praetor stroked his ears. 'The harpy Ella . . . it *was* a prophecy she spoke. We both know that, don't we?'

Annabeth swallowed. Something about Aurum's ruby eyes made her uneasy. She had heard that dogs could smell fear, even detect changes in a human's breathing and heartbeat. She didn't know if that applied to magical metal dogs, but she decided it would be better to tell the truth.

'It sounded like a prophecy,' she admitted. 'But I've never met Ella before today, and I've never heard those lines exactly.'

'I have,' Reyna murmured. 'At least some of them –'

A few yards away, the silver dog barked. A group of children spilled out of a nearby alleyway and gathered around Argentum, petting the dog and laughing, unfazed by its razor-sharp teeth.

'We should move on,' Reyna said.

They wound their way up the hill. The greyhounds followed, leaving the children behind. Annabeth kept glancing at Reyna's face. A vague memory started tugging at her – the way Reyna brushed her hair behind her ear, the silver ring she wore with the torch and sword design.

'We've met before,' Annabeth ventured. 'You were younger, I think.'

Reyna gave her a dry smile. 'Very good. Percy didn't remember me. Of course you spoke mostly with my older sister Hylla, who is now queen of the Amazons. She left just this morning, before you arrived. At any rate, when we last met, I was a mere handmaiden in the house of Circe.'

'Circe . . .' Annabeth remembered her trip to the island of the sorceress. She'd been thirteen. Percy and she had washed ashore from the Sea of Monsters. Hylla had welcomed them. She had helped Annabeth get cleaned up and given her a beautiful new dress and a complete makeover. Then Circe had made her sales pitch: if Annabeth stayed on the island, she could have magical training and incredible power. Annabeth had been tempted, maybe just a little, until she realized the place was a trap, and Percy had been turned into a rodent. (That last part seemed funny afterwards, but at the time it had been terrifying.) As for Reyna . . . she'd been one of the servants who had combed Annabeth's hair.

'You . . .' Annabeth said in amazement. 'And Hylla is queen of the Amazons? How did you two –?'

'Long story,' Reyna said. 'But I remember you well. You were brave. I'd never seen anyone refuse Circe's hospitality, much less outwit her. It's no wonder Percy cares for you.'

Her voice was wistful. Annabeth thought it might be safer not to respond.

They reached the top of the hill, where a terrace overlooked the entire valley.

'This is my favourite spot,' Reyna said. 'The Garden of Bacchus.'

Grapevine trellises made a canopy overhead. Bees buzzed through honeysuckle and jasmine, which filled the afternoon air with a dizzying mix of perfumes. In the middle of the terrace stood a statue of Bacchus in a sort of ballet position, wearing nothing but a loincloth, his cheeks puffed out and lips pursed, spouting water into a fountain.

Despite her worries, Annabeth almost laughed. She knew the god in his Greek form, Dionysus – or Mr D, as they called him back at Camp Half-Blood. Seeing their cranky old camp director immortalized in stone, wearing a nappy and spewing water from his mouth, made her feel a little better.

Reyna stopped at the edge of the terrace. The view was worth the climb. The whole city spread out below them like a 3-D mosaic. To the south, beyond the lake, a cluster of temples perched on a hill. To the north, an aqueduct marched towards the Berkeley Hills. Work crews were repairing a broken section, probably damaged in the recent battle.

'I wanted to hear it from you,' Reyna said.

Annabeth turned. 'Hear *what* from me?'

'The truth,' Reyna said. 'Convince me that I'm not making a mistake by trusting you. Tell me about yourself. Tell me about Camp Half-Blood. Your friend Piper has sorcery in her words. I spent enough time with Circe to know charmspeak when I hear it. I can't trust what she says. And Jason . . . well, he has changed. He seems distant, no longer quite Roman.'

The hurt in her voice was as sharp as broken glass. Annabeth wondered if *she* had sounded that way, all the months she'd spent searching for Percy. At least she'd found her boyfriend. Reyna had no one. She was responsible for running an entire camp all by herself. Annabeth could sense that Reyna wanted Jason to love her. But he had disappeared, only to come back with a new girlfriend. Meanwhile, Percy had risen to praetor, but he had rebuffed Reyna, too. Now Annabeth had come to take him away. Reyna would be left alone again, shouldering a job meant for two people.

When Annabeth had arrived at Camp Jupiter, she'd been prepared to negotiate with Reyna or even fight her if needed. She hadn't been prepared to feel sorry for her.

She kept that feeling hidden. Reyna didn't strike her as someone who would appreciate pity.

Instead, she told Reyna about her own life. She talked about her dad and stepmom and her two stepbrothers in San Francisco, and how she had felt like an outsider in her own family. She talked about how she had run away when she was only seven, finding her friends Luke and Thalia and making her way to Camp Half-Blood on Long Island. She described the camp and her years growing up there. She talked about meeting Percy and the adventures they'd had together.

Reyna was a good listener.

Annabeth was tempted to tell her about more recent problems: her fight with her mom, the gift of the silver coin and the nightmares she'd been having – about an old fear so paralysing she'd almost decided that she couldn't go on this quest. But she couldn't bring herself to open up quite that much.

When Annabeth was done talking, Reyna gazed over New Rome. Her metal greyhounds sniffed around the garden, snapping at bees in the honeysuckle. Finally Reyna pointed to the cluster of temples on the distant hill.

'The small red building,' she said, 'there on the northern side? That's the temple of my mother, Bellona.' Reyna turned towards Annabeth. 'Unlike your mother, Bellona has no Greek equivalent. She is fully, truly Roman. She's the goddess of protecting the homeland.'

Annabeth said nothing. She knew very little about the Roman goddess. She wished she had studied up, but Latin never came as easily to her as Greek. Down below, the hull of the *Argo II* gleamed as it floated over the forum, like some massive bronze party balloon.

'When the Romans go to war,' Reyna continued, 'we first visit the Temple of Bellona. Inside is a symbolic patch of ground that represents enemy soil. We throw a spear into that ground, indicating that we are now at war. You see, Romans have always believed that offence is the best defence. In ancient times, whenever our ancestors felt threatened by their neighbours, they would invade to protect themselves.'

'They conquered everyone around them,' Annabeth said. 'Carthage, the Gauls –'

'And the Greeks.' Reyna let that comment hang. 'My point, Annabeth, is that it isn't Rome's nature to cooperate with other powers. Every time Greek and Roman demigods have met, we've fought. Conflicts between our two sides have started some of the most horrible wars in human history – especially civil wars.'

'It doesn't have to be that way,' Annabeth said. 'We've got to work together, or Gaia will destroy us both.'

'I agree,' Reyna said. 'But is cooperation possible? What if Juno's plan is flawed? Even goddesses can make mistakes.'

Annabeth waited for Reyna to get struck by lightning or turned into a peacock. Nothing happened.

Unfortunately, Annabeth shared Reyna's doubts. Hera *did* make mistakes. Annabeth had had nothing but trouble from that overbearing goddess, and she'd never forgive Hera for taking Percy away, even if it was for a noble cause.

'I don't trust the goddess,' Annabeth admitted. 'But I do trust my friends. This isn't a trick, Reyna. We *can* work together.'

Reyna finished her cup of chocolate. She set the cup on the terrace railing and gazed over the valley as if imagining battle lines.

'I believe you mean it,' she said. 'But if you go to the ancient lands, especially Rome itself, there is something you should know about your mother.'

Annabeth's shoulders tensed. 'My – my mother?'

'When I lived on Circe's island,' Reyna said, 'we had many visitors. Once, perhaps a year before you and Percy arrived, a young man washed ashore. He was half mad from thirst and heat. He'd been drifting at sea for days. His words didn't make much sense, but he said he was a son of Athena.'

Reyna paused as if waiting for a reaction. Annabeth had no idea who the boy might have been. She wasn't aware of any other Athena kids who'd gone on a quest in the Sea of Monsters, but still she felt a sense of dread. The light filtering through the grapevines made shadows writhe across the ground like a swarm of bugs.

'What happened to this demigod?' she asked.

Reyna waved her hand as if the question was trivial. 'Circe turned him into a guinea pig, of course. He made quite a crazy little rodent. But *before* that he kept raving about his failed quest. He claimed that he'd gone to Rome, following the Mark of Athena.'

Annabeth grabbed the railing to keep her balance.

'Yes,' Reyna said, seeing her discomfort. 'He kept muttering about wisdom's child, the Mark of Athena and the giants' bane standing pale and gold. The same lines Ella was just reciting. But you say that you've never heard them before today?'

'Not – not the way Ella said them.' Annabeth's voice was weak. She wasn't lying. She'd never heard that prophecy, but her mother had charged her with following the Mark of Athena and, as she thought about the coin in her pocket, a horrible suspicion began taking root in her mind. She remembered her mother's scathing words. She thought about the strange nightmares she'd been having lately. 'Did this demigod – did he explain his quest?'

Reyna shook her head. 'At the time, I had no idea what

he was talking about. Much later, when I became praetor of Camp Jupiter, I began to suspect.'

'Suspect . . . what?'

'There is an old legend that the praetors of Camp Jupiter have passed down through the centuries. If it's true, it may explain why our two groups of demigods have never been able to work together. It may be the cause of our animosity. Until this old score is finally settled, so the legend goes, Romans and Greeks will never be at peace. And the legend centres on Athena –'

A shrill sound pierced the air. Light flashed in the corner of Annabeth's eye.

She turned in time to see an explosion blast a new crater in the forum. A burning couch tumbled through the air. Demigods scattered in panic.

'Giants?' Annabeth reached for her dagger, which of course wasn't there. 'I thought their army was defeated!'

'It isn't the giants.' Reyna's eyes seethed with rage. 'You've betrayed our trust.'

'What? No!'

As soon as she said it, the *Argo II* launched a second volley. Its port ballista fired a massive spear wreathed in Greek fire, which sailed straight through the broken dome of the Senate House and exploded inside, lighting up the building like a jack-o'-lantern. If anyone had been in there . . .

'Gods, no.' A wave of nausea almost made Annabeth's knees buckle. 'Reyna, it isn't possible. We'd never do this!'

The metal dogs ran to their mistress's side. They snarled at Annabeth but paced uncertainly, as if reluctant to attack.

'You're telling the truth,' Reyna judged. 'Perhaps you were not aware of this treachery, but *someone* must pay.'

Down in the forum, chaos was spreading. Crowds were pushing and shoving. Fistfights were breaking out.

'Bloodshed,' Reyna said.

'We have to stop it!'

Annabeth had a horrible feeling this might be the last time Reyna and she ever acted in agreement, but together they ran down the hill.

If weapons had been allowed in the city, Annabeth's friends would have already been dead. The Roman demigods in the forum had coalesced into an angry mob. Some threw plates, food and rocks at the *Argo II*, which was pointless, as most of the stuff fell back into the crowd.

Several dozen Romans had surrounded Piper and Jason, who were trying to calm them without much luck. Piper's charmspeak was useless against so many screaming, angry demigods. Jason's forehead was bleeding. His purple cloak had been ripped to shreds. He kept pleading, 'I'm on your side!' but his orange Camp Half-Blood T-shirt didn't help matters – nor did the warship overhead, firing flaming spears into New Rome. One landed nearby and blasted a toga shop to rubble.

'Pluto's pauldrons,' Reyna cursed. 'Look.'

Armed legionnaires were hurrying towards the forum. Two artillery crews had set up catapults just outside the Pomerian Line and were preparing to fire at the *Argo II*.

'That'll just make things worse,' Annabeth said.

'I hate my job,' Reyna growled. She rushed off towards the legionnaires, her dogs at her side.

Percy, Annabeth thought, scanning the forum desperately. *Where are you?*

Two Romans tried to grab her. She ducked past them, plunging into the crowd. As if the angry Romans, burning couches and exploding buildings weren't confusing enough, hundreds of purple ghosts drifted through the forum, passing straight through the demigods' bodies and wailing incoherently. The fauns had also taken advantage of the chaos. They swarmed the dining tables, grabbing food, plates and cups. One trotted by Annabeth with his arms full of tacos and an entire pineapple between his teeth.

A statue of Terminus exploded into being, right in front of Annabeth. He yelled at her in Latin, no doubt calling her a liar and a rule breaker, but she pushed the statue over and kept running.

Finally she spotted Percy. He and his friends, Hazel and Frank, were standing in the middle of a fountain as Percy repelled the angry Romans with blasts of water. Percy's toga was in tatters, but he looked unhurt.

Annabeth called to him as another explosion rocked the forum. This time the flash of light was directly overhead. One of the Roman catapults had fired, and the *Argo II* groaned and tilted sideways, flames bubbling over its bronze-plated hull.

Annabeth noticed a figure clinging desperately to the rope ladder, trying to climb down. It was Octavian, his robes steaming and his face black with soot.

Over by the fountain, Percy blasted the Roman mob with

more water. Annabeth ran towards him, ducking a Roman fist and a flying plate of sandwiches.

'Annabeth!' Percy called. 'What –?'

'I don't know!' she yelled.

'I'll tell you what!' cried a voice from above. Octavian had reached the bottom of the ladder. 'The Greeks have *fired* on us! Your boy Leo has trained his weapons on Rome!'

Annabeth's chest filled with liquid hydrogen. She felt like she might shatter into a million frozen pieces.

'You're lying,' she said. 'Leo would never –'

'I was just there!' Octavian shrieked. 'I saw it with my own eyes!'

The *Argo II* returned fire. Legionnaires in the field scattered as one of their catapults was blasted to splinters.

'You see?' Octavian screamed. 'Romans, kill the invaders!'

Annabeth growled in frustration. There was no time for anyone to figure out the truth. The crew from Camp Half-Blood was outnumbered a hundred to one, and even if Octavian had managed to stage some sort of trick (which she thought likely) they'd never be able to convince the Romans before they were overrun and killed.

'We have to leave,' she told Percy. '*Now.*'

He nodded grimly. 'Hazel, Frank, you've got to make a choice. Are you coming?'

Hazel looked terrified, but she donned her cavalry helmet. 'Of course we are. But you'll never make it to the ship unless we buy you some time.'

'How?' Annabeth asked.

Hazel whistled. Instantly a blur of beige shot across the

forum. A majestic horse materialized next to the fountain. He reared, whinnying and scattering the mob. Hazel climbed on his back like she'd been born to ride. Strapped to the horse's saddle was a Roman cavalry sword.

Hazel unsheathed her golden blade. 'Send me an Iris-message when you're safely away, and we'll rendezvous,' she said. 'Arion, ride!'

The horse zipped through the crowd with incredible speed, pushing back Romans and causing mass panic.

Annabeth felt a glimmer of hope. Maybe they could make it out of here alive. Then, from halfway across the forum, she heard Jason shouting.

'Romans!' he cried. 'Please!'

He and Piper were being pelted with plates and stones. Jason tried to shield Piper, but a brick caught him above the eye. He crumpled, and the crowd surged forward.

'Get back!' Piper screamed. Her charmspeak rolled over the mob, making them hesitate, but Annabeth knew the effect wouldn't last. She and Percy couldn't possibly reach them in time to help.

'Frank,' Percy said, 'it's up to you. Can you help them?'

Annabeth didn't understand how Frank could do that all by himself, but he swallowed nervously.

'Oh, gods,' he murmured. 'Okay, sure. Just get up the ropes. Now.'

Percy and Annabeth lunged for the ladder. Octavian was still clinging to the bottom, but Percy yanked him off and threw him into the mob.

They began to climb as armed legionnaires flooded into the

forum. Arrows whistled past Annabeth's head. An explosion almost knocked her off the ladder. Halfway up, she heard a roar below and glanced down.

Romans screamed and scattered as a full-sized dragon charged through the forum – a beast even scarier than the bronze dragon figurehead on the *Argo II*. It had rough grey skin like a Komodo lizard's and leathery bat wings. Arrows and rocks bounced harmlessly off its hide as it lumbered towards Piper and Jason, grabbed them with its front claws and vaulted into the air.

'Is that . . .?' Annabeth couldn't even put the thought into words.

'Frank,' Percy confirmed, a few feet above her. 'He has a few special talents.'

'Understatement,' Annabeth muttered. 'Keep climbing!'

Without the dragon and Hazel's horse to distract the archers, they never would have made it up the ladder, but finally they climbed past a row of broken aerial oars and onto the deck. The rigging was on fire. The foresail was ripped down the middle, and the ship listed badly to starboard.

There was no sign of Coach Hedge, but Leo stood amidships, calmly reloading the ballistae. Annabeth's gut twisted with horror.

'Leo!' she screamed. 'What are you *doing*?'

'Destroy them . . .' He faced Annabeth. His eyes were glazed. His movements were like a robot's. 'Destroy them all.'

He turned back to the ballistae, but Percy tackled him. Leo's head hit the deck hard, and his eyes rolled up so that only the whites showed.

The grey dragon soared into view. It circled the ship once and landed at the bow, depositing Jason and Piper, who both collapsed.

'Go!' Percy yelled. 'Get us out of here!'

With a shock, Annabeth realized he was talking to her.

She ran for the helm. She made the mistake of glancing over the rail and saw armed legionnaires closing ranks in the forum, preparing flaming arrows. Hazel spurred Arion, and they raced out of the city with a mob chasing after them. More catapults were being wheeled into range. All along the Pomerian Line, the statues of Terminus were glowing purple, as if building up energy for some kind of attack.

Annabeth looked over the controls. She cursed Leo for making them so complicated. No time for fancy manoeuvres, but she did know one basic command: *Up.*

She grabbed the aviation throttle and yanked it straight back. The ship groaned. The bow tilted up at a horrifying angle. The mooring lines snapped, and the *Argo II* shot into the clouds.

V

LEO

LEO WISHED HE COULD INVENT a time machine. He'd go back two hours and undo what had happened. Either that or he could invent a Slap-Leo-in-the-Face machine to punish himself, though he doubted it would hurt as badly as the look Annabeth was giving him.

'One more time,' she said. 'Exactly *what* happened?'

Leo slumped against the mast. His head still throbbed from hitting the deck. All around him, his beautiful new ship was in shambles. The aft crossbows were piles of kindling. The foresail was tattered. The satellite array that powered the onboard Internet and TV was blown to bits, which had really made Coach Hedge mad. Their bronze dragon figurehead, Festus, was coughing up smoke like he had a hairball, and Leo could tell from the groaning sounds on the port side that some of the aerial oars had been knocked out of alignment or broken off completely, which explained why the ship was listing and shuddering as it flew, the engine wheezing like an asthmatic steam train.

He choked back a sob. 'I don't know. It's fuzzy.'

Too many people were looking at him: Annabeth (Leo *hated* to make her angry; that girl scared him), Coach Hedge with his furry goat legs, his orange polo shirt and his baseball bat (did he have to carry that everywhere?) and the newcomer, Frank.

Leo wasn't sure what to make of Frank. He looked like a baby sumo wrestler, though Leo wasn't stupid enough to say that aloud. Leo's memory was hazy, but while he'd been half conscious, he was pretty sure he'd seen a dragon land on the ship – a dragon that had turned into Frank.

Annabeth crossed her arms. 'You mean you don't remember?'

'I . . .' Leo felt as if he was trying to swallow a marble. 'I remember, but it's like I was watching myself do things. I couldn't control it.'

Coach Hedge tapped his bat against the deck. In his gym clothes, with his cap pulled over his horns, he looked just like he used to at the Wilderness School, where he'd spent a year undercover as Jason, Piper and Leo's PE teacher. The way the old satyr was glowering, Leo almost wondered if the coach was going to order him to do push-ups.

'Look, kid,' Hedge said, 'you blew up some stuff. You attacked some Romans. Awesome! Excellent! But did you *have* to knock out the satellite channels? I was right in the middle of watching a cage match.'

'Coach,' Annabeth said, 'why don't you make sure all the fires are out?'

'But I already did that.'

'Do it again.'

The satyr trudged off, muttering under his breath. Even Hedge wasn't crazy enough to defy Annabeth.

She knelt next to Leo. Her grey eyes were as steely as ball bearings. Her blonde hair fell loose around her shoulders, but Leo didn't find that attractive. He had no idea where the stereotype of dumb giggly blondes came from. Ever since he'd met Annabeth at the Grand Canyon last winter, when she'd marched towards him with that *Give me Percy Jackson or I'll kill you* expression, Leo thought of blondes as much too smart and much too dangerous.

'Leo,' she said calmly, 'did Octavian trick you somehow? Did he frame you, or –'

'No.' Leo could have lied and blamed that stupid Roman, but he didn't want to make a bad situation worse. 'The guy was a jerk, but he didn't fire on the camp. I did.'

The new kid, Frank, scowled. 'On purpose?'

'No!' Leo squeezed his eyes shut. 'Well, yes . . . I mean, I didn't want to. But at the same time I *felt* like I wanted to. Something was making me do it. There was this cold feeling inside me –'

'A cold feeling.' Annabeth's tone changed. She sounded almost . . . scared.

'Yeah,' Leo said. 'Why?'

From belowdecks, Percy called up, 'Annabeth, we need you.'

Oh, gods, Leo thought. Please let Jason be okay.

As soon as they were on board, Piper had taken Jason below. The cut on his head had looked pretty bad. Leo had known Jason longer than anyone at Camp Half-Blood. They were best friends. If Jason didn't make it . . .

'He'll be fine.' Annabeth's expression softened. 'Frank, I'll be back. Just . . . watch Leo. Please.'

Frank nodded.

If it was possible for Leo to feel worse, he did. Annabeth now trusted a Roman demigod she'd known for, like, three seconds, more than she trusted Leo.

Once she was gone, Leo and Frank stared at each other. The big dude looked pretty odd in his bedsheet toga, with his grey pullover hoodie and jeans, and a bow and quiver from the ship's armoury slung over his shoulder. Leo remembered the time he had met the Hunters of Artemis – a bunch of cute lithe girls in silvery clothes, all armed with bows. He imagined Frank frolicking along with them. The idea was so ridiculous it almost made him feel better.

'So,' Frank said. 'Your name isn't Sammy?'

Leo scowled. 'What kind of question is that?'

'Nothing,' Frank said quickly. 'I just – Nothing. About the firing on the camp . . . Octavian could be behind it, like magically or something. He didn't want the Romans getting along with you guys.'

Leo wanted to believe that. He was grateful to this kid for not hating him. But he knew it hadn't been Octavian. *Leo* had walked to a ballista and started firing. Part of him had known it was wrong. He'd asked himself: *What the heck am I doing?* But he'd done it anyway.

Maybe he was going crazy. The stress of all those months working on the *Argo II* might've finally made him crack.

But he couldn't think about that. He needed to do something productive. His hands needed to be busy.

'Look,' he said, 'I should talk to Festus and get a damage report. You mind . . .?'

Frank helped him up. 'Who is Festus?'

'My friend,' Leo said. 'His name isn't Sammy either, in case you're wondering. Come on. I'll introduce you.'

Fortunately the bronze dragon wasn't damaged. Well, aside from the fact that last winter he'd lost everything except his head – but Leo didn't count that.

When they reached the bow of the ship, the figurehead turned a hundred and eighty degrees to look at them. Frank yelped and backed away.

'It's alive!' he said.

Leo would have laughed if he hadn't felt so bad. 'Yeah. Frank, this is Festus. He used to be a full bronze dragon, but we had an accident.'

'You have a lot of accidents,' Frank noted.

'Well, some of us can't turn into dragons, so we have to build our own.' Leo arched his eyebrows at Frank. 'Anyway, I revived him as a figurehead. He's kind of the ship's main interface now. How are things looking, Festus?'

Festus snorted smoke and made a series of squeaking, whirring sounds. Over the last few months, Leo had learned to interpret this machine language. Other demigods could understand Latin and Greek. Leo could speak Creak and Squeak.

'Ugh,' Leo said. 'Could be worse, but the hull is compromised in several places. The port aerial oars have to be fixed before we can go full speed again. We'll need some repair materials: Celestial bronze, tar, lime –'

'What do you need limes for?'

'Dude, *lime*. Calcium carbonate, used in cement and a bunch of other – Ah, never mind. The point is this ship isn't going far unless we can fix it.'

Festus made another click-creak noise that Leo didn't recognize. It sounded like *AY-zuhl*.

'Oh . . . *Hazel*,' he deciphered. 'That's the girl with the curly hair, right?'

Frank gulped. 'Is she okay?'

'Yeah, she's fine,' Leo said. 'According to Festus, her horse is racing along below. She's following us.'

'We've got to land, then,' Frank said.

Leo studied him. 'She's your girlfriend?'

Frank chewed his lip. 'Yes.'

'You don't sound sure.'

'Yes. Yes, definitely. I'm sure.'

Leo raised his hands. 'Okay, fine. The problem is we can only manage one landing. The way the hull and the oars are, we won't be able to lift off again until we repair, so we'll have to make sure we land somewhere with all the right supplies.'

Frank scratched his head. 'Where do you get Celestial bronze? You can't just stock up at Home Depot.'

'Festus, do a scan.'

'He can scan for magic bronze?' Frank marvelled. 'Is there anything he *can't* do?'

Leo thought: *You should've seen him when he had a body.* But he didn't say that. It was too painful, remembering the way Festus used to be.

Leo peered over the ship's bow. The Central California valley was passing below. Leo didn't hold out much hope that they could find what they needed all in one place, but they had to try. Leo also wanted to put as much distance as possible between himself and New Rome. The *Argo II* could cover vast distances pretty quickly, thanks to its magical engine, but Leo figured the Romans had magic travel methods of their own.

Behind him, the stairs creaked. Percy and Annabeth climbed up, their faces grim.

Leo's heart stumbled. 'Is Jason –?'

'He's resting,' Annabeth said. 'Piper's keeping an eye on him, but he should be fine.'

Percy gave him a hard look. 'Annabeth says you *did* fire that ballista?'

'Man, I – I don't understand how it happened. I'm so sorry –'

'*Sorry?*' Percy growled.

Annabeth put a hand on her boyfriend's chest. 'We'll figure it out later. Right now, we have to regroup and make a plan. What's the situation with the ship?'

Leo's legs trembled. The way Percy had looked at him made him feel the same as when Jason summoned lightning.

Leo's skin tingled, and every instinct in his body screamed, *Duck!*

He told Annabeth about the damage and the supplies they needed. At least he felt better talking about something fixable.

He was bemoaning the shortage of Celestial bronze when Festus began to whir and squeak.

'Perfect.' Leo sighed with relief.

'What's perfect?' Annabeth said. 'I could use some *perfect* about now.'

Leo managed a smile. 'Everything we need in one place. Frank, why don't you turn into a bird or something? Fly down and tell your girlfriend to meet us at the Great Salt Lake in Utah.'

Once they got there, it wasn't a pretty landing. With the oars damaged and the foresail torn, Leo could barely manage a controlled descent. The others strapped themselves in below – except for Coach Hedge, who insisted on clinging to the forward rail, yelling, 'YEAH! Bring it on, lake!' Leo stood astern, alone at the helm, and aimed as best he could.

Festus creaked and whirred warning signals, which were relayed through the intercom to the quarterdeck.

'I know, I know,' Leo said, gritting his teeth.

He didn't have much time to take in the scenery. To the southeast, a city was nestled in the foothills of a mountain range, blue and purple in the afternoon shadows. A flat desert landscape spread to the south. Directly beneath them the Great Salt Lake glittered like aluminum foil, the shoreline etched with white salt marshes that reminded Leo of aerial photos of Mars.

'Hang on, Coach!' he shouted. 'This is going to hurt.'

'I was *born* for hurt!'

WHOOM! A swell of salt water washed over the bow, dousing Coach Hedge. The *Argo II* listed dangerously to starboard, then righted itself and rocked on the surface of the lake. Machinery hummed as the aerial blades that were still working changed to nautical form.

Three banks of robotic oars dipped into the water and began moving them forward.

'Good job, Festus,' Leo said. 'Take us towards the south shore.'

'Yeah!' Coach Hedge pumped his fists in the air. He was drenched from his horns to hooves, but grinning like a crazy goat. 'Do it again!'

'Uh . . . maybe later,' Leo said. 'Just stay above deck, okay? You can keep watch, in case – you know, the lake decides to attack us or something.'

'On it,' Hedge promised.

Leo rang the *All clear* bell and headed for the stairs. Before he got there, a loud *clump-clump-clump* shook the hull. A tan stallion appeared on deck with Hazel Levesque on his back.

'How –?' Leo's question died in his throat. 'We're in the middle of a lake! Can that thing fly?'

The horse whinnied angrily.

'Arion can't fly,' Hazel said. 'But he can run across just about anything. Water, vertical surfaces, small mountains – none of that bothers him.'

'Oh.'

Hazel was looking at him strangely, the way she had during the feast in the forum – like she was searching for something in his face. He was tempted to ask if they had met before, but he was sure they hadn't. He would remember a pretty girl paying such close attention to him. That didn't happen a lot.

She's Frank's girlfriend, he reminded himself.

Frank was still below, but Leo almost wished the big guy would come up the stairs. The way Hazel was studying Leo made him feel uneasy and self-conscious.

Coach Hedge crept forward with his baseball bat, eyeing the magic horse suspiciously. 'Valdez, does this count as an invasion?'

'No!' Leo said. 'Um, Hazel, you'd better come with me. I built a stable belowdecks, if Arion wants to –'

'He's more of a free spirit.' Hazel slipped out of the saddle. 'He'll graze around the lake until I call him. But I want to see the ship. Lead the way.'

The *Argo II* was designed like an ancient trireme, only twice as big. The first deck had one central corridor with crew cabins on either side. On a normal trireme, most of the space would've been taken up with three rows of benches for a few hundred sweaty guys to do the manual labour, but Leo's oars were automated and retractable, so they took up very little room inside the hull. The ship's power came from the engine room on the second and lowest deck, which also housed sickbay, storage and the stables.

Leo led the way down the hall. He'd built the ship with eight cabins – seven for the demigods of the prophecy, and a room for Coach Hedge (seriously – Chiron considered him a responsible adult chaperone?). At the stern was a large mess hall/lounge, which was where Leo headed.

On the way, they passed Jason's room. The door was open. Piper sat at the side of his berth, holding Jason's hand while he snored with an ice pack on his head.

Piper glanced at Leo. She held a finger to her lips for quiet, but she didn't look angry. That was something. Leo tried to force down his guilt, and they kept walking. When they reached the mess hall, they found the others – Percy, Annabeth and Frank – sitting dejectedly around the dining table.

Leo had made the lounge as nice as possible, since he figured they'd be spending a lot of time there. The cupboard was lined with magic cups and plates from Camp Half-Blood, which would fill up with whatever food or drink you wanted on command. There was also a magical ice chest with canned drinks, perfect for picnics ashore. The chairs were cushy recliners with thousand-finger massage, built-in headphones, and sword and drink holders for all your demigod kicking-back needs. There were no windows, but the walls were enchanted to show real-time footage from Camp Half-Blood – the beach, the forest, the strawberry fields – although now Leo was wondering if this made people homesick rather than happy.

Percy was staring longingly at a sunset view of Half-Blood Hill, where the Golden Fleece glittered in the branches of the tall pine tree.

'So we've landed,' Percy said. 'What now?'

Frank plucked on his bowstring. 'Figure out the prophecy? I mean . . . that *was* a prophecy Ella spoke, right? From the Sibylline Books?'

'The what?' Leo asked.

Frank explained how their harpy friend was freakishly good at memorizing books. At some point in the past, she'd inhaled a collection of ancient prophecies that had supposedly been destroyed around the fall of Rome.

'That's why you didn't tell the Romans,' Leo guessed. 'You didn't want them to get hold of her.'

Percy kept staring at the image of Half-Blood Hill. 'Ella's sensitive. She was a captive when we found her. I just didn't want . . .' He made a fist. 'It doesn't matter now. I sent Tyson an Iris-message, told him to take Ella to Camp Half-Blood. They'll be safe there.'

Leo doubted that *any* of them would be safe, now that he had stirred up a camp of angry Romans on top of the problems they already had with Gaia and the giants, but he kept quiet.

Annabeth laced her fingers. 'Let me think about the prophecy – but right now we have more immediate problems. We have to get this ship fixed. Leo, what do we need?'

'The easiest thing is tar.' Leo was glad to change the subject. 'We can get that in the city, at a roofing-supply store or someplace like that. Also, Celestial bronze and lime. According to Festus, we can find both of those on an island in the lake, just west of here.'

'We'll have to hurry,' Hazel warned. 'If I know Octavian, he's searching for us with his auguries. The Romans will send a strike force after us. It's a matter of honour.'

Leo felt everyone's eyes on him. 'Guys . . . I don't know what happened. Honestly, I –'

Annabeth raised her hand. 'We've been talking. We agree it couldn't have been *you*, Leo. That cold feeling you mentioned . . . I felt it, too. It must have been some sort of magic, either Octavian or Gaia or one of her minions. But until we understand what happened –'

Frank grunted. 'How can we be sure it won't happen again?'

Leo's fingers heated up like they were about to catch fire. One of his powers as a son of Hephaestus was that he could summon flames at will, but he had to be careful not to do so by accident, especially on a ship filled with explosives and flammable supplies.

'I'm fine now,' he insisted, though he wished he could be sure. 'Maybe we should use the buddy system. Nobody goes anywhere alone. We can leave Piper and Coach Hedge on board with Jason. Send one team into town to get tar. Another team can go after the bronze and the lime.'

'Split up?' Percy said. 'That sounds like a really bad idea.'

'It'll be quicker,' Hazel put in. 'Besides, there's a reason a quest is usually limited to three demigods, right?'

Annabeth raised her eyebrows, as if reappraising Hazel's merits. 'You're right. The same reason we needed the *Argo II* . . . outside camp, seven demigods in one place will attract way too much monstrous attention. The ship is designed to conceal and protect us. We should be safe enough on board, but if we go on expeditions we shouldn't travel in groups larger than three. No sense alerting more of Gaia's minions than we have to.'

Percy still didn't look happy about it, but he took Annabeth's hand. 'As long as you're my buddy, I'm good.'

Hazel smiled. 'Oh, that's easy. Frank, you were amazing, turning into a dragon! Could you do it again to fly Annabeth and Percy into town for the tar?'

Frank opened his mouth like he wanted to protest. 'I . . . I suppose. But what about you?'

'I'll ride Arion with Sa– with Leo, here.' She fidgeted with her sword hilt, which made Leo uneasy. She had even more nervous energy than *he* did. 'We'll get the bronze and the lime. We can all meet back here by dark.'

Frank scowled. Obviously, he didn't like the idea of Leo going off with Hazel. For some reason, Frank's disapproval made Leo want to go. He *had* to prove he was trustworthy. He wasn't going to fire any random ballistae again.

'Leo,' said Annabeth, 'if we get the supplies, how long to fix the ship?'

'With luck, just a few hours.'

'Fine,' she decided. 'We'll meet you back here as soon as possible, but stay safe. We could use some good luck. That doesn't mean we'll get it.'

VI

LEO

RIDING ARION WAS THE BEST THING that had happened to Leo all day – which wasn't saying much, since his day had sucked. The horse's hooves turned the surface of the lake to salty mist. Leo put his hand against the horse's side and felt the muscles working like a well-oiled machine. For the first time, he understood why car engines were measured in horsepower. Arion was a four-legged Maserati.

Ahead of them lay an island – a line of sand so white it might have been pure table salt. Behind that rose an expanse of grassy dunes and weathered boulders.

Leo sat behind Hazel, one arm around her waist. The close contact made him a little uncomfortable, but it was the only way he could stay on board (or whatever you called it with a horse).

Before they left, Percy had pulled him aside to tell him Hazel's story. Percy made it sound like he was just doing Leo a favour, but there'd been an undertone like *If you mess with my friend, I will personally feed you to a great white shark.*

According to Percy, Hazel was a daughter of Pluto. She'd died in the 1940s and been brought back to life only a few months ago.

Leo found that hard to believe. Hazel seemed warm and very alive, not like the ghosts or the other reborn mortals Leo had tangled with.

She seemed good with people, too, unlike Leo, who was much more comfortable with machines. Living stuff, like horses and girls? He had no idea what made them work.

Hazel was also Frank's girlfriend, so Leo knew he should keep his distance. Still, her hair smelled good, and riding with her made his heart race almost against his will. It must've been the speed of the horse.

Arion thundered onto the beach. He stomped his hooves and whinnied triumphantly, like Coach Hedge yelling a battle cry.

Hazel and Leo dismounted. Arion pawed the sand.

'He needs to eat,' Hazel explained. 'He likes gold, but –'

'Gold?' Leo asked.

'He'll settle for grass. Go on, Arion. Thanks for the ride. I'll call you.'

Just like that, the horse was gone – nothing left but a steaming trail across the lake.

'Fast horse,' Leo said, 'and expensive to feed.'

'Not really,' Hazel said. 'Gold is easy for me.'

Leo raised his eyebrows. 'How is gold easy? Please tell

me you're not related to King Midas. I don't like that guy.'

Hazel pursed her lips, as if she regretted raising the subject. 'Never mind.'

That made Leo even more curious, but he decided it might be better not to press her. He knelt and cupped a handful of white sand. 'Well . . . one problem solved, anyway. This is lime.'

Hazel frowned. 'The whole beach?'

'Yeah. See? The granules are perfectly round. It's not really sand. It's calcium carbonate.' Leo pulled an airtight bag from his tool belt and dug his hand into the lime.

Suddenly he froze. He remembered all the times the earth goddess Gaia had appeared to him in the ground – her sleeping face made of dust or sand or soil. She loved to taunt him. He imagined her closed eyes and her dreaming smile swirling in the white calcium.

Walk away, little hero, Gaia said. *Without you, the ship cannot be fixed.*

'Leo?' Hazel asked. 'You okay?'

He took a shaky breath. Gaia wasn't here. He was just freaking himself out.

'Yeah,' he said. 'Yeah, fine.'

He started to fill the bag.

Hazel knelt next to him and helped. 'We should've brought a pail and shovels.'

The idea cheered Leo up. He even smiled. 'We could've made a sand castle.'

'A lime castle.'

Their eyes locked for a second too long.

Hazel looked away. 'You are *so* much like –'

'Sammy?' Leo guessed.

She fell backwards. 'You know?'

'I have no idea who Sammy is. But Frank asked me if I was sure that wasn't my name.'

'And . . . it isn't?'

'No! Jeez.'

'You don't have a twin brother or . . .' Hazel stopped. 'Is your family from New Orleans?'

'Nah. Houston. Why? Is Sammy a guy you used to know?'

'I . . . It's nothing. You just look like him.'

Leo could tell she was too embarrassed to say more. But, if Hazel was a kid from the past, did that mean Sammy was from the 1940s? If so, how could Frank know the guy? And why would Hazel think Leo was Sammy, all these decades later?

They finished filling the bag in silence. Leo stuffed it in his tool belt and the bag vanished – no weight, no mass, no volume – though Leo knew it would be there as soon as he reached for it. Anything that could fit into the pockets, Leo could tote around. He *loved* his tool belt. He just wished the pockets were large enough for a chain saw, or maybe a bazooka.

He stood and scanned the island – bleach-white dunes, blankets of grass and boulders encrusted with salt like frosting. 'Festus said there was Celestial bronze close by, but I'm not sure where –'

'That way.' Hazel pointed up the beach. 'About five hundred yards.'

'How do you –?'

'Precious metals,' Hazel said. 'It's a Pluto thing.'

Leo remembered what she'd said about gold being easy. 'Handy talent. Lead the way, Miss Metal Detector.'

The sun began to set. The sky turned a bizarre mix of purple and yellow. In another reality, Leo might've enjoyed a walk on the beach with a pretty girl, but the further they went the edgier he felt. Finally Hazel turned inland.

'You sure this is a good idea?' he asked.

'We're close,' she promised. 'Come on.'

Just over the dunes, they saw a woman.

She sat on a boulder in the middle of a grassy field. A black-and-chrome motorcycle was parked nearby, but each of the wheels had a big pie slice removed from the spokes and rim, so that they resembled Pac-Men. No way was the bike drivable in that condition.

The woman had curly black hair and a bony frame. She wore black leather biker's pants, tall leather boots and a blood-red leather jacket – sort of a *Michael Jackson joins the Hell's Angels* look. Around her feet, the ground was littered with what looked like broken shells. She was hunched over, pulling new ones out of a sack and cracking them open. Shucking oysters? Leo wasn't sure if there were oysters in the Great Salt Lake. He didn't think so.

He wasn't anxious to approach. He'd had bad experiences with strange ladies. His old babysitter, Tía Callida, had turned out to be Hera and had a nasty habit of putting him down for naps in a blazing fireplace. The earth goddess Gaia had killed his mother in a workshop fire when Leo was eight. The snow goddess Khione had tried to turn him into a frozen dairy treat in Sonoma.

But Hazel forged ahead, so he didn't have much choice except to follow.

As they got closer, Leo noticed disturbing details. Attached to the woman's belt was a curled whip. Her red-leather jacket had a subtle design to it – twisted branches of an apple tree populated with skeletal birds. The oysters she was shucking were actually fortune cookies.

A pile of broken cookies lay ankle-deep all around her. She kept pulling new ones from her sack, cracking them open and reading the fortunes. Most she tossed aside. A few made her mutter unhappily. She would swipe her finger over the slip of paper like she was smudging it, then magically reseal the cookie and toss it into a nearby basket.

'What are you doing?' Leo asked before he could stop himself.

The woman looked up. Leo's lungs filled so fast he thought they might burst.

'Aunt Rosa?' he asked.

It didn't make sense, but this woman looked *exactly* like his aunt. She had the same broad nose with a mole on one side, the same sour mouth and hard eyes. But it couldn't be Rosa. She would never wear clothes like that, and she was still down in Houston, as far as Leo knew. She wouldn't be cracking open fortune cookies in the middle of the Great Salt Lake.

'Is that what you see?' the woman asked. 'Interesting. And you, Hazel, dear?'

'How did you –?' Hazel stepped back in alarm. 'You – you look like Mrs Leer. My third-grade teacher. I hated you.'

The woman cackled. 'Excellent. You resented her, eh? She judged you unfairly?'

'You – she taped my hands to the desk for misbehaving,' Hazel said. 'She called my mother a witch. She blamed me for everything I didn't do and – No. She *has* to be dead. Who *are* you?'

'Oh, Leo knows,' the woman said. 'How do you feel about Aunt Rosa, *mijo*?'

Mijo. That's what Leo's mom had always called him. After his mom died, Rosa had rejected Leo. She'd called him a devil child. She'd blamed him for the fire that had killed her sister. Rosa had turned his family against him and left him – a scrawny orphaned eight-year-old – at the mercy of social services. Leo had bounced around from foster home to foster home until he'd finally found a home at Camp Half-Blood. Leo didn't hate many people, but after all these years Aunt Rosa's face made him boil with resentment.

How did he feel? He wanted to get even. He wanted revenge.

His eyes drifted to the motorcycle with the Pac-Man wheels. Where had he seen something like that before? Cabin 16, back at Camp Half-Blood – the symbol above their door was a broken wheel.

'Nemesis,' he said. 'You're the goddess of revenge.'

'You see?' The goddess smiled at Hazel. 'He recognizes me.'

Nemesis cracked another cookie and wrinkled her nose. *'You will have great fortune when you least expect it,'* she read. 'That's exactly the sort of nonsense I hate. Someone opens a cookie and suddenly they have a prophecy that they'll be rich! I blame that tramp Tyche. Always dispensing good luck to people who don't deserve it!'

Leo looked at the mound of broken cookies. 'Uh . . . you know those aren't real prophecies, right? They're just stuffed in the cookies at some factory —'

'Don't try to excuse it!' Nemesis snapped. 'It's just like Tyche to get people's hopes up. No, no. I *must* counter her.' Nemesis flicked a finger over the slip of paper, and the letters changed to red. *'You will die painfully when you most expect it.* There! Much better.'

'That's horrible!' Hazel said. 'You'd let someone read that in their fortune cookie, and it would come true?'

Nemesis sneered. It really was creepy, seeing that expression on Aunt Rosa's face. 'My dear Hazel, haven't you ever wished horrible things on Mrs Leer for the way she treated you?'

'That doesn't mean I'd want them to come true!'

'Bah.' The goddess resealed the cookie and tossed it in her basket. 'Tyche would be Fortuna for you, I suppose, being Roman. Like the others, she's in a horrible way right now. Me? I'm not affected. I am called Nemesis in both Greek and Roman. I do not change, because revenge is universal.'

'What are you talking about?' Leo asked. 'What are you doing here?'

Nemesis opened another cookie. 'Lucky numbers. Ridiculous! That's not even a proper fortune!' She crushed the cookie and scattered the pieces around her feet.

'To answer your question, Leo Valdez, the gods are in terrible shape. It always happens when a civil war is brewing between you Romans and Greeks. The Olympians are torn between their two natures, called on by both sides. They become quite schizophrenic, I'm afraid. Splitting headaches. Disorientation.'

'But we're not at war,' Leo insisted.

'Um, Leo . . .' Hazel winced. 'Except for the fact that you recently blew up large sections of New Rome.'

Leo stared at her, wondering whose side she was on. 'Not on purpose!'

'I know . . .' Hazel said, 'but the Romans don't realize that. And they'll be pursuing us in retaliation.'

Nemesis cackled. 'Leo, listen to the girl. War is coming. Gaia has seen to it, with your help. And can you guess whom the gods blame for their predicament?'

Leo's mouth tasted like calcium carbonate. 'Me.'

The goddess snorted. 'Well, don't *you* have a high opinion of yourself. You're just a pawn on the chessboard, Leo Valdez. I was referring to the player who set this ridiculous quest in motion, bringing the Greeks and Romans together. The gods blame Hera – or Juno, if you prefer! The queen of the heavens has fled Olympus to escape the wrath of her family. Don't expect any more help from your patron!'

Leo's head throbbed. He had mixed feelings about Hera.

She'd meddled in his life since he was a baby, moulding him to serve her purpose in this big prophecy, but at least she had been on their side, more or less. If she was out of the picture now . . .

'So why are you here?' he asked.

'Why, to offer *my* help!' Nemesis smiled wickedly.

Leo glanced at Hazel. She looked like she'd just been offered a free snake.

'Your help,' Leo said.

'Of course!' said the goddess. 'I enjoy tearing down the proud and powerful, and there are none who deserve tearing down like Gaia and her giants. Still, I must warn you that I will not suffer undeserved success. Good luck is a sham. The wheel of fortune is a Ponzi scheme. True success requires sacrifice.'

'Sacrifice?' Hazel's voice was tight. 'I lost my mother. I died and came back. Now my brother is missing. Isn't that enough sacrifice for you?'

Leo could totally relate. He wanted to scream that he'd lost his mom, too. His whole life had been one misery after another. He'd lost his dragon, Festus. He'd nearly killed himself trying to finish the *Argo II*. Now he'd fired on the Roman camp, most likely started a war and maybe lost the trust of his friends.

'Right now,' he said, trying to control his anger, 'all I want is some Celestial bronze.'

'Oh, that's easy,' Nemesis said. 'It's just over the rise. You'll find it with the sweethearts.'

'Wait,' Hazel said. 'What sweethearts?'

Nemesis popped a cookie in her mouth and swallowed it, fortune and all. 'You'll see. Perhaps they will teach you a lesson, Hazel Levesque. Most heroes cannot escape their nature, even when given a second chance at life.' She smiled. 'And speaking of your brother, Nico, you don't have much time. Let's see . . . it's June twenty-fifth? Yes, after today, six more days. Then he dies, along with the entire city of Rome.'

Hazel's eyes widened. 'How . . . what –?'

'And as for *you*, child of fire.' She turned to Leo. 'Your worst hardships are yet to come. You will always be the outsider, the seventh wheel. You will not find a place among your brethren. Soon you will face a problem you cannot solve, though I could help you . . . for a price.'

Leo smelled smoke. He realized the fingers on his left hand were ablaze, and Hazel was staring at him in terror.

He shoved his hand in his pocket to extinguish the flames. 'I like to solve my own problems.'

'Very well.' Nemesis brushed cookie dust off her jacket.

'But, um, what sort of price are we talking about?'

The goddess shrugged. 'One of my children recently traded an eye for the ability to make a real difference in the world.'

Leo's stomach churned. 'You . . . want an eye?'

'In your case, perhaps another sacrifice would do. But something just as painful. Here.' She handed him an unbroken fortune cookie. 'If you need an answer, break this. It will solve your problem.'

Leo's hand trembled as he held the fortune cookie. 'What problem?'

'You'll know when the time comes.'

'No, thanks,' Leo said firmly. But his hand, as though it had a will of its own, slipped the cookie into his tool belt.

Nemesis picked another cookie from her bag and cracked it open. '*You will have cause to reconsider your choices soon.* Oh, I like that one. No changes needed here.'

She resealed the cookie and tossed it into the basket. 'Very few gods will be able to help you on the quest. Most are already incapacitated, and their confusion will only grow worse. One thing might bring unity to Olympus again – an old wrong finally avenged. Ah, that would be sweet indeed, the scales finally balanced! But it will not happen unless you accept my help.'

'I suppose you won't tell us what you're talking about,' Hazel muttered. 'Or why my brother, Nico, has only six days to live. Or why Rome is going to be destroyed.'

Nemesis chuckled. She rose and slung her sack of cookies over her shoulder. 'Oh, it's all tied together, Hazel Levesque. As for my offer, Leo Valdez, give it some thought. You're a good child. A hard worker. We could do business. But I have detained you too long. You should visit the reflecting pool before the light fades. My poor cursed boy gets quite . . . agitated when the darkness comes.'

Leo didn't like the sound of that, but the goddess climbed on her motorcycle. Apparently, it *was* drivable, despite those Pac-Man-shaped wheels, because Nemesis revved her engine and disappeared in a mushroom cloud of black smoke.

Hazel bent down. All the broken cookies and fortunes had disappeared except for one crumpled slip of paper. She picked it up and read, '*You will see yourself reflected, and you will have reason to despair.*'

'Fantastic,' Leo grumbled. 'Let's go see what that means.'

VII

LEO

'WHO IS AUNT ROSA?' HAZEL ASKED.

Leo didn't want to talk about her. Nemesis's words were still buzzing in his ears. His tool belt seemed heavier since he'd put the cookie in there – which was impossible. Its pockets could carry anything without adding extra weight. Even the most fragile things would never break. Still, Leo imagined he could feel it in there, dragging him down, waiting to be cracked open.

'Long story,' he said. 'She abandoned me after my mom died, gave me to foster care.'

'I'm sorry.'

'Yeah, well . . .' Leo was anxious to change the subject. 'What about you? What Nemesis said about your brother?'

Hazel blinked like she'd got salt in her eyes. 'Nico . . . he found me in the Underworld. He brought me back to the mortal world and convinced the Romans at Camp Jupiter to accept me. I owe him for my second chance at life. If Nemesis is right and Nico's in danger . . . I *have* to help him.'

'Sure,' Leo said, though the idea made him uneasy. He doubted the revenge goddess ever gave advice out of the goodness of her heart. 'And what Nemesis said about your brother having six days to live and Rome getting destroyed . . . any idea what she meant?'

'None,' Hazel admitted. 'But I'm afraid . . .'

Whatever she was thinking, she decided not to share it. She climbed one of the largest boulders to get a better view. Leo tried to follow and lost his balance. Hazel caught his hand. She pulled him up and they found themselves atop the rock, holding hands, face to face.

Hazel's eyes glittered like gold.

Gold is easy, she'd said. It didn't seem that way to Leo – not when he looked at her. He wondered who Sammy was. Leo had a nagging suspicion that he *should* know, but he just couldn't place the name. Whoever he was, he was lucky if Hazel cared for him.

'Um, thanks.' He let go of her hand, but they were still standing so close that he could feel the warmth of her breath. She *definitely* didn't seem like a dead person.

'When we were talking to Nemesis,' Hazel said uneasily, 'your hands . . . I saw flames.'

'Yeah,' he said. 'It's a Hephaestus power. Usually I can keep it under control.'

'Oh.' She put one hand protectively on her denim shirt, like she was about to say the Pledge of Allegiance. Leo got the feeling she wanted to back away from him, but the boulder was too small.

Great, he thought. Another person who thinks I'm a scary freak.

He gazed across the island. The opposite shore was only a few hundred yards away. Between here and there were dunes and clumps of boulders, but nothing that looked like a reflecting pool.

You will always be the outsider, Nemesis had told him, *the seventh wheel. You will not find a place among your brethren.*

She might as well have poured acid in his ears. Leo didn't need anybody to tell him he was odd man out. He'd spent months alone in Bunker 9 at Camp Half-Blood, working on his ship while his friends trained together and shared meals and played capture the flag for fun and prizes. Even his two best friends, Piper and Jason, often treated him like an outsider. Since they'd started dating, their idea of 'quality time' didn't include Leo. His only other friend, Festus the dragon, had been reduced to a figurehead when his control disk had got destroyed on their last adventure. Leo didn't have the technical skill to repair it.

The seventh wheel. Leo had heard of a fifth wheel – an extra, useless piece of equipment. He figured a seventh wheel was worse.

He'd thought maybe this quest would be a fresh start for him. All his hard work on the *Argo II* would pay off. He'd have six good friends who would admire and appreciate him, and they'd go sailing off into the sunrise to fight giants. Maybe, Leo secretly hoped, he'd even find a girlfriend.

Do the maths, he chided himself.

Nemesis was right. He might be part of a group of seven,

but he was still isolated. He had fired on the Romans and brought his friends nothing but trouble. *You will not find a place among your brethren.*

'Leo?' Hazel asked gently. 'You can't take what Nemesis said to heart.'

He frowned. 'What if it's true?'

'She's the goddess of revenge,' Hazel reminded him. 'Maybe she's on our side, maybe not, but she exists to stir up resentment.'

Leo wished he could dismiss his feelings that easily. He couldn't. Still, it wasn't Hazel's fault.

'We should keep going,' he said. 'I wonder what Nemesis meant about finishing before dark.'

Hazel glanced at the sun, which was just touching the horizon. 'And who is the *cursed boy* she mentioned?'

Below them, a voice said, 'Cursed boy she mentioned.'

At first, Leo saw no one. Then his eyes adjusted. He realized a young woman was standing only ten feet from the base of the boulder. Her dress was a Greek-style tunic the same colour as the rocks. Her wispy hair was somewhere between brown and blonde and grey, so it blended with the dry grass. She wasn't invisible, exactly, but she was almost perfectly camouflaged until she moved. Even then, Leo had trouble focusing on her. Her face was pretty but not memorable. In fact, each time Leo blinked, he couldn't remember what she looked like, and he had to concentrate to find her again.

'Hello,' Hazel said. 'Who are you?'

'Who are you?' the girl answered. Her voice sounded weary, like she was tired of answering that question.

Hazel and Leo exchanged looks. With this demigod gig, you never knew what you'd run into. Nine times out of ten, it wasn't good. A ninja girl camouflaged in earth tones didn't strike Leo as something he wanted to deal with just then.

'Are you the cursed kid Nemesis mentioned?' Leo asked. 'But you're a girl.'

'You're a girl,' said the girl.

'Excuse me?' Leo said.

'Excuse me,' the girl said miserably.

'You're repeating . . .' Leo stopped. 'Oh. Hold it. Hazel, wasn't there some myth about a girl who repeated everything –?'

'Echo,' Hazel said.

'Echo,' the girl agreed. She shifted, her dress changing with the landscape. Her eyes were the colour of the salt water. Leo tried to home in on her features, but he couldn't.

'I don't remember the myth,' he admitted. 'You were cursed to repeat the last thing you heard?'

'You heard,' Echo said.

'Poor thing,' Hazel said. 'If I remember right, a goddess did this?'

'A goddess did this,' Echo confirmed.

Leo scratched his head. 'But wasn't that thousands of years . . . oh. You're one of the mortals who came back through the Doors of Death. I really wish we could stop running into dead people.'

'Dead people,' Echo said, like she was chastising him.

He realized Hazel was staring at her feet.

'Uh . . . sorry,' he muttered. 'I didn't mean it that way.'

'That way.' Echo pointed towards the far shore of the island.

'You want to show us something?' Hazel asked. She climbed down the boulder, and Leo followed.

Even up close, Echo was hard to see. In fact, she seemed to get more invisible the longer he looked at her.

'You sure you're real?' he asked. 'I mean . . . flesh and blood?'

'Flesh and blood.' She touched Leo's face and made him flinch. Her fingers were warm.

'So . . . you have to repeat everything?' he asked.

'Everything.'

Leo couldn't help smiling. 'That could be fun.'

'Fun,' she said unhappily.

'Blue elephants.'

'Blue elephants.'

'Kiss me, you fool.'

'You fool.'

'Hey!'

'Hey!'

'Leo,' Hazel pleaded, 'don't tease her.'

'Don't tease her,' Echo agreed.

'Okay, okay,' Leo said, though he had to resist the urge. It wasn't every day he met somebody with a built-in talkback feature. 'So what were you pointing at? Do you need our help?'

'Help,' Echo agreed emphatically. She gestured for them to follow and sprinted down the slope. Leo could only follow her progress by the movement of the grass and the shimmer of her dress as it changed to match the rocks.

'We'd better hurry,' Hazel said. 'Or we'll lose her.'

They found the problem – if you can call a mob of good-looking girls a problem. Echo led them down into a grassy meadow shaped like a blast crater, with a small pond in the middle. Gathered at the water's edge were several dozen nymphs. At least, Leo guessed they were nymphs. Like the ones at Camp Half-Blood, these wore gossamer dresses. Their feet were bare. They had elfish features, and their skin had a slightly greenish tinge.

Leo didn't understand what they were doing, but they were all crowded together in one spot, facing the pond and jostling for a better view. Several held up phone cameras, trying to get a shot over the heads of the others. Leo had never seen nymphs with phones. He wondered if they were looking at a dead body. If so, why were they bouncing up and down and giggling so excitedly?

'What are they looking at?' Leo wondered.

'Looking at,' Echo sighed.

'One way to find out.' Hazel marched forward and began nudging her way through the crowd. 'Excuse us. Pardon me.'

'Hey!' one nymph complained. 'We were here first!'

'Yeah,' another sniffed. 'He won't be interested in *you*.'

The second nymph had large red hearts painted on her cheeks. Over her dress, she wore a T-shirt that read: OMG, I <3 N!!!!

'Uh, demigod business,' Leo said, trying to sound official. 'Make room. Thanks.'

The nymphs grumbled, but they parted to reveal a young man kneeling at the edge of the pond, gazing intently at the water.

Leo usually didn't pay much attention to how other guys looked. He supposed that came from hanging around Jason – tall, blond, rugged and basically everything Leo could never be. Leo was used to not being noticed by girls. At least, he knew he'd never get a girl by his looks. He hoped his personality and sense of humour would do that someday, though it definitely hadn't worked yet.

At any rate, Leo couldn't miss the fact that the guy at the pond was one super good-looking dude. He had a chiselled face with lips and eyes that were somewhere between feminine beautiful and masculine handsome. Dark hair swept over his brow. He might've been seventeen or twenty, it was hard to say, but he was built like a dancer – with long graceful arms and muscular legs, perfect posture and an air of regal calm. He wore a simple white T-shirt and jeans, with a bow and quiver strapped to his back. The weapons obviously hadn't been used in a while. The arrows were covered in dust. A spider had woven a web in the top of the bow.

As Leo edged closer, he realized the guy's face was unusually golden. In the sunset, the light was bouncing off a large flat sheet of Celestial bronze that lay at the bottom of the pond, washing Mr Handsome's features in a warm glow.

The guy seemed fascinated with his reflection in the metal.

Hazel inhaled sharply. 'He's gorgeous.'

Around her, the nymphs squealed and clapped in agreement.

'I am,' the young man murmured dreamily, his gaze still fixed on the water. 'I am *so* gorgeous.'

One of the nymphs showed her iPhone screen. 'His latest YouTube video got a million hits in, like, an *hour*. I think I was half of those!'

The other nymphs giggled.

'YouTube video?' Leo asked. 'What does he do in the video, sing?'

'No, silly!' the nymph chided. 'He used to be a prince, and a wonderful hunter and stuff. But that doesn't matter. Now he just . . . well, look!' She showed Leo the video. It was exactly what they were seeing in real life – the guy staring at himself in the pond.

'He is sooooo hot!' said another girl. Her T-shirt read: MRS NARCISSUS.

'Narcissus?' Leo asked.

'Narcissus,' Echo agreed sadly.

Leo had forgotten Echo was there. Apparently none of the nymphs had noticed her either.

'Oh, not *you* again!' Mrs Narcissus tried to push Echo away, but she misjudged where the camouflaged girl was and ended up shoving several other nymphs.

'You had your chance, Echo!' said the nymph with the iPhone. 'He dumped you four thousand years ago! You are *so* not good enough for him.'

'For him,' Echo said bitterly.

'Wait.' Hazel clearly had trouble tearing her eyes away

from the handsome guy, but she managed it. 'What's going on here? Why did Echo bring us here?'

One nymph rolled her eyes. She was holding an autograph pen and a crumpled poster of Narcissus. 'Echo was a nymph like us, a long time ago, but she was a total chatterbox! Gossiping, blah, blah, blah, all the time.'

'I know!' another nymph shrieked. 'Like, who could stand that? Just the other day, I told Cleopeia – you know she lives in the boulder next to me? – I said: *Stop gossiping or you'll end up like Echo.* Cleopeia is such a big mouth! Did you hear what she said about that cloud nymph and the satyr?'

'Totally!' said the nymph with the poster. 'So anyway, as punishment for blabbing, Hera cursed Echo so she could only repeat things, which was *fine* with us. But then Echo fell in love with our gorgeous guy, Narcissus – as if he would ever notice her.'

'As if!' said half a dozen others. 'Now she's got some weird idea he needs saving,' said Mrs Narcissus. 'She should just go away.'

'Go away,' Echo growled back.

'I'm *so* glad Narcissus is alive again,' said another nymph in a grey dress. She had the words NARCISSUS + LAIEA written up and down her arms in black marker. 'He's like *the best*! And he's in *my* territory.'

'Oh, stop it, Laiea,' her friend said. '*I'm* the pond nymph. You're just the rock nymph.'

'Well, I'm the grass nymph,' another protested.

'No, he obviously came here because he likes the wild-flowers!' another said. 'Those are mine!'

The whole mob began arguing while Narcissus stared at the lake, ignoring them.

'Hold it!' Leo yelled. 'Ladies, hold it! I need to ask Narcissus something.'

Slowly the nymphs settled down and went back to taking pictures.

Leo knelt next to the handsome dude. 'So, Narcissus. What's up?'

'Could you move?' Narcissus asked distractedly. 'You're ruining the view.'

Leo looked in the water. His own reflection rippled next to Narcissus's on the surface of the submerged bronze. Leo didn't have any desire to stare at himself. Compared to Narcissus, he looked like an undergrown troll. But there was no doubt the metal was a sheet of hammered Celestial bronze, roughly circular, about five feet in diameter.

What it was doing in this pond, Leo wasn't sure. Celestial bronze fell to earth in odd places. He'd heard that most pieces were cast off from his dad's various workshops. Hephaestus would lose his temper when projects didn't work out, and he'd toss his scraps into the mortal world. This piece looked like it might have been meant as a shield for a god, but it hadn't turned out properly. If Leo could get it back to the ship, it would be just enough bronze for his repairs.

'Right, great view,' Leo said. 'Happy to move, but, if you're not using it, could I just take that sheet of bronze?'

'No,' Narcissus said. 'I love him. He's so gorgeous.'

Leo looked around to see if the nymphs were laughing. This *had* to be a huge joke. But they were swooning and nodding in agreement. Only Hazel seemed appalled. She wrinkled her nose as if she'd come to the conclusion that Narcissus smelled worse than he looked.

'Man,' Leo said to Narcissus. 'You *do* realize that you're looking at *yourself* in the water, right?'

'I am so great,' Narcissus sighed. He stretched out a hand longingly to touch the water, but held back. 'No, I can't make ripples. That ruins the image. Wow . . . I am *so* great.'

'Yeah,' Leo muttered. 'But if I took the bronze you could still see yourself in the water. Or here . . .' He reached in his tool belt and pulled out a simple mirror the size of a monocle. 'I'll trade you.'

Narcissus took the mirror, reluctantly, and admired himself. 'Even *you* carry a picture of me? I don't blame you. I am gorgeous. Thank you.' He set the mirror down and returned his attention to the pond. 'But I already have a much better image. The colour flatters me, don't you think?'

'Oh, gods, yes!' a nymph screamed. 'Marry me, Narcissus!'

'No, me!' another cried. 'Would you sign my poster?'

'No, sign my shirt!'

'No, sign my forehead!'

'No, sign my –'

'Stop it!' Hazel snapped.

'Stop it,' Echo agreed.

Leo had lost sight of Echo again, but now he realized she was kneeling on the other side of Narcissus, waving her hand in front of his face as if trying to break his concentration. Narcissus didn't even blink.

The nymph fan club tried to shove Hazel out of the way,

but she drew her cavalry sword and forced them back. 'Snap out of it!' she yelled.

'He won't sign your sword,' the poster nymph complained.

'He won't marry you,' said the iPhone girl. 'And you can't take his bronze mirror! That's what *keeps* him here!'

'You're all ridiculous,' Hazel said. 'He's so *full* of himself! How can you possibly like him?'

'Like him,' Echo sighed, still waving her hand in front of his face.

The others sighed along with her.

'I am so hot,' Narcissus said sympathetically.

'Narcissus, listen.' Hazel kept her sword at the ready. 'Echo brought us here to help you. Didn't you, Echo?'

'Echo,' said Echo.

'Who?' Narcissus said.

'The only girl who cares what happens to you, apparently,' Hazel said. 'Do you remember dying?'

Narcissus frowned. 'I . . . no. That can't be right. I am much too important to die.'

'You died staring at yourself,' Hazel insisted. 'I remember the story now. Nemesis was the goddess who cursed you, because you broke so many hearts. Your punishment was to fall in love with your own reflection.'

'I love me so, so much,' Narcissus agreed.

'You finally died,' Hazel continued. 'I don't know which version of the story is true. You either drowned yourself or turned into a flower hanging over the water or – Echo, which is it?'

'Which is it?' she said hopelessly.

Leo stood. 'It doesn't matter. The point is you're alive again, man. You have a second chance. That's what Nemesis was telling us. You can get up, and get on with your life. Echo is trying to save you. Or you can stay here and stare at yourself until you die again.'

'Stay here!' all the nymphs screamed.

'Marry me before you die!' another squeaked.

Narcissus shook his head. 'You just want my reflection. I don't blame you, but you can't have it. I belong to me.'

Hazel sighed in exasperation. She glanced at the sun, which was sinking fast. Then she gestured with her sword towards the edge of the crater. 'Leo, could we talk for a minute?'

'Excuse us,' Leo told Narcissus. 'Echo, want to come with?'

'Come with,' Echo confirmed.

The nymphs clustered around Narcissus again and began recording new videos and taking more photos.

Hazel led the way until they were out of earshot. 'Nemesis was right,' she said. 'Some demigods can't change their nature. Narcissus is going to stay there until he dies again.'

'No,' Leo said.

'No,' Echo agreed.

'We need that bronze,' Leo said. 'If we take it away, it might give Narcissus a reason to snap out of it. Echo could have a chance to save him.'

'A chance to save him,' Echo said gratefully.

Hazel stabbed her sword in the sand. 'It could also make several dozen nymphs very angry with us,' she said. 'And Narcissus might still know how to shoot his bow.'

Leo pondered that. The sun was just about down. Nemesis had mentioned that Narcissus got agitated after dark, probably because he couldn't see his reflection any more. Leo didn't want to stick around long enough to find out what the goddess meant by *agitated*. He'd also had experience with mobs of crazed nymphs. He wasn't anxious to repeat that.

'Hazel,' he said, 'your power with precious metal – Can you just detect it, or can you actually summon it to you?'

She frowned. 'Sometimes I can summon it. I've never tried with a piece of Celestial bronze that big before. I might be able to draw it to me through the earth, but I'd have to be fairly close. It would take a lot of concentration, and it wouldn't be fast.'

'Be fast,' Echo warned.

Leo cursed. He had hoped they could just go back to the ship, and Hazel could teleport the Celestial bronze from a safe distance.

'All right,' he said. 'We'll have to try something risky. Hazel, how about you try to summon the bronze from right here? Make it sink through the sand and tunnel over to you, then grab it and run for the ship.'

'But Narcissus is looking at it all the time,' she said.

'All the time,' Echo echoed.

'That'll be my job,' Leo said, hating his own plan already. 'Echo and I will cause a distraction.'

'Distraction?' Echo asked.

'I'll explain,' Leo promised. 'Are you willing?'

'Willing,' Echo said.

'Great,' Leo said. 'Now, let's hope we don't die.'

VIII

LEO

LEO PSYCHED HIMSELF UP FOR AN extreme makeover. He summoned some breath mints and a pair of welding goggles from his tool belt. The goggles weren't exactly sunglasses, but they'd have to do. He rolled up the sleeves of his shirt. He used some machine oil to grease back his hair. He stuck a wrench in his back pocket (why exactly, he wasn't sure) and he had Hazel draw a tattoo on his biceps with a marker: HOT STUFF, with a skull and crossbones.

'What in the world are you thinking?' She sounded pretty flustered.

'I try not to think,' Leo admitted. 'It interferes with being nuts. Just concentrate on moving that Celestial bronze. Echo, you ready?'

'Ready,' she said.

Leo took a deep breath. He strutted back towards the pond, hoping he looked awesome and not like he had some sort of nervous affliction. 'Leo is the coolest!' he shouted.

'Leo is the coolest!' Echo shouted back.

'Yeah, baby, check me out!'

'Check me out!' Echo said.

'Make way for the king!'

'The king!'

'Narcissus is weak!'

'Weak!'

The crowd of nymphs scattered in surprise. Leo shooed them away as if they were bothering him. 'No autographs, girls. I know you want some Leo time, but I'm way too cool. You better just hang around that ugly dweeb Narcissus. He's lame!'

'Lame!' Echo said with enthusiasm.

The nymphs muttered angrily.

'What are you talking about?' one demanded.

'*You're* lame,' said another.

Leo adjusted his goggles and smiled. He flexed his biceps, though he didn't have much to flex, and showed off his HOT STUFF tattoo. He had the nymphs' attention, if only because they were stunned, but Narcissus was still fixed on his own reflection.

'You know how ugly Narcissus is?' Leo asked the crowd. 'He's so ugly that when he was born his mama thought he was a backwards centaur – with a horse butt for a face.'

Some of the nymphs gasped. Narcissus frowned, as though he was vaguely aware of a gnat buzzing around his head.

'You know why his bow has cobwebs?' Leo continued. 'He uses it to hunt for dates, but he can't find one!'

One of the nymphs laughed. The others quickly elbowed her into silence.

Narcissus turned and scowled at Leo. 'Who *are* you?'

'I'm the Super-sized McShizzle, man!' Leo said. 'I'm Leo Valdez, bad boy supreme. And the ladies *love* a bad boy.'

'Love a bad boy!' Echo said, with a convincing squeal.

Leo took out a pen and autographed the arm of one of the nymphs. 'Narcissus is a loser! He's so weak he can't bench-press a Kleenex. He's so lame; when you look up *lame* on Wikipedia, it's got a picture of Narcissus – only the picture's so *ugly* no one ever checks it out.'

Narcissus knitted his handsome eyebrows. His face was turning from bronze to salmon pink. For the moment, he'd totally forgotten about the pond, and Leo could see the sheet of bronze sinking into the sand.

'What are you talking about?' Narcissus demanded. 'I am amazing. Everyone knows this.'

'Amazing at *pure suck*,' Leo said. 'If I was as *suck* as you, I'd drown myself. Oh wait, you already did that.'

Another nymph giggled. Then another. Narcissus growled, which did make him look a little less handsome. Meanwhile Leo beamed and wiggled his eyebrows over his goggles and spread his hands, gesturing for applause.

'That's right!' he said. 'Team Leo for the win!'

'Team Leo for the win!' Echo shouted. She'd wriggled into the mob of nymphs and, because she was so hard to see, the nymphs apparently thought the voice came from one of their own.

'Oh my god, I am so awesome!' Leo bellowed.

'So awesome!' Echo yelled back.

'He *is* funny,' a nymph ventured.

'And cute, in a scrawny way,' another said.

'Scrawny?' Leo asked. 'Baby, I *invented* scrawny. Scrawny is the new *sizzling hot*. And I GOT the scrawny. Narcissus? He's such a loser even the Underworld didn't want him. He couldn't get the ghost girls to date him.'

'Eww,' said a nymph.

'Eww!' Echo agreed.

'Stop!' Narcissus got to his feet. 'This is not right! This person is obviously not awesome, so he must be . . .' He struggled for the right words. It had probably been a long time since he'd talked about anything other than himself. 'He must be tricking us.'

Apparently Narcissus wasn't completely stupid. Realization dawned on his face. He turned back to the pond. 'The bronze mirror is gone! My reflection! Give me back to me!'

'Team Leo!' one of the nymphs squeaked. But the others returned their attention to Narcissus.

'*I'm* the beautiful one!' Narcissus insisted. 'He's stolen my mirror, and I'm going to leave unless we get it back!'

The girls gasped. One pointed. 'There!'

Hazel was at the top of the crater, running away as fast as she could while lugging a large sheet of bronze.

'Get it back!' cried a nymph.

Probably against her will, Echo muttered, 'Get it back.'

'Yes!' Narcissus unslung his bow and grabbed an arrow from his dusty quiver. 'The first one who gets that bronze, I will like you *almost* as much as I like me. I might even kiss you, right after I kiss my reflection!'

'Oh my gods!' the nymphs screamed.

'And kill those demigods!' Narcissus added, glaring very handsomely at Leo. 'They are *not* as cool as me!'

Leo could run pretty fast when someone was trying to kill him. Sadly, he'd had a lot of practice.

He overtook Hazel, which was easy, since she was struggling with fifty pounds of Celestial bronze. He took one side of the metal plate and glanced back. Narcissus was nocking an arrow, but it was so old and brittle it broke into splinters.

'Ow!' he yelled very attractively. 'My manicure!'

Normally nymphs were quick – at least the ones at Camp Half-Blood were – but these were burdened with posters, T-shirts and other Narcissus™ merchandise. The nymphs also weren't great at working as a team. They kept stumbling over one another, pushing and shoving. Echo made things worse by running among them, tripping and tackling as many as she could.

Still, they were closing rapidly.

'Call Arion!' Leo gasped.

'Already did!' Hazel said.

They ran for the beach. They made it to the edge of the water and could see the *Argo II*, but there was no way to get there. It was much too far to swim, even if they hadn't been toting bronze.

Leo turned. The mob was coming over the dunes, Narcissus in the lead, holding his bow like a band major's baton. The nymphs had conjured assorted weapons. Some held rocks. Some had wooden clubs wreathed in flowers. A few of the water nymphs had squirt guns – which seemed not quite as terrifying – but the look in their eyes was still murderous.

'Oh, man,' Leo muttered, summoning fire in his free hand. 'Straight-up fighting isn't my thing.'

'Hold the Celestial bronze.' Hazel drew her sword. 'Get behind me!'

'Get behind me!' Echo repeated. The camouflaged girl was racing ahead of the mob now. She stopped in front of Leo and turned, spreading her arms as if she meant to personally shield him.

'Echo?' Leo could hardly talk with the lump in his throat. 'You're one brave nymph.'

'Brave nymph?' Her tone made it a question.

'I'm proud to have you on Team Leo,' he said. 'If we survive this, you should forget Narcissus.'

'Forget Narcissus?' she said uncertainly.

'You're way too good for him.'

The nymphs surrounded them in a semicircle.

'Trickery!' Narcissus said. 'They don't love me, girls! *We* all love me, don't we?'

'Yes!' the girls screamed, except for one confused nymph in a yellow dress who squeaked, 'Team Leo!'

'Kill them!' Narcissus ordered.

The nymphs surged forward, but the sand in front of them exploded. Arion raced out of nowhere, circling the mob so quickly he created a sandstorm, showering the nymphs in white lime, spraying their eyes.

'I love this horse!' Leo said.

The nymphs collapsed, coughing and gagging. Narcissus

stumbled around blindly, swinging his bow like he was trying to hit a piñata.

Hazel climbed into the saddle, hoisted up the bronze and offered Leo a hand.

'We can't leave Echo!' Leo said.

'Leave Echo,' the nymph repeated.

She smiled, and for the first time Leo could clearly see her face. She really was pretty. Her eyes were bluer than he'd realized. How had he missed that?

'Why?' Leo asked. 'You don't think you can still save Narcissus . . .'

'Save Narcissus,' she said confidently. And even though it was only an echo Leo could tell that she meant it. She'd been given a second chance at life, and she was determined to use it to save the guy she loved – even if he was a completely hopeless (though very handsome) moron.

Leo wanted to protest, but Echo leaned forward and kissed him on the cheek, then pushed him gently away.

'Leo, come on!' Hazel called.

The other nymphs were starting to recover. They wiped the lime out of their eyes, which were now glowing green with anger. Leo looked for Echo again, but she had dissolved into the scenery.

'Yeah,' he said, his throat dry. 'Yeah, okay.'

He climbed up behind Hazel. Arion took off across the water, the nymphs screaming behind them and Narcissus shouting, 'Bring me back! Bring me back!'

As Arion raced towards the *Argo II*, Leo remembered what

Nemesis had said about Echo and Narcissus: *Perhaps they'll teach you a lesson.*

Leo had thought she'd meant Narcissus, but now he wondered if the real lesson for him was Echo – invisible to her brethren, cursed to love someone who didn't care for her. *A seventh wheel.* He tried to shake that thought. He clung to the sheet of bronze like a shield.

He was determined never to forget Echo's face. She deserved at least one person who saw her and knew how good she was. Leo closed his eyes, but the memory of her smile was already fading.

PIPER

PIPER DIDN'T WANT TO USE THE KNIFE.

But sitting in Jason's cabin, waiting for him to wake up, she felt alone and helpless.

Jason's face was so pale he might've been dead. She remembered the awful sound of that brick hitting his forehead – an injury that had happened only because he'd tried to shield her from the Romans.

Even with the nectar and ambrosia they'd managed to force-feed him, Piper couldn't be sure he would be okay when he woke up. What if he'd lost his memories again – but this time his memories of *her*?

That would be the cruellest trick the gods had played on her yet, and they'd played some pretty cruel tricks.

She heard Gleeson Hedge in his room next door, humming a military song – 'Stars and Stripes Forever' maybe? Since the satellite TV was out, the satyr was probably sitting on his bunk reading back issues of *Guns & Ammo* magazine. He wasn't a bad chaperone, but he was definitely the most warlike old goat Piper had ever met.

Of course she was grateful to the satyr. He had helped her dad, movie actor Tristan McLean, get back on his feet after being kidnapped by giants the past winter. A few weeks ago, Hedge had asked his girlfriend, Mellie, to take charge of the McLean household so he could come along to help with this quest.

Coach Hedge had tried to make it sound like returning to Camp Half-Blood had been all his idea, but Piper suspected there was more to it. The last few weeks, whenever Piper called home, her dad and Mellie had asked her what was wrong. Maybe something in her voice had tipped them off.

Piper couldn't share the visions she'd seen. They were too disturbing. Besides, her dad had taken a potion that had erased all of Piper's demigod secrets from his memory. But he could still tell when she was upset, and she was pretty sure her dad had encouraged Coach to look out for her.

She shouldn't draw her blade. It would only make her feel worse.

Finally the temptation was too great. She unsheathed Katoptris. It didn't look very special, just a triangular blade with an unadorned hilt, but it had once been owned by Helen of Troy. The dagger's name meant 'looking glass'.

Piper gazed at the bronze blade. At first, she saw only her reflection. Then light rippled across the metal. She saw a crowd of Roman demigods gathered in the forum. The blond scarecrow-looking kid, Octavian, was speaking to the mob, shaking his fist. Piper couldn't hear him, but the gist was obvious: *We need to kill those Greeks!*

Reyna, the praetor, stood to one side, her face tight with suppressed emotion. Bitterness? Anger? Piper wasn't sure.

She'd been prepared to hate Reyna, but she couldn't. During the feast in the forum, Piper had admired the way Reyna kept her feelings in check.

Reyna had sized up Piper and Jason's relationship right away. As a daughter of Aphrodite, Piper could tell stuff like that. Yet Reyna had stayed polite and in control. She'd put her camp's needs ahead of her emotions. She'd given the Greeks a fair chance . . . right up until the *Argo II* had started destroying her city.

She'd almost made Piper feel guilty about being Jason's girlfriend, though that was silly. Jason hadn't ever *been* Reyna's boyfriend, not really.

Maybe Reyna wasn't so bad, but it didn't matter now. They'd messed up the chance for peace. Piper's power of persuasion had, for once, done absolutely no good.

Her secret fear? Maybe she hadn't tried hard enough. Piper had never wanted to make friends with the Romans. She was too worried about losing Jason to his old life. Maybe unconsciously she hadn't put her best effort into the charmspeak.

Now Jason was hurt. The ship had been almost destroyed. And, according to her dagger, that crazy teddy-bear-strangling kid, Octavian, was whipping the Romans into a war frenzy.

The scene in her blade shifted. There was a rapid series

of images she'd seen before, but she still didn't understand them: Jason riding into battle on horseback, his eyes gold instead of blue; a woman in an old-fashioned Southern belle dress, standing in an oceanside park with palm trees; a bull with the face of a bearded man, rising out of a river; and two giants in matching yellow togas, hoisting a rope on a pulley system, lifting a large bronze vase out of a pit.

Then came the worst vision: she saw herself with Jason and Percy, standing waist-deep in water at the bottom of a dark circular chamber, like a giant well. Ghostly shapes moved through the water as it rose rapidly. Piper clawed at the walls, trying to escape, but there was nowhere to go. The water reached their chests. Jason was pulled under. Percy stumbled and disappeared.

How could a child of the sea god drown? Piper didn't know, but she watched herself in the vision, alone and thrashing in the dark, until the water rose over her head.

Piper shut her eyes. *Don't show me that again*, she pleaded. *Show me something helpful.*

She forced herself to look at the blade again.

This time, she saw an empty highway cutting between fields of wheat and sunflowers. A mileage marker read: Topeka 32. On the shoulder of the road stood a man in khaki shorts and a purple camp shirt. His face was lost in the shadow of a broad hat, the brim wreathed in leafy vines. He held up a silver goblet and beckoned to Piper. Somehow she knew he was offering her some sort of gift – a cure, or an antidote.

'Hey,' Jason croaked.

Piper was so startled she dropped the knife. 'You're awake!'

'Don't sound so surprised.' Jason touched his bandaged head and frowned. 'What . . . what happened? I remember the explosions, and –'

'You remember who I am?'

Jason tried to laugh, but it turned into a painful wince. 'Last I checked, you were my awesome girlfriend Piper. Unless something has changed since I was out?'

Piper was so relieved she almost sobbed. She helped him sit up and gave him some nectar to sip while she brought him up to speed. She was just explaining Leo's plan to fix the ship when she heard horse hooves clomping across the deck over their heads.

Moments later, Leo and Hazel stumbled to a stop in the doorway, carrying a large sheet of hammered bronze between them.

'Gods of Olympus.' Piper stared at Leo. 'What happened to *you*?'

His hair was greased back. He had welding goggles on his forehead, a lipstick mark on his cheek, tattoos all over his arms and a T-shirt that read HOT STUFF, BAD BOY and TEAM LEO.

'Long story,' he said. 'Others back?'

'Not yet,' Piper said.

Leo cursed. Then he noticed Jason sitting up, and his face brightened. 'Hey, man! Glad you're better. I'll be in the engine room.'

He ran off with the sheet of bronze, leaving Hazel in the doorway.

Piper raised an eyebrow at her. '*Team Leo?*'

'We met Narcissus,' Hazel said, which didn't really explain much. 'Also Nemesis, the revenge goddess.'

Jason sighed. 'I miss all the fun.'

On the deck above, something went *THUMP*, as if a heavy creature had landed. Annabeth and Percy came running down the hall. Percy was toting a steaming five-gallon plastic bucket that smelled horrible. Annabeth had a patch of black sticky stuff in her hair. Percy's shirt was covered in it.

'Roofing tar?' Piper guessed.

Frank stumbled up behind them, which made the hallway pretty jam-packed with demigods. Frank had a big smear of the black sludge down his face.

'Ran into some tar monsters,' Annabeth said. 'Hey, Jason, glad you're awake. Hazel, where's Leo?'

She pointed down. 'Engine room.'

Suddenly the entire ship listed to port. The demigods stumbled. Percy almost spilled his bucket of tar.

'Uh, what was that?' he demanded.

'Oh . . .' Hazel looked embarrassed. 'We may have angered the nymphs who live in this lake. Like . . . *all* of them.'

'Great.' Percy handed the bucket of tar to Frank and Annabeth. 'You guys help Leo. I'll hold off the water spirits as long as I can.'

'On it!' Frank promised.

The three of them ran off, leaving Hazel at the cabin door.

The ship listed again, and Hazel hugged her stomach like she was going to be sick.

'I'll just . . .' She swallowed, pointed weakly down the passageway and ran off.

Jason and Piper stayed below as the ship rocked back and forth. For a hero, Piper felt pretty useless. Waves crashed against the hull as angry voices came from above deck – Percy shouting, Coach Hedge yelling at the lake. Festus the figurehead breathed fire several times. Down the hall, Hazel moaned miserably in her cabin. In the engine room below, it sounded like Leo and the others were doing an Irish line dance with anvils tied to their feet. After what seemed like hours, the engine began to hum. The oars creaked and groaned, and Piper felt the ship lift into the air.

The rocking and shaking stopped. The ship became quiet except for the drone of machinery. Finally Leo emerged from the engine room. He was caked in sweat, lime dust and tar. His T-shirt looked like it had been caught in an escalator and chewed to shreds. The TEAM LEO on his chest now read: AM LEO. But he grinned like a madman and announced that they were safely under way.

'Meeting in the mess hall, one hour,' he said. 'Crazy day, huh?'

After everyone had cleaned up, Coach Hedge took the helm and the demigods gathered below for dinner. It was the first time they'd all sat down together – just the seven of them. Maybe their presence should've reassured Piper, but seeing all of them in one place only reminded her that the Prophecy of Seven was unfolding at last. No more waiting for Leo to finish the ship. No more easy days at Camp Half-Blood, pretending the future was still a long way off. They were under way, with a bunch of angry Romans behind them and the ancient lands ahead. The giants would be waiting. Gaia was rising. And unless they succeeded in this quest the world would be destroyed.

The others must've felt it, too. The tension in the mess hall was like an electrical storm brewing, which was totally possible, considering Percy's and Jason's powers. In an awkward moment, the two boys tried to sit in the same chair at the head of the table. Sparks literally flew from Jason's hands. After a brief silent standoff, like they were both thinking, *Seriously, dude?* they ceded the chair to Annabeth and sat at opposite sides of the table.

The crew compared notes on what had happened in Salt Lake City, but even Leo's ridiculous story about how he tricked Narcissus wasn't enough to cheer up the group.

'So where to now?' Leo asked with a mouthful of pizza. 'I did a quick repair job to get us out of the lake, but there's still a lot of damage. We should really put down again and fix things before we head across the Atlantic.'

Percy was eating a piece of pie, which for some reason was completely blue – filling, crust, even the whipped cream. 'We need to put some distance between us and Camp Jupiter,' he said. 'Frank spotted some eagles over Salt Lake City. We figure the Romans aren't far behind us.'

That didn't improve the mood around the table. Piper didn't want to say anything, but she felt obliged . . . and a little guilty. 'I don't suppose we should go back and try to reason with the Romans? Maybe – maybe I didn't try hard enough with the charmspeak.'

Jason took her hand. 'It wasn't your fault, Pipes. Or Leo's,' he added quickly. 'Whatever happened, it was Gaia's doing, to drive the two camps apart.'

Piper was grateful for his support, but she still felt uneasy. 'Maybe if we could explain that, though –'

'With no proof?' Annabeth asked. 'And no idea what really happened? I appreciate what you're saying, Piper. I don't want the Romans on our bad side, but, until we understand what Gaia's up to, going back is suicide.'

'She's right,' Hazel said. She still looked a little queasy from seasickness, but she was trying to eat a few saltine crackers. The rim of her plate was embedded with rubies, and Piper was pretty sure they hadn't been there at the beginning of the meal. 'Reyna might listen, but Octavian won't. The Romans have honour to think about. They've been attacked. They'll shoot first and ask questions *posthac.*'

Piper stared at her own dinner. The magical plates could conjure up a great selection of vegetarian stuff. She especially liked the avocado and grilled pepper quesadilla, but tonight she didn't have much of an appetite.

She thought about the visions she'd seen in her knife: Jason with golden eyes; the bull with the human head; the two giants in yellow togas hoisting a bronze jar from a pit. Worst of all, she remembered herself drowning in black water.

Piper had always liked the water. She had good memories of surfing with her dad. But since she'd started seeing that vision in Katoptris she'd been thinking more and more of an old Cherokee story her granddad used to tell to keep her away from the river near his cabin. He told her the Cherokees believed in good water spirits, like the naiads of the Greeks, but they also believed in evil water spirits, the water cannibals, who hunted mortals with invisible arrows and were especially fond of drowning small children.

'You're right,' she decided. 'We have to keep going. Not just because of the Romans. We have to hurry.'

Hazel nodded. 'Nemesis said we have only six days until Nico dies and Rome is destroyed.'

Jason frowned. 'You mean *Rome* Rome, not New Rome?'

'I think,' Hazel said. 'But, if so, that's not much time.'

'Why six days?' Percy wondered. 'And how are they going to destroy Rome?'

No one answered. Piper didn't want to add further bad news, but she felt she had to.

'There's more,' she said. 'I've been seeing some things in my knife.'

The big kid, Frank, froze with a forkful of spaghetti halfway to his mouth. 'Things such as . . .?'

'They don't really make sense,' Piper said, 'just garbled images, but I saw two giants, dressed alike. Maybe twins.'

Annabeth stared at the magical video feed from Camp Half-Blood on the wall. Right now it showed the living room in the Big House: a cosy fire on the hearth and Seymour, the stuffed leopard head, snoring contentedly above the mantel.

'Twins, like in Ella's prophecy,' Annabeth said. 'If we could figure out those lines, it might help.'

'*Wisdom's daughter walks alone*,' Percy said. '*The Mark of Athena burns through Rome*. Annabeth, that's got to mean you. Juno told me . . . well, she said you had a hard task ahead of you in Rome. She said she doubted you could do it. But I know she's wrong.'

Annabeth took a long breath. 'Reyna was about to tell me something right before the ship fired on us. She said there was an old legend among the Roman praetors – something that had to do with Athena. She said it might be the reason Greeks and Romans could never get along.'

Leo and Hazel exchanged nervous looks.

'Nemesis mentioned something similar,' Leo said. 'She talked about an old score that had to be settled –'

'The one thing that might bring the gods' two natures into harmony,' Hazel recalled. '"An old wrong finally avenged."'

Percy drew a frowny face in his blue whipped cream. 'I was only a praetor for about two hours. Jason, you ever hear a legend like that?'

Jason was still holding Piper's hand. His fingers had turned clammy.

'I . . . uh, I'm not sure,' he said. 'I'll give it some thought.'

Percy narrowed his eyes. 'You're not *sure*?'

Jason didn't respond. Piper wanted to ask him what was wrong. She could tell he didn't want to discuss this old legend. She caught his eye, and he pleaded silently, *Later*.

Hazel broke the silence. 'What about the other lines?' She turned her ruby-encrusted plate. '*Twins snuff out the angel's breath, Who holds the key to endless death*.'

'*Giants' bane stands gold and pale,*' Frank added, '*Won through pain from a woven jail.*'

'Giants' bane,' Leo said. 'Anything that's a giants' bane is good for us, right? That's probably what we need to find. If it can help the gods get their schizophrenic act together, that's good.'

Percy nodded. 'We can't kill the giants without the help of the gods.'

Jason turned to Frank and Hazel. 'I thought you guys killed that one giant in Alaska without a god's help, just the two of you.'

'Alcyoneus was a special case,' Frank said. 'He was only immortal in the territory where he was reborn – Alaska. But not in Canada. I wish I could kill *all* the giants by dragging them across the border from Alaska into Canada, but . . .' He shrugged. 'Percy's right, we'll need the gods.'

Piper gazed at the walls. She really wished Leo hadn't enchanted them with images of Camp Half-Blood. It was like a doorway to home that she could never go through. She watched the hearth of Hestia burning in the middle of the green as the cabins turned off their lights for curfew.

She wondered how the Roman demigods, Frank and Hazel, felt about those images. They'd never even been to Camp Half-Blood. Did it seem alien to them, or unfair that Camp Jupiter wasn't represented? Did it make them miss their own home?

The other lines of the prophecy turned in Piper's mind. What was a woven jail? How could twins snuff out an angel's breath? The key to endless death didn't sound very cheerful, either.

'So . . .' Leo pushed his chair away from the table. 'First things first, I guess. We'll have to put down in the morning to finish repairs.'

'Someplace close to a city,' Annabeth suggested, 'in case we need supplies. But somewhere out of the way, so the Romans will have trouble finding us. Any ideas?'

No one spoke. Piper remembered her vision in the knife: the strange man in purple, holding out a goblet and beckoning to her. He'd been standing in front of a sign that read TOPEKA 32.

'Well,' she ventured, 'how do you guys feel about Kansas?'

X

PIPER

PIPER HAD TROUBLE FALLING ASLEEP.

Coach Hedge spent the first hour after curfew doing his nightly duty, walking up and down the passageway yelling, 'Lights out! Settle down! Try to sneak out, and I'll smack you back to Long Island!'

He banged his baseball bat against a cabin door whenever he heard a noise, shouting at everyone to go to sleep, which made it impossible for *anyone* to go to sleep. Piper figured this was the most fun the satyr had had since he'd pretended to be a gym teacher at the Wilderness School.

She stared at the bronze beams on the ceiling. Her cabin was pretty cosy. Leo had programmed their quarters to adjust automatically to the occupant's preferred temperature, so it was never too cold or too hot. The mattress and the pillows were stuffed with pegasus down (no pegasi were harmed in the making of these products, Leo had assured her), so they were über-comfortable. A bronze lantern hung from the ceiling, glowing at whatever brightness Piper wished. The lantern's sides were perforated with pinholes, so at night glimmering constellations drifted across her walls.

Piper had so many things on her mind she thought she'd never sleep. But there was something peaceful about the rocking of the boat and the drone of the aerial oars as they scooped through the sky.

Finally her eyelids got heavy, and she drifted off.

It seemed like only a few seconds had passed before she woke to the breakfast bell.

'Yo, Piper!' Leo knocked on her door. 'We're landing!'

'Landing?' She sat up groggily.

Leo opened her door and poked his head in. He had his hand over his eyes, which would've been a nice gesture if he hadn't been peeking through his fingers. 'You decent?'

'Leo!'

'Sorry.' He grinned. 'Hey, nice Power Ranger jammies.'

'They are not Power Rangers! They're Cherokee eagles!'

'Yeah, sure. Anyway, we're setting down a few miles outside Topeka, as requested. And, um . . .' He glanced out in the passageway, then leaned inside again. 'Thanks for not hating me, for blowing up the Romans yesterday.'

Piper rubbed her eyes. The feast in New Rome had been only yesterday? 'That's okay, Leo. You weren't in control of yourself.'

'Yeah, but still . . . you didn't have to stick up for me.'

'Are you kidding? You're like the annoying little brother I never had. Of course I'll stick up for you.'

'Uh . . . thanks?'

From above, Coach Hedge yelled, 'Thar she blows! Kansas, ahoy!'

'Holy Hephaestus,' Leo muttered. 'He really needs to work on his shipspeak. I'd better get above deck.'

By the time Piper had showered, changed and grabbed a bagel from the mess hall, she could hear the ship's landing gear extending. She climbed on deck and joined the others as the *Argo II* settled in the middle of a field of sunflowers. The oars retracted. The gangplank lowered itself.

The morning air smelled of irrigation, warm plants and fertilized earth. Not a bad smell. It reminded Piper of Grandpa Tom's place in Tahlequah, Oklahoma, back on the reservation.

Percy was the first to notice her. He smiled in greeting, which for some reason surprised Piper. He was wearing faded jeans and a fresh orange Camp Half-Blood T-shirt, as if he'd never been away from the Greek side. The new clothes had probably helped his mood – and of course the fact that he was standing at the rail with his arm around Annabeth.

Piper was happy to see Annabeth with a sparkle in her eyes, because Piper had never had a better friend. For months, Annabeth had been tormenting herself, her every waking moment consumed with the search for Percy. Now, despite the dangerous quest they were facing, at least she had her boyfriend back.

'So!' Annabeth plucked the bagel out of Piper's hand and took a bite, but that didn't bother Piper. Back at camp, they'd had a running joke about stealing each other's breakfast. 'Here we are. What's the plan?'

'I want to check out the highway,' Piper said. 'Find the sign that says Topeka 32.'

Leo spun his Wii controller in a circle, and the sails lowered themselves. 'We shouldn't be far,' he said. 'Festus and I calculated the landing as best we could. What do you expect to find at the mile marker?'

Piper explained what she'd seen in the knife – the man in purple with a goblet. She kept quiet about the other images, though, like the vision of Percy, Jason and herself drowning. She wasn't sure what it meant, anyway; and everyone seemed in such better spirits this morning that she didn't want to ruin the mood.

'Purple shirt?' Jason asked. 'Vines on his hat? Sounds like Bacchus.'

'Dionysus,' Percy muttered. 'If we came all the way to Kansas to see *Mr D* –'

'Bacchus isn't so bad,' Jason said. 'I don't like his followers much . . .'

Piper shuddered. Jason, Leo and she had had an encounter with the maenads a few months ago and had almost got torn to pieces.

'But the god himself is okay,' Jason continued. 'I did him a favour once up in the wine country.'

Percy looked appalled. 'Whatever, man. Maybe he's better on the Roman side. But why would he be hanging around in Kansas? Didn't Zeus order the gods to cease all contact with mortals?'

Frank grunted. The big guy was wearing a blue tracksuit this morning, like he was ready to go for a jog in the sunflowers.

'The gods haven't been very good at following *that* order,' he noted. 'Besides, if the gods *have* gone schizophrenic like Hazel said –'

'And *Leo* said,' added Leo.

Frank scowled at him. 'Then who knows what's going on with the Olympians? Could be some pretty bad stuff out there.'

'Sounds dangerous!' Leo agreed cheerfully. 'Well . . . you guys have fun. I've got to finish repairs on the hull. Coach Hedge is gonna work on the broken crossbows. And, uh, Annabeth – I could really use your help. You're the only other person who even *sort of* understands engineering.'

Annabeth looked apologetically at Percy. 'He's right. I should stay and help.'

'I'll come back to you.' He kissed her on the cheek. 'Promise.'

They were so easy together it made Piper's heart ache.

Jason was great, of course. But sometimes he acted so distant, like last night, when he'd been reluctant to talk about that old Roman legend. So often he seemed to be thinking of his old life at Camp Jupiter. Piper wondered if she would ever be able to break through that barrier.

The trip to Camp Jupiter, seeing Reyna in person, hadn't helped. Neither did the fact that Jason had chosen to wear a purple shirt today – the colour of the Romans.

Frank slid his bow off his shoulder and propped it against the rail. 'I think I should turn into a crow or something and fly around, keep an eye out for Roman eagles.'

'Why a crow?' Leo asked. 'Man, if you can turn into a dragon, why don't you just turn into a dragon every time? That's the coolest.'

Frank's face looked like it was being infused with cranberry juice. 'That's like asking why you don't bench-press your maximum weight every time you lift. Because it's hard and you'd hurt yourself. Turning into a dragon isn't easy.'

'Oh.' Leo nodded. 'I wouldn't know. I don't lift weights.'

'Yeah. Well, maybe you should consider it, Mr –'

Hazel stepped between them.

'I'll help you, Frank,' she said, shooting Leo an evil look. 'I can summon Arion and scout around below.'

'Sure,' Frank said, still glaring at Leo. 'Yeah, thanks.'

Piper wondered what was going on with those three. The boys showing off for Hazel and razzing each other – *that* she understood. But it almost seemed like Hazel and Leo had a history. As far as she knew, they'd met for the first time just yesterday. She wondered if something else had happened on their trip to the Great Salt Lake – something they hadn't mentioned.

Hazel turned to Percy. 'Just be careful when you go out there. Lots of fields, lots of crops. Could be *karpoi* on the loose.'

'*Karpoi?*' Piper asked.

'Grain spirits,' Hazel said. 'You don't want to meet them.'

Piper didn't see how a grain spirit could be so bad, but Hazel's tone convinced her not to ask.

'That leaves three of us to check on the mile marker,' Percy said. 'Me, Jason, Piper. I'm not psyched about seeing Mr D again. That guy is a pain. But, Jason, if you're on better terms with him –'

'Yeah,' Jason said. 'If we find him, I'll talk to him. Piper, it's your vision. You should take the lead.'

Piper shivered. She'd seen the three of them drowning in that dark well. Was Kansas where it would happen? That didn't seem right, but she couldn't be sure.

'Of course,' she said, trying to sound upbeat. 'Let's find the highway.'

Leo had said they were close. His idea of 'close' needed some work.

After trudging half a mile through hot fields, getting bitten by mosquitoes and whacked in the face with scratchy sunflowers, they finally reached the road. An old billboard for Bubba's Gas 'n' Grub indicated they were still forty miles from the first Topeka exit.

'Correct my maths,' Percy said, 'but doesn't that mean we have eight miles to walk?'

Jason peered both ways down the deserted road. He looked better today, thanks to the magical healing of ambrosia and nectar. His colour was back to normal, and the scar on his forehead had almost vanished. The new *gladius* that Hera had given him last winter hung at his belt. Most guys would look pretty awkward walking around with a scabbard strapped to their jeans, but on Jason it seemed perfectly natural.

'No cars . . .' he said. 'But I guess we wouldn't want to hitchhike.'

'No,' Piper agreed, gazing nervously down the highway. 'We've already spent too much time going overland. The earth is Gaia's territory.'

'Hmm . . .' Jason snapped his fingers. 'I can call a friend for a ride.'

Percy raised his eyebrows. 'Oh, yeah? Me, too. Let's see whose friend gets here first.'

Jason whistled. Piper knew what he was doing, but he'd succeeded in summoning Tempest only three times since they'd met the storm spirit at the Wolf House last winter. Today, the sky was so blue Piper didn't see how it could work.

Percy simply closed his eyes and concentrated.

Piper hadn't studied him up close before. After hearing so much at Camp Half-Blood about Percy Jackson *this* and Percy Jackson *that*, she thought he looked . . . well, unimpressive, especially next to Jason. Percy was more slender, about an inch shorter, with slightly longer, much darker hair.

He wasn't really Piper's type. If she'd seen him in the mall somewhere, she probably would've thought he was a skater – cute in a scruffy way, a little on the wild side, definitely a troublemaker. She would have steered clear. She had enough trouble in her life. But she could see why Annabeth liked him, and she could definitely see why Percy needed Annabeth in his life. If anybody could keep a guy like that under control, it was Annabeth.

Thunder crackled in the clear sky.

Jason smiled. 'Soon.'

'Too late.' Percy pointed east, where a black winged shape was spiralling towards them. At first, Piper thought it might be Frank in crow form. Then she realized it was much too big to be a bird.

'A black pegasus?' she said. 'Never seen one like that.'

The winged stallion came in for a landing. He trotted over to Percy and nuzzled his face, then turned his head inquisitively towards Piper and Jason.

'Blackjack,' Percy said, 'this is Piper and Jason. They're friends.'

The horse nickered.

'Uh, maybe later,' Percy answered.

Piper had heard that Percy could speak to horses, being the son of the horse lord Poseidon, but she'd never seen it in action.

'What does Blackjack want?' she asked.

'Doughnuts,' Percy said. 'Always doughnuts. He can carry all three of us if –'

Suddenly the air turned cold. Piper's ears popped. About fifty yards away, a miniature cyclone three storeys tall tore across the tops of the sunflowers like a scene from *The Wizard of Oz*. It touched down on the road next to Jason and took the form of a horse – a misty steed with lightning flickering through its body.

'Tempest,' Jason said, grinning broadly. 'Long time, my friend.'

The storm spirit reared and whinnied. Blackjack backed up skittishly.

'Easy, boy,' Percy said. 'He's a friend, too.' He gave Jason an impressed look. 'Nice ride, Grace.'

Jason shrugged. 'I made friends with him during our fight

at the Wolf House. He's a free spirit, literally, but once in a while he agrees to help me.'

Percy and Jason climbed on their respective horses. Piper had never been comfortable with Tempest. Riding full gallop on a beast that could vaporize at any moment made her a bit nervous. Nevertheless, she accepted Jason's hand and climbed on.

Tempest raced down the road with Blackjack soaring overhead. Fortunately, they didn't pass any cars, or they might have caused a wreck. In no time, they arrived at the thirty-two-mile marker, which looked exactly as Piper had seen it in her vision.

Blackjack landed. Both horses pawed the tarmac. Neither looked pleased to have stopped so suddenly, just when they'd found their stride.

Blackjack whinnied.

'You're right,' Percy said. 'No sign of the wine dude.'

'I beg your pardon?' said a voice from the fields.

Tempest turned so quickly Piper almost fell off.

The wheat parted, and the man from her vision stepped into view. He wore a wide-brimmed hat wreathed in grapevines, a purple short-sleeved shirt, khaki shorts and Birkenstocks with white socks. He looked maybe thirty, with a slight potbelly, like a frat boy who hadn't yet realized college was over.

'Did someone just call me the *wine dude*?' he asked in a lazy drawl. 'It's Bacchus, please. Or Mr Bacchus. Or Lord Bacchus. Or, sometimes, Oh-My-Gods-Please-Don't-Kill-Me, Lord Bacchus.'

Percy urged Blackjack forward, though the pegasus didn't seem happy about it.

'You look different,' Percy told the god. 'Skinnier. Your hair is longer. And your shirt isn't so loud.'

The wine god squinted up at him. 'What in blazes are you talking about? Who are you, and where is Ceres?'

'Uh . . . what series?'

'I think he means Ceres,' Jason said. 'The goddess of agriculture. You'd call her Demeter.' He nodded respectfully to the god. 'Lord Bacchus, do you remember me? I helped you with that missing leopard in Sonoma.'

Bacchus scratched his stubbly chin. 'Ah . . . yes. John Green.'

'Jason Grace.'

'Whatever,' the god said. 'Did Ceres send you, then?'

'No, Lord Bacchus,' Jason said. 'Were you expecting to meet her here?'

The god snorted. 'Well, I didn't come to Kansas to *party*, my boy. Ceres asked me here for a council of war. What with Gaia rising, the crops are withering. Droughts are spreading. The *karpoi* are in revolt. Even my grapes aren't safe. Ceres wanted a united front in the plant war.'

'The plant war,' Percy said. 'You're going to arm all the little grapes with tiny assault rifles?'

The god narrowed his eyes. 'Have we met?'

'At Camp Half-Blood,' Percy said, 'I know you as Mr D – Dionysus.'

'Agh!' Bacchus winced and pressed his hands to his temples. For a moment, his image flickered. Piper saw a different person – fatter, dumpier, in a much louder, leopard-patterned shirt. Then Bacchus returned to being Bacchus. 'Stop that!' he demanded. 'Stop thinking about me in Greek!'

Percy blinked. 'Uh, but –'

'Do you have any idea how *hard* it is to stay focused? Splitting headaches all the time! I never know what I'm doing or where I'm going! Constantly grumpy!'

'That sounds pretty normal for you,' Percy said.

The god's nostrils flared. One of the grape leaves on his hat burst into flame. 'If we know each other from that *other* camp, it's a wonder I haven't already turned you into a dolphin.'

'It was discussed,' Percy assured him. 'I think you were just too lazy to do it.'

Piper had been watching with horrified fascination, the way she might watch a car wreck in progress. Now she realized Percy was *not* making things better, and Annabeth wasn't around to rein him in. Piper figured her friend would never forgive her if she brought Percy back transformed into a sea mammal.

'Lord Bacchus!' she interrupted, slipping off Tempest's back.

'Piper, careful,' Jason said.

She shot him a warning glance: *I've got this.*

'Sorry to trouble you, my lord,' she told the god, 'but actually we came here to get your advice. Please, we need your wisdom.'

She used her most agreeable tone, pouring respect into her charmspeak.

The god frowned, but the purple glow faded in his eyes.

'You're well-spoken, girl. Advice, eh? Very well. I would avoid karaoke. Really, theme parties in general are out. In these austere times, people are looking for a simple, low-key affair, with locally produced organic snacks and –'

'Not about parties,' Piper interrupted. 'Although that's incredibly useful advice, Lord Bacchus. We were hoping you'd help us on our quest.'

She explained about the *Argo II* and their voyage to stop the giants from awakening Gaia. She told him what Nemesis had said: that in six days, Rome would be destroyed. She described the vision reflected in her knife, where Bacchus offered her a silver goblet.

'Silver goblet?' The god didn't sound very excited. He grabbed a Diet Pepsi from nowhere and popped the top of the can.

'You drink Diet Coke,' Percy said.

'I don't know what you're talking about,' Bacchus snapped. 'As to this vision of the goblet, young lady, I have nothing for you to drink unless you want a Pepsi. Jupiter has put me under strict orders to avoid giving wine to minors. Bothersome, but there you have it. As for the giants, I know them well. I fought in the first Giant War, you know.'

'You can fight?' Percy asked.

Piper wished he hadn't sounded so incredulous.

Dionysus snarled. His Diet Pepsi transformed into a five-foot staff wreathed in ivy, topped with a pinecone.

'A *thyrsus*!' Piper said, hoping to distract the god before he whacked Percy on the head. She'd seen weapons like that before in the hands of crazy nymphs and wasn't thrilled to see one again, but she tried to sound impressed. 'Oh, what a mighty weapon!'

'Indeed,' Bacchus agreed. 'I'm glad *someone* in your group is smart. The pinecone is a fearsome tool of destruction! I was a demigod myself in the first Giant War, you know. The son of Jupiter!'

Jason flinched. Probably he wasn't thrilled to be reminded that the Wine Dude was technically his big brother.

Bacchus swung his staff through the air, though his potbelly almost threw him off balance. 'Of course that was long before I invented wine and became an immortal. I fought side by side with the gods and some other demigod . . . Harry Cleese, I think.'

'Heracles?' Piper suggested politely.

'Whatever,' Bacchus said. 'Anyway, I killed the giant Ephialtes and his brother Otis. Horrible boors, those two. Pinecone in the face for both of them!'

Piper held her breath. All at once, several ideas came together in her head – the visions in the knife, the lines of the prophecy they'd been discussing the night before. She felt like she used to when she was scuba diving with her father, and he would wipe her mask for her underwater. Suddenly, everything was clearer.

'Lord Bacchus,' she said, trying to control the nervousness in her voice. 'Those two giants, Ephialtes and Otis . . . would they happen to be twins?'

'Hmm?' The god seemed distracted by his *thyrsus*-swinging, but he nodded. 'Yes, twins. That's right.'

Piper turned to Jason. She could tell he was following her thoughts: *Twins snuff out the angel's breath.*

In the blade of Katoptris, she'd seen two giants in yellow robes, lifting a jar from a deep pit.

'That's why we're here,' Piper told the god. 'You're part of our quest!'

Bacchus frowned. 'I'm sorry, my girl. I'm not a demigod any more. I don't *do* quests.'

'But giants can only be killed by heroes and gods working together,' she insisted. 'You're a god now, and the two giants we have to fight are Ephialtes and Otis. I think . . . I think they're waiting for us in Rome. They're going to destroy the city somehow. The silver goblet I saw in my vision – maybe it's meant as a symbol for your help. You *have* to help us kill the giants!'

Bacchus glared at her, and Piper realized she'd chosen her words poorly.

'My girl,' he said coldly, 'I don't *have* to do anything. Besides, I only help those who give me proper tribute, which no one has managed to do in many, many centuries.'

Blackjack whinnied uneasily.

Piper couldn't blame him. She didn't like the sound of *tribute*. She remembered the maenads, the crazed followers of Bacchus, who would tear up nonbelievers with their bare hands. And that was when they were in a *good* mood.

Percy voiced the question that she was too scared to ask. 'What kind of tribute?'

Bacchus waved his hand dismissively. 'Nothing *you* could

handle, insolent Greek. But I will give you some free advice, since this girl does have *some* manners. Seek out Gaia's son, Phorcys. He always hated his mother, not that I can blame him. He didn't have much use for his siblings the twins, either. You'll find him in the city they named after that heroine – Atalanta.'

Piper hesitated. 'You mean Atlanta?'

'That's the one.'

'But this Phorcys,' Jason said. 'Is he a giant? A Titan?'

Bacchus laughed. 'Neither. Seek out the salt water.'

'Salt water . . .' Percy said. 'In Atlanta?'

'Yes,' Bacchus said. 'Are you hard of hearing? If anyone can give you insight on Gaia and the twins, it's Phorcys. Just watch out for him.'

'What do you mean?' Jason asked.

The god glanced at the sun, which had climbed almost to high noon. 'It's unlike Ceres to be late, unless she sensed something dangerous in this area. Or . . .'

The god's face suddenly went slack. 'Or a trap. Well, I must be going! And if I were you I'd do the same!'

'Lord Bacchus, wait!' Jason protested.

The god shimmered and disappeared with a sound like a soda-can top being popped.

The wind rustled through the sunflowers. The horses paced in agitation. Despite the dry, hot day, Piper shivered. A cold feeling . . . Annabeth and Leo had both described a cold feeling . . .

'Bacchus is right,' she said. 'We need to leave –'

Too late, said a sleepy voice, humming through the fields all around them and resonating in the ground at Piper's feet.

Percy and Jason drew their swords. Piper stood on the road between them, frozen with fear. The power of Gaia was suddenly everywhere. The sunflowers turned to look at them. The wheat bent towards them like a million scythes.

Welcome to my party, Gaia murmured. Her voice reminded Piper of corn growing – a crackling, hissing, hot and persistent noise she used to hear at Grandpa Tom's on those quiet nights in Oklahoma.

What did Bacchus say? the goddess mocked. *A simple, low-key affair with organic snacks? Yes. For my snacks, I need only two: the blood of a female demigod and the blood of a male. Piper, my dear, choose which hero will die with you.*

'Gaia!' Jason yelled. 'Stop hiding in the wheat. Show yourself!'

Such bravado, Gaia hissed. *But the other one, Percy Jackson, also has appeal. Choose, Piper McLean, or I will.*

Piper's heart raced. Gaia meant to kill her. That was no surprise. But what was this about choosing one of the boys? Why would Gaia let either of them go? It had to be a trap.

'You're insane!' she shouted. 'I'm not choosing anything for you!'

Suddenly Jason gasped. He sat up straight in his saddle.

'Jason!' Piper cried. 'What's wrong –?'

He looked down at her, his expression deadly calm. His eyes were no longer blue. They glowed solid gold.

'Percy, help!' Piper stumbled back from Tempest.

But Percy galloped away from them. He stopped thirty feet down the road and wheeled his pegasus around. He raised his sword and pointed the tip towards Jason.

'*One will die,*' Percy said, but the voice wasn't his. It was deep and hollow, like someone whispering from inside the barrel of a cannon.

'*I will choose,*' Jason answered, in the same hollow voice.

'No!' Piper yelled.

All around her, the fields crackled and hissed, laughing in Gaia's voice as Percy and Jason charged at each other, their weapons ready.

XI

PIPER

IF NOT FOR THE HORSES, PIPER WOULD'VE DIED.

Jason and Percy charged each other, but Tempest and Blackjack baulked long enough for Piper to leap out of the way.

She rolled to the edge of the road and looked back, dazed and horrified, as the boys crossed swords, gold against bronze. Sparks flew. Their blades blurred – strike and parry – and the ground trembled. The first exchange took only a second, but Piper couldn't believe the speed of their sword fighting. The horses pulled away from each other – Tempest thundering in protest, Blackjack flapping his wings.

'Stop it!' Piper yelled.

For a moment, Jason heeded her voice. His golden eyes turned towards her, and Percy charged, slamming his blade into Jason. Thank the gods, Percy turned his sword – maybe on purpose, maybe accidentally – so the flat of it hit Jason's chest, but the impact was still enough to knock Jason off his mount.

Blackjack cantered away as Tempest reared in confusion. The spirit horse charged into the sunflowers and dissipated into vapour.

Percy struggled to turn his pegasus around.

'Percy!' Piper yelled. 'Jason's your friend. Drop your weapon!'

Percy's sword arm dipped. Piper might have been able to bring him under control, but unfortunately Jason got to his feet.

Jason roared. A bolt of lightning arced out of the clear blue sky. It ricocheted off his *gladius* and blasted Percy off his horse.

Blackjack whinnied and fled into the wheat fields. Jason charged at Percy, who was now on his back, his clothes smoking from the lightning blast.

For a horrible moment, Piper couldn't find her voice. Gaia seemed to be whispering to her: *You must choose one. Why not let Jason kill him?*

'No!' she screamed. 'Jason, stop!'

He froze, his sword six inches from Percy's face.

Jason turned, the gold light in his eyes flickering uncertainly. '*I cannot stop. One must die.*'

Something about that voice . . . it wasn't Gaia. It wasn't Jason. Whoever it was spoke haltingly, as if English was its second language.

'Who are you?' Piper demanded.

Jason's mouth twisted in a gruesome smile. '*We are the eidolons. We will live again.*'

'Eidolons . . .?' Piper's mind raced. She'd studied all sorts of monsters at Camp Half-Blood, but that term wasn't familiar. 'You're – you're some sort of ghost?'

'*He must die.*' Jason turned his attention back to Percy, but Percy had recovered more than either of them realized. He swept out his leg and knocked Jason off his feet.

Jason's head hit the tarmac with a nauseating *conk*.

Percy rose.

'Stop it!' Piper screamed again, but there was no charmspeak in her voice. She was shouting in sheer desperation.

Percy raised Riptide over Jason's chest.

Panic closed up Piper's throat. She wanted to attack Percy with her dagger, but she knew that wouldn't help. Whatever was controlling him had all of Percy's skill. There was no way she could beat him in combat.

She forced herself to focus. She poured all of her anger into her voice. 'Eidolon, stop.'

Percy froze.

'Face me,' Piper ordered.

The son of the sea god turned. His eyes were gold instead of green, his face pale and cruel, not at all like Percy's.

'*You have not chosen,*' he said. '*So this one will die.*'

'You're a spirit from the Underworld,' Piper guessed. 'You're possessing Percy Jackson. Is that it?'

Percy sneered. '*I will live again in this body. The Earth Mother has promised. I will go where I please, control whom I wish.*'

A wave of cold washed over Piper. 'Leo . . . that's what happened to Leo. He was being controlled by an eidolon.'

The thing in Percy's form laughed without humour. *'Too late you realize. You can trust no one.'*

Jason still wasn't moving. Piper had no help, no way to protect him.

Behind Percy, something rustled in the wheat. Piper saw the tip of a black wing, and Percy began to turn towards the sound.

'Ignore it!' she yelped. 'Look at me.'

Percy obeyed. *'You cannot stop me. I will kill Jason Grace.'*

Behind him, Blackjack emerged from the wheat field, moving with surprising stealth for such a large animal.

'You won't kill him,' Piper ordered. But she wasn't looking at Percy. She locked eyes with the pegasus, pouring all her power into her words and hoping Blackjack would understand. 'You will knock him out.'

The charmspeak washed over Percy. He shifted his weight indecisively. *'I . . . will knock him out?'*

'Oh, sorry.' Piper smiled. 'I wasn't talking to you.'

Blackjack reared and brought his hoof down on Percy's head.

Percy crumpled to the road next to Jason.

'Oh, gods!' Piper ran to the boys. 'Blackjack, you didn't *kill* him, did you?'

The pegasus snorted. Piper couldn't speak Horse, but she thought he might have said: *Please. I know my own strength.*

Tempest was nowhere to be seen. The lightning steed had apparently returned to wherever storm spirits live on clear days.

Piper checked on Jason. He was breathing steadily, but

two knocks on the skull in two days couldn't have been good for him. Then she examined Percy's head. She didn't see any blood, but a large knot was forming where the horse had kicked him. 'We have to get them both back to the ship,' she told Blackjack.

The pegasus bobbed his head in agreement. He knelt on the ground, so that Piper could drape Percy and Jason over his back. After a lot of hard work (unconscious boys are heavy), she got them reasonably secured, climbed onto Blackjack's back herself and they took off for the ship.

The others were a little surprised when Piper came back on a pegasus with two unconscious demigods. While Frank and Hazel tended to Blackjack, Annabeth and Leo helped get Piper and the boys to the sickbay.

'At this rate, we're going to run out of ambrosia,' Coach Hedge grumbled as he tended their wounds. 'How come I never get invited on these violent trips?'

Piper sat at Jason's side. She herself felt fine after a swig of nectar and some water, but she was still worried about the boys.

'Leo,' Piper said, 'are we ready to sail?'

'Yeah, but –'

'Set course for Atlanta. I'll explain later.'

'But . . . okay.' He hurried off.

Annabeth didn't argue with Piper either. She was too busy examining the horseshoe-shaped dent on the back of Percy's head.

'What *hit* him?' she demanded.

'Blackjack,' Piper said.

'*What?*'

Piper tried to explain while Coach Hedge applied some healing paste to the boys' heads. She'd never been impressed with Hedge's nursing abilities before, but he must have done something right. Either that, or the spirits that possessed the boys had also made them extra resilient. They both groaned and opened their eyes.

Within a few minutes, Jason and Percy were sitting up in their berths and able to talk in complete sentences. Both had fuzzy memories of what had happened. When Piper described their duel on the highway, Jason winced.

'Knocked out twice in two days,' he muttered. 'Some demigod.' He glanced sheepishly at Percy. 'Sorry, man. I didn't mean to blast you.'

Percy's shirt was peppered with burn holes. His hair was even more dishevelled than normal. Despite that, he managed a weak laugh. 'Not the first time. Your big sister got me good once at camp.'

'Yeah, but . . . I could have killed you.'

'Or I could have killed you,' Percy said.

Jason shrugged. 'If there'd been an ocean in Kansas, maybe.'

'I don't need an ocean –'

'Boys,' Annabeth interrupted, 'I'm sure you both would've been wonderful at killing each other. But right now you need some rest.'

'Food first,' Percy said. 'Please? And we really need to talk. Bacchus said some things that don't –'

'Bacchus?' Annabeth raised her hand. 'Okay, fine. We need to talk. Mess hall. Ten minutes. I'll tell the others. And please, Percy . . . change your clothes. You smell like you've been run over by an electric horse.'

Leo gave the helm to Coach Hedge again, after making the satyr promise he would not steer them to the nearest military base 'for fun'.

They gathered around the dining table, and Piper explained what had happened at TOPEKA 32 – their conversation with Bacchus, the trap sprung by Gaia, the eidolons that had possessed the boys.

'Of course!' Hazel slapped the table, which startled Frank so much he dropped his burrito. 'That's what happened to Leo, too.'

'So it wasn't my fault.' Leo exhaled. 'I didn't start World War Three. I just got possessed by an evil spirit. That's a relief!'

'But the Romans don't know that,' Annabeth said. 'And why would they take our word for it?'

'We could contact Reyna,' Jason suggested. 'She would believe us.'

Hearing the way Jason said her name, like it was a lifeline to his past, made Piper's heart sink.

Jason turned to her with a hopeful gleam in his eyes. 'You could convince her, Pipes. I know you could.'

Piper felt like all the blood in her body was draining into her feet. Annabeth looked at her sympathetically, as if to say: *Boys are so clueless.* Even Hazel winced.

'I could try,' she said halfheartedly. 'But Octavian is the one we have to worry about. In my dagger blade, I saw him taking control of the Roman crowd. I'm not sure Reyna can stop him.'

Jason's expression darkened. Piper didn't get any pleasure from bursting his bubble, but the other Romans – Hazel and Frank – nodded in agreement.

'She's right,' Frank said. 'This afternoon when we were scouting, we saw eagles again. They were a long way off, but closing fast. Octavian is on the warpath.'

Hazel grimaced. 'This is exactly the sort of opportunity Octavian has always wanted. He'll try to seize power. If Reyna objects, he'll say she's soft on the Greeks. As for those eagles . . . it's like they could smell us.'

'They can,' Jason said. 'Roman eagles can hunt demigods by their magical scent even better than monsters can. This ship might conceal us somewhat, but not completely – not from them.'

Leo drummed his fingers. 'Great. I should have installed a smoke screen that makes the ship smell like a giant chicken nugget. Remind me to invent that, next time.'

Hazel frowned. 'What is a chicken nugget?'

'Oh, man . . .' Leo shook his head in amazement. 'That's right. You've missed the last, like, seventy years. Well, my apprentice, a chicken nugget –'

'Doesn't matter,' Annabeth interrupted. 'The point is we'll have a hard time explaining the truth to the Romans. Even if they believe us –'

'You're right.' Jason leaned forward. 'We should just keep

going. Once we're over the Atlantic, we'll be safe – at least from the legion.'

He sounded so depressed Piper didn't know whether to feel sorry for him or resentful. 'How can you be sure?' she asked. 'Why wouldn't they follow us?'

He shook his head. 'You heard Reyna talking about the ancient lands. They're much too dangerous. Roman demigods have been forbidden to go there for generations. Even Octavian couldn't get around that rule.'

Frank swallowed a bite of burrito like it had turned to cardboard in his mouth. 'So, if *we* go there . . .'

'We'll be outlaws as well as traitors,' Jason confirmed. 'Any Roman demigod would have the right to kill us on sight. But I wouldn't worry about that. If we get across the Atlantic, they'll give up on chasing us. They'll assume that we'll die in the Mediterranean – the Mare Nostrum.'

Percy pointed his pizza slice at Jason. 'You, sir, are a ray of sunshine.'

Jason didn't argue. The other demigods stared at their plates, except for Percy, who continued to enjoy his pizza. Where he put all that food, Piper didn't know. The guy could eat like a satyr.

'So let's plan ahead,' Percy suggested, 'and make sure we *don't* die. Mr D – Bacchus – ugh, do I have to call him Mr *B* now? Anyway, he mentioned the twins in Ella's prophecy. Two giants. Otis and, uh, something that started with an F?'

'Ephialtes,' Jason said.

'Twin giants, like Piper saw in her blade . . .' Annabeth ran her finger along the rim of her cup. 'I remember a story about twin giants. They tried to reach Mount Olympus by piling up a bunch of mountains.'

Frank nearly choked. 'Well, that's great. Giants who can use mountains like building blocks. And you say Bacchus killed these guys with a pinecone on a stick?'

'Something like that,' Percy said. 'I don't think we should count on his help this time. He wanted a tribute, and he made it pretty clear it would be a tribute we couldn't handle.'

Silence fell around the table. Piper could hear Coach Hedge above deck singing 'Blow the Man Down', except he didn't know the lyrics, so he mostly sang, 'Blah-blah-hum-de-dum-dum.'

Piper couldn't shake the feeling that Bacchus was *meant* to help them. The giant twins were in Rome. They were keeping something the demigods needed – something in that bronze jar. Whatever it was, she got the feeling it held the answer to sealing the Doors of Death – *the key to endless death*. She also felt sure they could never defeat the giants without Bacchus's help. And, if they couldn't do that in five days, Rome would be destroyed and Hazel's brother, Nico, would die.

On the other hand, if the vision of Bacchus offering her a silver goblet was false, maybe the other visions didn't have to come true either – especially the one of her, Percy and Jason drowning. Maybe that was just symbolic.

The blood of a female demigod, Gaia had said, *and the blood of a male. Piper, my dear, choose which hero will die with you.*

'She wants two of us,' Piper murmured.

Everyone turned to look at her.

Piper hated being the centre of attention. Maybe that was

strange for a child of Aphrodite, but she'd watched her dad, the movie star, deal with fame for years. She remembered when Aphrodite had claimed her at the bonfire in front of the entire camp, zapping her with a magic beauty-queen makeover. That had been the most embarrassing moment of her life. Even here, with only six other demigods, Piper felt exposed.

They're my friends, she told herself. It's okay.

But she had a strange feeling . . . as if more than six sets of eyes were watching her.

'Today on the highway,' she said, 'Gaia told me that she needed the blood of only two demigods – one female, one male. She – she asked me to choose which boy would die.'

Jason squeezed her hand. 'But neither of us died. You saved us.'

'I know. It's just . . . Why would she want that?'

Leo whistled softly. 'Guys, remember at the Wolf House? Our favourite ice princess, Khione? She talked about spilling Jason's blood, how it would taint the place for generations. Maybe demigod blood has some kind of power.'

'Oh . . .' Percy set down his third pizza slice. He leaned back and stared at nothing, as if the horse kick to his head had just now registered.

'Percy?' Annabeth gripped his arm.

'Oh, bad,' he muttered. 'Bad. Bad.' He looked across the table at Frank and Hazel. 'You guys remember Polybotes?'

'The giant who invaded Camp Jupiter,' Hazel said. 'The anti-Poseidon you whacked in the head with a Terminus statue. Yes, I think I remember.'

'I had a dream,' Percy said, 'when we were flying to Alaska. Polybotes was talking to the gorgons, and he said – he said he wanted me taken prisoner, not killed. He said: "I want that one chained at my feet, so I can kill him when the time is ripe. His blood shall water the stones of Mount Olympus and wake Earth Mother!"'

Piper wondered if the room's temperature controls were broken, because suddenly she couldn't stop shaking. It was the same way she'd felt on the highway outside Topeka. 'You think the giants would use our blood . . . the blood of two of us –'

'I don't know,' Percy said. 'But until we figure it out I suggest we all try to avoid getting captured.'

Jason grunted. '*That* I agree with.'

'But how do we figure it out?' Hazel asked. 'The Mark of Athena, the twins, Ella's prophecy . . . how does it all fit together?'

Annabeth pressed her hands against the edge of the table. 'Piper, you told Leo to set our course for Atlanta.'

'Right,' Piper said. 'Bacchus told us we should seek out . . . what was his name?'

'Phorcys,' Percy said.

Annabeth looked surprised, like she wasn't used to her boyfriend having the answers. 'You know him?'

Percy shrugged. 'I didn't recognize the name at first. Then Bacchus mentioned salt water, and it rang a bell. Phorcys is an old sea god from before my dad's time. Never met him, but supposedly he's a son of Gaia. I still don't understand what a sea god would be doing in Atlanta.'

Leo snorted. 'What's a wine god doing in Kansas? Gods are weird. Anyway, we should reach Atlanta by noon tomorrow, unless something *else* goes wrong.'

'Don't even say that,' Annabeth muttered. 'It's getting late. We should all get some sleep.'

'Wait,' Piper said.

Once more, everyone looked at her.

She was rapidly losing her courage, wondering if her instincts were wrong, but she forced herself to speak.

'There's one last thing,' she said. 'The eidolons – the possessing spirits. They're still here, in this room.'

XII

PIPER

PIPER COULDN'T EXPLAIN HOW SHE KNEW.

Stories of phantoms and tortured souls had always freaked her out. Her dad used to joke about Grandpa Tom's Cherokee legends from back on the rez, but even at home in their big Malibu mansion, looking out over the Pacific, whenever her dad recounted the ghost stories for her, she could never get them out of her head.

Cherokee spirits were always restless. They often lost their way to the Land of the Dead, or stayed behind with the living out of sheer stubbornness. Sometimes they didn't even realize they *were* dead.

The more Piper learned about being a demigod, the more convinced she was that Cherokee legends and Greek myths weren't so different. These eidolons acted a lot like the spirits in her dad's stories.

Piper had a gut sense they were still present, simply because no one had told them to go away.

When she was done explaining, the others looked at her uncomfortably. Up on deck, Hedge sang something that sounded like 'In the Navy' while Blackjack stomped his hooves, whinnying in protest.

Finally Hazel exhaled. 'Piper is right.'

'How can you be sure?' Annabeth asked.

'I've met eidolons,' Hazel said. 'In the Underworld, when I was . . . you know.'

Dead.

Piper had forgotten that Hazel was a second-timer. In her own way, Hazel too was a ghost reborn.

'So . . .' Frank rubbed his hand across his buzz-cut hair as if some ghosts might have invaded his scalp. 'You think these things are lurking on the ship, or –'

'Possibly lurking inside some of us,' Piper said. 'We don't know.'

Jason clenched his fist. 'If that's true –'

'We have to take steps,' Piper said. 'I think I can do this.'

'Do what?' Percy asked.

'Just listen, okay?' Piper took a deep breath. 'Everybody listen.'

Piper met their eyes, one person at a time.

'Eidolons,' she said, using her charmspeak, 'raise your hands.'

There was tense silence.

Leo laughed nervously. 'Did you really think that was going to –?'

His voice died. His face went slack. He raised his hand.

Jason and Percy did the same. Their eyes had turned

glassy and gold. Hazel caught her breath. Next to Leo, Frank scrambled out of his chair and put his back against the wall.

'Oh, gods.' Annabeth looked at Piper imploringly. 'Can you cure them?'

Piper wanted to whimper and hide under the table, but she *had* to help Jason. She couldn't believe she'd held hands with . . . No, she refused to think about it.

She focused on Leo because he was the least intimidating.

'Are there more of you on this ship?' she asked.

'*No*,' Leo said in a hollow voice. '*The Earth Mother sent three. The strongest, the best. We will live again.*'

'Not here, you won't,' Piper growled. 'All three of you, listen carefully.'

Jason and Percy turned towards her. Those gold eyes were unnerving, but seeing all three boys like that fuelled Piper's anger.

'You will leave those bodies,' she commanded.

'*No*,' Percy said.

Leo let out a soft hiss. '*We must live.*'

Frank fumbled for his bow. 'Mars Almighty, that's creepy! Get out of here, spirits! Leave our friends alone!'

Leo turned towards him. '*You cannot command us, child of war. Your own life is fragile. Your soul could burn at any moment.*'

Piper wasn't sure what that meant, but Frank staggered like he'd been punched in the gut. He drew an arrow, his hands shaking. 'I – I've faced down worse things than you. If you want a fight –'

'Frank, don't.' Hazel rose.

Next to her, Jason drew his sword.

'Stop!' Piper ordered, but her voice quavered. She was rapidly losing faith in her plan. She'd made the eidolons appear, but what now? If she couldn't persuade them to leave, any bloodshed would be her fault. In the back of her mind, she could almost hear Gaia laughing.

'Listen to Piper.' Hazel pointed at Jason's sword. The gold blade seemed to grow heavy in his hand. It clunked to the table and Jason sank back into his chair.

Percy growled in a very un-Percy-like way. *'Daughter of Pluto, you may control gems and metals. You do not control the dead.'*

Annabeth reached towards him as if to restrain him, but Hazel waved her off.

'Listen, eidolons,' Hazel said sternly, 'you do not belong here. I may not command you, but Piper does. Obey her.'

She turned towards Piper, her expression clear: *Try again. You can do this.*

Piper mustered all her courage. She looked straight at Jason – straight into the eyes of the thing that was controlling him. 'You will leave those bodies,' Piper repeated, even more forcefully.

Jason's face tightened. His forehead beaded with sweat. *'We – we will leave these bodies.'*

'You will vow on the River Styx never to return to this ship,' Piper continued, 'and never to possess any member of this crew.'

Leo and Percy both hissed in protest.

'You will promise on the River Styx,' Piper insisted.

A moment of tension – she could feel their wills fighting

against hers. Then all three eidolons spoke in unison: '*We promise on the River Styx.*'

'You are dead,' Piper said.

'*We are dead,*' they agreed.

'Now, leave.'

All three boys slumped forward. Percy fell face-first into his pizza.

'Percy!' Annabeth grabbed him.

Piper and Hazel caught Jason's arms as he slipped out of his chair.

Leo wasn't so lucky. He fell towards Frank, who made no attempt to intercept him. Leo hit the floor.

'Ow!' he groaned.

'Are you all right?' Hazel asked.

Leo pulled himself up. He had a piece of spaghetti in the shape of a *3* stuck to his forehead. 'Did it work?'

'It worked,' Piper said, feeling pretty sure she was right. 'I don't think they'll be back.'

Jason blinked. 'Does that mean I can stop getting head injuries now?'

Piper laughed, exhaling all her nervousness. 'Come on, Lightning Boy. Let's get you some fresh air.'

Piper and Jason walked back and forth along the deck. Jason was still wobbly, so Piper encouraged him to wrap his arm around her for support.

Leo stood at the helm, conferring with Festus through the intercom; he knew from experience to give Jason and Piper some space. Since the satellite TV was up again, Coach

Hedge was in his cabin happily catching up on his mixed martial arts cage matches. Percy's pegasus Blackjack had flown off somewhere. The other demigods were settling in for the night.

The *Argo II* raced east, cruising several hundred feet above the ground. Below them small towns passed by like lit-up islands in a dark sea of prairie.

Piper remembered last winter, flying Festus the dragon over the city of Quebec. She had never seen anything so beautiful, or felt so happy to have Jason's arms around her – but this was even better.

The night was warm. The ship sailed along more smoothly than a dragon. Best of all, they were flying away from Camp Jupiter as fast as they possibly could. No matter how dangerous the ancient lands were, Piper couldn't wait to get there. She hoped Jason was right that the Romans wouldn't follow them across the Atlantic.

Jason stopped amidships and leaned against the rail. The moonlight turned his blond hair silver.

'Thanks, Pipes,' he said. 'You saved me again.'

He put his arm around her waist. She thought about the day they'd fallen into the Grand Canyon – the first time she'd learned that Jason could control the air. He'd held her so tightly she could feel his heartbeat. Then they'd stopped falling and floated in midair. Best. Boyfriend. Ever.

She wanted to kiss him now, but something held her back.

'I don't know if Percy will trust me any more,' she said. 'Not after I let his horse knock him out.'

Jason laughed. 'Don't worry about that. Percy's a nice guy,

but I get the feeling he needs a knock on the head every once in a while.'

'You could have killed him.'

Jason's smile faded. 'That wasn't me.'

'But I almost *let* you,' Piper said. 'When Gaia said I had to choose, I hesitated and . . .'

She blinked, cursing herself for crying.

'Don't be so hard on yourself,' Jason said. 'You saved us both.'

'But if two of our crew really have to die, a boy and a girl –'

'I don't accept that. We're going to stop Gaia. All seven of us are going to come back alive. I promise you.'

Piper wished that he hadn't *promised*. The word only reminded her of the Prophecy of Seven: *an oath to keep with a final breath.*

Please, she thought, wondering if her mom, the goddess of love, could hear her. *Don't let it be Jason's final breath. If love means anything, don't take him away.*

As soon as she had made the wish, she felt guilty. How could she stand to see Annabeth in that kind of pain if Percy died? How could she live with herself if *any* of the seven demigods died? Already, each of them had endured so much. Even the two new Roman kids, Hazel and Frank, whom Piper barely knew, felt like kin. At Camp Jupiter, Percy had recounted their trip to Alaska, which sounded as harrowing as anything Piper had experienced. And, from the way Hazel and Frank tried to help during the exorcism, she could tell they were brave, good people.

'The legend that Annabeth mentioned,' she said, 'about the Mark of Athena . . . why didn't you want to talk about it?'

She was afraid Jason might shut her out, but he just lowered his head like he'd been expecting the question. 'Pipes, I don't know what's true and what's not. That legend . . . it could be really dangerous.'

'For who?'

'All of us,' he said grimly. 'The story goes that the Romans stole something important from the Greeks, back in ancient times, when the Romans conquered the Greeks' cities.'

Piper waited, but Jason seemed lost in thought.

'What did they steal?' she asked.

'I don't know,' he said. 'I'm not sure anyone in the legion has ever known. But, according to the story, this thing was taken away to Rome and hidden there. The children of Athena, Greek demigods, have hated us ever since. They've always stirred up their brethren against the Romans. Like I said, I don't know how much of that is true –'

'But why not just tell Annabeth?' Piper asked. 'She's not going to suddenly hate you.'

He seemed to have trouble focusing on her. 'I hope not. But the legend says that the children of Athena have been searching for this thing for millennia. Every generation, a few are chosen by the goddess to find it. Apparently, they're led to Rome by some sign . . . the Mark of Athena.'

'If Annabeth is one of those searchers . . . we should help her.'

Jason hesitated. 'Maybe. When we get closer to Rome, I'll tell her what little I know. Honest. But the story, at least the way I heard it – it claims that if the Greeks ever found what was stolen they'd never forgive us. They'd destroy the legion and Rome, once and for all. After what Nemesis told Leo, about Rome being destroyed five days from now . . .'

Piper studied Jason's face. He was, without a doubt, the bravest person she'd ever known, but she realized he was afraid. This legend – the idea that it might tear apart their group and level a city – absolutely terrified him.

Piper wondered what could have been stolen from the Greeks that would be so important. She couldn't imagine anything that would make Annabeth suddenly turn vengeful.

Then again, Piper couldn't imagine choosing one demigod's life over another, and today on that deserted road, just for a moment, Gaia had almost tempted her . . .

'I'm sorry, by the way,' Jason said.

Piper wiped the last tear from her face. 'Sorry for what? It was the eidolon who attacked –'

'Not about that.' The little scar on Jason's upper lip seemed to glow white in the moonlight. She'd always loved that scar. The imperfection made his face much more interesting.

'I was stupid to ask you to contact Reyna,' he said. 'I wasn't thinking.'

'Oh.' Piper looked up at the clouds and wondered if her mother, Aphrodite, was somehow influencing him. His apology seemed too good to be true.

But don't stop, she thought. 'Really, it's okay.'

'It's just . . . I never felt that way towards Reyna,' Jason said, 'so I didn't think about it making you uncomfortable. You've got nothing to worry about, Pipes.'

'I wanted to hate her,' Piper admitted. 'I was so afraid you'd go back to Camp Jupiter.'

Jason looked surprised. 'That would never happen. Not unless you came with me. I promise.'

Piper held his hand. She managed a smile, but she was thinking: *Another promise. An oath to keep with a final breath.*

She tried to put those thoughts out of her mind. She knew she should just enjoy this quiet moment with Jason. But, as she looked over the side of the ship, she couldn't help remembering how much the prairie at night looked like dark water – like the drowning room she'd seen in the blade of her knife.

XIII

PERCY

FORGET THE CHICKEN-NUGGET SMOKE SCREEN. Percy wanted Leo to invent an anti-dream hat.

That night he had horrible nightmares. First he dreamed he was back in Alaska on the quest for the legion's eagle. He was hiking along a mountain road, but as soon as he stepped off the shoulder he was swallowed by the bog – muskeg, Hazel had called it. He found himself choking in mud, unable to move or see or breathe. For the first time in his life, he understood what it was like to drown.

It's just a dream, he told himself. *I'll wake up.*

But that didn't make it any less terrifying.

Percy had never been scared of water. It was his father's element. But since the muskeg experience he'd developed a fear of suffocation. He could never admit this to anyone, but it had even made him nervous about going in the water. He knew that was silly. He couldn't drown. But he also suspected that if he didn't control the fear it might start controlling him.

He thought about his friend Thalia, who was scared of heights even though she was the daughter of the sky god. Her brother, Jason, could fly by summoning the winds. Thalia couldn't, maybe because she was too afraid to try. If Percy started to believe he could drown . . .

The muskeg pressed against his chest. His lungs wanted to burst.

Stop panicking, he told himself. *This isn't real.*

Just when he couldn't hold his breath any longer, the dream changed.

He stood in a vast gloomy space like an underground parking garage. Rows of stone pillars marched off in every direction, holding up the ceiling about twenty feet above. Freestanding braziers cast a dim red glow over the floor.

Percy couldn't see very far in the shadows, but hanging from the ceiling were pulley systems, sandbags and rows of dark theatre lights. Piled around the chamber, wooden crates were labelled PROPS, WEAPONS and COSTUMES. One read: ASSORTED ROCKET LAUNCHERS.

Percy heard machinery creaking in the darkness, huge gears turning and water rushing through pipes.

Then he saw the giant . . . or at least Percy guessed that he was a giant.

He was about twelve feet tall – a respectable height for a Cyclops, but only half as tall as other giants Percy had dealt with. He also looked more human than a typical giant, without the dragonlike legs of his larger kin. Nevertheless, his long purple hair was braided in a ponytail of dreadlocks, woven with gold and silver coins, which struck Percy as a giantish hairstyle. He had a ten-foot spear strapped to his back – a giantish weapon.

He wore the largest black turtleneck Percy had ever seen, black trousers and black leather shoes with points so long and curly they might have been jester slippers. He paced back and forth in front of a raised platform, examining a bronze jar about the size of Percy.

'No, no, no,' the giant muttered to himself. 'Where's the splash? Where's the value?' He yelled into the darkness, 'Otis!'

Percy heard something shuffling in the distance. Another giant appeared out of the gloom. He wore exactly the same black outfit, right down to the curly shoes. The only difference between the two giants was that the second one's hair was green rather than purple.

The first giant cursed. 'Otis, why do you do this to me *every day?* I told you *I* was wearing the black turtleneck today. You could wear anything *but* the black turtleneck!'

Otis blinked as if he'd just woken up. 'I thought you were wearing the yellow toga today.'

'That was yesterday! When *you* showed up in the yellow toga!'

'Oh. Right. Sorry, Ephie.'

His brother snarled. They had to be twins, because their faces were identically ugly.

'And don't call me Ephie,' Ephie demanded. 'Call me

Ephialtes. That's my name. Or you can use my stage name: The BIG F!'

Otis grimaced. 'I'm still not sure about that stage name.'

'Nonsense! It's perfect. Now, how are the preparations coming along?'

'Fine.' Otis didn't sound very enthusiastic. 'The man-eating tigers, the spinning blades . . . But I still think a few ballerinas would be nice.'

'No ballerinas!' Ephialtes snapped. 'And *this* thing.' He waved at the bronze jar in disgust. 'What does it do? It's not exciting.'

'But that's the whole point of the show. He dies unless the others rescue him. And if they arrive on schedule –'

'Oh, they'd better!' Ephialtes said. 'July first, the Kalends of July, sacred to Juno. That's when Mother wants to destroy those stupid demigods and *really* rub it in Juno's face. Besides, I'm not paying overtime for those gladiator ghosts!'

'Well, then, they all die,' Otis said, 'and we start the destruction of Rome. Just like Mother wants. It'll be perfect. The crowd will love it. Roman ghosts adore this sort of thing.'

Ephialtes looked unconvinced. 'But the jar just *stands* there. Couldn't we suspend it above a fire, or dissolve it in a pool of acid or something?'

'We need him alive for a few more days,' Otis reminded his brother. 'Otherwise, the seven won't take the bait and rush to save him.'

'Hmm. I suppose. I'd still like a little more screaming. This slow death is boring. Ah, well, what about our talented friend? Is she ready to receive her visitor?'

Otis made a sour face. 'I *really* don't like talking to her. She makes me nervous.'

'But is she ready?'

'Yes,' Otis said reluctantly. 'She's been ready for centuries. No one will be removing *that* statue.'

'Excellent.' Ephialtes rubbed his hands together in anticipation. 'This is our big chance, my brother.'

'That's what you said about our last stunt,' Otis mumbled. 'I was hanging in that block of ice suspended over the River Lethe for six months, and we didn't even get any media attention.'

'This is different!' Ephialtes insisted. 'We will set a new standard for entertainment! If Mother is pleased, we can write our own ticket to fame and fortune!'

'If you say so,' Otis sighed. 'Though I still think those ballerina costumes from *Swan Lake* would look lovely –'

'No ballet!'

'Sorry.'

'Come,' Ephialtes said. 'Let's examine the tigers. I want to be sure they are hungry!'

The giants lumbered off into the gloom, and Percy turned towards the jar.

I need to see inside, he thought.

He willed his dream forward, right to the surface of the jar. Then he passed through.

The air in the jar smelled of stale breath and tarnished metal. The only light came from the dim purple glow of a dark sword, its Stygian iron blade set against one side of the container. Huddled next to it was a dejected-looking boy in tattered jeans, a black shirt and an old aviator jacket. On his right hand, a silver skull ring glittered.

'Nico,' Percy called. But the son of Hades couldn't hear him.

The container was completely sealed. The air was turning poisonous. Nico's eyes were closed, his breathing shallow. He appeared to be meditating. His face was pale, and thinner than Percy remembered.

On the inner wall of the jar, it looked as though Nico had scratched three hash marks with his sword – maybe it had been three days that he'd been imprisoned?

It didn't seem possible he could have survived so long without suffocating. Even in a dream, Percy was already starting to feel panicky, struggling to get enough oxygen.

Then he noticed something between Nico's feet – a small collection of glistening objects no bigger than baby teeth.

Seeds, Percy realized. Pomegranate seeds. Three had been eaten and spat out. Five were still encased in dark red pulp.

'Nico,' Percy said, 'where is this place? We'll save you . . .'

The image faded, and a girl's voice whispered: 'Percy.'

At first, Percy thought he was still asleep. When he'd lost his memory, he'd spent weeks dreaming about Annabeth, the only person he remembered from his past. As his eyes opened and his vision cleared, he realized she was really there.

She was standing by his berth, smiling down at him.

Her blonde hair fell across her shoulders. Her storm-grey eyes were bright with amusement. He remembered his first day at Camp Half-Blood, five years ago, when he'd woken from a daze and found Annabeth standing over him. She had said, *You drool when you sleep.*

She was sentimental that way.

'Wh– what's going on?' he asked. 'Are we there?'

'No,' she said, her voice low. 'It's the middle of the night.'

'You mean . . .' Percy's heart started to race. He realized he was in his pyjamas, in bed. He probably *had* been drooling, or at least making weird noises as he dreamed. No doubt he had a severe case of pillow hair and his breath didn't smell great. 'You sneaked into my cabin?'

Annabeth rolled her eyes. 'Percy, you'll be seventeen in two months. You can't seriously be worried about getting into trouble with Coach Hedge.'

'Uh, have you seen his baseball bat?'

'Besides, Seaweed Brain, I just thought we could take a walk. We haven't had any time to be together alone. I want to show you something – my favourite place aboard the ship.'

Percy's pulse was still in overdrive, but it wasn't from fear of getting into trouble. 'Can I, you know, brush my teeth first?'

'You'd better,' Annabeth said. 'Because I'm not kissing you until you do. And brush your hair while you're at it.'

For a trireme, the ship was huge, but it still felt cosy to Percy – like his dorm building back at Yancy Academy, or any of the other boarding schools he'd been kicked out of. Annabeth and he crept downstairs to the second deck, which Percy hadn't explored except for sickbay.

She led him past the engine room, which looked like a very dangerous, mechanized jungle gym, with pipes and pistons and tubes jutting from a central bronze sphere. Cables resembling giant metal noodles snaked across the floor and ran up the walls.

'How does that thing even work?' Percy asked.

'No idea,' Annabeth said. 'And I'm the only one besides Leo who can operate it.'

'That's reassuring.'

'It should be fine. It's only threatened to blow up once.'

'You're kidding, I hope.'

She smiled. 'Come on.'

They worked their way past the supply rooms and the armoury. Towards the stern of the ship, they reached a set of wooden double doors that opened into a large stable. The room smelled of fresh hay and wool blankets. Lining the left wall were three empty horse stalls like the ones they used for pegasi back at camp. The right wall had two empty cages big enough for large zoo animals.

In the centre of the floor was a twenty-foot-square see-through panel. Far below, the night landscape whisked by – miles of dark countryside crisscrossed with illuminated highways like the strands of a web.

'A glass-bottomed boat?' Percy asked.

Annabeth grabbed a blanket from the nearest stable gate and spread it across part of the glass floor. 'Sit with me.'

They relaxed on the blanket, as if they were having a picnic, and watched the world go by below.

'Leo built the stables so pegasi could come and go easily,'

Annabeth said. 'Only he didn't realize that pegasi prefer to roam free, so the stables are always empty.'

Percy wondered where Blackjack was – roaming the skies somewhere, hopefully following their progress. Percy's head still throbbed from getting whopped by Blackjack's hoof, but he didn't hold that against the horse.

'What do you mean, *come and go easily*?' he asked. 'Wouldn't a pegasus have to make it down two flights of stairs?'

Annabeth rapped her knuckles on the glass. 'These are bay doors, like on a bomber.'

Percy gulped. 'You mean we're sitting on *doors*? What if they opened?'

'I suppose we'd fall to our deaths. But they won't open. Most likely.'

'Great.'

Annabeth laughed. 'You know why I like it here? It's not just the view. What does this place remind you of?'

Percy looked around: the cages and stables, the Celestial bronze lamp hanging from the beam, the smell of hay and of course Annabeth sitting close to him, her face ghostly and beautiful in the soft amber light.

'That zoo truck,' Percy decided. 'The one we took to Las Vegas.'

Her smile told him he'd got the answer right.

'That was so long ago,' Percy said. 'We were in bad shape, struggling to get across the country to find that stupid lightning bolt, trapped in a truck with a bunch of mistreated animals. How can you be nostalgic about that?'

'Because, Seaweed Brain, it's the first time we really talked, you and me. I told you about my family, and . . .' She took out her camp necklace, strung with her dad's college ring and a colourful clay bead for each year at Camp Half-Blood. Now there was something else on the leather cord: a red coral pendant Percy had given her when they had started dating. He'd brought it from his father's palace at the bottom of the sea.

'And,' Annabeth continued, 'it reminds me how long we've known each other. We were *twelve*, Percy. Can you believe that?'

'No,' he admitted. 'So . . . you knew you liked me from that moment?'

She smirked. 'I hated you at first. You annoyed me. Then I tolerated you for a few years. Then –'

'Okay, fine.'

She leaned over and kissed him: a good, proper kiss without anyone watching – no Romans anywhere, no screaming satyr chaperones.

She pulled away. 'I missed you, Percy.'

Percy wanted to tell her the same thing, but it seemed too small a comment. While he had been on the Roman side, he'd kept himself alive almost solely by thinking of Annabeth. *I missed you* didn't really cover that.

He remembered earlier in the night, when Piper had forced the eidolon to leave his mind. Percy hadn't been aware of its presence until she had used her charmspeak. After the eidolon was gone, he felt as if a hot spike had been removed from his forehead. He hadn't realized how much pain he had been in until the spirit left. Then his thoughts became clearer. His soul settled comfortably back into his body.

Sitting here with Annabeth made him feel the same way. The past few months could have been one of his strange dreams. The events at Camp Jupiter seemed as fuzzy and unreal as that fight with Jason, when they had both been controlled by the eidolons.

Yet he didn't regret the time he'd spent at Camp Jupiter. It had opened his eyes in a lot of ways.

'Annabeth,' he said hesitantly, 'in New Rome, demigods can live their whole lives in peace.'

Her expression turned guarded. 'Reyna explained it to me. But, Percy, you belong at Camp Half-Blood. That other life –'

'I know,' Percy said. 'But while I was there I saw so many demigods living without fear: kids going to college, couples getting married and raising families. There's nothing like that at Camp Half-Blood. I kept thinking about you and me . . . and maybe some day when this war with the giants is over . . .'

It was hard to tell in the golden light, but he thought Annabeth was blushing. 'Oh,' she said.

Percy was afraid he'd said too much. Maybe he'd scared her with his big dreams of the future. She was usually the one with the plans. Percy cursed himself silently.

As long as he'd known Annabeth, he still felt like he understood so little about her. Even after they'd been dating several months, their relationship had always felt new and delicate, like a glass sculpture. He was terrified of doing something wrong and breaking it.

'I'm sorry,' he said. 'I just . . . I had to think of that to keep going. To give me hope. Forget I mentioned –'

'No!' she said. 'No, Percy. Gods, that's so sweet. It's just . . . we may have burned that bridge. If we can't repair things with the Romans – well, the two sets of demigods have *never* got along. That's why the gods kept us separate. I don't know if we could ever belong there.'

Percy didn't want to argue, but he couldn't let go of the hope. It felt important – not just for Annabeth and him, but for all the other demigods. It *had* to be possible to belong in two different worlds at once. After all, that's what being a demigod was all about – not quite belonging in the mortal world or on Mount Olympus, but trying to make peace with both sides of their nature.

Unfortunately, that got him thinking about the gods, the war they were facing and his dream about the twins Ephialtes and Otis.

'I was having a nightmare when you woke me up,' he admitted.

He told Annabeth what he'd seen.

Even the most troubling parts didn't seem to surprise her. She shook her head sadly when he described Nico's imprisonment in the bronze jar. She got an angry glint in her eyes when he told her about the giants planning some sort of Rome-destroying extravaganza that would include their painful deaths as the opening event.

'Nico is the bait,' she murmured. 'Gaia's forces must have captured him somehow. But we don't know exactly where they're holding him.'

'Somewhere in Rome,' Percy said. 'Somewhere underground. They made it sound like Nico still had a few days to live, but I don't see how he could hold out so long with no oxygen.'

'Five more days, according to Nemesis,' Annabeth said. 'The Kalends of July. At least the deadline makes sense now.'

'What's a Kalends?'

Annabeth smirked, like she was pleased they were back in their old familiar pattern – Percy being ignorant, she herself explaining stuff. 'It's just the Roman term for the first of the month. That's where we get the word *calendar*. But how can Nico survive that long? We should talk to Hazel.'

'Now?'

She hesitated. 'No. It can wait until morning. I don't want to hit her with this news in the middle of the night.'

'The giants mentioned a statue,' Percy recalled. 'And something about a talented friend who was guarding it. Whoever this friend was, she scared Otis. Anyone who can scare a giant . . .'

Annabeth gazed down at a highway snaking through dark hills. 'Percy, have you seen Poseidon lately? Or had any kind of sign from him?'

He shook his head. 'Not since . . . Wow. I guess I haven't thought about it. Not since the end of the Titan War. I saw him at Camp Half-Blood, but that was last August.' A sense of dread settled over him. 'Why? Have you seen Athena?'

She didn't meet his eyes.

'A few weeks ago,' she admitted. 'It . . . it wasn't good. She didn't seem like herself. Maybe it's the Greek/Roman schizophrenia that Nemesis described. I'm not sure. She said some hurtful things. She said I had failed her.'

'Failed her?' Percy wasn't sure he'd heard her right. Annabeth was the *perfect* demigod child. She was everything a daughter of Athena should be. 'How could you ever –?'

'I don't know,' she said miserably. 'On top of that, I've been having nightmares of my own. They don't make as much sense as yours.'

Percy waited, but Annabeth didn't share any more details. He wanted to make her feel better and tell her it would be okay, but he knew he couldn't. He wanted to fix everything for both of them so they could have a happy ending. After all these years, even the cruellest gods would have to admit they deserved it.

But he had a gut feeling that there was nothing he could do to help Annabeth this time, other than simply *be* there. *Wisdom's daughter walks alone.*

He felt as trapped and helpless as when he'd sunk into the muskeg.

Annabeth managed a faint smile. 'Some romantic evening, huh? No more bad things until the morning.' She kissed him again. 'We'll figure everything out. I've got you back. For now, that's all that matters.'

'Right,' Percy said. 'No more talk about Gaia rising, Nico being held hostage, the world ending, the giants –'

'Shut up, Seaweed Brain,' she ordered. 'Just hold me for a while.'

They sat together cuddling, enjoying each other's warmth. Before Percy knew it, the drone of the ship's engine, the dim light and the comfortable feeling of being with Annabeth made his eyes heavy, and he drifted to sleep.

When he woke, daylight was coming through the glass floor, and a boy's voice said, 'Oh . . . You are in *so* much trouble.'

XIV

PERCY

PERCY HAD SEEN FRANK SURROUNDED by cannibal ogres, facing down an unkillable giant, and even unleashing Thanatos, the god of death. But he'd never seen Frank look as terrified as he did now, finding the two of them passed out in the stables.

'What . . . ?' Percy rubbed his eyes. 'Oh, we just fell asleep.'

Frank swallowed. He was dressed in running shoes, dark cargo pants and a Vancouver Winter Olympics T-shirt with his Roman centurion badge pinned to the neck (which seemed either sad or hopeful to Percy, now that they were renegades). Frank averted his eyes as if the sight of them together might burn him.

'Everyone thinks you've been kidnapped,' he said. 'We've been scouring the ship. When Coach Hedge finds out – oh, gods, you've been here *all night*?'

'Frank!' Annabeth's ears were as red as strawberries. 'We

just came down here to talk. We fell asleep. Accidentally. That's *it*.'

'Kissed a couple of times,' Percy said.

Annabeth glared at him. 'Not helping!'

'We'd better . . .' Frank pointed to the stable doors. 'Uh, we're supposed to meet for breakfast. Would you explain what you did – I mean didn't do? I mean . . . I really don't want that faun – I mean satyr – to kill me.'

Frank ran.

When everyone finally gathered in the mess hall, it wasn't quite as bad as Frank had feared. Jason and Piper were mostly relieved. Leo couldn't stop grinning and muttering, 'Classic. Classic.' Only Hazel seemed scandalized, maybe because she was from the 1940s. She kept fanning her face and wouldn't meet Percy's eyes.

Naturally, Coach Hedge went ballistic, but Percy found it hard to take the satyr seriously since he was barely five feet tall.

'Never in my life!' Coach bellowed, waving his bat and knocking over a plate of apples. 'Against the rules! Irresponsible!'

'Coach,' Annabeth said, 'it was an accident. We were talking and we fell asleep.'

'Besides,' Percy said, 'you're starting to sound like Terminus.'

Hedge narrowed his eyes. 'Is that an insult, Jackson? 'Cause I'll – I'll terminus you, buddy!'

Percy tried not to laugh. 'It won't happen again, Coach. I promise. Now, don't we have other things to discuss?'

Hedge fumed. 'Fine! But I'm watching you, Jackson. And you, Annabeth Chase, I thought you had more sense –'

Jason cleared his throat. 'So grab some food, everybody. Let's get started.'

The meeting was like a war council with doughnuts. Then again, back at Camp Half-Blood they used to have their most serious discussions around the ping-pong table in the rec room with crackers and Cheez Whiz, so Percy felt right at home.

He told them about his dream – the twin giants planning a reception for them in an underground parking lot with rocket launchers; Nico di Angelo trapped in a bronze jar, slowly dying from asphyxiation with pomegranate seeds at his feet.

Hazel choked back a sob. 'Nico . . . Oh, gods. The seeds.'

'You know what they are?' Annabeth asked.

Hazel nodded. 'He showed them to me once. They're from our stepmother's garden.'

'Your step– oh,' Percy said. 'You mean Persephone.'

Percy had met the wife of Hades once. She hadn't been exactly warm and sunny. He had also been to her Underworld garden – a creepy place full of crystal trees and flowers that bloomed blood red and ghost white.

'The seeds are a last-resort food,' Hazel said. Percy could tell she was nervous, because all the silverware on the table was starting to move towards her. 'Only children of Hades can eat them. Nico always kept some in case he got stuck somewhere. But if he's really imprisoned –'

'The giants are trying to lure us,' Annabeth said. 'They're assuming we'll try to rescue him.'

'Well, they're right!' Hazel looked around the table, her confidence apparently crumbling. 'Won't we?'

'Yes!' Coach Hedge yelled with a mouthful of napkins. 'It'll involve fighting, right?'

'Hazel, of course we'll help him,' Frank said. 'But how long do we have before . . . uh, I mean, how long can Nico hold out?'

'One seed a day,' Hazel said miserably. 'That's if he puts himself in a death trance.'

'A death trance?' Annabeth scowled. 'That doesn't sound fun.'

'It keeps him from consuming all his air,' Hazel said. 'Like hibernation or a coma. One seed can sustain him one day, barely.'

'And he has five seeds left,' Percy said. 'That's five days, including today. The giants must have planned it that way, so we'd have to arrive by July first. Assuming Nico is hidden somewhere in Rome –'

'That's not much time,' Piper summed up. She put her hand on Hazel's shoulder. 'We'll find him. At least we know what the lines of the prophecy mean now. "Twins snuff out the angel's breath, who holds the key to endless death." Your brother's last name: di Angelo. *Angelo* is Italian for "angel".'

'Oh, gods,' Hazel muttered. 'Nico . . .'

Percy stared at his jam doughnut. He had a rocky history with Nico di Angelo. The guy had once tricked him into visiting Hades's palace, and Percy had ended up in a cell. But most of the time Nico sided with the good guys. He certainly didn't deserve slow suffocation in a bronze jar, and Percy couldn't stand seeing Hazel in pain.

'We'll rescue him,' he promised her. 'We *have* to. The prophecy says he holds the key to endless death.'

'That's right,' Piper said encouragingly. 'Hazel, your brother went searching for the Doors of Death in the Underworld, right? He must've found them.'

'He can tell us where the doors are,' Percy said, 'and how to close them.'

Hazel took a deep breath. 'Yes. Good.'

'Uh . . .' Leo shifted in his chair. 'One thing. The giants are expecting us to do this, right? So we're walking into a trap?'

Hazel looked at Leo like he'd made a rude gesture. 'We have no choice!'

'Don't get me wrong, Hazel. It's just that your brother, Nico . . . he knew about both camps, right?'

'Well, yes,' Hazel said.

'He's been going back and forth,' Leo said, 'and he didn't tell either side.'

Jason sat forward, his expression grim. 'You're wondering if we can trust the guy. So am I.'

Hazel shot to her feet. 'I don't believe this. He's my *brother*. He brought me back from the Underworld, and you don't want to help him?'

Frank put his hand on her shoulder. 'Nobody's saying that.' He glared at Leo. 'Nobody had *better* be saying that.'

Leo blinked. 'Look, guys. All I mean is –'

'Hazel,' Jason said. 'Leo is raising a fair point. I remember Nico from Camp Jupiter. Now I find out he also visited Camp Half-Blood. That does strike me as . . . well, a little shady. Do we really know where his loyalties lie? We just have to be careful.'

Hazel's arms shook. A silver platter zoomed towards her and hit the wall to her left, splattering scrambled eggs. 'You . . . the *great* Jason Grace . . . the praetor I looked up to. You were supposed to be so fair, such a good leader. And now you . . .' Hazel stomped her foot and stormed out of the mess hall.

'Hazel!' Leo called after her. 'Ah, jeez. I should –'

'You've done enough,' Frank growled. He got up to follow her, but Piper gestured for him to wait.

'Give her time,' Piper advised. Then she frowned at Leo and Jason. 'You guys, that *was* pretty cold.'

Jason looked shocked. 'Cold? I'm just being cautious!'

'Her brother is dying,' Piper said.

'I'll go talk to her,' Frank insisted.

'No,' Piper said. 'Let her cool down first. Trust me on this. I'll go check on her in a few minutes.'

'But . . .' Frank huffed like an irritated bear. 'Fine. I'll wait.'

From up above came a whirring sound like a large drill.

'That's Festus,' Leo said. 'I've got him on autopilot, but we must be nearing Atlanta. I'll have to get up there . . . uh, assuming we know where to land.'

Everyone turned to Percy.

Jason raised an eyebrow. 'You're Captain Salt Water. Any ideas from the expert?'

Was that resentment in his voice? Percy wondered if Jason was secretly miffed about the duel in Kansas. Jason had joked about it, but Percy figured that they both harboured a little grudge. You couldn't put two demigods in a fight and not have them wonder who was stronger.

'I'm not sure,' he admitted. 'Somewhere central, high up so we can get a good view of the city. Maybe a park with some woods? We don't want to land a warship in the middle of downtown. I doubt even the Mist could cover up something that huge.'

Leo nodded. 'On it.' He raced for the stairs.

Frank settled back in his chair uneasily. Percy felt bad for him. On the trip to Alaska, he had watched Hazel and Frank grow close. He knew how protective Frank felt towards her. He also noticed the baleful look Frank was giving Leo. He decided it might be a good idea to get Frank off the ship for a while.

'When we land, I'll scout around in Atlanta,' Percy said. 'Frank, I could use your help.'

'You mean turn into a dragon again? Honestly, Percy, I don't want to spend the whole quest being everyone's flying taxi.'

'No,' Percy said. 'I want you with me because you've got the blood of Poseidon. Maybe you can help me figure out where to find salt water. Besides, you're good in a fight.'

That seemed to make Frank feel a little better. 'Sure. I guess.'

'Great,' Percy said. 'We should take one more. Annabeth –'

'Oh, no!' Coach Hedge barked. 'Young lady, you are *grounded*.'

Annabeth stared at him like he was speaking a foreign language. 'Excuse me?'

'You and Jackson are not going *anywhere* together!' Hedge insisted. He glared at Percy, daring him to mouth off. '*I'll* go with Frank and Mr Sneaky Jackson. The rest of you guard the ship and make sure Annabeth doesn't break any more rules!'

Wonderful, Percy thought. A boys' day out with Frank and a bloodthirsty satyr, to find salt water in a landlocked city.

'This,' he said, 'is going to be *so* much fun.'

PERCY

PERCY CLIMBED OUT ON DECK AND SAID, 'Wow.'

They had landed near the summit of a forested hill. A complex of white buildings, like a museum or a university, nestled in a grove of pines to the left. Below them spread the city of Atlanta – a cluster of brown and silver downtown skyscrapers two miles away, rising from what looked like an endless flat sprawl of highways, railroad tracks, houses and green swathes of forest.

'Ah, lovely spot.' Coach Hedge inhaled the morning air. 'Good choice, Valdez.'

Leo shrugged. 'I just picked a tall hill. That's a presidential library or something over there. At least that's what Festus says.'

'I don't know about that!' Hedge barked. 'But do you realize what happened on this hill? Frank Zhang, you should know!'

Frank flinched. 'I should?'

'A son of Ares stood here!' Hedge cried indignantly.

'I'm Roman . . . so Mars, actually.'

'Whatever! Famous spot in the American Civil War!'

'I'm Canadian, actually.'

'Whatever! General Sherman, Union leader. He stood on this hill watching the city of Atlanta burn. Cut a path of destruction all the way from here to the sea. Burning, looting, pillaging – now *there* was a demigod!'

Frank inched away from the satyr. 'Uh, okay.'

Percy didn't care much about history, but he wondered whether landing here was a bad omen. He'd heard that most human civil wars started as fights between Greek and Roman demigods. Now they were standing on the site of one such battle. The entire city below them had been levelled on orders of a child of Ares.

Percy could imagine some of the kids at Camp Half-Blood giving such a command. Clarisse La Rue, for instance, wouldn't hesitate. But he couldn't imagine Frank being so harsh.

'Anyway,' Percy said, 'let's try not to burn down the city this time.'

The coach looked disappointed. 'All right. But where to?'

Percy pointed towards downtown. 'When in doubt, start in the middle.'

Catching a ride there was easier than they thought. The three of them headed to the presidential library – which turned out to be the Carter Center – and asked the staff if they could call a taxi or give them directions to the nearest bus stop. Percy could have summoned Blackjack, but he was reluctant to ask the pegasus for help so soon after their last disaster. Frank didn't want to polymorph into anything. And, besides, Percy was kind of hoping to travel like a regular mortal for a change.

One of the librarians, whose name was Esther, insisted on driving them personally. She was so nice about it that Percy thought she must be a monster in disguise, but Hedge pulled him aside and assured him that Esther smelled like a normal human.

'With a hint of potpourri,' he said. 'Cloves. Rose petals. Tasty!'

They piled into Esther's big black Cadillac and drove towards downtown. Esther was so tiny she could barely see over the steering wheel, but that didn't seem to bother her. She muscled her car through traffic while regaling them with stories about the crazy families of Atlanta – the old plantation owners, the founders of Coca-Cola, the sports stars and the CNN news people. She sounded so knowledgeable that Percy decided to try his luck.

'Uh, so, Esther,' he said, 'here's a hard question for you. Salt water in Atlanta. What's the first thing that comes to mind?'

The old lady chuckled. 'Oh, sugar. That's easy. Whale sharks!'

Frank and Percy exchanged looks.

'Whale sharks?' Frank asked nervously. 'You have those in Atlanta?'

'At the aquarium, sugar,' Esther said. 'Very famous! Right downtown. Is that where you wanted to go?'

An aquarium. Percy considered that. He didn't know what an Ancient Greek sea god would be doing at a Georgia aquarium, but he didn't have any better ideas.

'Yes,' Percy said. 'That's where we're going.'

Esther dropped them at the main entrance, where a queue was already forming. She insisted on giving them her cell phone number for emergencies, money for a taxi ride back to the Carter Center and a jar of homemade peach preserves, which for some reason she kept in a box in her trunk. Frank stuck the jar in his backpack and thanked Esther, who had already switched from calling him *sugar* to *son*.

As she drove away, Frank said, 'Are all people in Atlanta that nice?'

Hedge grunted. 'Hope not. I can't fight them if they're nice. Let's go beat up some whale sharks. They sound dangerous!'

It hadn't occurred to Percy that they might have to pay admission, or stand in line behind a bunch of families and kids from summer camps.

Looking at the elementary schoolers in their colourful T-shirts from various day camps, Percy felt a twinge of sadness. He should be at Camp Half-Blood right now, settling into his cabin for the summer, teaching sword-fighting lessons in the arena, planning pranks on the other counsellors. These kids had no idea just how crazy a summer camp could be.

He sighed. 'Well, I guess we wait in line. Anybody have money?'

Frank checked his pockets. 'Three denarii from Camp Jupiter. Five dollars Canadian.'

Hedge patted his gym shorts and pulled out what he

found. 'Three quarters, two dimes, a rubber band and – score! A piece of celery.'

He started munching on the celery, eyeing the change and the rubber band like they might be next.

'Great,' Percy said. His own pockets were empty except for his pen/sword, Riptide. He was pondering whether or not they could sneak in somehow when a woman in a blue-and-green Georgia Aquarium shirt came up to them, smiling brightly.

'Ah, VIP visitors!' She had perky dimpled cheeks, thick-framed glasses, braces and frizzy black hair pulled to the sides in pigtails, so that even though she was probably in her late twenties she looked like a schoolgirl nerd – sort of cute, but sort of odd. Along with her Georgia Aquarium polo shirt, she wore dark slacks and black trainers, and she bounced on the balls of her feet like she simply couldn't contain her energy. Her name tag read KATE.

'You have your payment, I see,' she said. 'Excellent!'

'What?' Percy asked.

Kate scooped the three denarii out of Frank's hand. 'Yes, that's fine. Right this way!'

She spun and trotted off towards the main entrance.

Percy looked at Coach Hedge and Frank. 'A trap?'

'Probably,' Frank said.

'She's not mortal,' Hedge said, sniffing the air. 'Probably some sort of goat-eating, demigod-destroying fiend from Tartarus.'

'No doubt,' Percy agreed.

'Awesome.' Hedge grinned. 'Let's go.'

Kate got them past the ticket queue and into the aquarium with no problem.

'Right this way.' Kate grinned at Percy. 'It's a *wonderful* exhibit. You won't be disappointed. So rare we get VIPs.'

'Uh, you mean demigods?' Frank asked.

Kate winked at him impishly and put a finger to her mouth. 'So over here is the cold-water experience, with your penguins and beluga whales and whatnot. And over there . . . well, those are some fish, obviously.'

For an aquarium worker, she didn't seem to know much or care much about the smaller fish. They passed one huge tank full of tropical species, and when Frank pointed to a particular fish and asked what it was Kate said, 'Oh, those are the yellow ones.'

They passed the gift shop. Frank slowed down to check out a clearance table with clothes and toys.

'Take what you want,' Kate told him.

Frank blinked. 'Really?'

'Of course! You're a VIP!'

Frank hesitated. Then he stuffed some T-shirts in his backpack.

'Dude,' Percy said, 'what are you doing?'

'She said I could,' Frank whispered. 'Besides, I need more clothes. I didn't pack for a long trip!'

He added a snow globe to his stash, which didn't seem like clothing to Percy. Then Frank picked up a braided cylinder about the size of a candy bar.

He squinted at it. 'What is −?'

'Chinese handcuffs,' Percy said.

Frank, who was Chinese Canadian, looked offended. 'How is this Chinese?'

'I don't know,' Percy said. 'That's just what it's called. It's like a gag gift.'

'Come along, boys!' Kate called from across the hall.

'I'll show you later,' Percy promised.

Frank stuffed the handcuffs in his backpack, and they kept walking.

They passed through an acrylic tunnel. Fish swam over their heads, and Percy felt irrational panic building in his throat.

This is dumb, he told himself. *I've been underwater a million times. And I'm not even* in *the water.*

The real threat was Kate, he reminded himself. Hedge had already detected that she wasn't human. Any minute she might turn into some horrible creature and attack them. Unfortunately, Percy didn't see much choice but to play along with her VIP tour until they could find the sea god Phorcys, even if they were walking deeper into a trap.

They emerged in a viewing room awash with blue light. On the other side of a glass wall was the biggest aquarium tank Percy had ever seen. Cruising in circles were dozens of huge fish, including two spotted sharks, each twice Percy's size. They were fat and slow, with open mouths and no teeth.

'Whale sharks,' Coach Hedge growled. 'Now we shall battle to the death!'

Kate giggled. 'Silly satyr. Whale sharks are peaceful. They only eat plankton.'

Percy scowled. He wondered how Kate knew the coach

was a satyr. Hedge was wearing trousers and specially fitted shoes over his hooves, like satyrs usually did to blend in with mortals. His baseball cap covered his horns. The more Kate giggled and acted friendly, the more Percy didn't like her, but Coach Hedge didn't seem fazed.

'Peaceful sharks?' the coach said with disgust. 'What's the point of that?'

Frank read the plaque next to the tank. 'The only whale sharks in captivity in the world,' he mused. 'That's kind of amazing.'

'Yes, and these are small,' Kate said. 'You should see some of my other babies out in the wild.'

'Your babies?' Frank asked.

Judging from the wicked glint in Kate's eyes, Percy was pretty sure he didn't want to meet Kate's *babies*. He decided it was time to get to the point. He didn't want to go any further into this aquarium than he had to.

'So, Kate,' he said, 'we're looking for a guy . . . I mean a god, named Phorcys. Would you happen to know him?'

Kate snorted. '*Know* him? He's my brother. That's where we're going, sillies. The *real* exhibits are right through here.'

She gestured at the far wall. The solid black surface rippled and another tunnel appeared, leading through a luminous purple tank.

Kate strolled inside. The last thing Percy wanted to do was follow, but if Phorcys was really on the other side, and if he had information that would help their quest . . . Percy took a deep breath and followed his friends into the tunnel.

As soon as they entered, Coach Hedge whistled. 'Now *that's* interesting.'

Gliding above them were multicoloured jellyfish the size of trash cans, each with hundreds of tentacles that looked like silky barbed wire. One jellyfish had a paralysed ten-foot-long swordfish tangled in its grasp. The jellyfish slowly wrapped its tendrils tighter and tighter around its prey.

Kate beamed at Coach Hedge. 'You see? Forget the whale sharks! And there's much more.'

Kate led them into an even larger chamber, lined with more aquariums. On one wall, a glowing red sign proclaimed: DEATH IN THE DEEP SEAS! *Sponsored by Monster Doughnut.*

Percy had to read the sign twice because of his dyslexia and then twice more to let the message sink in. 'Monster Doughnut?'

'Oh, yes,' Kate said. 'One of our corporate sponsors.'

Percy gulped. His last experience with Monster Doughnut hadn't been pleasant. It had involved acid-spitting serpent heads, much screaming and a cannon.

In one aquarium, a dozen hippocampi – horses with the tails of fish – drifted aimlessly. Percy had seen many hippocampi in the wild. He'd even ridden a few, but he had never seen any in an aquarium. He tried to speak with them, but they just floated around, occasionally bumping against the glass. Their minds seemed addled.

'This isn't right,' Percy muttered.

He turned and saw something even worse. At the bottom of a smaller tank, two Nereids – female sea spirits – sat cross-legged, facing each other, playing a game of Go Fish. They looked incredibly bored. Their long green hair floated listlessly around their faces. Their eyes were half closed.

Percy felt so angry he could hardly breathe. He glared at Kate. 'How can you keep them here?'

'I know.' Kate sighed. 'They aren't very interesting. We tried to teach them some tricks, but with no luck, I'm afraid. I think you'll like this tank over here much better.'

Percy started to protest, but Kate had already moved on.

'Holy mother of goats!' cried Coach Hedge. 'Look at these beauties!'

He was gawking at two sea serpents – thirty-foot-long monsters with glowing blue scales and jaws that could have bitten a whale shark in half. In another tank, peeking out from its cement cave, was a squid the size of an eighteen-wheeler, with a beak like a giant bolt cutter.

A third tank held a dozen humanoid creatures with sleek seal bodies, doglike faces, and human hands. They sat on the sand at the bottom of the tank, building things out of Lego, though the creatures seemed just as dazed as the Nereids.

'Are those –?' Percy struggled to form the question.

'Telkhines?' Kate said. 'Yes! The only ones in captivity.'

'But they fought for Kronos in the last war!' Percy said. 'They're dangerous!'

Kate rolled her eyes. 'Well, we couldn't call it "Death in the Deep Seas" if these exhibits weren't dangerous. Don't worry. We keep them well sedated.'

'Sedated?' Frank asked. 'Is that legal?'

Kate appeared not to have heard. She kept walking,

pointing out other exhibits. Percy looked back at the telkhines. One was obviously a youngster. He was trying to make a sword out of Lego, but he seemed too groggy to put the pieces together. Percy had never liked sea demons, but now he felt sorry for them.

'And *these* sea monsters,' Kate narrated up ahead, 'can grow five hundred feet long in the deep ocean. They have over a thousand teeth. And these? Their favourite food is demigod –'

'Demigod?' Frank yelped.

'But they will eat whales or small boats, too.' Kate turned to Percy and blushed. 'Sorry . . . I'm *such* a monster nerd! I'm sure you know all this, being the son of Poseidon and all.'

Percy's ears were ringing like alarm bells. He didn't like how much Kate knew about him. He didn't like the way she casually tossed out information about drugging captive creatures or which of her *babies* liked to devour demigods.

'Who *are* you?' he demanded. 'Does Kate stand for something?'

'Kate?' She looked momentarily confused. Then she glanced at her name tag. 'Oh . . .' She laughed. 'No, it's –'

'Hello!' said a new voice, booming through the aquarium.

A small man scuttled out of the darkness. He walked sideways on bowed legs like a crab, his back hunched, his arms raised on either side like he was holding invisible plates.

He wore a wet suit that was several horrible shades of green. Glittery silver words printed down the side read: PORKY'S FOLLIES. A headset microphone was clamped over his greasy wiry hair. His eyes were milky blue, one higher than the other, and though he smiled he didn't look friendly – more like his face was being peeled back in a wind tunnel.

'Visitors!' the man said, the word thundering through the microphone. He had a DJ's voice, deep and resonant, which did not match his appearance at all. 'Welcome to Phorcys's Follies!'

He swept his arms in one direction, as if directing their attention to an explosion. Nothing happened.

'Curse it,' the man grumbled. 'Telkhines, that's your cue! I wave my hands, and you leap energetically in your tank, do a synchronized double spin and land in pyramid formation. We practised this!'

The sea demons paid him no attention.

Coach Hedge leaned towards the crab man and sniffed his glittery wet suit. *'Nice* outfit.'

He didn't sound like he was kidding. Of course, the satyr wore gym uniforms for fun.

'Thank you!' The man beamed. 'I am Phorcys.'

Frank shifted his weight from foot to foot. 'Why does your suit say *Porky?*'

Phorcys snarled. 'Stupid uniform company! They can't get anything right.'

Kate tapped her name tag. 'I told them my name was *Keto.* They misspelled it as *Kate.* My brother . . . well, now he's Porky.'

'I am not!' the man snapped. 'I'm not even a *little* porky. The name doesn't work with Follies, either. What kind of show is called Porky's Follies? But you folks don't want to hear us complain. Behold, the wondrous majesty of the giant killer squid!'

He gestured dramatically towards the squid tank. This time, fireworks shot off in front of the glass right on cue, sending up geysers of golden sparkles. Music swelled from the loudspeakers. The lights brightened and revealed the wondrous majesty of an empty tank.

The squid had apparently skulked back into its cave.

'Curse it!' Phorcys yelled again. He wheeled on his sister. 'Keto, training the squid was *your* job. Juggling, I said. Maybe a bit of flesh-rending for the finale. Is that too much to ask?'

'He's shy,' Keto said defensively. 'Besides, each of his tentacles has sixty-two razorlike barbs that have to be sharpened daily.' She turned towards Frank. 'Did you know the monstrous squid is the only beast known to eat demi-gods whole, armour and all, without getting indigestion? It's true!'

Frank stumbled away from her, hugging his gut as if making sure he was still in one piece.

'Keto!' Porky snapped – literally, since he clicked his fingers to his thumbs like crab claws. 'You'll bore our guests with so much information. Less education, more entertainment! We've discussed this.'

'But –'

'No buts! We're here to present "Death in the Deep Seas!" Sponsored by Monster Doughnut!'

The last words reverberated through the room with extra echo. Lights flashed. Smoke clouds billowed from the floor, making doughnut-shaped rings that smelled like real doughnuts.

'Available at the concession stand,' Phorcys advised. 'But you've spent your hard-earned denarii to get the VIP tour and so you shall! Come with me!'

'Um, hold it,' Percy said.

Phorcys's smile melted in an ugly way. 'Yes?'

'You're a sea god, aren't you?' Percy asked. 'Son of Gaia?'

The crab man sighed. 'Five thousand years, and I'm still known as Gaia's little boy. Never mind that I'm one of the oldest sea gods in existence. Older than *your* upstart father, by the way. I'm god of the hidden depths! Lord of watery terrors! Father of a thousand monsters! But, no . . . nobody even knows me. I make one little mistake, supporting the Titans in their war, and I'm exiled from the ocean – to Atlanta, of all places.'

'We thought the Olympians said *Atlantis*,' Keto explained. 'Their idea of a joke, I guess, sending us here instead.'

Percy narrowed his eyes. 'And you're a goddess?'

'Keto, yes!' She smiled happily. 'Goddess of sea monsters, naturally! Whales, sharks, squids and other giant sea life, but my heart always belonged to the monsters. Did you know that young sea serpents can regurgitate the flesh of their victims and keep themselves fed for up to six years on the same meal? It's true!'

Frank was still clutching his stomach like he was going to be sick.

Coach Hedge whistled. 'Six years? That's fascinating.'

'I know!' Keto beamed.

'And how exactly does a killer squid rend the flesh from its victims?' Hedge asked. 'I *love* nature.'

'Oh, well –'

'Stop!' Phorcys demanded. 'You're ruining the show! Now, witness our Nereid gladiators fight to the death!'

A mirrored disco ball descended into the Nereid exhibit, making the water dance with multicoloured light. Two swords fell to the bottom and plunked in the sand. The Nereids ignored them and kept playing Go Fish.

'Curse it!' Phorcys stomped his legs sideways.

Keto grimaced at Coach Hedge. 'Don't mind Porky. He's *such* a windbag. Come with me, my fine satyr. I'll show you full-colour diagrams of the monsters' hunting habits.'

'Excellent!'

Before Percy could object, Keto led Coach Hedge away through a maze of aquarium glass, leaving Frank and him alone with the crabby sea god.

A bead of sweat traced its way down Percy's neck. He exchanged a nervous look with Frank. This felt like a *divide-and-conquer* strategy. He didn't see any way the encounter was going to end well. Part of him wanted to attack Phorcys now – at least that might give them the element of surprise – but they hadn't found out any useful information yet. Percy wasn't sure he could find Coach Hedge again. He wasn't even sure he could find the exit.

Phorcys must've read his expression.

'Oh, it's fine!' the god assured him. 'Keto might be a little boring, but she'll take good care of your friend. And, honestly, the best part of the tour is still to come!'

Percy tried to think, but he was starting to get a headache. He wasn't sure if it was from yesterday's head injury, Phorcys's special effects or Keto's lectures on nauseating sea monster facts. 'So . . .' he managed. 'Dionysus sent us here.'

'Bacchus,' Frank corrected.

'Right.' Percy tried to keep his annoyance in check. He could barely remember one name for each god. Two was pushing it. 'The wine god. Whatever.' He looked at Phorcys. 'Bacchus said you might know what your mom Gaia is up to, and these twin giant brothers of yours – Ephialtes and Otis. And if you happen to know anything about this Mark of Athena –'

'Bacchus thought I would help you?' Phorcys asked.

'Well, yeah,' Percy said. 'I mean, you're Phorcys. Everybody talks about you.'

Phorcys tilted his head so that his mismatched eyes almost lined up. 'They do?'

'Of course. Don't they, Frank?'

'Oh . . . sure!' Frank said. 'People talk about you all the time.'

'What do they say?' the god asked.

Frank looked uncomfortable. 'Well, you have great pyrotechnics. And a good announcer's voice. And, um, a disco ball –'

'It's true!' Phorcys clacked his fingers and thumbs excitedly. 'I also have the largest collection of captive sea monsters in the world!'

'And you *know* stuff,' Percy added. 'Like about the twins and what they're up to.'

'The twins!' Phorcys made his voice echo. Sparklers blazed to life in front of the sea-serpent tank. 'Yes, I know all about Ephialtes and Otis. Those wannabes! They never fitted in with the other giants. Too puny – and those snakes for feet.'

'Snakes for feet?' Percy remembered the long, curly shoes the twins had been wearing in his dream.

'Yes, yes,' Phorcys said impatiently. 'They knew they couldn't get by on their strength, so they decided to go for drama – illusions, stage tricks, that sort of thing. You see, Gaia *shaped* her giant children with specific enemies in mind. Each giant was born to kill a certain god. Ephialtes and Otis . . . well, together they were sort of the anti-Dionysus.'

Percy tried to wrap his mind around that idea. 'So . . . they want to replace all wine with cranberry juice or something?'

The sea god snorted. 'Nothing like that! Ephialtes and Otis always wanted to do things better, flashier, more spectacular! Oh, of course they wanted to kill Dionysus. But first they wanted to humiliate him by making his revelries look tame!'

Frank glanced at the sparklers. 'By using stuff like fireworks and disco balls?'

Phorcys's mouth stretched into that wind tunnel smile. 'Exactly! I taught the twins everything they know, or at least I tried to. They never listened. Their first big trick? They tried to reach Olympus by piling mountains on top of one another. It was just an illusion, of course. I told them it was ridiculous. "You should start small," I said. "Sawing each other in half, pulling gorgons out of a hat. That sort of thing. And matching sequined outfits. Twins need those!"'

'Good advice,' Percy agreed. 'And now the twins are –'

'Oh, preparing for their doomsday show in Rome,' Phorcys sneered. 'It's one of Mother's silly ideas. They're keeping some prisoner in a large bronze jar.' He turned towards Frank. 'You're a child of Ares, aren't you? You've got that smell. The twins imprisoned your father the same way, once.'

'Child of Mars,' Frank corrected. 'Wait . . . these giants trapped my dad in a bronze jar?'

'Yes, another stupid stunt,' said the sea god. 'How can you show off your prisoner if he's in a bronze jar? No entertainment value. Not like my lovely specimens!'

He gestured to the hippocampi, who were bumping their heads apathetically against the glass.

Percy tried to think. He felt like the lethargy of the addled sea creatures was starting to affect him. 'You said this – this doomsday show was Gaia's idea?'

'Well . . . Mother's plans always have lots of layers.' He laughed. 'The earth has layers! I suppose that makes sense!'

'Uh-huh,' Percy said. 'And so her plan . . .'

'Oh, she's put out a general bounty on some group of demigods,' Phorcys said. 'She doesn't really care *who* kills them, as long as they're killed. Well . . . I take that back. She was very specific that *two* must be spared. One boy and one girl. Tartarus only knows why. At any rate, the twins have their little show planned, hoping it will lure these demigods to Rome. I suppose the prisoner in the jar is a friend of theirs or some such. That, or perhaps they think this group of demigods will be foolish enough to come into their territory searching for the Mark of Athena.' Phorcys elbowed Frank in the ribs. 'Ha! Good luck with that, eh?'

Frank laughed nervously. 'Yeah. Ha-ha. That would be really dumb because, uh . . .'

Phorcys narrowed his eyes.

Percy slipped his hand into his pocket. He closed his fingers around Riptide. Even this old sea god must be smart enough to realize they were the demigods with the bounty on their heads.

But Phorcys just grinned and elbowed Frank again. 'Ha! Good one, child of Mars. I suppose you're right. No point talking about it. Even if the demigods found that map in Charleston they'd never make it to Rome alive!'

'Yes, the MAP IN CHARLESTON,' Frank said loudly, giving Percy a wide-eyed look to make sure he hadn't missed the information. He couldn't have been more obvious if he had held up a large sign that read *CLUE!!!!!*

'But enough boring educational stuff!' Phorcys said. 'You've paid for the VIP treatment. Won't you *please* let me finish the tour? The three denarii entrance fee is non-refundable, you know.'

Percy wasn't excited about more fireworks, doughnut-scented smoke or depressing captive sea creatures. But he glanced at Frank and decided they'd better humour the crabby old god, at least until they found Coach Hedge and got safely to the exit. Besides, they might be able to get more information out of Phorcys.

'Afterwards,' Percy said, 'can we ask questions?'

'Of course! I'll tell you everything you need to know.' Phorcys clapped his hands twice. On the wall under the glowing red sign, a new tunnel appeared, leading into another tank.

'Walk this way!' Phorcys scuttled sideways through the tunnel.

Frank scratched his head. 'Do we have to –?' He turned sideways.

'It's just a figure of speech, man,' Percy said. 'Come on.'

XVI

PERCY

THE TUNNEL RAN ALONG THE FLOOR of a gymnasium-sized tank. Except for water and some cheap decorations, it seemed majestically empty. Percy guessed there were about fifty thousand gallons of water over their heads. If the tunnel were to shatter for some reason . . .

No big deal, Percy thought. I've been surrounded by water thousands of times. This is my home court.

But his heart was pounding. He remembered sinking into the cold Alaskan bog – black mud covering his eyes, mouth and nose.

Phorcys stopped in the middle of the tunnel and spread his arms proudly. 'Beautiful exhibit, isn't it?'

Percy tried to distract himself by concentrating on details. In one corner of the tank, snuggled in a forest of fake kelp, was a life-sized plastic gingerbread cottage with bubbles coming out of the chimney. In the opposite corner, a plastic sculpture of a guy in an old-fashioned diving suit knelt beside a treasure chest, which popped open every few seconds, spewed bubbles and closed again. Littered across the white sand floor were glass marbles the size of bowling balls and a strange assortment of weapons like tridents and spearguns. Outside the tank's display wall was an amphitheatre with seating for several hundred.

'What do you keep in here?' Frank asked. 'Giant killer goldfish?'

Phorcys raised his eyebrows. 'Oh, that would be good! But, no, Frank Zhang, descendant of Poseidon. This tank is not for goldfish.'

At *descendant of Poseidon*, Frank flinched. He stepped back, gripping his backpack like a mace he was prepared to swing.

A sense of dread trickled down Percy's throat like cough syrup. Unfortunately, it was a feeling he was used to.

'How do you know Frank's last name?' he demanded. 'How do you know he's descended from Poseidon?'

'Well . . .' Phorcys shrugged, trying to look modest. 'It was probably in the descriptions Gaia provided. You know, for the bounty, Percy Jackson.'

Percy uncapped his pen. Instantly, Riptide appeared in his hand. 'Don't double-cross me, Phorcys. You promised me answers.'

'After the VIP treatment, yes,' Phorcys agreed. 'I promised to tell you everything you need to know. The thing is, however, you don't really need to know anything.' His grotesque smile stretched wide. 'You see, even if you made it to Rome, which is *quite* unlikely, you'd never defeat my giant brothers without a god fighting at your side. And what god would help you? So

I have a better plan. You're not leaving. You're VIPs – Very Important Prisoners!'

Percy lunged. Frank hurled his backpack at the sea god's head. Phorcys simply disappeared.

The god's voice reverberated through the aquarium's sound system, echoing down the tunnel. 'Yes, good! Fighting is good! You see, Mother never trusted me with big assignments, but she *did* agree that I could keep anything I caught. You two will make an excellent exhibit – the only demigod spawn of Poseidon in captivity. "Demigod Terrors" – yes, I like that! We already have sponsorship lined up with Bargain Mart. You can fight each other every day at eleven a.m. and one p.m., with an evening show at seven p.m.'

'You're crazy!' Frank yelled.

'Don't sell yourself short!' Phorcys said. 'You'll be our biggest draw!'

Frank ran for the exit, only to slam into a glass wall. Percy ran the other way and found it blocked as well. Their tunnel had become a bubble. He put his hand against the glass and realized it was softening, melting like ice. Soon the water would come crashing in.

'We won't cooperate, Phorcys!' he shouted.

'Oh, I'm optimistic,' the sea god's voice boomed. 'If you won't fight each other at first, no problem! I can send in fresh sea monsters every day. After you get used to the food here, you'll be properly sedated and will follow directions. Believe me, you'll come to love your new home.'

Over Percy's head, the glass dome cracked and began to leak.

'I'm the son of Poseidon!' Percy tried to keep the fear out of his voice. 'You can't imprison me in water. This is where I'm strongest.'

Phorcys's laugh seemed to come from all around them. 'What a coincidence! It's also where *I'm* strongest. This tank is specially designed to contain demigods. Now, have fun, you two. I'll see you at feeding time!'

The glass dome shattered, and the water crashed in.

Percy held his breath until he couldn't stand it. When he finally filled his lungs with water, it felt just like normal breathing. The water pressure didn't bother him. His clothes didn't even get wet. His underwater abilities were as good as ever.

It's just a stupid phobia, he assured himself. I'm not going to drown.

Then he remembered Frank, and he immediately felt a surge of panic and guilt. Percy had been so worried about himself that he'd forgotten his friend was only a distant descendant of Poseidon. *Frank* couldn't breathe underwater.

But where *was* he?

Percy turned in a full circle. Nothing. Then he glanced up. Hovering above him was a giant goldfish. Frank had turned – clothes, backpack, and all – into a koi the size of a teenaged boy.

Dude. Percy sent his thoughts through the water, the way he spoke with other sea creatures. *A goldfish?*

Frank's voice came back to him: *I freaked. We were talking about goldfish, so it was on my mind. Sue me.*

I'm having a telepathic conversation with a giant koi, Percy said. *Great. Can you turn into something more . . . useful?*

Silence. Maybe Frank was concentrating, though it was impossible to tell, since koi don't have many expressions.

Sorry. Frank sounded embarrassed. *I'm stuck. That happens sometimes when I panic.*

Fine. Percy gritted his teeth. *Let's figure out how to escape.*

Frank swam around the tank and reported no exits. The top was covered with Celestial bronze mesh, like the curtains that roll down over closed storefronts at the mall. Percy tried to cut through with Riptide, but he couldn't make a dent. He tried to smash the glass wall with his sword hilt – again, no luck. Then he repeated his efforts with several of the weapons lying around the bottom of the tank and managed to break three tridents, a sword and a speargun.

Finally he tried to control the water. He wanted it to expand and break the tank, or explode out of the top. The water didn't obey. Maybe it was enchanted, or under the power of Phorcys. Percy concentrated until his ears popped, but the best he could do was blow the lid off the plastic treasure chest.

Well, that's it, he thought dejectedly. I'll have to live in a plastic gingerbread house the rest of my life, fighting my giant goldfish friend and waiting for feeding time.

Phorcys had promised they'd learn to love it. Percy thought about the dazed telkhines, the Nereids and hippocampi, all swimming in bored, lazy circles. The thought of ending up like that didn't help to lower his anxiety level.

He wondered if Phorcys was right. Even if they managed to escape, how could they defeat the giants if the gods were all incapacitated? Bacchus might be able to help. He had killed the twin giants once before, but he would only join the fight if he got an impossible tribute, and the idea of giving Bacchus *any* kind of tribute made Percy want to gag himself with a Monster Doughnut.

Look! Frank said.

Outside the glass, Keto was leading Coach Hedge through the amphitheatre, lecturing him on something while the coach nodded and admired the stadium seating.

Coach! Percy yelled. Then he realized it was hopeless. The coach couldn't hear telepathic yelling.

Frank bumped his head against the glass.

Hedge didn't seem to notice. Keto walked him briskly across the amphitheatre. She didn't even look through the glass, probably because she assumed the tank was still empty. She pointed to the far end of the room as if saying, *Come on. More gruesome sea monsters this way.*

Percy realized he had only a few seconds before the coach would be gone. He swam after them, but the water didn't help him move as it usually did. In fact, it seemed to be pushing him back. He dropped Riptide and used both arms.

Coach Hedge and Keto were five feet from the exit.

In desperation, Percy scooped up a giant marble and hurled it underhanded like a bowling ball.

It hit the glass with a *thunk* – not nearly loud enough to attract attention.

Percy's heart sank.

But Coach Hedge had the ears of a satyr. He glanced over his shoulder. When he saw Percy, his expression went

through several changes in a matter of microseconds –
incomprehension, surprise, outrage, then a mask of calm.

Before Keto could notice, Hedge pointed towards the top
of the amphitheatre. It looked like he might be screaming,
Gods of Olympus, what is that?

Keto turned. Coach Hedge promptly took off his fake foot
and ninja-kicked her in the back of the head with his goat
hoof. Keto crumpled to the floor.

Percy winced. His own recently whopped head throbbed in
sympathy, but he had never been happier to have a chaperone
who liked mixed martial arts cage matches.

Hedge ran to the glass. He held up his palms like: *What
are you doing in there, Jackson?* Percy pounded his fist on the
glass and mouthed: *Break it!*

Hedge yelled a question that might have been: *Where's
Frank?*

Percy pointed at the giant koi.

Frank waved his left dorsal fin. *'Sup?*

Behind Hedge, the sea goddess began to move. Percy
pointed frantically.

Hedge shook his leg like he was warming up his kicking
hoof, but Percy waved his arms, *No.* They couldn't keep
whopping Keto on the head forever. Since she was immortal,
she wouldn't stay down, and it wouldn't get them out of this
tank. It was only a matter of time before Phorcys came back
to check on them.

On three, Percy mouthed, holding up three fingers and
then gesturing at the glass. *All of us hit it at the same time.*

Percy had never been good at charades, but Hedge nodded

like he understood. Hitting things was a language the satyr knew well.

Percy hefted another giant marble. *Frank, we'll need you, too. Can you change form yet?*

Maybe back to human.

Human is fine! Just hold your breath. If this works . . .

Keto rose to her knees. No time to waste.

Percy counted on his fingers. *One, two, three!*

Frank turned to human and shoved his shoulder against the glass. The coach did a Chuck Norris roundhouse kick with his hoof. Percy used all his strength to slam the marble into the wall, but he did more than that. He called on the water to obey him, and this time he refused to take no for an answer. He felt all the pent-up pressure inside the tank, and he put it to use. Water liked to be free. Given time, water could overcome any barrier, and it *hated* to be trapped, just like Percy. He thought about getting back to Annabeth. He thought about destroying this horrible prison for sea creatures. He thought about shoving Phorcys's microphone down his ugly throat. Fifty thousand gallons of water responded to his anger.

The glass wall cracked. Fracture lines zigzagged from the point of impact, and suddenly the tank burst. Percy was sucked out in a torrent of water. He tumbled across the amphitheatre floor with Frank, some large marbles and a clump of plastic seaweed. Keto was just getting to her feet when the diver statue slammed into her like it wanted a hug.

Coach Hedge spat salt water. 'Pan's pipes, Jackson! What were you *doing* in there?'

'Phorcys!' Percy spluttered. 'Trap! Run!'

Alarms blared as they fled the exhibits. They ran past the Nereids' tank, then the telkhines. Percy wanted to free them, but how? They were drugged and sluggish, and they were sea creatures. They wouldn't survive unless he found a way to transport them to the ocean.

Besides, if Phorcys caught them, Percy was pretty sure the sea god's power would overcome his. And Keto would be after them, too, ready to feed them to her sea monsters.

I'll be back, Percy promised, but if the creatures in the exhibits could hear him they gave no sign.

Over the sound system, Phorcys's voice boomed: 'Percy Jackson!'

Flash pots and sparklers exploded randomly. Doughnut-scented smoke filled the halls. Dramatic music – five or six different tracks – blared simultaneously from the speakers. Lights popped and caught fire as all the special effects in the building were triggered at once.

Percy, Coach Hedge and Frank stumbled out of the glass tunnel and found themselves back in the whale-shark room. The mortal section of the aquarium was filled with screaming crowds – families and day-camp groups running in every direction while the staff raced around frantically, trying to assure everyone it was just a faulty alarm system.

Percy knew better. He and his friends joined the mortals and ran for the exit.

XVII

ANNABETH

ANNABETH WAS TRYING TO CHEER UP HAZEL, regaling her with Percy's greatest Seaweed Brain moments, when Frank stumbled down the hall and burst into her cabin.

'Where's Leo?' he gasped. 'Take off! Take off!'

Both girls shot to their feet.

'Where's *Percy*?' Annabeth demanded. 'And the goat?'

Frank grabbed his knees, trying to breathe. His clothes were stiff and damp, like they'd been washed in pure starch. 'On deck. They're fine. We're being followed!'

Annabeth pushed past him and took the stairs three at a time, Hazel right behind her and Frank trailing, still gasping for air. Percy and Hedge lay on the deck, looking exhausted. Hedge was missing his shoes. He grinned at the sky, muttering, 'Awesome. Awesome.' Percy was covered with nicks and scratches, like he'd jumped through a window. He didn't say anything, but he grasped Annabeth's hand weakly as if to say, *Be right with you, as soon as the world stops spinning.*

Leo, Piper and Jason, who'd been eating in the mess hall, came rushing up the stairs.

'What? What?' Leo cried, holding a half-eaten grilled cheese sandwich. 'Can't a guy even take a lunch break? What's wrong?'

'Followed!' Frank yelled again.

'Followed by *what*?' Jason asked.

'I don't know!' Frank panted. 'Whales? Sea monsters? Maybe Kate and Porky!'

Annabeth wanted to strangle the guy, but she wasn't sure her hands would fit around his thick neck. 'That makes absolutely no sense. Leo, you'd better get us out of here.'

Leo put his sandwich between his teeth, pirate style, and ran for the helm.

Soon the *Argo II* was rising into the sky. Annabeth manned the aft crossbow. She saw no sign of pursuit by whales or otherwise, but Percy, Frank and Hedge didn't start to recover until the Atlanta skyline was a hazy smudge in the distance.

'Charleston,' Percy said, hobbling around the deck like an old man. He still sounded pretty shaken up. 'Set course for Charleston.'

'Charleston?' Jason said the name as if it brought back bad memories. 'What exactly did you find in Atlanta?'

Frank unzipped his backpack and starting bringing out souvenirs. 'Some peach preserves. A couple of T-shirts. A snow globe. And, um, these not-really-Chinese handcuffs.'

Annabeth forced herself to stay calm. 'How about you start from the top – of the story, not the backpack.'

They gathered on the quarterdeck so Leo could hear the

conversation as he navigated. Percy and Frank took turns relating what had happened at the Georgia Aquarium, with Coach Hedge interjecting from time to time: 'That was awesome!' or 'Then I kicked her in the head!'

At least the coach seemed to have forgotten about Percy and Annabeth falling asleep in the stable the night before. But, judging from Percy's story, Annabeth had worse problems to worry about than being grounded.

When Percy explained about the captive sea creatures in the aquarium, she understood why he seemed so upset.

'That's terrible,' she said. 'We need to help them.'

'We will,' Percy promised. 'In time. But I have to figure out *how*. I wish . . .' He shook his head. 'Never mind. First we have to deal with this bounty on our heads.'

Coach Hedge had lost interest in the conversation – probably because it was no longer about him – and wandered towards the bow of the ship, practising his roundhouse kicks and complimenting himself on his technique.

Annabeth gripped the hilt of her dagger. 'A bounty on our heads . . . as if we didn't attract enough monsters already.'

'Do we get WANTED posters?' Leo asked. 'And do they have our bounties, like, broken down on a price list?'

Hazel wrinkled her nose. '*What* are you talking about?'

'Just curious how much I'm going for these days,' Leo said. 'I mean, I can understand not being as pricey as Percy or Jason, maybe . . . but am I worth, like, two Franks or three Franks?'

'Hey!' Frank complained.

'Knock it off,' Annabeth ordered. 'At least we know our next step is to go to Charleston, to find this map.'

Piper leaned against the control panel. She'd done her braid with white feathers today, which looked good with her dark brown hair. Annabeth wondered how she found the time. Annabeth could barely remember to *brush* her hair.

'A map,' Piper said. 'But a map to *what*?'

'The Mark of Athena.' Percy looked cautiously at Annabeth, like he was afraid he'd overstepped. She must have been putting out a strong *I don't want to talk about it* vibe.

'*Whatever* that is,' he continued. 'We know it leads to something important in Rome, something that might heal the rift between the Romans and Greeks.'

'*Giants' bane*,' Hazel added.

Percy nodded. 'And in my dream the twin giants said something about a statue.'

'Um . . .' Frank rolled his not-exactly-Chinese handcuffs between his fingers. 'According to Phorcys, we'd have to be insane to try to find it. But what *is* it?'

Everyone looked at Annabeth. Her scalp tingled, as if the thoughts in her brain were agitating to get out: a statue . . . Athena . . . Greek and Roman, her nightmares and her argument with her mom. She saw how the pieces were coming together, but she couldn't believe it was true. The answer was too big, too important and much too scary.

She noticed Jason studying her, as if he knew *exactly* what she was thinking and didn't like it any more than she did. Again she couldn't help but wonder: *Why does this guy make me so nervous? Is he really on my side?* Or maybe that was her mom talking . . .

'I – I'm close to an answer,' she said. 'I'll know more if we find this map. Jason, the way you reacted to the name *Charleston* . . . have you been there before?'

Jason glanced uneasily at Piper, though Annabeth wasn't sure why.

'Yeah,' he admitted. 'Reyna and I did a quest there about a year ago. We were salvaging Imperial gold weapons from the CSS *Hunley*.'

'The what?' Piper asked.

'Whoa!' Leo said. 'That's the first successful military submarine. From the Civil War. I always wanted to see that.'

'It was designed by Roman demigods,' Jason said. 'It held a secret stash of Imperial gold torpedoes – until we rescued them and brought them back to Camp Jupiter.'

Hazel crossed her arms. 'So the Romans fought on the Confederate side? As a girl whose grandmother was a slave, can I just say . . . not cool?'

Jason put his hands in front of him, palms up. 'I personally was not alive then. And it wasn't *all* Greeks on one side and *all* Romans on the other. But, yes. Not cool. Sometimes demigods make bad choices.' He looked sheepishly at Hazel. 'Like sometimes we're too suspicious. And we speak without thinking.'

Hazel stared at him. Slowly it seemed to dawn on her that he was apologizing.

Jason elbowed Leo.

'Ow!' Leo yelped. 'I mean, yeah . . . bad choices. Like not

trusting people's brothers who, you know, might need saving. Hypothetically speaking.'

Hazel pursed her lips. 'Fine. Back to Charleston. Are you saying we should check that submarine again?'

Jason shrugged. 'Well . . . I can think of *two* places in Charleston we might search. The museum where they keep the *Hunley* – that's one of them. It has a lot of relics from the Civil War. A map could be hidden in one. I know the layout. I could lead a team inside.'

'I'll go,' Leo said. 'That sounds cool.'

Jason nodded. He turned to Frank, who was trying to pull his fingers out of the Chinese handcuffs. 'You should come, too, Frank. We might need you.'

Frank looked surprised. 'Why? Not like I was much good at that aquarium.'

'You did fine,' Percy assured him. 'It took all three of us to break that glass.'

'Besides, you're a child of Mars,' Jason said. 'The ghosts of defeated causes are bound to serve you. And the museum in Charleston has *plenty* of Confederate ghosts. We'll need you to keep them in line.'

Frank gulped. Annabeth remembered Percy's comment about Frank turning into a giant goldfish, and she resisted the urge to smile. She would never be able to look at the big guy again without seeing him as a koi.

'Okay.' Frank relented. 'Sure.' He frowned at his fingers, trying to pull them out of the trap. 'Uh, how do you –?'

Leo chuckled. 'Man, you've never seen those before? There's a simple trick to getting out.'

Frank tugged again with no luck. Even Hazel was trying not to laugh.

Frank grimaced with concentration. Suddenly, he disappeared. On the deck where he'd been standing, a green iguana crouched next to an empty set of Chinese handcuffs.

'Well done, Frank Zhang,' Leo said dryly, doing his impression of Chiron the centaur. 'That is exactly how people beat Chinese handcuffs. They turn into iguanas.'

Everybody busted out laughing. Frank turned back to human, picked up the handcuffs and shoved them in his backpack. He managed an embarrassed smile.

'Anyway,' he said, clearly anxious to change the subject. 'The museum is one place to search. But, uh, Jason, you said there were two?'

Jason's smile faded. Whatever he was thinking about, Annabeth could tell it wasn't pleasant.

'Yeah,' he said. 'The other place is called the Battery – it's a park right by the harbour. The last time I was there . . . with Reyna . . .' He glanced at Piper, then rushed on. 'We saw something in the park. A ghost or some sort of spirit, like a Southern belle from the Civil War, glowing and floating along. We tried to approach it, but it disappeared whenever we got close. Then Reyna had this feeling – she said she should try it alone. Like maybe it would only talk to a girl. She went up to the spirit by herself and, sure enough, it spoke to her.'

Everyone waited.

'What did it say?' Annabeth asked.

'Reyna wouldn't tell me,' Jason admitted. 'But it must have been important. She seemed . . . shaken up. Maybe she got a prophecy or some bad news. Reyna never acted the same around me after that.'

Annabeth considered that. After their experience with the eidolons, she didn't like the idea of approaching a ghost, especially one that changed people with bad news or prophecies. On the other hand, her mom was the goddess of knowledge, and knowledge was the most powerful weapon. Annabeth couldn't turn down a possible source of information.

'A girls' adventure, then,' Annabeth said. 'Piper and Hazel can come with me.'

Both nodded, though Hazel looked nervous. No doubt her time in the Underworld had given her enough ghost experiences for two lifetimes. Piper's eyes flashed defiantly, like anything Reyna could do, she could do.

Annabeth realized that if six of them went on these two quests it would leave Percy alone on the ship with Coach Hedge, which was maybe not a situation a caring girlfriend should put him in. Nor was she eager to let Percy out of her sight again – not after they'd been apart for so many months. On the other hand, Percy looked so troubled by his experience with those imprisoned sea creatures she thought maybe he could use a rest. She met his eyes, asking him a silent question. He nodded as if to say, *Yeah. It'll be fine.*

'So that's settled.' Annabeth turned to Leo, who was studying his console, listening to Festus creak and click over the intercom. 'Leo, how long until we reach Charleston?'

'Good question,' he muttered. 'Festus just detected a large group of eagles behind us – long-range radar, still not in sight.'

Piper leaned over the console. 'Are you sure they're Roman?'

Leo rolled his eyes. 'No, Pipes. It could be a random group of giant eagles flying in perfect formation. Of course they're Roman! I suppose we could turn the ship around and fight –'

'Which would be a very bad idea,' Jason said, 'and remove any doubt that we're enemies of Rome.'

'Or I've got another idea,' Leo said. 'If we went straight to Charleston, we could be there in a few hours. But the eagles would overtake us and things would get complicated. *Instead* we could send out a decoy to trick the eagles. We take the ship on a detour, go the long way to Charleston and get there tomorrow morning –'

Hazel started to protest, but Leo raised his hand. 'I know, I know. Nico's in trouble and we have to hurry.'

'It's June twenty-seventh,' Hazel said. 'After today, four more days. Then he dies.'

'I know! But this might throw the Romans off our trail. We still should have enough time to reach Rome.'

Hazel scowled. 'When you say *should have enough* . . .'

Leo shrugged. 'How do you feel about *barely enough*?'

Hazel put her face in her hands for a count of three. 'Sounds about typical for us.'

Annabeth decided to take that as a green light. 'Okay, Leo. What kind of decoy are we talking about?'

'I'm so glad you asked!' He punched a few buttons on the console, rotated the turntable and repeatedly pressed the *A* button on his Wii controller really, really fast. He called into the intercom, 'Buford? Report for duty, please.'

Frank took a step back. 'There's somebody else on the ship? Who is Buford?'

A puff of steam shot from the stairwell and Leo's automatic table climbed on deck.

Annabeth hadn't seen much of Buford during the trip. He mostly stayed in the engine room. (Leo insisted that Buford had a secret crush on the engine.) He was a three-legged table with a mahogany top. His bronze base had several drawers, spinning gears and a set of steam vents. Buford was toting a bag like a mail sack tied to one of his legs. He clattered to the helm and made a sound like a train whistle.

'This is Buford,' Leo announced.

'You name your furniture?' Frank asked.

Leo snorted. 'Man, you just *wish* you had furniture this cool. Buford, are you ready for Operation End Table?'

Buford spewed steam. He stepped to the railing. His mahogany top split into four pie slices, which elongated into wooden blades. The blades spun and Buford took off.

'A helicopter table,' Percy muttered. 'Gotta admit, that's cool. What's in the bag?'

'Dirty demigod laundry,' Leo said. 'I hope you don't mind, Frank.'

Frank choked. 'What?'

'It'll throw the eagles off our scent.'

'Those were my only extra jeans!'

Leo shrugged. 'I asked Buford to get them laundered and folded while he's out. Hopefully he will.' He rubbed his hands and grinned. 'Well! I call that a good day's work. I'm gonna calculate our detour route now. See you all at dinner!'

Percy passed out early, which left Annabeth with nothing to do in the evening except stare at her computer.

She'd brought Daedalus's laptop with her, of course. Two years ago, she'd inherited the machine from the greatest inventor of all time, and it was loaded with invention ideas, schematics and diagrams, most of which Annabeth was still trying to figure out. After two years, a typical laptop would have been out of date, but Annabeth figured Daedalus's machine was still about fifty years ahead of its time. It could expand into a full-size laptop, shrink into a tablet computer, or fold into a wafer of metal smaller than a cell phone. It ran faster than any computer she'd ever had, could access satellites or Hephaestus-TV broadcasts from Mount Olympus and ran custom-made programs that could do just about anything except tie shoelaces. There might have been an app for that, too, but Annabeth hadn't found it yet.

She sat on her bunk, using one of Daedalus's 3-D-rendering programs to study a model of the Parthenon in Athens. She'd always yearned to visit it, both because she loved architecture and because it was the most famous temple to her mother.

Now she might get her wish, if they lived long enough to reach Greece. But the more she thought about the Mark of Athena, and the old Roman legend Reyna had mentioned, the more nervous she got.

She didn't want to, but she recalled her argument with her mother. Even after so many weeks, the words still stung.

Annabeth had been riding the subway back from the Upper East Side after visiting Percy's mom. During those long months when Percy was missing, Annabeth made the trip at least once a week – partly to give Sally Jackson and her husband, Paul, an update on the search, and partly because Annabeth and Sally needed to lift each other's spirits and convince one another that Percy would be fine.

The spring had been especially hard. By then, Annabeth had reason to hope Percy was alive, since Hera's plan seemed to involve sending him to the Roman side, but she couldn't be sure where he was. Jason had remembered his old camp's location more or less, but all the Greeks' magic – even that of the campers of Hecate's cabin – couldn't confirm that Percy was there, or anywhere. He seemed to have disappeared from the planet. Rachel the Oracle had tried to read the future and, while she couldn't see much, she'd been certain that Leo needed to finish the *Argo II* before they could contact the Romans.

Nevertheless, Annabeth had spent every spare moment scouring all sources for any rumours of Percy. She had talked to nature spirits, read legends about Rome, dug for clues on Daedalus's notebook and spent hundreds of golden drachmas on Iris-messages to every friendly spirit, demigod or monster she'd ever met, all with no luck.

That particular afternoon, coming back from Sally's, Annabeth had felt even more drained than usual. She and Sally had first cried and then attempted to pull themselves together, but their nerves were frayed. Finally Annabeth took the Lexington Avenue subway down to Grand Central.

There were other ways to get back to her high-school dorm from the Upper East Side, but Annabeth liked going through Grand Central Terminal. The beautiful design and the vast open space reminded her of Mount Olympus. Grand buildings made her feel better – maybe because being in a place so permanent made *her* feel more permanent.

She had just passed Sweet on America, the candy shop where Percy's mom used to work, and was thinking about going inside to buy some blue candy for old times' sake, when she saw Athena studying the subway map on the wall.

'Mother!' Annabeth couldn't believe it. She hadn't seen her mom in months – not since Zeus had closed the gates of Olympus and forbade all communication with demigods.

Many times, Annabeth had tried to call on her mom anyway, pleading for guidance, sending up burnt offerings with every meal at camp. She'd had no response. Now here was Athena, dressed in jeans and hiking boots and a red flannel shirt, her dark hair cascading over her shoulders. She held a backpack and a walking stick like she was prepared for a long journey.

'I must return home,' Athena murmured, studying the map. 'The way is complex. I wish Odysseus were here. He would understand.'

'Mom!' Annabeth said. 'Athena!'

The goddess turned. She seemed to look right through Annabeth with no recognition.

'That was my name,' the goddess said dreamily. 'Before they sacked my city, took my identity, made me *this*.' She looked at her clothes in disgust. 'I must return home.'

Annabeth stepped back in shock. 'You're . . . you're Minerva?'

'Don't call me that!' The goddess's grey eyes flared with anger. 'I used to carry a spear and a shield. I held victory in the palm of my hand. I was so much more than this.'

'Mom.' Annabeth's voice trembled. 'It's me, Annabeth. Your *daughter*.'

'My daughter . . .' Athena repeated. 'Yes, my children will avenge me. They must destroy the Romans. Horrible, dishonourable, copycat Romans. Hera argued that we must keep the two camps apart. I said, "No, let them fight. Let my children destroy the usurpers."'

Annabeth's heartbeat thumped in her ears. 'You *wanted* that? But you're wise. You understand warfare better than any –'

'Once!' the goddess said. 'Replaced. Sacked. Looted like a trophy and carted off – away from my beloved homeland. I lost so much. I swore I would never forgive. Neither would my children.' She focused more closely on Annabeth. 'You are my daughter?'

'Yes.'

The goddess fished something from the pocket of her shirt – an old-fashioned subway token – and pressed it into Annabeth's hand.

'Follow the Mark of Athena,' the goddess said. 'Avenge me.'

Annabeth had looked at the coin. As she watched, it changed from a New York subway token to an ancient silver drachma, the kind used by Athenians. It showed an owl,

Athena's sacred animal, with an olive branch on one side and a Greek inscription on the other.

The Mark of Athena.

At the time, Annabeth had had no idea what it meant. She didn't understand why her mom was acting like this. Minerva or not, she shouldn't be so confused.

'Mom . . .' She tried to make her tone as reasonable as possible. 'Percy is missing. I need your help.' She had started to explain Hera's plan for bringing the camps together to battle Gaia and the giants, but the goddess stamped her walking stick against the marble floor.

'Never!' she said. 'Anyone who helps Rome must perish. If you would join them, you are no child of mine. You have already failed me.'

'Mother!'

'I care nothing about this *Percy*. If he has gone over to the Romans, let him perish. Kill him. Kill all the Romans. Find the Mark, follow it to its source. Witness how Rome has disgraced me, and pledge your vengeance.'

'Athena isn't the goddess of revenge.' Annabeth's nails bit into her palms. The silver coin seemed to grow warmer in her hand. 'Percy is everything to me.'

'And revenge is everything to me,' the goddess snarled. 'Which of us is wiser?'

'Something is *wrong* with you. What's happened?'

'Rome happened!' the goddess said bitterly. 'See what they have done, making a *Roman* of me. They wish me to be their goddess? Then let them taste their own evil. Kill them, child.'

'No!'

'Then you are nothing.' The goddess turned to the subway map. Her expression softened, becoming confused and unfocused. 'If I could find the route . . . the way home, then perhaps – But, no. Avenge me or leave me. You are no child of mine.'

Annabeth's eyes stung. She thought of a thousand horrible things she wanted to say, but she couldn't. She had turned and fled.

She'd tried to throw away the silver coin, but it simply reappeared in her pocket, the way Riptide did for Percy. Unfortunately, Annabeth's drachma had no magical powers – at least nothing useful. It only gave her nightmares and, no matter what she tried, she couldn't get rid of it.

Now, sitting in her cabin aboard the *Argo II*, she could feel the coin growing warm in her pocket. She stared at the model of the Parthenon on her computer screen and thought about the argument with Athena. Phrases she'd heard over the last few days swirled in her head: *A talented friend, ready for her visitor. No one will retrieve that statue. Wisdom's daughter walks alone.*

She was afraid she finally understood what it all meant. She prayed to the gods that she was wrong.

A knock on her door made her jump.

She hoped it might be Percy, but instead Frank Zhang poked his head in.

'Um, sorry,' he said. 'Could I –?'

She was so startled to see him that it took her a moment to realize he wanted to come in.

'Sure,' she said. 'Yes.'

He stepped inside, looking around the cabin. There wasn't much to see. On her desk sat a stack of books, a journal and pen, and a picture of her dad flying his Sopwith Camel biplane, grinning and giving a thumbs-up. Annabeth liked that photo. It reminded her of the time she'd felt closest to him, when he'd strafed an army of monsters with Celestial-bronze machine guns just to protect her – pretty much the best present a girl could hope for.

Hanging from a hook on the wall was her New York Yankees cap, her most prized possession from her mom. Once, the cap had had the power to turn its wearer invisible. Since Annabeth's argument with Athena, the cap had lost its magic. Annabeth wasn't sure why, but she'd stubbornly brought it along on the quest. Every morning she would try it on, hoping it would work again. So far it had only served as a reminder of her mother's wrath.

Otherwise, her cabin was bare. She kept it clean and simple, which helped her to think. Percy didn't believe it because she always made excellent grades, but, like most demigods, she was ADHD. When there were too many distractions in her personal space, she was never able to focus.

'So . . . Frank,' she ventured. 'What can I do for you?'

Out of all the kids on the ship, Frank was the one she thought least likely to pay her a visit. She didn't feel any less confused when he blushed and pulled his Chinese handcuffs out of his pocket.

'I don't like being in the dark about this,' he muttered.

'Could you show me the trick? I didn't feel comfortable asking anyone else.'

Annabeth processed his words with a slight delay. Wait . . . Frank was asking *her* for help? Then it dawned on her: of course, Frank was embarrassed. Leo had been razzing him pretty hard. Nobody liked being a laughing stock. Frank's determined expression said he never wanted that to happen again. He wanted to understand the puzzle, without the iguana solution.

Annabeth felt strangely honoured. Frank trusted her not to make fun of him. Besides, she had a soft spot for anyone who was seeking knowledge – even about something as simple as Chinese handcuffs.

She patted the bunk next to her. 'Absolutely. Sit down.'

Frank sat on the edge of the mattress, as if preparing for a quick escape. Annabeth took the Chinese handcuffs and held them next to her computer.

She hit the key for an infrared scan. A few seconds later a 3-D model of the Chinese handcuffs appeared on the screen. She turned the laptop so that Frank could see.

'How did you do that?' he marvelled.

'Cutting-edge Ancient Greek technology,' she said. 'Okay, look. The structure is a cylindrical biaxial braid, so it has excellent resilience.' She manipulated the image so it squeezed in and out like an accordion. 'When you put your fingers inside, it loosens. But when you try to remove them the circumference shrinks as the braid catches and tightens. There's no way you can pull free by struggling.'

Frank stared at her blankly. 'But what's the answer?'

'Well . . .' She showed him some of her calculations – how the handcuffs could resist tearing under incredible stress, depending on the material used in the braid. 'Pretty amazing for a woven structure, right? Doctors use it for traction and electrical contractors –'

'Uh, but the answer?'

Annabeth laughed. 'You don't fight *against* the handcuffs. You push your fingers in, not out. That loosens the braid.'

'Oh.' Frank tried it. It worked. 'Thanks, but . . . couldn't you have just shown me on the handcuffs without the 3-D program and the calculations?'

Annabeth hesitated. Sometimes wisdom came from strange places, even from giant teenaged goldfish. 'I guess you're right. That was silly. I learned something, too.'

Frank tried the handcuffs again. 'It's easy when you know the solution.'

'Many of the best traps are simple,' Annabeth said. 'You just have to think about it, and hope your victim doesn't.'

Frank nodded. He seemed reluctant to leave.

'You know,' Annabeth said, 'Leo doesn't intend to be mean. He's just got a big mouth. When people make him nervous, he uses humour as a defence.'

Frank frowned. 'Why would I make him nervous?'

'You're twice his size. You can turn into a dragon.' *And Hazel likes you*, Annabeth thought, though she didn't say that.

Frank didn't look convinced. 'Leo can summon fire.' He twisted the handcuffs. 'Annabeth . . . sometime, maybe could you help me with another problem that's not so simple? I've got . . . I guess you'd call it an Achilles' heel.'

Annabeth felt like she'd just had a drink of Roman hot chocolate. She'd never really got the term *warm and fuzzy*, but Frank gave her that sensation. He was just a big teddy bear. She could see why Hazel liked him. 'I'd be happy to,' she said. 'Does anyone else know about this Achilles' heel?'

'Percy and Hazel,' he said. 'That's it. Percy . . . he's a really good guy. I would follow him anywhere. Thought you should know.'

Annabeth patted his arm. 'Percy has a knack for picking good friends. Like you. But, Frank, you can trust anyone on this ship. Even Leo. We're all a team. We have to trust each other.'

'I – I suppose.'

'So what's the weakness you're worried about?'

The dinner bell sounded, and Frank jumped.

'Maybe . . . maybe later,' he said. 'It's hard to talk about. But thanks, Annabeth.' He held up the Chinese handcuffs. 'Keep it simple.'

XVIII

ANNABETH

THAT NIGHT, ANNABETH SLEPT WITHOUT NIGHTMARES, which just made her uneasy when she woke up – like the calm before a storm.

Leo docked the ship at a pier in Charleston Harbor, right next to the seawall. Along the shore was a historical district with tall mansions, palm trees and wrought-iron fences. Antique cannons pointed at the water.

By the time Annabeth came up on deck, Jason, Frank and Leo had already left for the museum. According to Coach Hedge, they'd promised to be back by sunset. Piper and Hazel were ready to go, but first Annabeth turned to Percy, who was leaning on the starboard rail, gazing over the bay.

Annabeth took his hand. 'What are you going to do while we're gone?'

'Jump into the harbour,' he said casually, like another kid might say, *I'm going to get a snack.* 'I want to try communicating with the local Nereids. Maybe they can give me some advice about how to free those captives in Atlanta. Besides, I think the sea might be good for me. Being in that aquarium made me feel . . . unclean.'

His hair was dark and tangled as usual, but Annabeth thought about the streak of grey he used to have on one side. When the two of them were fourteen, they'd taken turns (unwillingly) holding the weight of the sky. The strain left them both with some grey hair. Over the last year, while Percy had been missing, the grey streaks had finally disappeared from both of them, which made Annabeth sad and a little worried. She felt like she'd lost a symbolic bond with Percy.

Annabeth kissed him. 'Good luck, Seaweed Brain. Just come back to me, okay?'

'I will,' he promised. 'You do the same.'

Annabeth tried to push down her growing unease.

She turned to Piper and Hazel. 'Okay, ladies. Let's find the ghost of the Battery.'

Afterwards, Annabeth wished she'd jumped into the harbour with Percy. She even would've preferred a museum full of ghosts.

Not that she minded hanging out with Hazel and Piper. At first, they had a pretty good time walking along the Battery. According to the signs, the seaside park was called White Point Gardens. The ocean breeze swept away the muggy heat of the summer afternoon, and it was pleasantly cool under the shade of the palmetto trees. Lining the road were old Civil War cannons and bronze statues of historical figures, which made Annabeth shudder. She thought about the statues in

New York City during the Titan War, which had come to life thanks to Daedalus's command sequence twenty-three. She wondered how many other statues around the country were secretly automatons, waiting to be triggered.

Charleston Harbor glittered in the sun. To the north and south, strips of land stretched out like arms enclosing the bay, and sitting in the mouth of the harbour, about a mile out, was an island with a stone fort. Annabeth had a vague memory of that fort being important in the Civil War, but she didn't spend much time thinking about it.

Mostly she breathed in the sea air and thought about Percy. Gods forbid she ever had to break up with him. She'd never be able to visit the sea again without remembering her broken heart. She was relieved when they turned away from the seawall and explored the inland side of the gardens.

The park wasn't crowded. Annabeth imagined that most of the locals had gone on summer vacation, or were holed up at home taking a siesta. They strolled along South Battery Street, which was lined with four-storey colonial mansions. The brick walls were blanketed with ivy. The facades had soaring white columns like Roman temples. The front gardens were bursting with rosebushes, honeysuckle and flowering bougainvillea. It looked like Demeter had set the timer on all the plants to *grow* several decades ago, then forgotten to come back and check on them.

'Kind of reminds me of New Rome,' Hazel said. 'All the big mansions and the gardens. The columns and arches.'

Annabeth nodded. She remembered reading how the American South had often compared itself to Rome back before the Civil War. In the old days their society had been all about impressive architecture, honour and codes of chivalry. And on the evil side it had also been about slavery. *Rome had slaves*, some Southerners had argued, *so why shouldn't we?*

Annabeth shivered. She loved the architecture here. The houses and the gardens were very beautiful, very Roman. But she wondered why beautiful things had to be wrapped up with evil history. Or was it the other way around? Maybe the evil history made it necessary to build beautiful things, to mask the darker aspects.

She shook her head. Percy would hate her getting so philosophical. If she tried to talk to him about stuff like that, his eyes glazed over.

The other girls didn't say much.

Piper kept looking around like she expected an ambush. She had said she'd seen this park in the blade of her knife, but she wouldn't elaborate. Annabeth guessed she was afraid to. After all, the last time Piper had tried to interpret a vision from her knife, Percy and Jason had almost killed each other in Kansas.

Hazel also seemed preoccupied. Maybe she was taking in their surroundings, or maybe she was worrying about her brother. In less than four days, unless they found him and freed him, Nico would be dead.

Annabeth felt that deadline weighing on her, too. She'd always had mixed feelings about Nico di Angelo. She suspected that he'd had a crush on her ever since they rescued him and his big sister, Bianca, from that military academy in Maine, but Annabeth had never felt any attraction to Nico.

He was too young and too moody. There was a darkness in him that made her uneasy.

Still, she felt responsible for him. Back when they had met, neither of them had known about his half-sister, Hazel. At the time, Bianca had been Nico's only living family. When she had died, Nico became a homeless orphan, drifting through the world alone. Annabeth could relate to that.

She was so deep in thought she might have kept walking around the park forever, but Piper grabbed her arm.

'There.' She pointed across the harbour. A hundred yards out, a shimmering white figure floated on the water. At first, Annabeth thought it might be a buoy or a small boat reflecting the sunlight, but it was definitely glowing, and it was moving more smoothly than a boat, making a straight line towards them. As it got closer, Annabeth could tell it was the figure of a woman.

'The ghost,' she said.

'That's not a ghost,' Hazel said. 'No kind of spirit glows that brightly.'

Annabeth decided to take her word for it. She couldn't imagine being Hazel, dying at such a young age and coming back from the Underworld, knowing more about the dead than the living.

As if in a trance, Piper walked across the street towards the edge of the seawall, narrowly avoiding a horse-drawn carriage.

'Piper!' Annabeth called.

'We'd better follow her,' Hazel said.

By the time Annabeth and Hazel caught up to her, the ghostly apparition was only a few yards away.

Piper glared at it like the sight offended her.

'It *is* her,' she grumbled.

Annabeth squinted at the ghost, but it blazed too brightly to make out details. Then the apparition floated up the seawall and stopped in front of them. The glow faded.

Annabeth gasped. The woman was breathtakingly beautiful and strangely familiar. Her face was hard to describe. Her features seemed to shift from those of one glamorous movie star to another. Her eyes sparkled playfully – sometimes green or blue or amber. Her hair changed from long, straight blonde to dark chocolatey curls.

Annabeth was instantly jealous. She'd always wished she had dark hair. She felt like nobody took her seriously as a blonde. She had to work twice as hard to get recognition as a strategist, an architect, a senior counsellor – anything that had to do with brains.

The woman was dressed like a Southern belle, just as Jason had described. Her gown had a low-cut bodice of pink silk and a three-tiered hoop skirt with white scalloped lace. She wore long white silk gloves, and held a feathered pink-and-white fan to her chest.

Everything about her seemed calculated to make Annabeth feel inadequate: the easy grace with which she wore her dress, the perfect yet understated makeup, the way she radiated feminine charm that no man could possibly resist.

Annabeth realized that her jealousy was irrational. The woman was *making* her feel this way. She'd had this experience before. She recognized this person, even though her face changed by the second, becoming more and more beautiful.

'Aphrodite,' she said.

'Venus?' Hazel asked in amazement.

'Mom,' Piper said, with no enthusiasm.

'Girls!' The goddess spread her arms like she wanted a group hug.

The three demigods did not oblige. Hazel backed into a palmetto tree.

'I'm so glad you're here,' Aphrodite said. 'War is coming. Bloodshed is inevitable. So there's really only one thing to do.'

'Uh . . . and that is?' Annabeth ventured.

'Why, have tea and chat, obviously. Come with me!'

Aphrodite knew how to do tea.

She led them to the central pavilion in the gardens – a white-pillared gazebo, where a table was set with silverware, china cups and of course a steaming pot of tea, the fragrance shifting as easily as Aphrodite's appearance – sometimes cinnamon, or jasmine, or mint. There were plates of scones, cookies and muffins, fresh butter and jam – all of which, Annabeth figured, were incredibly fattening; unless, of course, you were the immortal goddess of love.

Aphrodite sat – or held court, rather – in a wicker peacock chair. She poured tea and served cakes without getting a speck on her clothes, her posture always perfect, her smile dazzling.

Annabeth hated her more and more the longer they sat.

'Oh, my sweet girls,' the goddess said. 'I do love Charleston! The weddings I've attended in this gazebo – they bring tears to my eyes. And the elegant balls in the days of the Old South. Ah, they were lovely. Many of these mansions still have statues of me in their gardens, though they called me Venus.'

'Which are you?' Annabeth asked. 'Venus or Aphrodite?'

The goddess sipped her tea. Her eyes sparkled mischievously. 'Annabeth Chase, you've grown into quite a beautiful young lady. You really should do something with your hair, though. And Hazel Levesque, your clothes –'

'My clothes?' Hazel looked down at her rumpled denim, not self-consciously but baffled, as if she couldn't imagine what was wrong with them.

'Mother!' Piper said. 'You're embarrassing me.'

'Well, I don't see why,' the goddess said. 'Just because *you* don't appreciate my fashion tips, Piper, doesn't mean the others won't. I could do a quick makeover for Annabeth and Hazel, perhaps silk ball gowns like mine –'

'Mother!'

'Fine,' Aphrodite sighed. 'To answer your question, Annabeth, I am *both* Aphrodite and Venus. Unlike many of my fellow Olympians, I changed hardly at all from one age to the other. In fact, I like to think I haven't aged a bit!' Her fingers fluttered around her face appreciatively. 'Love is love, after all, whether you're Greek or Roman. This civil war won't affect me as much as it will the others.'

Wonderful, Annabeth thought. Her own mother, the most levelheaded Olympian, was reduced to a raving, vicious scatterbrain in a subway station. And, of all the gods who might help them, the only ones not affected by the Greek–Roman schism seemed to be Aphrodite, Nemesis and Dionysus. Love, revenge, wine. Very helpful.

Hazel nibbled a sugar cookie. 'We're not in a war yet, my lady.'

'Oh, dear Hazel.' Aphrodite folded her fan. 'Such optimism, yet you have heartrending days ahead of you. Of *course* war is coming. Love and war always go together. They are the peaks of human emotion! Evil and good, beauty and ugliness.'

She smiled at Annabeth as if she knew what Annabeth had been thinking earlier about the Old South.

Hazel set down her sugar cookie. She had a few crumbs on her chin, and Annabeth liked the fact that Hazel either didn't know or didn't care.

'What do you mean,' Hazel asked, 'heartrending days?'

The goddess laughed as if Hazel were a cute puppy. 'Well, Annabeth could give you some idea. I once promised to make *her* love life interesting. And didn't I?'

Annabeth almost snapped the handle off her teacup. For years, her heart had been torn. First there was Luke Castellan, her first crush, who had seen her only as a little sister, then he'd turned evil and decided he liked her – right before he died. Next came Percy, who was infuriating but sweet, yet he had seemed to be falling for another girl named Rachel, and then *he* almost died, several times. Finally Annabeth had got Percy to herself, only to have him vanish for six months and lose his memory.

'Interesting,' Annabeth said, 'is a mild way of putting it.'

'Well, I can't take credit for *all* your troubles,' the goddess said. 'But I adore twists and turns in a love story. Oh, all of you are such excellent stories – I mean, girls. You do me proud!'

'Mother,' Piper said, 'is there a reason you're here?'

'Hmm? Oh, you mean besides the tea? I often come here. I love the view, the food, the atmosphere – you can just smell the romance and heartbreak in the air, can't you? Centuries of it.'

She pointed to a nearby mansion. 'Do you see that rooftop balcony? We had a party there the night the American Civil War began. The shelling of Fort Sumter.'

'That's it,' Annabeth remembered. 'The island in the harbour. That's where the first fighting of the Civil War happened. The Confederates shelled the Union troops and took the fort.'

'Oh, such a party!' Aphrodite said. 'A string quartet, and all the men in their elegant new officers' uniforms. The women's dresses – you should've seen them! I danced with Ares – or was he Mars? I'm afraid I was a little giddy. And the beautiful bursts of light across the harbour, the roar of the cannons giving the men an excuse to put their arms around their frightened sweethearts!'

Annabeth's tea was cold. She hadn't eaten anything, but she felt like she wanted to throw up. 'You're talking about the beginning of the bloodiest war in U.S. history. Over six hundred thousand people died – more Americans than in World War One and World War Two combined.'

'And the refreshments!' Aphrodite continued. 'Ah, they were divine. General Beauregard himself made an appearance. He was such a scoundrel. He was on his second wife then, but you should have seen the way he looked at Lisbeth Cooper –'

'Mother!' Piper tossed her scone to the pigeons.

'Yes, sorry,' the goddess said. 'To make the story short,

I'm here to help you, girls. I doubt you'll be seeing Hera much. Your little quest has hardly made her welcome in the throne room. And the other gods are rather indisposed, as you know, torn between their Roman and Greek sides. Some more than others.' Aphrodite fixed her gaze on Annabeth. 'I suppose you've told your friends about your falling-out with your mother?'

Heat rose to Annabeth's cheeks. Hazel and Piper looked at her curiously.

'Falling-out?' Hazel asked.

'An argument,' Annabeth said. 'It's nothing.'

'Nothing!' the goddess said. 'Well, I don't know about that. Athena was the most Greek of all goddesses. The patron of Athens, after all. When the Romans took over . . . oh, they adopted Athena after a fashion. She became Minerva, the goddess of crafts and cleverness. But the Romans had *other* war gods who were more to their taste, more reliably Roman – like Bellona –'

'Reyna's mom,' Piper muttered.

'Yes, indeed,' the goddess agreed. 'I had a lovely talk with Reyna a while back, right here in the park. And the Romans had Mars, of course. And later, there was Mithras – not even properly Greek or Roman, but the legionnaires were crazy about his cult. I always found him crass and terribly *nouveau dieu*, personally. At any rate, the Romans quite sidelined poor Athena. They took away most of her military importance. The Greeks never forgave the Romans for that insult. Neither did Athena.'

Annabeth's ears buzzed.

'The Mark of Athena,' she said. 'It leads to a statue, doesn't it? It leads to . . . to *the* statue.'

Aphrodite smiled. 'You are clever, like your mother. Understand, though, your siblings, the children of Athena, have been searching for centuries. None has succeeded in recovering the statue. In the meantime, they've been keeping alive the Greek feud with the Romans. Every civil war . . . so much bloodshed and heartbreak . . . has been orchestrated largely by Athena's children.'

'That's . . .' Annabeth wanted to say *impossible*, but she remembered Athena's bitter words in Grand Central Station, the burning hatred in her eyes.

'Romantic?' Aphrodite offered. 'Yes, I supposed it is.'

'But . . .' Annabeth tried to clear the fog from her brain. 'The Mark of Athena, how does it work? Is it a series of clues, or a trail set by Athena –'

'Hmm.' Aphrodite looked politely bored. 'I couldn't say. I don't believe Athena created the Mark consciously. If she knew where her statue was, she'd simply tell you where to find it. No . . . I'd guess the Mark is more like a spiritual trail of bread crumbs. It's a connection between the statue and the children of the goddess. The statue *wants* to be found, you see, but it can only be freed by the most worthy.'

'And for thousands of years,' Annabeth said, 'no one has managed.'

'Hold on,' Piper said. 'What *statue* are we talking about?'

The goddess laughed. 'Oh, I'm sure Annabeth can fill you in. At any rate, the clue you need is close by: a map of sorts, left by the children of Athena in 1861 – a remembrance that will start you on your path, once you reach Rome. But as you said, Annabeth Chase, no one has ever succeeded in following the Mark of Athena to its end. There you will face your worst fear – the fear of every child of Athena. And even if you survive, how will you use your reward? For war or for peace?'

Annabeth was glad about the tablecloth, because under the table, her legs were trembling. 'This map,' she said, 'where is it?'

'Guys!' Hazel pointed to the sky.

Circling above the palmetto trees were two large eagles. Higher up, descending rapidly, was a flying chariot pulled by pegasi. Apparently Leo's diversion with Buford the end table hadn't worked – at least not for long.

Aphrodite spread butter on a muffin as if she had all the time in the world. 'Oh, the map is at Fort Sumter, of course.' She pointed her butter knife towards the island across the harbour. 'It looks like the Romans have arrived to cut you off. I'd get back to your ship in a hurry if I were you. Would you care for some tea cakes to go?'

XIX

ANNABETH

THEY DIDN'T MAKE IT TO THE SHIP.

Halfway across the dock, three giant eagles descended in front of them. Each deposited a Roman commando in purple and denim with glittering gold armour, sword and shield. The eagles flew away, and the Roman in the middle, who was scrawnier than the others, raised his visor.

'Surrender to Rome!' Octavian shrieked.

Hazel drew her cavalry sword and grumbled, 'Fat chance, Octavian.'

Annabeth cursed under her breath. By himself, the skinny augur wouldn't have bothered her, but the two other guys looked like seasoned warriors – a lot bigger and stronger than Annabeth wanted to deal with, especially since Piper and she were armed only with daggers.

Piper raised her hands in a placating gesture. 'Octavian, what happened at camp was a set-up. We can explain.'

'Can't hear you!' Octavian yelled. 'Wax in our ears – standard procedure when battling evil sirens. Now, throw down your weapons and turn around slowly so I can bind your hands.'

'Let me skewer him,' Hazel muttered. 'Please.'

The ship was only fifty feet away, but Annabeth saw no sign of Coach Hedge on deck. He was probably below, watching his stupid martial arts programmes. Jason's group wasn't due back until sunset, and Percy would be underwater, unaware of the invasion. If Annabeth could get on board, she could use the ballistae, but there was no way to get around these three Romans.

She was running out of time. The eagles circled overhead, crying out as if to alert their brethren: *Hey, some tasty Greek demigods over here!* Annabeth couldn't see the flying chariot any more, but she assumed it was close by. She had to figure out something before more Romans arrived.

She needed help . . . some kind of distress signal to Coach Hedge, or even better – Percy.

'Well?' Octavian demanded. His two friends brandished their swords.

Very slowly, using only two fingers, Annabeth drew her dagger. Instead of dropping it, she tossed it as far as she could into the water.

Octavian made a squeaking sound. 'What was that for? I didn't say *toss* it! That could've been evidence. Or spoils of war!'

Annabeth tried for a dumb-blonde smile, like: *Oh, silly me.*

Nobody who knew her would have been fooled. But Octavian seemed to buy it. He huffed in exasperation.

'You other two . . .' He pointed his blade at Hazel and Piper. 'Put your weapons on the dock. No funny bus—'

All around the Romans, Charleston Harbor erupted like a Las Vegas fountain putting on a show. When the wall of seawater subsided, the three Romans were in the bay, spluttering and frantically trying to stay afloat in their armour. Percy stood on the dock, holding Annabeth's dagger.

'You dropped this,' he said, totally poker-faced.

Annabeth threw her arms around him. 'I love you!'

'Guys,' Hazel interrupted. She had a little smile on her face. 'We need to hurry.'

Down in the water, Octavian yelled, 'Get me out of here! I'll kill you!'

'Tempting,' Percy called down.

'What?' Octavian shouted. He was holding on to one of his guards, who was having trouble keeping them both afloat.

'Nothing!' Percy shouted back. 'Let's go, guys.'

Hazel frowned. 'We can't let them drown, can we?'

'They won't,' Percy promised. 'I've got the water circulating around their feet. As soon as we're out of range, I'll spit them ashore.'

Piper grinned. 'Nice.'

They climbed aboard the *Argo II*, and Annabeth ran to the helm. 'Piper, get below. Use the sink in the galley for an Iris-message. Warn Jason to get back here!'

Piper nodded and raced off.

'Hazel, go find Coach Hedge and tell him to get his furry hindquarters on deck!'

'Right!'

'And, Percy – you and I need to get this ship to Fort Sumter.'

Percy nodded and ran to the mast. Annabeth took the helm. Her hands flew across the controls. She'd just have to hope she knew enough to operate them.

Annabeth had seen Percy control full-sized sailing ships before with only his willpower. This time, he didn't disappoint. Ropes flew on their own – releasing the dock ties, weighing the anchor. The sails unfurled and caught the wind. Meanwhile Annabeth fired the engine. The oars extended with a sound like machine-gun fire, and the *Argo II* turned from the dock, heading for the island in the distance.

The three eagles still circled overhead, but they made no attempt to land on the ship, probably because Festus the figurehead blew fire whenever they got close. More eagles were flying in formation towards Fort Sumter – at least a dozen. If each of them carried a Roman demigod . . . that was a lot of enemies.

Coach Hedge came pounding up the stairs with Hazel at his hooves.

'Where are they?' he demanded. 'Who do I kill?'

'No killing!' Annabeth ordered. 'Just defend the ship!'

'But they interrupted a Chuck Norris movie!'

Piper emerged from below. 'Got a message through to Jason. Kind of fuzzy, but he's already on his way. He should be – oh! There!'

Soaring over the city, heading in their direction, was a giant bald eagle, unlike the golden Roman birds.

'Frank!' Hazel said.

Leo was holding on to the eagle's feet, and even from the ship Annabeth could hear him screaming and cursing.

Behind them flew Jason, riding the wind.

'Never seen Jason fly before,' Percy grumbled. 'He looks like a blond Superman.'

'This isn't the time!' Piper scolded him. 'Look, they're in trouble!'

Sure enough, the Roman flying chariot had descended from a cloud and was diving straight towards them. Jason and Frank veered out of the way, pulling up to avoid getting trampled by the pegasi. The charioteers fired their bows. Arrows whistled under Leo's feet, which led to more screaming and cursing. Jason and Frank were forced to overshoot the *Argo II* and fly towards Fort Sumter.

'I'll get 'em!' yelled Coach Hedge.

He spun the port ballista. Before Annabeth could yell, 'Don't be stupid!' Hedge fired. A flaming spear rocketed towards the chariot.

It exploded over the heads of the pegasi and threw them into a panic. Unfortunately it also singed Frank's wings and sent him spiralling out of control. Leo slipped from his grasp. The chariot shot towards Fort Sumter, slamming into Jason.

Annabeth watched in horror as Jason – obviously dazed and in pain – lunged for Leo, caught him, then struggled to gain altitude. He only managed to slow their fall. They disappeared behind the ramparts of the fort. Frank tumbled after them. Then the chariot dropped somewhere inside and hit with a bone-shattering *CRACK!* One broken wheel spun into the air.

'Coach!' Piper screamed.

'What?' Hedge demanded. 'That was just a warning shot!'

Annabeth gunned the engines. The hull shuddered as they picked up speed. The docks of the island were only a hundred yards away now, but a dozen more eagles were soaring overhead, each carrying a Roman demigod in its claws.

The *Argo II*'s crew would be outnumbered at least three to one.

'Percy,' Annabeth said, 'we're going to come in hard. I need you to control the water so we don't smash into the docks. Once we're there, you're going to have to hold off the attackers. The rest of you help him guard the ship.'

'But – Jason!' Piper said.

'Frank and Leo!' Hazel added.

'I'll find them,' Annabeth promised. 'I've got to figure out where the map is. And I'm pretty sure I'm the only one who can do that.'

'The fort is crawling with Romans,' Percy warned. 'You'll have to fight your way through, find our friends – assuming they're okay – find this map and get everybody back alive. All on your own?'

'Just an average day.' Annabeth kissed him. 'Whatever you do, don't let them take this ship!'

ANNABETH

THE NEW CIVIL WAR HAD BEGUN.

Leo had somehow survived his fall unharmed. Annabeth saw him ducking from portico to portico, blasting fire at the giant eagles swooping down on him. Roman demigods tried to chase him, tripping over piles of cannonballs and dodging tourists, who screamed and ran in circles.

Tour guides kept yelling, 'It's just a re-enactment!' Though they didn't sound sure. The Mist could only do so much to change what mortals saw.

In the middle of the courtyard, a full-grown elephant – could that be Frank? – rampaged around the flagpoles, scattering Roman warriors. Jason stood about fifty yards away, sword-fighting with a stocky centurion whose lips were stained cherry red, like blood. A wannabe vampire, or maybe a Kool-Aid freak?

As Annabeth watched, Jason yelled, 'Sorry about this, Dakota!'

He vaulted straight over the centurion's head like an acrobat and slammed the hilt of his *gladius* into the back of the Roman's head. Dakota crumpled.

'Jason!' Annabeth called.

He scanned the battlefield until he saw her.

She pointed to where the *Argo II* was docked. 'Get the others aboard! Retreat!'

'What about you?' he called.

'Don't wait for me!'

Annabeth bolted off before he could protest.

She had a hard time manoeuvring through the mobs of tourists. Why did so many people want to see Fort Sumter on a sweltering summer day? But Annabeth quickly realized the crowds had saved their lives. Without the chaos of all these panicked mortals, the Romans would have already surrounded their outnumbered crew.

Annabeth dodged into a small room that must have been part of the garrison. She tried to steady her breathing. She imagined what it would have been like to be a Union soldier on this island in 1861. Surrounded by enemies. Dwindling food and supplies, no reinforcements coming.

Some of the Union defenders had been children of Athena. They'd hidden an important map here – something they didn't want falling into enemy hands. If Annabeth had been one of those demigods, where would she have put it?

Suddenly the walls glistened. The air became warm. Annabeth wondered if she was hallucinating. She was about to run for the exit when the door slammed shut. The mortar between the stones blistered. The bubbles popped and thousands of tiny black spiders swelled forth.

Annabeth couldn't move. Her heart seemed to have stopped. The spiders blanketed the walls, crawling over one another, spreading across the floor and gradually surrounding her. It was impossible. This couldn't be *real*.

Terror plunged her into memories. She was seven years old again, alone in her bedroom in Richmond, Virginia. The spiders came at night. They crawled in waves from her closet and waited in the shadows. She yelled for her father, but her father was away for work. He *always* seemed to be away for work.

Her stepmother came instead.

I don't mind being the bad cop, she had once told Annabeth's father, when she didn't think Annabeth could hear.

It's only your imagination, her stepmother said about the spiders. *You're scaring your baby brothers.*

They're not my brothers, Annabeth argued, which made her stepmother's expression harden. Her eyes were almost as scary as the spiders.

Go to sleep now, her stepmother insisted. *No more screaming.*

The spiders came back as soon as her stepmother had left the room. Annabeth tried to hide under the covers, but it was no good. Eventually she fell asleep from sheer exhaustion. She woke up in the morning, freckled with bites, cobwebs covering her eyes, her mouth and nose.

The bites faded before she even got dressed, so she had nothing to show her stepmother except cobwebs, which her stepmother thought was some sort of clever trick.

No more talk of spiders, her stepmother said firmly. *You're a big girl now.*

The second night, the spiders came again. Her stepmother continued to be the bad cop. Annabeth wasn't allowed to call her father and bother him with this nonsense. No, he would *not* come home early.

The third night, Annabeth ran away from home.

Later, at Camp Half-Blood, she learned that all children of Athena feared spiders. Long ago, Athena had taught the mortal weaver Arachne a hard lesson – cursing her for her pride by turning her into the first spider. Ever since, spiders had hated the children of Athena.

But that didn't make her fear easier to deal with. Once, she'd almost killed Connor Stoll at camp for putting a tarantula in her bunk. Years later, she'd had a panic attack at a water park in Denver, when she and Percy were assaulted by mechanical spiders. And the past few weeks Annabeth had dreamed of spiders almost every night – crawling over her, suffocating her, wrapping her in webs.

Now, standing in the barracks at Fort Sumter, she was surrounded. Her nightmares had come true.

A sleepy voice murmured in her head: *Soon, my dear. You will meet the weaver soon.*

'Gaia?' Annabeth murmured. She feared the answer, but she asked: 'Who – who is the weaver?'

The spiders became excited, swarming over the walls, swirling around Annabeth's feet like a glistening black whirlpool. Only the hope that it might be an illusion kept Annabeth from passing out from fear.

I hope you survive, child, the woman's voice said. *I would prefer you as my sacrifice. But we must let the weaver take her revenge . . .*

Gaia's voice faded. On the far wall, in the centre of the spider swarm, a red symbol blazed to life: the figure of an owl like the one on the silver drachma, staring straight at Annabeth. Then, just as in her nightmares, the Mark of Athena burned across the walls, incinerating the spiders until the room was empty except for the smell of sickly sweet ashes.

Go, said a new voice – Annabeth's mother. *Avenge me. Follow the Mark.*

The blazing symbol of the owl faded. The garrison door burst open. Annabeth stood stunned in the middle of the room, unsure whether she'd seen something real or just a vision.

An explosion shook the building. Annabeth remembered that her friends were in danger. She'd stayed here much too long.

She forced herself to move. Still trembling, she stumbled outside. The ocean air helped clear her mind. She gazed across the courtyard – past the panicked tourists and fighting demigods – to the edge of the battlements, where a large mortar pointed out to sea.

It might have been Annabeth's imagination, but the old artillery piece seemed to be glowing red. She dashed towards it. An eagle swooped at her, but she ducked and kept running. Nothing could possibly scare her as much as those spiders.

Roman demigods had formed ranks and were advancing towards the *Argo II*, but a miniature storm had gathered over their heads. Though the day was clear all around them, thunder rumbled, and lightning flashed above the Romans. Rain and wind pushed them back.

Annabeth didn't stop to think about it.

She reached the mortar and put her hand on the muzzle. On the plug that blocked the opening, the Mark of Athena began to glow – the red outline of an owl.

'In the mortar,' she said. 'Of course.'

She pulled at the plug with her fingers. No luck. Cursing, she drew her dagger. As soon as the Celestial bronze touched the plug, the plug shrank and loosened. Annabeth pulled it off and stuck her hand inside the cannon.

Her fingers touched something cold, smooth and metal. She pulled out a small disc of bronze the size of a tea saucer, etched with delicate letters and illustrations. She decided to examine it later. She thrust it in her pack and turned.

'Rushing off?' Reyna asked.

The praetor stood ten feet away in full battle armour, holding a golden javelin. Her two metal greyhounds growled at her side.

Annabeth scanned the area. They were more or less alone. Most of the combat had moved towards the docks. Hopefully her friends had all made it on board, but they'd have to set sail immediately or risk being overrun. Annabeth had to hurry.

'Reyna,' she said, 'what happened at Camp Jupiter was Gaia's fault. Eidolons, possessing spirits –'

'Save your explanations,' Reyna said. 'You'll need them for the trial.'

The dogs snarled and inched forward. This time, it didn't

seem to matter to them that Annabeth was telling the truth. She tried to think of an escape plan. She doubted she could take Reyna in one-on-one combat. With those metal dogs, she stood no chance at all.

'If you let Gaia drive our camps apart,' Annabeth said, 'the giants have already won. They'll destroy the Romans, the Greeks, the gods, the whole mortal world.'

'You think I don't know that?' Reyna's voice was as hard as iron. 'What choice have you left me? Octavian smells blood. He's whipped the legion into a frenzy, and I can't stop it. Surrender to me. I'll bring you back to New Rome for trial. It won't be fair. You'll be painfully executed. But it *may* be enough to stop further violence. Octavian won't be satisfied, of course, but I think I can convince the others to stand down.'

'It wasn't me!'

'It doesn't *matter*!' Reyna snapped. 'Someone must pay for what happened. Let it be you. It's the better option.'

Annabeth's skin crawled. 'Better than what?'

'Use that wisdom of yours,' Reyna said. 'If you escape today, we won't follow. I told you – not even a madman would cross the sea to the ancient lands. If Octavian can't have vengeance on your ship, he'll turn his attention to Camp Half-Blood. The legion will march on your territory. We will raze it and salt the earth.'

Kill the Romans, she heard her mother urging. *They can never be your allies.*

Annabeth wanted to sob. Camp Half-Blood was the only real home she'd ever known, and in a bid for friendship she had told Reyna exactly where to find it. She couldn't leave it at the mercy of the Romans and travel halfway around the world.

But their quest, and everything she'd suffered to get Percy back . . . if she didn't go to the ancient lands, it would all mean nothing. Besides, the Mark of Athena didn't have to lead to revenge.

If I could find the route, her mother had said, *the way home . . .*

How will you use your reward? Aphrodite had asked. *For war or peace?*

There *was* an answer. The Mark of Athena could lead her there – if she survived.

'I'm going,' she told Reyna. 'I'm following the Mark of Athena to Rome.'

The praetor shook her head. 'You have no idea what awaits you.'

'Yes, I do,' Annabeth said. 'This grudge between our camps . . . I can fix it.'

'Our grudge is thousands of years old. How can one person fix it?'

Annabeth wished she could give a convincing answer, show Reyna a 3-D diagram or a brilliant schematic, but she couldn't. She just knew she had to try. She remembered that lost look on her mother's face: *I must return home.*

'The quest has to succeed,' she said. 'You can try to stop me, in which case we'll have to fight to the death. Or you can let me go and I'll try to save both our camps. If you must march on Camp Half-Blood, at least try to delay. Slow Octavian down.'

Reyna's eyes narrowed. 'One daughter of a war goddess

to another, I respect your boldness. But if you leave now you doom your camp to destruction.'

'Don't underestimate Camp Half-Blood,' Annabeth warned.

'You've never seen the legion at war,' Reyna countered.

Over by the docks, a familiar voice shrieked over the wind: 'Kill them! Kill them all!'

Octavian had survived his swim in the harbour. He crouched behind his guards, screaming encouragement at the other Roman demigods as they struggled towards the ship, holding up their shields as if that would deflect the storm raging all around them.

On the deck of the *Argo II*, Percy and Jason stood together, their swords crossed. Annabeth got a tingle down her spine as she realized the boys were working as one, summoning the sky and the sea to do their bidding. Water and wind churned together. Waves heaved against the ramparts and lightning flashed. Giant eagles were knocked out of the sky. Wreckage of the flying chariot burned in the water, and Coach Hedge swung a mounted crossbow, taking potshots at the Roman birds as they flew overhead.

'You see?' Reyna said bitterly. 'The spear is thrown. Our people are at war.'

'Not if I succeed,' Annabeth said.

Reyna's expression looked the same as it had at Camp Jupiter when she realized Jason had found another girl. The praetor was too alone, too bitter and betrayed to believe anything could go right for her ever again. Annabeth waited for her to attack.

Instead, Reyna flicked her hand. The metal dogs backed away. 'Annabeth Chase,' she said, 'when we meet again, we will be enemies on the field of battle.'

The praetor turned and walked across the ramparts, her greyhounds behind her.

Annabeth feared it might be some sort of trick, but she had no time to wonder. She ran for the ship.

The winds that battered the Romans didn't seem to affect her.

Annabeth sprinted through their lines. Octavian yelled, 'Stop her!'

A spear flew past her ear. The *Argo II* was already pulling away from the dock. Piper was at the gangplank, her hand outstretched.

Annabeth leaped and grabbed Piper's hand. The gangplank fell into the sea, and the two girls tumbled onto the deck.

'Go!' Annabeth screamed. 'Go, go, go!'

The engines rumbled beneath her. The oars churned. Jason changed the course of the wind, and Percy called up a massive wave, which lifted the ship higher than the fort's walls and pushed it out to sea. By the time the *Argo II* reached top speed, Fort Sumter was only a blot in the distance, and they were racing across the waves towards the ancient lands.

XXI

LEO

AFTER RAIDING A MUSEUM FULL OF Confederate ghosts, Leo didn't think his day could get any worse. He was wrong.

They hadn't found anything in the Civil War sub or elsewhere in the museum: just a few elderly tourists, a dozing security guard and – when they tried to inspect the artefacts – a whole battalion of glowing zombie dudes in grey uniforms.

The idea that Frank should be able to control the spirits? Yeah . . . that pretty much failed. By the time Piper sent her Iris-message warning them about the Roman attack, they were already halfway back to the ship, having been chased through downtown Charleston by a pack of angry dead Confederates.

Then – oh, boy! – Leo got to hitch a ride with Frank the Friendly Eagle so they could fight a bunch of Romans. Rumour must've got around that Leo was the one who had fired on their little city, because those Romans seemed especially anxious to kill him.

But wait! There was more! Coach Hedge shot them out of the sky, Frank dropped him (that was no accident) and they crash-landed in Fort Sumter.

Now, as the *Argo II* raced across the waves, Leo had to use all his skill just to keep the ship in one piece. Percy and Jason were a little *too* good at cooking up massive storms.

At one point, Annabeth stood next to him, yelling against the roar of the wind: 'Percy says he talked to a Nereid in Charleston Harbor!'

'Good for him!' Leo yelled back.

'The Nereid said we should seek help from Chiron's brothers.'

'What does that mean? The Party Ponies?' Leo had never met Chiron's crazy centaur relatives, but he'd heard rumours of Nerf sword-fights, root-beer-chugging contests and Super Soakers filled with pressurized whipped cream.

'Not sure,' Annabeth said. 'But I've got coordinates. Can you input latitude and longitude in this thing?'

'I can input star charts and order you a smoothie, if you want. Of *course* I can do latitude and longitude!'

Annabeth rattled off the numbers. Leo somehow managed to punch them in while holding the wheel with one hand. A red dot popped up on the bronze display screen.

'That location is in the middle of the Atlantic,' he said. 'Do the Party Ponies have a yacht?'

Annabeth shrugged helplessly. 'Just hold the ship together until we get further from Charleston. Jason and Percy will keep up the winds!'

'Happy fun time!'

It seemed like forever, but finally the sea calmed and the winds died.

'Valdez,' said Coach Hedge, with surprising gentleness. 'Let me take the wheel. You've been steering for two hours.'

'Two hours?'

'Yeah. Give me the wheel.'

'Coach?'

'Yeah, kid?'

'I can't unclench my hands.'

It was true. Leo's fingers felt like they had turned to stone. His eyes burned from staring at the horizon. His knees were marshmallows. Coach Hedge managed to prise him from the wheel.

Leo took one last look at the console, listening to Festus chatter and whir a status report. Leo felt like he was forgetting something. He stared at the controls, trying to think, but it was no good. His eyes could hardly focus. 'Just watch for monsters,' he told the coach. 'And be careful with the damaged stabilizer. And –'

'I've got it covered,' Coach Hedge promised. 'Now, go away!'

Leo nodded wearily. He staggered across the deck towards his friends.

Percy and Jason sat with their backs against the mast, their heads slumped in exhaustion. Annabeth and Piper were trying to get them to drink some water.

Hazel and Frank stood just out of earshot, having an

argument that involved lots of arm waving and head shaking. Leo should not have felt pleased about that, but part of him did. The other part of him felt bad that he felt pleased.

The argument stopped abruptly when Hazel saw Leo. Everybody gathered at the mast.

Frank scowled like he was trying hard to turn into a bulldog. 'No sign of pursuit,' he said.

'Or land,' Hazel added. She looked a little green, though Leo wasn't sure if that was from the rocking of the boat or from arguing.

Leo scanned the horizon. Nothing but ocean in every direction. That shouldn't have surprised him. He'd spent six months building a ship that he knew would cross the Atlantic. But until today their embarking on a journey to the ancient lands hadn't seemed real. Leo had never been outside the U.S. before – except for a quick dragon flight up to Quebec. Now they were in the middle of the open sea, completely on their own, sailing to the Mare Nostrum, where all the scary monsters and nasty giants had come from. The Romans might not follow them, but they couldn't count on any help from Camp Half-Blood, either.

Leo patted his waist to make sure his tool belt was still there. Unfortunately that just reminded him of Nemesis's fortune cookie, tucked inside one of the pockets.

You will always be an outsider. The goddess's voice still wriggled around in his head. *The seventh wheel.*

Forget her, Leo told himself. Concentrate on the stuff you can fix.

He turned to Annabeth. 'Did you find the map you wanted?'

She nodded, though she looked pale. Leo wondered what she'd seen at Fort Sumter that could have shaken her up so badly.

'I'll have to study it,' she said, as if that was the end of the subject. 'How far are we from those coordinates?'

'At top rowing speed, about an hour,' Leo said. 'Any idea what we're looking for?'

'No,' she admitted. 'Percy?'

Percy raised his head. His green eyes were bloodshot and droopy. 'The Nereid said Chiron's brothers were there, and they'd want to hear about that aquarium in Atlanta. I don't know what she meant, but . . .' He paused, like he'd used up all his energy saying that much. 'She also warned me to be careful. Keto, the goddess at the aquarium: she's the mother of sea monsters. She might be stuck in Atlanta, but she can still send her children after us. The Nereid said we should expect an attack.'

'Wonderful,' Frank muttered.

Jason tried to stand, which wasn't a good idea. Piper grabbed him to keep him from falling over, and he slid back down the mast.

'Can we get the ship aloft?' he asked. 'If we could fly –'

'That'd be great,' Leo said. 'Except Festus tells me the port aerial stabilizer got pulverized when the ship raked against the dock at Fort Sumter.'

'We were in a hurry,' Annabeth said. 'Trying to save you.'

'And saving me is a very noble cause,' Leo agreed. 'I'm just saying it'll take some time to fix. Until then, we're not flying anywhere.'

Percy flexed his shoulders and winced. 'Fine with me. The sea is good.'

'Speak for yourself.' Hazel glanced at the evening sun, which was almost to the horizon. 'We need to go fast. We've burned another day, and Nico only has three more left.'

'We can do it,' Leo promised. He hoped Hazel had forgiven him for not trusting her brother (hey, it had seemed like a reasonable suspicion to Leo), but he didn't want to reopen that wound. 'We can make it to Rome in three days – assuming, you know, nothing unexpected happens.'

Frank grunted. He looked like he was still working on that bulldog transformation. 'Is there any *good* news?'

'Actually, yes,' Leo said. 'According to Festus, our flying table, Buford, made it back safely while we were in Charleston, so those eagles didn't get him. Unfortunately, he lost the laundry bag with your pants.'

'Dang it!' Frank barked, which Leo figured was probably severe profanity for him.

No doubt Frank would've cursed some more – busting out the *golly gee*s and the *gosh darn*s – but Percy interrupted by doubling over and groaning.

'Did the world just turn upside down?' he asked.

Jason pressed his hands to his head. 'Yeah, and it's spinning. Everything is yellow. Is it supposed to be yellow?'

Annabeth and Piper exchanged concerned looks.

'Summoning that storm really sapped your strength,' Piper told the boys. 'You've got to rest.'

Annabeth nodded agreement. 'Frank, can you help us get the guys belowdecks?'

Frank glanced at Leo, no doubt reluctant to leave him alone with Hazel.

'It's fine, man,' Leo said. 'Just try not to drop them on the way down the stairs.'

Once the others were below, Hazel and Leo faced each other awkwardly. They were alone except for Coach Hedge, who was back on the quarterdeck singing the *Pokémon* theme song. The coach had changed the words to 'Gotta kill 'em all' and Leo really didn't want to know why.

The song didn't seem to help Hazel's nausea.

'Ugh . . .' She leaned over and hugged her sides. She had nice hair – frizzy and golden brown like curls of cinnamon. Her hair reminded Leo of a place in Houston that made excellent *churros*. The thought made him hungry.

'Don't lean over,' he advised. 'Don't close your eyes. It makes the queasiness worse.'

'It does? Do you get seasick, too?'

'Not seasick. But cars make me nauseous, and . . .'

He stopped himself. He wanted to say *talking to girls*, but he decided to keep that to himself.

'Cars?' Hazel straightened with difficulty. 'You can sail a ship or fly a dragon, but cars make you sick?'

'I know, right?' Leo shrugged. 'I'm special that way. Look, keep your eyes on the horizon. That's a fixed point. It'll help.'

Hazel took a deep breath and stared into the distance. Her eyes were lustrous gold, like the copper and bronze discs inside Festus's mechanical head.

'Any better?' he asked.

'Maybe a little.' She sounded like she was just being polite. She kept her eyes on the horizon, but Leo got the feeling she was gauging his mood, considering what to say.

'Frank didn't drop you on purpose,' she said. 'He's not like that. He's just a little clumsy sometimes.'

'*Oops*,' Leo said, in his best Frank Zhang voice. '*Dropped Leo into a squad of enemy soldiers. Dang it!*'

Hazel tried to suppress a smile. Leo figured smiling was better than throwing up.

'Go easy on him,' Hazel said. 'You and your fireballs make Frank nervous.'

'The guy can turn into an elephant, and *I* make *him* nervous?'

Hazel kept her eyes on the horizon. She didn't look quite so queasy, despite the fact that Coach Hedge was still singing his *Pokémon* song at the helm.

'Leo,' she said, 'about what happened at the Great Salt Lake . . .'

Here it comes, Leo thought.

He remembered their meeting with the revenge goddess Nemesis. The fortune cookie in his tool belt started to feel heavier. Last night, as they flew from Atlanta, Leo had lain in his cabin and thought about how angry he'd made Hazel. He had thought about ways he could make it right.

Soon you will face a problem you cannot solve, Nemesis had said, *though I could help you . . . for a price.*

Leo had taken the fortune cookie out of his tool belt and turned it in his fingers, wondering what price he would have to pay if he broke it open.

Maybe now was the moment.

'I'd be willing,' he told Hazel. 'I could use the fortune cookie to find your brother.'

Hazel looked stunned. 'What? No! I mean . . . I'd never ask you to do that. Not after what Nemesis said about the horrible cost. We barely *know* each other!'

The *barely know each other* comment kind of hurt, though Leo knew it was true.

'So . . . that's not what you wanted to talk about?' he asked. 'Uh, did you want to talk about the holding-hands-on-the-boulder moment? Because –'

'No!' she said quickly, fanning her face in that cute way she did when she was flustered. 'No, I was just thinking about the way you tricked Narcissus and those nymphs . . .'

'Oh, right.' Leo glanced self-consciously at his arm. The HOT STUFF tattoo hadn't completely faded. 'Seemed like a good idea at the time.'

'You were amazing,' Hazel said. 'I've been mulling it over, how much you reminded me of –'

'Sammy,' Leo guessed. 'I wish you'd tell me who he is.'

'Who he *was*,' Hazel corrected. The evening air was warm, but she shivered. 'I've been thinking . . . I might be able to show you.'

'You mean like a photo?'

'No. There's a sort of flashback that happens to me. I haven't had one in a long time, and I've never tried to make one happen on purpose. But I shared one with Frank once, so I thought . . .'

Hazel locked eyes with him. Leo started to feel jittery, like he'd been injected with coffee. If this flashback was something Frank had shared with Hazel . . . well, either Leo didn't want any part of it, or he *definitely* wanted to try it. He wasn't sure which.

'When you say flashback . . .' He swallowed. 'What exactly are we talking about? Is it safe?'

Hazel held out her hand. 'I wouldn't ask you to do this, but I'm sure it's important. It *can't* be a coincidence we met. If this works, maybe we can finally understand how we're connected.'

Leo glanced back at the helm. He still had a nagging suspicion he'd forgotten something, but Coach Hedge seemed to be doing fine. The sky ahead was clear. There was no sign of trouble.

Besides, a flashback sounded like a pretty brief thing. It couldn't hurt to let the coach be in charge for a few more minutes, could it?

'Okay,' he relented. 'Show me.'

He took Hazel's hand, and the world dissolved.

XXII

LEO

THEY STOOD IN THE COURTYARD of an old compound, like a monastery. Redbrick walls were overgrown with vines. Big magnolia trees had cracked the ground. The sun beat down, and the humidity was about two hundred percent, even stickier than in Houston. Somewhere nearby, Leo smelled fish frying. Overhead, the cloud cover was low and grey, striped like a tiger's pelt.

The courtyard was about the size of a basketball court. An old deflated football sat in one corner, at the base of a Virgin Mary statue.

Along the sides of the buildings, windows were open. Leo could see flickers of movement inside, but it was eerily quiet. He saw no sign of air conditioning, which meant it must have been a thousand degrees in there.

'Where are we?' he asked.

'My old school,' Hazel said next to him. 'St Agnes's Academy for Coloured Children and Indians.'

'What kind of name —?'

He turned towards Hazel and yelped. She was a ghost — just a vaporous silhouette in the steamy air. Leo looked down and realized his own body had turned to mist, too.

Everything around him seemed solid and real, but he was a spirit. After having been possessed by an eidolon three days ago, he didn't appreciate the feeling.

Before he could ask questions, a bell rang inside: not a modern electronic sound but the old-fashioned buzz of a hammer on metal.

'This is a memory,' Hazel said, 'so no one will see us. Look, here we come.'

'*We?*'

From every door, dozens of children spilled into the courtyard, yelling and jostling each other. They were mostly African American, with a sprinkling of Hispanic-looking kids, as young as kindergartners and as old as high schoolers. Leo could tell this was in the past, because all the girls wore dresses and buckled leather shoes. The boys wore white collared shirts and trousers held up by suspenders. Many wore caps like horse jockeys wear. Some kids carried lunches. Many didn't. Their clothes were clean, but worn and faded. Some had holes in the knees of their trousers, or shoes with the heels coming apart.

A few of the girls began a skipping game with an old piece of clothesline. The older guys tossed a ratty baseball back and forth. Kids with lunches sat together and ate and chatted.

No one paid Ghost Hazel or Leo any attention.

Then Hazel — Hazel from the *past* — stepped into the courtyard. Leo recognized her with no problem, though she looked about two years younger than now. Her hair was pinned back in a bun. Her gold eyes darted around the courtyard uneasily. She wore a dark dress, unlike the other girls in their white cotton or pastel flowery prints, so she stood out like a mourner at a wedding.

She gripped a canvas lunch bag and moved along the wall, as if trying hard not to be noticed.

It didn't work. A boy called out, 'Witch girl!' He lumbered towards her, backing her into a corner. The boy could have been fourteen or nineteen. It was hard to tell because he was so big and tall, easily the largest guy on the playground. Leo figured he'd been held back a few times. He wore a dirty shirt the colour of grease rags, threadbare wool trousers (in this heat, they couldn't have been comfortable) and no shoes at all. Maybe the teachers were too terrified to insist that this kid wear shoes, or maybe he just didn't have any.

'That's Rufus,' said Ghost Hazel with distaste.

'Seriously? No way his name is Rufus,' Leo said.

'Come on,' said Ghost Hazel. She drifted towards the confrontation. Leo followed. He wasn't used to drifting, but he'd ridden a Segway once and it was kind of like that. He simply leaned in the direction he wanted to go and glided along.

The big kid Rufus had flat features, as if he spent most of his time face-planting on the sidewalk. His hair was cut just as flat on top, so miniature aeroplanes could've used it for a landing strip.

Rufus thrust out his hand. 'Lunch.'

Hazel from the past didn't protest. She handed over her canvas bag like this was an everyday occurrence.

A few older girls drifted over to watch the fun. One giggled at Rufus. 'You don't want to eat that,' she warned. 'It's probably poison.'

'You're right,' Rufus said. 'Did your witch mom make this, Levesque?'

'She's not a witch,' Hazel muttered.

Rufus dropped the bag and stepped on it, smashing the contents under his bare heel. 'You can have it back. I want a diamond, though. I hear your momma can make those out of thin air. Gimme a diamond.'

'I don't have diamonds,' Hazel said. 'Go away.'

Rufus balled his fists. Leo had been in enough rough schools and foster homes to sense when things were about to turn ugly. He wanted to step in and help Hazel, but he was a ghost. Besides, all this had happened decades ago.

Then another kid stumbled outside into the sunlight.

Leo sucked in his breath. The boy looked exactly like him. 'You see?' asked Ghost Hazel.

Fake Leo was the same height as Regular Leo – meaning he was short. He had the same nervous energy – tapping his fingers against his trousers, brushing at his white cotton shirt, adjusting the jockey cap on his curly brown hair. (Really, Leo thought, short people should not wear jockey caps unless they were jockeys.) Fake Leo had the same devilish smile that greeted Regular Leo whenever he looked in a mirror – an expression that made teachers immediately shout, 'Don't even think about it!' and plop him in the front row.

Apparently, Fake Leo had just been scolded by a teacher. He was holding a dunce cap – an honest-to-goodness cardboard cone that said DUNCE. Leo thought those were something you only saw in cartoons.

He could understand why Fake Leo wasn't wearing it. Bad enough to look like a jockey. With that cone on his head, he would've looked like a gnome.

Some kids backed up when Fake Leo burst onto the scene. Others nudged each other and ran towards him like they were expecting a show.

Meanwhile, Flathead Rufus was still trying to punk Hazel out of a diamond, oblivious to Fake Leo's arrival.

'Come on, girl.' Rufus loomed over Hazel with his fists clenched. 'Give it!'

Hazel pressed herself against the wall. Suddenly the ground at her feet went *snap*, like a twig breaking. A perfect diamond the size of a pistachio glittered between her feet.

'Ha!' Rufus barked when he saw it. He started to lean down, but Hazel yelped, 'No, please!' as if she was genuinely concerned for the big goon.

That's when Fake Leo strolled over.

Here it comes, Leo thought. Fake Leo is gonna bust out some Coach Hedge-style jujitsu and save the day.

Instead, Fake Leo put the top of the dunce cap to his mouth like a megaphone and yelled, 'CUT!'

He said it with such authority all the other kids momentarily froze. Even Rufus straightened and backed away in confusion.

One of the little boys snickered under his breath: 'Hammy Sammy.'

Sammy . . . Leo shivered. *Who the heck* was *this kid?*

Sammy/Fake Leo stormed up to Rufus with his dunce cap in his hand, looking angry. 'No, no, no!' he announced, waving his free hand wildly at the other kids, who were gathering to watch the entertainment.

Sammy turned to Hazel. 'Miss Lamarr, your line is . . .' Sammy looked around in exasperation. 'Script! What is Hedy Lamarr's line?'

'"*No, please, you villain!*"' one of the boys called out.

'Thank you!' Sammy said. 'Miss Lamarr, you're supposed to say, *No, please, you villain!* And you, Clark Gable –'

The whole courtyard burst into laughter. Leo vaguely knew Clark Gable was an old-timey actor, but he didn't know much else. Apparently, though, the idea that Flathead Rufus could be Clark Gable was hilarious to the kids.

'Mr Gable –'

'No!' one of the girls cried. 'Make him Gary Cooper.'

More laughter. Rufus looked as if he were about to blow a valve. He balled his fists like he wanted to hit somebody, but he couldn't attack the entire school. He clearly hated being laughed at, but his slow little mind couldn't quite work out what Sammy was up to.

Leo nodded in appreciation. Sammy *was* like him. Leo had done the same kind of stuff to bullies for years.

'Right!' Sammy yelled imperiously. 'Mr Cooper, you say, *Oh, but the diamond is mine, my treacherous darling!* And then you scoop up the diamond like this!'

'Sammy, no!' Hazel protested, but Sammy snatched up the stone and slipped it into his pocket in one smooth move.

He wheeled on Rufus. 'I want emotion! I want the ladies

in the audience swooning! Ladies, did Mr Cooper make you swoon just now?'

'No,' several of them called back.

'There, you see?' Sammy cried. 'Now, from the top!' he yelled into his dunce cap. 'Action!'

Rufus was just starting to get over his confusion. He stepped towards Sammy and said, 'Valdez, I'm gonna –'

The bell rang. Kids swarmed towards the doors. Sammy pulled Hazel out of the way as the little ones – who acted like they were on Sammy's payroll – herded Rufus along with them so he was carried inside on a tide of kindergartners.

Soon Sammy and Hazel were alone except for the ghosts.

Sammy scooped up Hazel's smashed lunch, made a show of dusting off the canvas bag and presented it to her with a deep bow, as if it were her crown. 'Miss Lamarr.'

Hazel from the past took her ruined lunch. She looked like she was about to cry, but Leo couldn't tell if that was from relief or misery or admiration. 'Sammy . . . Rufus is going to kill you.'

'Ah, he knows better than to tangle with me.' Sammy plopped the dunce cap on top of his jockey cap. He stood up straight and stuck out his scrawny chest. The dunce cap fell off.

Hazel laughed. 'You are ridiculous.'

'Why, thank you, Miss Lamarr.'

'You're welcome, *my treacherous darling.*'

Sammy's smile wavered. The air became uncomfortably charged. Hazel stared at the ground. 'You shouldn't have touched that diamond. It's dangerous.'

'Ah, come on,' Sammy said. 'Not for me!'

Hazel studied him warily, like she wanted to believe it. 'Bad things might happen. You shouldn't –'

'I won't sell it,' Sammy said. 'I promise! I'll just keep it as a token of your flavour.'

Hazel forced a smile. 'I think you mean *token of my favour*.'

'There you are! We should get going. It's time for our next scene: *Hedy Lamarr nearly dies of boredom in English class*.'

Sammy held out his elbow like a gentleman, but Hazel pushed him away playfully. 'Thanks for being there, Sammy.'

'Miss Lamarr, I will *always* be there for you!' he said brightly. The two of them raced back into the schoolhouse.

Leo felt more like a ghost than ever. Maybe he had actually been an eidolon his whole life, because this kid he'd just seen should have been the *real* Leo. He was smarter, cooler and funnier. He flirted so well with Hazel that he had obviously stolen her heart.

No wonder Hazel had looked at Leo so strangely when they first met. No wonder she had said *Sammy* with so much feeling. But Leo wasn't Sammy, any more than Flathead Rufus was Clark Gable.

'Hazel,' he said. 'I – I don't –'

The schoolyard dissolved into a different scene.

Hazel and Leo were still ghosts, but now they stood in front of a rundown house next to a drainage ditch overgrown with weeds. A clump of banana trees drooped in the yard. Perched on the steps, an old-fashioned radio played *conjunto* music, and on the shaded porch, sitting in a rocking chair, a skinny old man gazed at the horizon.

'Where *are* we?' Hazel asked. She was still only vapour, but her voice was full of alarm. 'This isn't from my life!'

Leo felt as if his ghostly self was thickening, becoming more real. This place seemed strangely familiar.

'It's Houston,' he realized. 'I know this view. That drainage ditch . . . This is my mom's old neighbourhood, where she grew up. Hobby Airport is over that way.'

'This is *your* life?' Hazel said. 'I don't understand! How –?'

'You're asking me?' Leo demanded.

Suddenly the old man murmured, 'Ah, Hazel . . .'

A shock went up Leo's spine. The old man's eyes were still fixed on the horizon. How did he know they were here?

'I guess we ran out of time,' the old man continued dreamily. 'Well . . .'

He didn't finish the thought.

Hazel and Leo stayed very still. The old man made no further sign that he saw them or heard them. It dawned on Leo that the guy had been talking to himself. But then why had he said Hazel's name?

He had leathery skin, curly white hair and gnarled hands, like he'd spent a lifetime working in a machine shop. He wore a pale yellow shirt, spotless and clean, with grey slacks and suspenders and polished black shoes.

Despite his age, his eyes were sharp and clear. He sat with a kind of quiet dignity. He looked at peace – amused, even, like he was thinking, *Dang, I lived this long? Cool!*

Leo was pretty sure he had never seen this man before.

So why did he seem familiar? Then he realized the man was tapping his fingers on the arm of his chair, but the tapping wasn't random. He was using Morse code, just like Leo's mother used to do with him . . . and the old man was tapping the same message: *I love you.*

The screen door opened. A young woman came out. She wore jeans and a turquoise blouse. Her hair was cut in a short black wedge. She was pretty, but not delicate. She had well-muscled arms and calloused hands. Like the old man's, her brown eyes glinted with amusement. In her arms was a baby, wrapped in a blue blanket.

'Look, *mijo*,' she said to the baby. 'This is your *bisabuelo*. *Bisabuelo*, you want to hold him?'

When Leo heard her voice, he sobbed.

It was his mother – younger than he remembered her, but very much alive. That meant the baby in her arms . . .

The old man broke into a huge grin. He had perfect teeth, as white as his hair. His face crinkled with smile lines. 'A boy! *Mi bebito*, Leo!'

'Leo?' Hazel whispered. 'That – that's you? What is *bisabuelo*?'

Leo couldn't find his voice. *Great-grandfather*, he wanted to say.

The old man took baby Leo in his arms, chuckling with appreciation and tickling the baby's chin – and Ghost Leo finally realized what he was seeing.

Somehow, Hazel's power to revisit the past had found the one event that connected both of their lives – where Leo's time line touched Hazel's.

This old man . . .

'Oh . . .' Hazel seemed to realize who he was at the same moment. Her voice became very small, on the verge of tears. 'Oh, Sammy, no . . .'

'Ah, little Leo,' said Sammy Valdez, aged well into his seventies. 'You'll have to be my stunt double, eh? That's what they call it, I think. Tell her for me. I hoped I would be alive, but, *ay*, the curse won't have it!'

Hazel sobbed. 'Gaia . . . Gaia told me that he died of a heart attack, in the 1960s. But this isn't – this can't be . . .'

Sammy Valdez kept talking to the baby, while Leo's mother, Esperanza, looked on with a pained smile – perhaps a little worried that Leo's *bisabuelo* was rambling, a little sad that he was speaking nonsense.

'That lady, Doña Callida, she warned me.' Sammy shook his head sadly. 'She said Hazel's great danger would not happen in my lifetime. But I promised I would be there for her. You will have to tell her I'm sorry, Leo. Help her if you can.'

'*Bisabuelo*,' Esperanza said, 'you must be tired.'

She extended her arms to take the baby, but the old man cuddled him a moment longer. Baby Leo seemed perfectly fine with it.

'Tell her I'm sorry I sold the diamond, eh?' Sammy said. 'I broke my promise. When she disappeared in Alaska . . . ah, so long ago, I finally used that diamond, moved to Texas as I always dreamed. I started my machine shop. Started my family! It was a good life, but Hazel was right. The diamond came with a curse. I never saw her again.'

'Oh, Sammy,' Hazel said. 'No, a curse didn't keep me away. I *wanted* to come back. I died!'

The old man didn't seem to hear. He smiled down at the baby, and kissed him on the head. 'I give you my blessing, Leo. First male great-grandchild! I have a feeling you are special, like Hazel was. You are more than a regular baby, eh? You will carry on for me. You will see her some day. Tell her hello for me.'

'*Bisabuelo*,' Esperanza said, a little more insistently.

'Yes, yes.' Sammy chuckled. '*El viejo loco* rambles on. I am tired, Esperanza. You are right. But I'll rest soon. It's been a good life. Raise him well, *nieta*.'

The scene faded.

Leo was standing on the deck of the *Argo II*, holding Hazel's hand. The sun had gone down, and the ship was lit only by bronze lanterns. Hazel's eyes were puffy from crying.

What they'd seen was too much. The whole ocean heaved under them, and now for the first time Leo felt as if they were totally adrift.

'Hello, Hazel Levesque,' he said, his voice gravelly.

Her chin trembled. She turned away and opened her mouth to speak, but, before she could, the ship lurched to one side.

'Leo!' Coach Hedge yelled.

Festus whirred in alarm and blew flames into the night sky. The ship's bell rang.

'Those monsters you were worried about?' Hedge shouted. 'One of 'em found us!'

XXIII

LEO

LEO DESERVED A DUNCE CAP.

If he'd been thinking straight, he would've switched the ship's detection system from radar to sonar as soon as they left Charleston Harbor. *That's* what he had forgotten. He'd designed the hull to resonate every few seconds, sending waves through the Mist and alerting Festus to any nearby monsters, but it only worked in one mode at a time: water or air.

He'd been so rattled by the Romans, then the storm, then Hazel, that he had completely forgotten. Now, a monster was right underneath them.

The ship tilted to starboard. Hazel gripped the rigging. Hedge yelled, 'Valdez, which button blows up monsters? Take the helm!'

Leo climbed the tilting deck and managed to grab the port rail. He started clambering sideways towards the helm, but when he saw the monster surface he forgot how to move.

The thing was the length of their ship. In the moonlight,

it looked like a cross between a giant shrimp and a cockroach, with a pink chitinous shell, a flat crayfish tail and millipede-type legs undulating hypnotically as the monster scraped against the hull of the *Argo II*.

Its head surfaced last – the slimy pink face of an enormous catfish with glassy dead eyes, a gaping toothless maw and a forest of tentacles sprouting from each nostril, making the bushiest nose beard Leo had ever had the displeasure to behold.

Leo remembered special Friday night dinners he and his mom used to share at a local seafood restaurant in Houston. They would eat shrimp and catfish. The idea now made him want to throw up.

'Come on, Valdez!' Hedge yelled. 'Take the wheel so I can get my baseball bat!'

'A bat's not going to help,' Leo said, but he made his way towards the helm.

Behind him, the rest of his friends stumbled up the stairs. Percy yelled, 'What's going – Gah! Shrimpzilla!'

Frank ran to Hazel's side. She was clutching the rigging, still dazed from her flashback, but she gestured that she was all right.

The monster rammed the ship again. The hull groaned. Annabeth, Piper and Jason tumbled to starboard and almost rolled overboard.

Leo reached the helm. His hands flew across the controls. Over the intercom, Festus clacked and clicked about leaks belowdecks, but the ship didn't seem to be in danger of sinking – at least not yet.

Leo toggled the oars. They could convert into spears, which should be enough to drive the creature away. Unfortunately, they were jammed. Shrimpzilla must have knocked them out of alignment, and the monster was in spitting distance, which meant that Leo couldn't use the ballistae without setting the *Argo II* on fire as well.

'How did it get so close?' Annabeth shouted, pulling herself up on one of the rail shields.

'I don't know!' Hedge snarled. He looked around for his bat, which had rolled across the quarterdeck.

'I'm stupid!' Leo scolded himself. 'Stupid, stupid! I forgot the sonar!'

The ship tilted further to starboard. Either the monster was trying to give them a hug, or it was about to capsize them.

'Sonar?' Hedge demanded. 'Pan's pipes, Valdez! Maybe if you hadn't been staring into Hazel's eyes, holding hands for so long –'

'*What?*' Frank yelped.

'It wasn't like that!' Hazel protested.

'It doesn't matter!' Piper said. 'Jason, can you call some lightning?'

Jason struggled to his feet. 'I –' He only managed to shake his head. Summoning the storm earlier had taken too much out of him. Leo doubted the poor guy could pop a spark plug in the shape he was in.

'Percy!' Annabeth said. 'Can you *talk* to that thing? Do you know what it is?'

The son of the sea god shook his head, clearly mystified. 'Maybe it's just curious about the ship. Maybe –'

The monster's tendrils lashed across the deck so fast Leo didn't even have time to yell, *Look out!*

One slammed Percy in the chest and sent him crashing down the steps. Another wrapped around Piper's legs and dragged her, screaming, towards the rail. Dozens more tendrils curled around the masts, encircling the crossbows and ripping down the rigging.

'Nose-hair attack!' Hedge snatched up his bat and leaped into action, but his hits just bounced harmlessly off the tendrils.

Jason drew his sword. He tried to free Piper, but he was still weak. His gold blade cut through the tendrils with no problem, but, faster than he could sever them, more took their place.

Annabeth unsheathed her dagger. She ran through the forest of tentacles, dodging and stabbing at whatever target she could find. Frank pulled out his bow. He fired over the side at the creature's body, lodging arrows in the chinks of its shell, but that only seemed to annoy the monster. It bellowed, and rocked the ship. The mast creaked like it might snap off.

They needed more firepower, but they couldn't use ballistae. They needed to deliver a blast that wouldn't destroy the ship. But how . . .?

Leo's eyes fixed on a supply crate next to Hazel's feet.

'Hazel!' he yelled. 'That box! Open it!'

She hesitated, then saw the box he meant. The label read: WARNING. DO NOT OPEN.

'Open it!' Leo yelled again. 'Coach, take the wheel! Turn us towards the monster, or we'll capsize.'

Hedge danced through the tentacles with his nimble goat hooves, smashing away with gusto. He bounded towards the helm and took the controls.

'Hope you got a plan!' he shouted.

'A bad one.' Leo raced towards the mast.

The monster pushed against the *Argo II*. The deck lurched to forty-five degrees. Despite everyone's efforts, the tentacles were just too numerous to fight. They seemed able to elongate as much as they wanted. Soon they'd have the *Argo II* completely entangled. Percy hadn't appeared from below. The others were fighting for their lives against nose hair.

'Frank!' Leo called as he ran towards Hazel. 'Buy us some time! Can you turn into a shark or something?'

Frank glanced over, scowling, and in that moment a tentacle slammed into the big guy, knocking him overboard.

Hazel screamed. She'd opened the supply box and almost dropped the two glass vials she was holding.

Leo caught them. Each was the size of an apple, and the liquid inside glowed poisonous green. The glass was warm to the touch. Leo's chest felt like it might implode from guilt. He'd just distracted Frank and possibly got him killed, but he couldn't think about it. He had to save the ship.

'Come on!' He handed Hazel one of the vials. 'We can kill the monster – and save Frank!'

He hoped he wasn't lying. Getting to the port rail was more like rock climbing than walking, but finally they made it.

'What is this stuff?' Hazel gasped, cradling her glass vial.

'Greek fire!'

Her eyes widened. 'Are you *crazy*? If these break, we'll burn the whole ship!'

'Its mouth!' Leo said. 'Just chuck it down its –'

Suddenly Leo was crushed against Hazel, and the world turned sideways. As they were lifted into the air, he realized they'd been wrapped together in a tentacle. Leo's arms were free, but it was all he could do to keep hold of his Greek fire vial. Hazel struggled. Her arms were pinned, which meant at any moment the vial trapped between them might break . . . and that would be extremely bad for their health.

They rose ten feet, twenty feet, thirty feet above the monster. Leo caught a glimpse of his friends in a losing battle, yelling and slashing at the monster's nose hairs. He saw Coach Hedge struggling to keep the ship from capsizing. The sea was dark, but in the moonlight he thought he saw a glistening object floating near the monster – maybe the unconscious body of Frank Zhang.

'Leo,' Hazel gasped, 'I can't – my arms –'

'Hazel,' he said. 'Do you trust me?'

'No!'

'Me neither,' Leo admitted. 'When this thing drops us, hold your breath. Whatever you do, try to chuck your vial as far *away* from the ship as possible.'

'Why – why would it drop us?'

Leo stared down at the monster's head. This would be a tough shot, but he had no choice. He raised the vial in his left hand. He pressed his right hand against the tentacle and summoned fire to his palm – a narrowly focused, white-hot burst.

That got the creature's attention. A tremble went all the way down the tentacle as its flesh blistered under Leo's touch. The monster raised its maw, bellowing in pain, and Leo threw his Greek fire straight down its throat.

After that, things got fuzzy. Leo felt the tentacle release them. They fell. He heard a muffled explosion and saw a green flash of light inside the giant pink lampshade of the monster's body. The water hit Leo's face like a brick wrapped in sandpaper, and he sank into darkness. He clamped his mouth shut, trying not to breathe, but he could feel himself losing consciousness.

Through the sting of the salt water, he thought he saw the hazy silhouette of the ship's hull above – a dark oval surrounded by a green fiery corona, but he couldn't tell if the ship was actually on fire.

Killed by a giant shrimp, Leo thought bitterly. *At least let the* Argo II *survive. Let my friends be okay.*

His vision began to dim. His lungs burned.

Just as he was about to give up, a strange face hovered over him – a man who looked like Chiron, their trainer back at Camp Half-Blood. He had the same curly hair, shaggy beard and intelligent eyes – a look somewhere between wild hippie and fatherly professor, except this man's skin was the colour of a lima bean. The man silently held up a dagger. His expression was grim and reproachful, as if to say: *Now, hold still, or I can't kill you properly.*

Leo blacked out.

• • •

When Leo woke, he wondered if he was a ghost in another flashback, because he was floating weightlessly. His eyes slowly adjusted to the dim light.

'About time.' Frank's voice had too much reverb, like he was speaking through several layers of plastic wrap.

Leo sat up . . . or rather he drifted upright. He was underwater, in a cave about the size of a two-car garage. Phosphorescent moss covered the ceiling, bathing the room in a blue-and-green glow. The floor was a carpet of sea urchins, which would have been uncomfortable to walk on, so Leo was glad he was floating. He didn't understand how he could be breathing with no air.

Frank levitated nearby in meditation position. With his chubby face and his grumpy expression, he looked like a Buddha who'd achieved enlightenment and wasn't thrilled about it.

The only exit to the cave was blocked by a massive abalone shell – its surface glistening in pearl and rose and turquoise. If this cave was a prison, at least it had an awesome door.

'Where are we?' Leo asked. 'Where is everyone else?'

'*Everyone?*' Frank grumbled. 'I don't know. As far as I can tell, it's just you and me and Hazel down here. The fish-horse guys took Hazel about an hour ago, leaving me with you.'

Frank's tone made it obvious he didn't approve of those arrangements. He didn't look injured, but Leo realized that he no longer had his bow or quiver. In a panic, Leo patted his waist. His tool belt was gone.

'They searched us,' Frank said. 'Took anything that could be a weapon.'

'Who?' Leo demanded. 'Who are these fish-horse –?'

'Fish-horse guys,' Frank clarified, which wasn't very clear. 'They must have grabbed us when we fell in the ocean and dragged us . . . wherever this is.'

Leo remembered the last thing he'd seen before he passed out – the lima-bean-coloured face of the bearded man with the dagger. 'The shrimp monster. The *Argo II* – is the ship okay?'

'I don't know,' Frank said darkly. 'The others might be in trouble or hurt, or – or worse. But I guess you care more about your ship than your friends.'

Leo felt like his face had just hit the water again. 'What kind of stupid thing –?'

Then he realized why Frank was so angry: the flashback. Things had happened so fast with the monster attack that Leo had almost forgotten. Coach Hedge had made that stupid comment about Leo and Hazel holding hands and gazing into each other's eyes. It probably hadn't helped that Leo had got Frank knocked overboard right after that.

Suddenly Leo found it hard to meet Frank's gaze.

'Look, man . . . I'm sorry I got us into this mess. I totally jacked things up.' He took a deep breath, which felt surprisingly normal, considering he was underwater. 'Me and Hazel holding hands . . . it's not what you think. She was showing me this flashback from her past, trying to figure out my connection with Sammy.'

Frank's angry expression started to unknot, replaced by curiosity. 'Did she . . . did you figure it out?'

'Yeah,' Leo said. 'Well, sort of. We didn't get a chance to

talk about it afterwards because of Shrimpzilla, but Sammy was my great-grandfather.'

He told Frank what they'd seen. The weirdness hadn't fully registered yet, but now, trying to explain it aloud, Leo could hardly believe it. Hazel had been sweet on his *bisabuelo*, a guy who had died when Leo was a baby. Leo hadn't made the connection before, but he had a vague memory of older family members calling his grandfather Sam Junior. Which meant Sam Senior was Sammy, Leo's *bisabuelo*. At some point, Tía Callida – Hera herself – had talked with Sammy, consoling him and giving him a glimpse into the future, which meant that Hera had been shaping Leo's life generations before he was even born. If Hazel had stayed in the 1940s, if she'd married Sammy, Leo might've been her great-grandson.

'Oh, man,' Leo said when he had finished the story. 'I don't feel so good. But I swear on the Styx that's what we saw.'

Frank had the same expression as the monster catfish head – wide glassy eyes and an open mouth. 'Hazel . . . Hazel liked your *great-grandfather*? That's why she likes you?'

'Frank, I know this is weird. *Believe* me. But I don't like Hazel – not *that* way. I'm not moving in on your girl.'

Frank knitted his eyebrows. 'No?'

Leo hoped he wasn't blushing. Truthfully, he had no idea how he felt about Hazel. She was awesome and cute, and Leo had a weakness for awesome cute girls. But the flashback had complicated his feelings *a lot*.

Besides, his ship was in trouble.

I guess you care more about your ship than your friends, Frank had said.

That wasn't true, was it? Leo's dad, Hephaestus, had admitted once that he wasn't good with organic life forms. And, yes, Leo had always been more comfortable with machines than people. But he *did* care about his friends. Piper and Jason . . . he'd known them the longest, but the others were important to him, too. Even Frank. They were like family.

The problem was it had been so long since Leo had *had* a family he couldn't even remember how it felt. Sure, last winter he'd become senior counsellor of Hephaestus cabin, but most of his time had been spent building the ship. He liked his cabin mates. He knew how to work with them – but did he really know them?

If Leo had a family, it was the demigods on the *Argo II* – and maybe Coach Hedge, which Leo would never admit aloud.

You will always be the outsider, warned Nemesis's voice, but Leo tried to push that thought aside.

'Right, so . . .' He looked around him. 'We need to make a plan. How are we breathing? If we're under the ocean, shouldn't we be crushed by the water pressure?'

Frank shrugged. 'Fish-horse magic, I guess. I remember the green guy touching my head with the point of a dagger. Then I could breathe.'

Leo studied the abalone door. 'Can you bust us out? Turn into a hammerhead shark or something?'

Frank shook his head glumly. 'My shape-shifting doesn't

work. I don't know why. Maybe they cursed me, or maybe I'm too messed up to focus.'

'Hazel could be in trouble,' Leo said. 'We've got to get out of here.'

He swam to the door and ran his fingers along the abalone. He couldn't feel any kind of latch or other mechanism. Either the door could only be opened by magic, or sheer force was required – neither of which was Leo's speciality.

'I've already tried,' Frank said. 'Even if we get out, we have no weapons.'

'Hmm . . .' Leo held up his hand. 'I wonder.'

He concentrated, and fire flickered over his fingers. For a split second, Leo was excited, because he hadn't expected it to work underwater. Then his plan started working a little too well. Fire raced up his arm and over his body until he was completely shrouded in a thin veil of flame. He tried to breathe, but he was inhaling pure heat.

'Leo!' Frank flailed backwards like he was falling off a bar stool. Instead of racing to Leo's aid, he hugged the wall to get as far away as possible.

Leo forced himself to stay calm. He understood what was going on. The fire itself couldn't hurt him. He willed the flames to die and counted to five. He took a shallow breath. He had oxygen again.

Frank stopped trying to merge with the cave wall. 'You're . . . you're okay?'

'Yeah,' Leo grumbled. 'Thanks for the assist.'

'I – I'm sorry.' Frank looked so horrified and ashamed

it was hard for Leo to stay mad at him. 'I just . . . what happened?'

'Clever magic,' Leo said. 'There's a thin layer of oxygen around us, like an extra skin. Must be self-regenerating. That's how we're breathing and staying dry. The oxygen gave the fire fuel – except the fire also suffocated me.'

'I really don't . . .' Frank gulped. 'I don't like that fire summoning you do.' He started getting cosy with the wall again.

Leo didn't mean to, but he couldn't help laughing. 'Man, I'm not going to attack you.'

'Fire,' Frank repeated, like that one word explained everything.

Leo remembered what Hazel had said – that his fire made Frank nervous. He'd seen the discomfort in Frank's face before, but Leo hadn't taken it seriously. Frank seemed *way* more powerful and scary than Leo was.

Now it occurred to him that Frank might have had a bad experience with fire. Leo's own mom had died in a machine-shop blaze. Leo had been blamed for it. He'd grown up being called a freak, an arsonist, because whenever he got angry things burned.

'Sorry I laughed,' he said, and he meant it. 'My mom died in a fire. I understand being afraid of it. Did, uh . . . did something like that happen with you?'

Frank seemed to be weighing up how much to say. 'My house . . . my grandmother's place. It burned down. But it's more than that . . .' He stared at the sea urchins on the floor. 'Annabeth said I could trust the crew. Even you.'

'Even me, huh?' Leo wondered how *that* had come up in conversation. 'Wow, high praise.'

'My weakness . . .' Frank started, like the words cut his mouth. 'There's this piece of firewood –'

The abalone door rolled open.

Leo turned and found himself face to face with Lima Bean Man, who wasn't actually a man at all. Now that Leo could see him clearly, the guy was by far the weirdest creature he'd ever met, and that was saying a lot.

From the waist up, he was more or less human – a thin, bare-chested dude with a dagger in his belt and a band of seashells strapped across his chest like a bandolier. His skin was green, his beard scraggly brown, and his longish hair was tied back in a seaweed bandanna. A pair of lobster claws stuck up from his head like horns, turning and snapping at random.

Leo decided he didn't look so much like Chiron. He looked more like the poster Leo's mom used to keep in her workspace – that old Mexican bandit Pancho Villa, except with seashells and lobster horns.

From the waist down, the guy was more complicated. He had the forelegs of a blue-green horse, sort of like a centaur, but towards the back his horse body morphed into a long fishy tail about ten feet long, with a rainbow-coloured, V-shaped tail fin.

Now Leo understood what Frank meant about fish-horse guys.

'I am Bythos,' said the green man. 'I will interrogate Frank Zhang.'

His voice was calm and firm, leaving no room for debate.

'Why did you capture us?' Leo demanded. 'Where's Hazel?'

Bythos narrowed his eyes. His expression seemed to say: *Did this tiny creature just talk to me?* 'You, Leo Valdez, will go with my brother.'

'Your brother?'

Leo realized that a much larger figure was looming behind Bythos, with a shadow so wide it filled the entire cave entrance.

'Yes,' Bythos said with a dry smile. 'Try not to make Aphros mad.'

XXIV

LEO

APHROS LOOKED LIKE HIS BROTHER, except he was blue instead of green and much, much bigger. He had Arnold-as-Terminator abs and arms, and a square, brutish head. A huge Conan-approved sword was strapped across his back. Even his hair was bigger – a massive globe of blue-black frizz so thick that his lobster claw horns appeared to be drowning as they tried to swim their way to the surface.

'Is that why they named you Aphros?' Leo asked as they glided down the path from the cave. 'Because of the Afro?'

Aphros scowled. 'What do you mean?'

'Nothing,' Leo said quickly. At least he would never have trouble remembering which fish dude was which. 'So what *are* you guys, exactly?'

'Ichthyocentaurs,' Aphros said, like it was a question he was tired of answering.

'Uh, icky what?'

'Fish centaurs. We are the half brothers of Chiron.'

'Oh, he's a friend of mine!'

Aphros narrowed his eyes. 'The one called Hazel told us this, but we will determine the truth. Come.'

Leo didn't like the sound of *determine the truth*. It made him think of torture racks and red-hot pokers.

He followed the fish centaur through a massive forest of kelp. Leo could've darted to one side and got lost in the plants pretty easily, but he didn't try. For one thing, he figured Aphros could travel much faster in the water, and the guy might be able to shut off the magic that let Leo move and breathe. Inside or outside the cave, Leo was just as much a captive.

Also, Leo had no clue where he was.

They drifted between rows of kelp as tall as apartment buildings. The green-and-yellow plants swayed weightlessly, like columns of helium balloons. High above, Leo saw a smudge of white that might have been the sun.

He guessed that meant they'd been here overnight. Was the *Argo II* all right? Had it sailed on without them, or were their friends still searching?

Leo couldn't even be sure how deep they were. Plants could grow here – so not *too* deep, right? Still, he knew he couldn't just swim for the surface. He'd heard about people who ascended too quickly and developed nitrogen bubbles in their blood. Leo wanted to avoid carbonated blood.

They drifted along for maybe half a mile. Leo was tempted to ask where Aphros was taking him, but the big sword strapped to the centaur's back sort of discouraged conversation.

Finally the kelp forest opened up. Leo gasped. They were

standing (swimming, whatever) at the summit of a high underwater hill. Below them stretched an entire town of Greek-style buildings on the seafloor.

The roofs were tiled with mother-of-pearl. The gardens were filled with coral and sea anemones. Hippocampi grazed in a field of seaweed. A team of Cyclopes was placing the domed roof on a new temple, using a blue whale as a crane. And swimming through the streets, hanging out in the courtyards, practising combat with tridents and swords in the arena, were dozens of mermen and mermaids – honest-to-goodness fish-people.

Leo had seen a lot of crazy stuff, but he had always thought merpeople were silly fictional creatures, like Smurfs or Muppets.

There was nothing silly or cute about these merpeople, though. Even from a distance, they looked fierce and not at all human. Their eyes glowed yellow. They had sharklike teeth and leathery skin in colours ranging from coral red to ink black.

'It's a training camp,' Leo realized. He looked at Aphros in awe. 'You train heroes, the same way Chiron does?'

Aphros nodded, a glint of pride in his eyes. 'We have trained all the famous mer-heroes! Name a mer-hero, and we have trained him or her!'

'Oh, sure,' Leo said. 'Like . . . um, the Little Mermaid?'

Aphros frowned. 'Who? No! Like Triton, Glaucus, Weissmuller and Bill!'

'Oh.' Leo had no idea who any of those people were. 'You trained Bill? Impressive.'

'Indeed!' Aphros pounded his chest. 'I trained Bill myself. A great merman.'

'You teach combat, I guess.'

Aphros threw up his hands in exasperation. 'Why does everyone assume that?'

Leo glanced at the massive sword on the fish-guy's back. 'Uh, I don't know.'

'I teach music and poetry!' Aphros said. 'Life skills! Homemaking! These are important for heroes.'

'Absolutely.' Leo tried to keep a straight face. 'Sewing? Cookie baking?'

'Yes. I'm glad you understand. Perhaps later, if I don't have to kill you, I will share my brownie recipe.' Aphros gestured behind him contemptuously. 'My brother Bythos – *he* teaches combat.'

Leo wasn't sure whether he felt relieved or insulted that the combat trainer was interrogating Frank, while Leo got the home economics teacher. 'So, great. This is Camp . . . what do you call it? Camp Fish-Blood?'

Aphros frowned. 'I hope that was a joke. This is Camp _____.' He made a sound that was a series of sonar pings and hisses.

'Silly me,' Leo said. 'And, you know, I could really go for some of those brownies! So what do we have to do to get to the *not killing me* stage?'

'Tell me your story,' Aphros said.

Leo hesitated, but not for long. Somehow he sensed that he should tell the truth. He started at the beginning – how

Hera had been his babysitter and placed him in the flames; how his mother had died because of Gaia, who had identified Leo as a future enemy. He talked about how he had spent his childhood bouncing around in foster homes, until he and Jason and Piper had been taken to Camp Half-Blood. He explained the Prophecy of Seven, the building of the *Argo II* and their quest to reach Greece and defeat the giants before Gaia woke.

As he talked, Aphros drew some wicked-looking metal spikes from his belt. Leo was afraid he had said something wrong, but Aphros pulled some seaweed yarn from his pouch and started knitting. 'Go on,' he urged. 'Don't stop.'

By the time Leo had explained the eidolons, the problem with the Romans and all the troubles the *Argo II* had encountered crossing the United States and embarking from Charleston, Aphros had knitted a complete baby bonnet.

Leo waited while the fish centaur put away his supplies. Aphros's lobster-claw horns kept swimming around in his thick hair, and Leo had to resist the urge to try to rescue them.

'Very well,' Aphros said. 'I believe you.'

'As simple as that?'

'I am quite good at discerning lies. I hear none from you. Your story also fits with what Hazel Levesque told us.'

'Is she –?'

'Of course,' Aphros said. 'She's fine.' He put his fingers to his mouth and whistled, which sounded strange underwater – like a dolphin screaming. 'My people will bring her here shortly. You must understand . . . our location is a carefully guarded secret. You and your friends showed up in a warship, pursued by one of Keto's sea monsters. We did not know whose side you were on.'

'Is the ship all right?'

'Damaged,' Aphros said, 'but not terribly. The skolopendra withdrew after it got a mouthful of fire. Nice touch.'

'Thank you. Skolopendra? Never heard of it.'

'Consider yourself lucky. They are nasty creatures. Keto must really hate you. At any rate, we rescued you and the other two from the creature's tentacles as it retreated into the deep. Your friends are still above, searching for you, but we have obscured their vision. We had to be sure you were not a threat. Otherwise, we would have had to . . . take measures.'

Leo gulped. He was pretty sure *taking measures* did not mean baking extra brownies. And if these guys were so powerful that they could keep their camp hidden from Percy, who had all those Poseidonish water powers, they were not fish dudes to mess with. 'So . . . we can go?'

'Soon,' Aphros promised. 'I must check with Bythos. When he is done talking with your friend Gank –'

'Frank.'

'Frank. When they are done, we will send you back to your ship. And we may have some warnings for you.'

'Warnings?'

'Ah.' Aphros pointed. Hazel emerged from the kelp forest, escorted by two vicious-looking mermaids, who were baring their fangs and hissing. Leo thought Hazel might be in danger. Then he saw she was completely at ease, grinning and talking with her escorts, and Leo realized that the mermaids were laughing.

'Leo!' Hazel paddled towards him. 'Isn't this place amazing?'

They were left alone at the ridge, which must have meant Aphros really did trust them. While the centaur and the mermaids went off to fetch Frank, Leo and Hazel floated above the hill and gazed down at the underwater camp.

Hazel told him how the mermaids had warmed up to her right away. Aphros and Bythos had been fascinated by her story, as they had never met a child of Pluto before. On top of that, they had heard many legends about the horse Arion, and they were amazed that Hazel had befriended him.

Hazel had promised to visit again with Arion. The mermaids had written their phone numbers in waterproof ink on Hazel's arm so that she could keep in touch. Leo didn't even want to ask how mermaids got cell-phone coverage in the middle of the Atlantic.

As Hazel talked, her hair floated around her face in a cloud – like brown earth and gold dust in a miner's pan. She looked very sure of herself and very beautiful – not at all like the shy, nervous girl in that New Orleans schoolyard with her smashed canvas lunch bag at her feet.

'We didn't get to talk,' Leo said. He was reluctant to bring up the subject, but he knew this might be their only chance to be alone. 'I mean about Sammy.'

Her smile faded. 'I know . . . I just need some time to let it sink in. It's strange to think that you and he . . .'

She didn't need to finish the thought. Leo knew exactly how strange it was.

'I'm not sure I can explain this to Frank,' she added. 'About you and me holding hands.'

She wouldn't meet Leo's eyes. Down in the valley, the Cyclopes work crew cheered as the temple roof was set in place.

'I talked to him,' Leo said. 'I told him I wasn't trying to . . . you know. Make trouble between you two.'

'Oh. Good.'

Did she sound disappointed? Leo wasn't sure, and he wasn't sure he wanted to know.

'Frank, um, seemed pretty freaked out when I summoned fire.' Leo explained what had happened in the cave.

Hazel looked stunned. 'Oh, no. That *would* terrify him.'

Her hand went to her denim jacket, like she was checking for something in the inside pocket. She always wore that jacket, or some sort of overshirt, even when it was hot outside. Leo had assumed that she did it out of modesty, or because it was better for horseback riding, like a motorcycle jacket. Now he began to wonder.

His brain shifted into high gear. He remembered what Frank had said about his weakness . . . a piece of firewood. He thought about why this kid would have a fear of fire, and why Hazel would be so attuned to those feelings. Leo thought about some of the stories he'd heard at Camp Half-Blood. For obvious reasons, he tended to pay attention to legends about fire. Now he remembered one he hadn't thought about in months.

'There was an old legend about a hero,' he recalled. 'His lifeline was tied to a stick in a fireplace, and when that piece of wood burned up . . .'

Hazel's expression turned dark. Leo knew he'd struck on the truth.

'Frank has that problem,' he guessed. 'And the piece of firewood . . .' He pointed at Hazel's jacket. 'He gave it to you for safekeeping?'

'Leo, please don't . . . I can't talk about it.'

Leo's instincts as a mechanic kicked in. He started thinking about the properties of wood and the corrosiveness of salt water. 'Is the firewood okay in the ocean like this? Does the layer of air around you protect it?'

'It's fine,' Hazel said. 'The wood didn't even get wet. Besides, it's wrapped up in several layers of cloth and plastic and –' She bit her lip in frustration. 'And I'm not supposed to *talk* about it! Leo, the point is if Frank seems afraid of you, or uneasy, you've got to understand . . .'

Leo was glad he was floating, because he probably would've been too dizzy to stand. He imagined being in Frank's position, his life so fragile it literally could burn up at any time. He imagined how much trust it would take to give his lifeline – his entire fate – to another person.

Frank had chosen Hazel, obviously. So when he had seen Leo – a guy who could summon fire at will – moving in on his girl . . .

Leo shuddered. No wonder Frank didn't like him. And suddenly Frank's ability to turn into a bunch of different animals didn't seem so awesome – not if it came with a big catch like that.

Leo thought about his least favourite line in the Prophecy of Seven: *To storm or fire the world must fall*. For a long time, he'd figured that Jason or Percy stood for storm – maybe both of them together. Leo was the fire guy. Nobody said that, but it was pretty clear. Leo was one of the wild cards. If he did the wrong thing, the world could fall. No . . . it *must* fall. Leo wondered if Frank and his firewood had something to do with that line. Leo had already made some epic mistakes. It would be so easy for him to accidentally send Frank Zhang up in flames.

'There you are!' Bythos's voice made Leo flinch.

Bythos and Aphros floated over with Frank between them, looking pale but okay. Frank studied Hazel and Leo carefully, as if trying to read what they'd been talking about.

'You are free to go,' Bythos said. He opened his saddlebags and returned their confiscated supplies. Leo had never been so glad to fit his tool belt around his waist.

'Tell Percy Jackson not to worry,' Aphros said. 'We have understood your story about the imprisoned sea creatures in Atlanta. Keto and Phorcys must be stopped. We will send a quest of mer-heroes to defeat them and free their captives. Perhaps Cyrus?'

'Or Bill,' Bythos offered.

'Yes! Bill would be perfect,' Aphros agreed. 'At any rate, we are grateful that Percy brought this to our attention.'

'You should talk to him in person,' Leo suggested. 'I mean, son of Poseidon, and all.'

Both fish-centaurs shook their heads solemnly. 'Sometimes it is best not to interact with Poseidon's brood,' Aphros said. 'We are friendly with the sea god, of course, but the politics of undersea deities is . . . complicated. And we value our independence. Nevertheless, tell Percy thank you. We will do what we can to speed you safely across the Atlantic without further interference from Keto's monsters, but be warned: in the ancient sea, the Mare Nostrum, more dangers await.'

Frank sighed. 'Naturally.'

Bythos clapped the big guy on the shoulder. 'You will be fine, Frank Zhang. Keep practising those sealife transformations. The koi fish is good, but try for a Portuguese man-of-war. Remember what I showed you. It's all in the breathing.'

Frank looked mortally embarrassed. Leo bit his lip, determined not to smile.

'And you, Hazel,' Aphros said, 'come visit again, and bring that horse of yours! I know you are concerned about the time you lost, spending the night in our realm. You are worried about your brother, Nico . . .'

Hazel gripped her cavalry sword. 'Is he – do you know where he is?'

Aphros shook his head. 'Not exactly. But when you get closer you should be able to sense his presence. Never fear! You must reach Rome the day after tomorrow if you are to save him, but there is still time. And you *must* save him.'

'Yes,' Bythos agreed. 'He will be essential for your journey. I am not sure how, but I sense it is true.'

Aphros planted his hand on Leo's shoulder. 'As for you, Leo Valdez, stay close to Hazel and Frank when you reach Rome. I sense they will face . . . ah, *mechanical* difficulties that only you can overcome.'

'Mechanical difficulties?' Leo asked.

Aphros smiled as if that was great news. 'And I have gifts for you, the brave navigator of the *Argo II*!'

'I like to think of myself as captain,' Leo said. 'Or supreme commander.'

'Brownies!' Aphros said proudly, shoving an old-fashioned picnic basket into Leo's arms. It was surrounded by a bubble of air, which Leo hoped would keep the brownies from turning into saltwater fudge sludge. 'In this basket you will also find the recipe. Not too much butter! That's the trick. And I've given you a letter of introduction to Tiberinus, the god of the Tiber River. Once you reach Rome, your friend the daughter of Athena will need this.'

'Annabeth . . .' Leo said. 'Okay, but why?'

Bythos laughed. 'She follows the Mark of Athena, doesn't she? Tiberinus can guide her in this quest. He's an ancient, proud god who can be . . . difficult, but letters of introduction are everything to Roman spirits. This will convince Tiberinus to help her. Hopefully.'

'Hopefully,' Leo repeated.

Bythos produced three small pink pearls from his saddlebags. 'And now, off with you, demigods! Good sailing!'

He threw a pearl at each of them in turn, and three shimmering pink bubbles of energy formed around them.

They began to rise through the water. Leo just had time to think: *A hamster ball elevator?* Then he gained speed and rocketed towards the distant glow of the sun above.

XXV

PIPER

PIPER HAD A NEW ENTRY IN her top-ten list of *Times Piper Felt Useless*.

Fighting Shrimpzilla with a dagger and a pretty voice? Not so effective. Then the monster had sunk into the deep and disappeared along with three of her friends, and she'd been powerless to help them.

Afterwards, Annabeth, Coach Hedge and Buford the table rushed around repairing things so that the ship wouldn't sink. Percy, despite being exhausted, searched the ocean for their missing friends. Jason, also exhausted, flew around the rigging like a blond Peter Pan, putting out fires from the second green explosion that had lit up the sky just above the mainmast.

As for Piper, all she could do was stare at her knife Katoptris, trying to locate Leo, Hazel and Frank. The only images that came to her were ones she didn't want to see: three black SUVs driving north from Charleston, packed with Roman demigods, Reyna sitting at the wheel of the lead car. Giant eagles escorted them from above. Every so often, glowing purple spirits in ghostly chariots appeared out of the countryside and fell in behind them, thundering up I-95 towards New York and Camp Half-Blood.

Piper concentrated harder. She saw the nightmarish images she had seen before: the human-headed bull rising from the water, then the dark well-shaped room filling with black water as Jason, Percy and she struggled to stay afloat.

She sheathed Katoptris, wondering how Helen of Troy had stayed sane during the Trojan War if this blade had been her only source of news. Then she remembered that everyone around Helen had been slaughtered by the invading Greek army. Maybe she *hadn't* stayed sane.

By the time the sun rose, none of them had slept. Percy had scoured the seafloor and found nothing. The *Argo II* was no longer in danger of sinking, though without Leo they couldn't do full repairs. The ship was capable of sailing, but no one suggested leaving the area – not without their missing friends.

Piper and Annabeth sent a dream vision to Camp Half-Blood, warning Chiron of what had happened with the Romans at Fort Sumter. Annabeth explained her exchange of words with Reyna. Piper relayed the vision from her knife about the SUVs racing north. The kindly centaur's face seemed to age thirty years during the course of their conversation, but he assured them he would see to the defences of the camp. Tyson, Mrs O'Leary and Ella had arrived safely. If necessary, Tyson could summon an army of Cyclopes to the camp's defence, and Ella and Rachel Dare were already comparing prophecies, trying to learn more about what the future held. The job of the seven demigods aboard the *Argo II*, Chiron reminded them, was to finish the quest and come back safely.

After the Iris-message, the demigods paced the deck in silence, staring at the water and hoping for a miracle.

When it finally came – three giant pink bubbles bursting at the surface off the starboard bow and ejecting Frank, Hazel and Leo – Piper went a little crazy. She cried out with relief and dived straight into the water.

What was she thinking? She didn't take a rope or a life vest or anything. But at the moment she was just so happy that she paddled over to Leo and kissed him on the cheek, which kind of surprised him.

'Miss me?' Leo laughed.

Piper was suddenly furious. 'Where *were* you? How are you guys alive?'

'Long story,' he said. A picnic basket bobbed to the surface next to him. 'Want a brownie?'

Once they got on board and changed into dry clothes (poor Frank had to borrow a pair of too-small jeans from Jason) the crew all gathered on the quarterdeck for a celebratory breakfast – except for Coach Hedge, who grumbled that the atmosphere was getting too cuddly for his tastes and went below to hammer out some dents in the hull. While Leo fussed over his helm controls, Hazel and Frank related the story of the fish-centaurs and their training camp.

'Incredible,' Jason said. 'These are *really* good brownies.'

'That's your only comment?' Piper demanded.

He looked surprised. 'What? I heard the story. Fish-centaurs. Merpeople. Letter of intro to the Tiber River god. Got it. But these brownies –'

'I know,' Frank said, his mouth full. 'Try them with Esther's peach preserves.'

'That,' Hazel said, 'is *incredibly* disgusting.'

'Pass me the jar, man,' Jason said.

Hazel and Piper exchanged a look of total exasperation. *Boys.*

Percy, for his part, wanted to hear every detail about the aquatic camp. He kept coming back to one point: 'They didn't want to meet me?'

'It wasn't that,' Hazel said. 'Just . . . undersea politics, I guess. The merpeople are territorial. The good news is they're taking care of that aquarium in Atlanta. And they'll help protect the *Argo II* as we cross the Atlantic.'

Percy nodded absently. 'But they didn't want to meet me?'

Annabeth swatted his arm. 'Come on, Seaweed Brain! We've got other things to worry about.'

'She's right,' Hazel said. 'After today, Nico has less than two days. The fish-centaurs said we *have* to rescue him. He's essential to the quest somehow.'

She looked around defensively, as if waiting for someone to argue. No one did. Piper tried to imagine what Nico di Angelo was feeling, stuck in a jar with only two pomegranate seeds left to sustain him and no idea whether he would be rescued. It made Piper anxious to reach Rome, even though she had a horrible feeling she was sailing towards her own sort of prison – a dark room filled with water.

'Nico must have information about the Doors of Death,' Piper said. 'We'll save him, Hazel. We can make it in time. Right, Leo?'

'What?' Leo tore his eyes away from the controls. 'Oh, yeah. We should reach the Mediterranean tomorrow morning. Then spend the rest of that day sailing to Rome, or *flying*, if I can get the stabilizer fixed by then . . .'

Jason suddenly looked as though his brownie with peach preserves didn't taste so good. 'Which will put us in Rome on the last possible day for Nico. Twenty-four hours to find him – at most.'

Percy crossed his legs. 'And that's only part of the problem. There's the Mark of Athena, too.'

Annabeth didn't seem happy with the change of topic. She rested her hand on her backpack, which, since they'd left Charleston, she always seemed to have with her.

She opened the bag and brought out a thin bronze disc the diameter of a doughnut. 'This is the map that I found at Fort Sumter. It's . . .'

She stopped abruptly, staring at the smooth bronze surface. 'It's blank!'

Percy took it and examined both sides. 'It wasn't like this earlier?'

'No! I was looking at it in my cabin and . . .' Annabeth muttered under her breath. 'It must be like the Mark of Athena. I can only see it when I'm alone. It won't show itself to other demigods.'

Frank scooted back like the disc might explode. He had

an orange-juice moustache and a brownie-crumb beard that made Piper want to hand him a napkin.

'What did it have on it?' Frank asked nervously. 'And what *is* the Mark of Athena? I still don't get it.'

Annabeth took the disc from Percy. She turned it in the sunlight, but it remained blank. 'The map was hard to read, but it showed a spot on the Tiber River in Rome. I think that's where my quest starts . . . the path I've got to take to follow the Mark.'

'Maybe that's where you meet the river god Tiberinus,' Piper said. 'But what *is* the Mark?'

'The coin,' Annabeth murmured.

Percy frowned. 'What coin?'

Annabeth dug into her pocket and brought out a silver drachma. 'I've been carrying this ever since I saw my mom at Grand Central. It's an Athenian coin.'

She passed it around. While each demigod looked at it, Piper had a ridiculous memory of show-and-tell in elementary school.

'An owl,' Leo noted. 'Well, that makes sense. I guess the branch is an olive branch? But what's this inscription, *AΘE* – Area Of Effect?'

'It's alpha, theta, epsilon,' Annabeth said. 'In Greek it stands for *of the Athenians* . . . or you could read it as *the children of Athena*. It's sort of the Athenian motto.'

'Like SPQR for the Romans,' Piper guessed.

Annabeth nodded. 'Anyway, the Mark of Athena is an owl, just like that one. It appears in fiery red. I've seen it in my dreams. Then twice at Fort Sumter.'

She described what had happened at the fort – the voice

of Gaia, the spiders in the garrison, the Mark burning them away. Piper could tell it wasn't easy for her to talk about.

Percy took Annabeth's hand. 'I should have been there for you.'

'But that's the point,' Annabeth said. '*No one* can be there for me. When I get to Rome, I'll have to strike out on my own. Otherwise, the Mark won't appear. I'll have to follow it to . . . to the source.'

Frank took the coin from Leo. He stared at the owl. '*Giants' bane stands gold and pale, Won with pain from a woven jail.*' He looked up at Annabeth. 'What is it . . . this thing at the source?'

Before Annabeth could answer, Jason spoke up.

'A statue,' he said. 'A statue of Athena. At least . . . that's my guess.'

Piper frowned. 'You said you didn't know.'

'I *don't*. But the more I think about it . . . there's only one artefact that could fit the legend.' He turned to Annabeth. 'I'm sorry. I should have told you everything I've heard, much earlier. But, honestly, I was scared. If this legend is true –'

'I know,' Annabeth said. 'I figured it out, Jason. I don't blame you. But if we manage to save the statue, Greek and Romans together . . . Don't you see? It could heal the rift.'

'Hold on.' Percy made a *time-out* gesture. '*What* statue?'

Annabeth took back the silver coin and slipped it into her pocket. 'The Athena Parthenos,' she said. 'The most famous Greek statue of all time. It was forty feet tall, covered in ivory and gold. It stood in the middle of the Parthenon in Athens.'

The ship went silent, except for the waves lapping against the hull.

'Okay, I'll bite,' Leo said at last. 'What happened to it?'

'It disappeared,' Annabeth said.

Leo frowned. 'How does a forty-foot-tall statue in the middle of the Parthenon just *disappear*?'

'That's a good question,' Annabeth said. 'It's one of the biggest mysteries in history. Some people thought the statue was melted down for its gold or destroyed by invaders. Athens was sacked a number of times. Some thought the statue was carried off –'

'By Romans,' Jason finished. 'At least, that's one theory, and it fits the legend I heard at Camp Jupiter. To break the Greeks' spirit, the Romans carted off the Athena Parthenos when they took over the city of Athens. They hid it in an underground shrine in Rome. The Roman demigods swore it would never see the light of day. They literally *stole* Athena, so she could no longer be the symbol of Greek military power. She became Minerva, a much tamer goddess.'

'And the children of Athena have been searching for the statue ever since,' Annabeth said. 'Most don't know about the legend, but in each generation a few are chosen by the goddess. They're given a coin like mine. They follow the Mark of Athena . . . a kind of magical trail that links them to the statue . . . hoping to find the resting place of the Athena Parthenos and get the statue back.'

Piper watched the two of them – Annabeth and Jason – with quiet amazement. They spoke like a team, without any hostility or blame. The two of them had never really trusted each other. Piper was close enough to both of them to know that. But now . . . if they could discuss such a huge problem so calmly – the ultimate source of Greek/Roman hatred – maybe there was hope for the two camps, after all.

Percy seemed be having similar thoughts, judging from his surprised expression. 'So if we – I mean *you* – find the statue . . . what would we do with it? Could we even *move* it?'

'I'm not sure,' Annabeth admitted. 'But, if we could save it somehow, it could unite the two camps. It could heal my mother of this hatred she's got, tearing her two aspects apart. And maybe . . . maybe the statue has some sort of power that could help us against the giants.'

Piper stared at Annabeth with awe, just starting to appreciate the huge responsibility her friend had taken on. And Annabeth meant to do it alone.

'This could change everything,' Piper said. 'It could end thousands of years of hostility. It might be the key to defeating Gaia. But if we can't help you . . .'

She didn't finish, but the question seemed to hang in the air: *Was saving the statue even possible?*

Annabeth squared her shoulders. Piper knew she must be terrified inside, but she did a good job hiding it.

'I have to succeed,' Annabeth said simply. 'The risk is worth it.'

Hazel twirled her hair pensively. 'I don't like the idea of you risking your life alone, but you're right. We saw what recovering the golden eagle standard did for the Roman legion. If this statue is the most powerful symbol of Athena ever created –'

'It could kick some serious booty,' Leo offered.

Hazel frowned. 'That wasn't the way *I'd* put it, but yes.'

'Except . . .' Percy took Annabeth's hand again. 'No child of Athena has *ever* found it. Annabeth, what's *down* there? What's guarding it? If it's got to do with spiders –?'

'*Won through pain from a woven jail*,' Frank recalled. 'Woven, like webs?'

Annabeth's face turned as white as printer paper. Piper suspected that Annabeth knew what awaited her . . . or at least that she had a very good idea. She was trying to hold down a wave of panic and terror.

'We'll deal with that when we get to Rome,' Piper suggested, putting a little charmspeak in her voice to soothe her friend's nerves. 'It's going to work out. Annabeth is going to kick some serious booty, too. You'll see.'

'Yeah,' Percy said. 'I learned a long time ago: *never* bet against Annabeth.'

Annabeth looked at them both gratefully.

Judging from their half-eaten breakfasts, the others still felt uneasy, but Leo managed to shake them out of it. He pushed a button, and a loud blast of steam exploded from Festus's mouth, making everyone jump.

'Well!' he said. 'Good pep rally, but there's still a ton of things to fix on this ship before we get to the Mediterranean. Please report to Supreme Commander Leo for your superfun list of chores!'

Piper and Jason took charge of cleaning the lower deck, which had been thrown into chaos during the monster attack. Reorganizing sickbay and battening down the storage area took them most of the day, but Piper didn't mind. For one thing, she got to spend time with Jason. For another, last night's explosions had given Piper a healthy respect for Greek fire. She didn't want any loose vials of that stuff rolling through the corridors in the middle of the night.

As they were fixing up the stables, Piper thought about the night Annabeth and Percy had spent down here accidentally. Piper wished that she could talk with Jason all night – just curl up on the stable floor and enjoy being with him. Why didn't *they* get to break the rules?

But Jason wasn't like that. He was hardwired to be a leader and set a good example. Breaking the rules didn't come naturally to him.

No doubt Reyna admired that about him. Piper did, too . . . mostly.

The one time she'd convinced him to be a rebel was back at the Wilderness School, when they had sneaked onto the roof at night to watch a meteor shower. That's where they'd had their first kiss.

Unfortunately, that memory was a trick of the Mist, a magical lie implanted in her head by Hera. Piper and Jason were together *now*, in real life, but their relationship had been founded on an illusion. If Piper tried to get the *real* Jason to sneak out at night, would he do it?

She swept the hay into piles. Jason fixed a broken door on one of the stables. The glass floor hatch glowed from the ocean below – a green expanse of light and shadow that seemed to go down forever. Piper kept glancing over, afraid she'd see a monster's face peeping in, or the water cannibals from her grandfather's old stories, but all she saw was an occasional school of herring.

As she watched Jason work, she admired how easily he did each task, whether it was fixing a door or oiling saddles. It wasn't just his strong arms and his skilful hands, though Piper liked those just fine, but the way he acted so upbeat and confident. He did what needed to be done without complaint. He kept his sense of humour, despite the fact that the guy had to be dead on his feet after not having slept the night before. Piper couldn't blame Reyna for having a crush on him. When it came to work and duty, Jason was Roman to the core.

Piper thought about her mother's tea party in Charleston. She wondered what the goddess had told Reyna a year ago, and why it had changed the way Reyna treated Jason. Had Aphrodite encouraged her to like or dislike Jason?

Piper wasn't sure, but she wished her mom hadn't appeared in Charleston. Regular mothers were embarrassing enough. Godly glamour moms who invited your friends over for tea and guy talk – that was just mortifying.

Aphrodite had paid so much attention to Annabeth and Hazel that it had made Piper uneasy. When her mom got interested in somebody's love life, usually that was a bad sign. It meant trouble was coming. Or, as Aphrodite would say, *twists and turns.*

But, also, Piper was secretly hurt not to have her mother to herself. Aphrodite had barely looked at her. She hadn't said a word about Jason. She hadn't bothered explaining her conversation with Reyna at all.

It was almost as if Aphrodite no longer found Piper interesting. Piper had got her guy. Now it was up to her to make things work, and Aphrodite had moved on to newer gossip as easily as she might toss out an old copy of a tabloid magazine.

All of you are such excellent stories, Aphrodite had said. *I mean, girls.*

Piper hadn't appreciated that, but part of her had thought: *Fine. I don't want to be a story. I want a nice steady life with a nice steady boyfriend.*

If only she knew more about making relationships work. She was supposed to be an expert, being the head counsellor for Aphrodite cabin. Other campers at Camp Half-Blood came to her for advice all the time. Piper had tried to do her best, but with her own boyfriend she was clueless. She was constantly second-guessing herself, reading too much into Jason's expressions, his moods, his offhand comments. Why did it have to be so hard? Why couldn't there be a happily-ever-after ride-into-the-sunset feeling all the time?

'What are you thinking?' Jason asked.

Piper realized she'd been making a sour face. In the reflection of the glass bay doors, she looked like she'd swallowed a teaspoon of salt.

'Nothing,' she said. 'I mean . . . a lot of things. Kind of all at once.'

Jason laughed. The scar on his lip almost disappeared when he smiled. Considering all the stuff he'd been through, it was amazing that he could be in such a good mood.

'It's going to work out,' he promised. 'You said so yourself.'

'Yeah,' Piper agreed. 'Except I was just saying that to make Annabeth feel better.'

Jason shrugged. 'Still, it's true. We're almost to the ancient lands. We've left the Romans behind.'

'And now they're on their way to Camp Half-Blood to attack our friends.'

Jason hesitated, as if it were hard for him to put a positive spin on that. 'Chiron will find a way to stall them. The Romans might take weeks to actually find the camp and plan their attack. Besides, Reyna will do what she can to slow things down. She's still on our side. I know she is.'

'You trust her.' Piper's voice sounded hollow, even to herself.

'Look, Pipes. I told you, you've got nothing to be jealous about.'

'She's beautiful. She's powerful. She's so . . . Roman.'

Jason put down his hammer. He took her hand, which sent a tingle up her arm. Piper's dad had once taken her to the Aquarium of the Pacific and shown her an electric eel. He told her that the eel sent out pulses that shocked and paralysed its prey. Every time Jason looked at her or touched her hand, Piper felt like that.

'*You're* beautiful and powerful,' he said. 'And I don't want you to be Roman. I want you to be Piper. Besides, we're a team, you and me.'

She wanted to believe him. They'd been together, really, for months now. Still, she couldn't get rid of her doubts, any more than Jason could get rid of the SPQR tattoo burned on his forearm.

Above them, the ship's bell rang for dinner.

Jason smirked. 'We'd better get up there. We don't want Coach Hedge tying bells around our necks.'

Piper shuddered. Coach Hedge had threatened to do that after the Percy/Annabeth scandal, so he'd know if anyone sneaked out at night.

'Yeah,' she said regretfully, looking at the glass doors below their feet. 'I guess we need dinner . . . and a good night's sleep.'

XXVI

PIPER

THE NEXT MORNING PIPER WOKE TO a different ship's horn
– a blast so loud it literally shook her out of bed.

She wondered if Leo was pulling another joke. Then
the horn boomed again. It sounded like it was coming from
several hundred yards away – from another vessel.

She rushed to get dressed. By the time she got up on deck,
the others had already gathered – all hastily dressed except
for Coach Hedge, who had pulled the night watch.

Frank's Vancouver Winter Olympics shirt was inside out.
Percy wore pyjama bottoms and a bronze breastplate, which
was an interesting fashion statement. Hazel's hair was all
blown to one side, as though she'd walked through a cyclone;
and Leo had accidentally set himself on fire. His T-shirt was
in charred tatters. His arms were smoking.

About a hundred yards to port, a massive cruise ship glided
past. Tourists waved at them from fifteen or sixteen rows
of balconies. Some smiled and took pictures. None of them

looked surprised to see an Ancient Greek trireme. Maybe the Mist made it look like a fishing boat, or perhaps the cruisers thought the *Argo II* was a tourist attraction.

The cruise ship blew its horn again, and the *Argo II* had a shaking fit.

Coach Hedge plugged his ears. 'Do they have to be so loud?'

'They're just saying hi,' Frank speculated.

'WHAT?' Hedge yelled back.

The ship edged past them, heading out to sea. The tourists kept waving. If they found it strange that the *Argo II* was populated by half-asleep kids in armour and pyjamas and a man with goat legs, they didn't let on.

'Bye!' Leo called, raising his smoking hand.

'Can I man the ballistae?' Hedge asked.

'No,' Leo said through a forced smile.

Hazel rubbed her eyes and looked across the glittering green water. 'Where are – oh . . . Wow.'

Piper followed her gaze and gasped. Without the cruise ship blocking their view, she saw a mountain jutting from the sea less than half a mile to the north. Piper had seen impressive cliffs before. She'd driven Highway 1 along the California coast. She'd even fallen down the Grand Canyon with Jason and flown back up. But neither was as amazing as this massive fist of blinding white rock thrust into the sky. On one side, the limestone cliffs were almost completely sheer, dropping into the sea over a thousand feet below, as near as Piper could figure. On the other side, the mountain sloped in tiers, covered in green forest, so that the whole thing reminded

Piper of a colossal sphinx, worn down over the millennia, with a massive white head and chest, and a green cloak over its back.

'The Rock of Gibraltar,' Annabeth said in awe. 'At the tip of Spain. And over there –' She pointed south, to a more distant stretch of red and ochre hills. 'That must be Africa. We're at the mouth of the Mediterranean.'

The morning was warm, but Piper shivered. Despite the wide stretch of sea in front of them, she felt like she was standing at an impassable barrier. Once in the Mediterranean – the Mare Nostrum – they would be in the ancient lands. If the legends were true, their quest would become ten times more dangerous.

'What now?' she asked. 'Do we just sail in?'

'Why not?' Leo said. 'It's a big shipping channel. Boats go in and out all the time.'

Not triremes full of demigods, Piper thought.

Annabeth gazed at the Rock of Gibraltar. Piper recognized that brooding expression on her friend's face. It almost always meant that she anticipated trouble.

'In the old days,' Annabeth said, 'they called this area the Pillars of Hercules. The Rock was supposed to be one pillar. The other was one of the African mountains. Nobody is sure which one.'

'Hercules, huh?' Percy frowned. 'That guy was like the Starbucks of Ancient Greece. Everywhere you turn – there he is.'

A thunderous *boom* shook the *Argo II*, though Piper wasn't sure where it came from this time. She didn't see any other ships, and the skies were clear.

Her mouth suddenly felt dry. 'So . . . these Pillars of Hercules. Are they dangerous?'

Annabeth stayed focused on the white cliffs, as if waiting for the Mark of Athena to blaze into life. 'For Greeks, the Pillars marked the end of the known world. The Romans said the pillars were inscribed with a Latin warning –'

'*Non plus ultra,*' Percy said.

Annabeth looked stunned. 'Yeah. *Nothing further beyond.* How did you know?'

Percy pointed. 'Because I'm looking at it.'

Directly ahead of them, in the middle of the straits, an island had shimmered into existence. Piper was positive no island had been there before. It was a small hilly mass of land, covered in forests and ringed with white beaches. Not very impressive compared to Gibraltar, but in front of the island, jutting from waves about a hundred yards offshore, were two white Grecian columns as tall as the *Argo*'s masts. Between the columns, huge silver words glittered underwater – maybe an illusion, or maybe inlaid in the sand: *NON PLUS ULTRA.*

'Guys, do I turn around?' Leo asked nervously. 'Or . . .'

No one answered – maybe because, like Piper, they had noticed the figure standing on the beach. As the ship approached the columns, she saw a dark-haired man in purple robes, his arms crossed, staring intently at their ship as if he were expecting them. Piper couldn't tell much else about him from this distance, but, judging from his posture, he wasn't happy.

Frank inhaled sharply. 'Could that be –?'

'Hercules,' Jason said. 'The most powerful demigod of all time.'

The *Argo II* was only a few hundred yards from the columns now.

'Need an answer,' Leo said urgently. 'I can turn, or we can take off. The stabilizers are working again. But I need to know quick –'

'We have to keep going,' Annabeth said. 'I think he's guarding these straits. If that's really Hercules, sailing or flying away wouldn't do any good. He'll want to talk to us.'

Piper resisted the urge to use charmspeak. She wanted to yell at Leo: *Fly! Get us out of here!* Unfortunately, she had a feeling that Annabeth was right. If they wanted to pass into the Mediterranean, they couldn't avoid this meeting.

'Won't Hercules be on our side?' she asked hopefully. 'I mean . . . he's one of us, right?'

Jason grunted. 'He was a son of Zeus, but when he died he became a god. You can never be sure with gods.'

Piper remembered their meeting with Bacchus in Kansas – another god who used to be a demigod. He hadn't been exactly helpful.

'Great,' Percy said. 'Seven of us against Hercules.'

'And a satyr!' Hedge added. 'We can take him.'

'I've got a better idea,' Annabeth said. 'We send ambassadors ashore. A small group – one or two at most. Try to talk with him.'

'I'll go,' Jason said. 'He's a son of Zeus. I'm the son of Jupiter. Maybe he'll be friendly to me.'

'Or maybe he'll hate you,' Percy suggested. 'Half brothers don't always get along.'

Jason scowled. 'Thank you, Mr Optimism.'

'It's worth a shot,' Annabeth said. 'At least Jason and Hercules have something in common. And we need our best diplomat. Somebody who's good with words.'

All eyes turned to Piper.

She tried to avoid screaming and jumping over the side. A bad premonition gnawed at her gut. But if Jason was going ashore, she wanted to be with him. Maybe this hugely powerful god would turn out to be helpful. They had to have good luck once in a while, didn't they?

'Fine,' she said. 'Just let me change my clothes.'

Once Leo had anchored the *Argo II* between the pillars, Jason summoned the wind to carry him and Piper ashore.

The man in purple was waiting for them.

Piper had heard tons of stories about Hercules. She'd seen several cheesy movies and cartoons. Before today, if she had thought about him at all, she'd just roll her eyes and imagine some stupid hairy dude in his thirties with a barrel chest and a gross hippie beard, with a lion skin over his head and a big club, like a caveman. She imagined he would smell bad, belch and scratch himself a lot, and speak mostly in grunts.

She was not expecting *this*.

His feet were bare, covered in white sand. His robes made him look like a priest, though Piper couldn't remember which rank of priest wore purple. Was that cardinals? Bishops? And did the purple colour mean he was the Roman version of

Hercules rather than the Greek? His beard was fashionably scruffy, like Piper's dad and his actor friends wore theirs – the sort of *I just happened not to shave for two days and I still look awesome* look.

He was well built, but not too stocky. His ebony hair was close-cropped, Roman style. He had startling blue eyes like Jason's, but his skin was coppery, as if he'd spent his entire life on a tanning bed. The most surprising thing: he looked about twenty. Definitely no older. He was handsome in a rugged but not-at-all-caveman way.

He did in fact have a club, which lay in the sand next to him, but it was more like an oversized baseball bat – a five-foot-long polished cylinder of mahogany with a leather handgrip studded in bronze. Coach Hedge would have been jealous.

Jason and Piper landed at the edge of the surf. They approached slowly, careful not to make any threatening moves. Hercules watched them with no particular emotion, as if they were some form of seabird he had never noticed before.

'Hello,' Piper said. Always a good start.

'What's up?' Hercules said. His voice was deep but casual, very modern. He could've been greeting them in the high-school locker room.

'Uh, not much.' Piper winced. 'Well, actually, a lot. I'm Piper. This is Jason. We –'

'Where's your lion skin?' Jason interrupted.

Piper wanted to elbow him, but Hercules looked more amused than annoyed.

'It's ninety degrees out here,' he said. 'Why would I wear my lion skin? Do you wear a fur coat to the beach?'

'I guess that makes sense.' Jason sounded disappointed. 'It's just that the pictures always show you with a lion skin.'

Hercules glared at the sky accusingly, like he wanted to have words with his father, Zeus. 'Don't believe everything you hear about me. Being famous isn't as fun as you might think.'

'Tell me about it,' Piper sighed.

Hercules fixed those brilliant blue eyes on her. 'Are you famous?'

'My dad . . . he's in the movies.'

Hercules snarled. 'Don't get me started with the movies. Gods of Olympus, they never get *anything* right. Have you seen one movie about me where I look like me?'

Piper had to admit he had a point. 'I'm surprised you're so young.'

'Ha! Being immortal helps. But, yes, I wasn't so old when I died. Not by modern standards. I did a lot during my years as a hero . . . too much, really.' His eyes drifted to Jason. 'Son of Zeus, eh?'

'Jupiter,' Jason said.

'Not much difference,' Hercules grumbled. 'Dad's annoying in either form. Me? I was called Heracles. Then the Romans came along and named me Hercules. I didn't really change that much, though lately just thinking about it gives me splitting headaches . . .'

The left side of his face twitched. His robes shimmered, momentarily turning white, then back to purple.

'At any rate,' Hercules said, 'if you're Jupiter's son, you might understand. It's a lot of pressure. Enough is never enough. Eventually it can make a guy snap.'

He turned to Piper. She felt like a thousand ants were crawling up her back. There was a mixture of sadness and darkness in his eyes that seemed not quite sane, and definitely not safe.

'As for you, my dear,' Hercules said, 'be careful. Sons of Zeus can be . . . well, never mind.'

Piper wasn't sure what that meant. Suddenly she wanted to get as far from this god as possible, but she tried to maintain a calm, polite expression.

'So, Lord Hercules,' she said, 'we're on a quest. We'd like permission to pass into the Mediterranean.'

Hercules shrugged. 'That's why I'm here. After I died, Dad made me the doorkeeper of Olympus. I said, *Great! Palace duty! Party all the time!* What he didn't mention is that I'd be guarding the doors to the ancient lands, stuck on this island for the rest of eternity. Lots of fun.'

He pointed at the pillars rising from the surf. 'Stupid columns. Some people claim I created the whole Strait of Gibraltar by shoving mountains apart. Some people say the mountains *are* the pillars. What a bunch of Augean manure. The pillars are *pillars*.'

'Right,' Piper said. 'Naturally. So . . . can we pass?'

The god scratched his fashionable beard. 'Well, I have to give you the standard warning about how dangerous the ancient lands are. Not just any demigod can survive the Mare Nostrum. Because of that, I have to give you a quest to complete. Prove your worth, blah, blah, blah. Honestly, I don't make a big deal of it. Usually I give demigods something simple like a shopping trip, singing a funny song, that sort of thing. After all those labours I had to complete for my evil cousin Eurystheus, well . . . I don't want to be *that guy*, you know?'

'Appreciate it,' Jason said.

'Hey, no problem.' Hercules sounded relaxed and easygoing, but he still made Piper nervous. That dark glint in his eyes reminded her of charcoal soaked in kerosene, ready to go up at a moment's notice.

'So anyway,' Hercules said, 'what's your quest?'

'Giants,' Jason said. 'We're off to Greece to stop them from awakening Gaia.'

'Giants,' Hercules muttered. 'I hate those guys. Back when I was a demigod hero . . . ah, but never mind. So which god put you up to this – Dad? Athena? Maybe Aphrodite?' He raised an eyebrow at Piper. 'As pretty as you are, I'm guessing that's your mom.'

Piper should've been thinking faster, but Hercules had unsettled her. Too late, she realized the conversation had become a minefield.

'Hera sent us,' Jason said. 'She brought us together to –'

'Hera.' Suddenly Hercules's expression was like the cliffs of Gibraltar – a solid, unforgiving sheet of stone.

'We hate her, too,' Piper said quickly. Gods, why hadn't it occurred to her? Hera had been Hercules's mortal enemy. 'We didn't want to help her. She didn't give us much choice, but –'

'But here you are,' Hercules said, all friendliness gone. 'Sorry, you two. I don't care how worthy your quest is. I don't do *anything* that Hera wants. Ever.'

Jason looked mystified. 'But I thought you made up with her when you became a god.'

'Like I said,' Hercules grumbled, 'don't believe everything you hear. If you want to pass into the Mediterranean, I'm afraid I've got to give you an extra-hard quest.'

'But we're like brothers,' Jason protested. 'Hera's messed with my life, too. I understand –'

'You understand nothing,' Hercules said coldly. 'My first family: dead. My life wasted on ridiculous quests. My second wife dead, after being tricked into poisoning me and leaving me to a painful demise. And my compensation? I got to become a *minor* god. Immortal, so I can never forget my pain. Stuck here as a gatekeeper, a doorman, a . . . a butler for the Olympians. No, you don't understand. The only god who understands me even a little bit is Dionysus. And at least *he* invented something useful. I have nothing to show except bad film adaptations of my life.'

Piper turned on the charmspeak. 'That's horribly sad, Lord Hercules. But please go easy on us. We're not bad people.'

She thought she'd succeeded. Hercules hesitated. Then his jaw tightened, and he shook his head. 'On the opposite side of this island, over those hills, you'll find a river. In the middle of that river lives the old god Achelous.'

Hercules waited, as if this information should send them running in terror.

'And . . .?' Jason asked.

'*And*,' Hercules said, 'I want you to break off his other horn and bring it to me.'

'He has horns,' Jason said. 'Wait . . . his *other* horn? What –?'

'Figure it out,' the god snapped. 'Here, this should help.'

He said the word *help* like it meant *hurt*. From under his robes, Hercules took a small book and tossed it to Piper. She barely caught it.

The book's glossy cover showed a photographic montage of Greek temples and smiling monsters. The Minotaur was giving the thumbs-up. The title read: *The Hercules Guide to the Mare Nostrum.*

'Bring me that horn by sundown,' Hercules said. 'Just the two of you. No contacting your friends. Your ship will remain where it is. If you succeed, you may pass into the Mediterranean.'

'And if we don't?' Piper asked, pretty sure she didn't want the answer.

'Well, Achelous will kill you, obviously,' Hercules said. 'And I will break your ship in half with my bare hands and send your friends to an early grave.'

Jason shifted his feet. 'Couldn't we just sing a funny song?'

'I'd get going,' Hercules said coldly. 'Sundown. Or your friends are dead.'

XXVII

PIPER

THE HERCULES GUIDE TO THE MARE NOSTRUM didn't help much with snakes and mosquitoes.

'If this is a magic island,' Piper grumbled, 'why couldn't it be a *nice* magic island?'

They tromped up a hill and down into a heavily wooded valley, careful to avoid the black-and-red-striped snakes sunning themselves on the rocks. Mosquitoes swarmed over stagnant ponds in the lowest areas. The trees were mostly stunted olives, cypress and pines. The chirring of the cicadas and the oppressive heat reminded Piper of the rez in Oklahoma during the summer.

So far they hadn't found any river.

'We could fly,' Jason suggested again.

'We might miss something,' Piper said. 'Besides, I'm not sure I want to drop in on an unfriendly god. What was his name? Etch-a-Sketch?'

'Achelous.' Jason was trying to read the guidebook while

they walked, so he kept running into trees and stumbling over rocks. 'Says here he's a *potamus*.'

'He's a hippopotamus?'

'No. *Potamus*. A river god. According to this, he's the spirit of some river in Greece.'

'Since we're not in Greece, let's assume he's moved,' Piper said. 'Doesn't bode well for how useful that book is going to be. Anything else?'

'Says Hercules fought him one time,' Jason offered.

'Hercules fought ninety-nine percent of everything in Ancient Greece.'

'Yeah. Let's see. Pillars of Hercules . . .' Jason flipped a page. 'Says here this island has no hotels, no restaurants, no transportation. Attractions: Hercules and two pillars. Huh, this is interesting. Supposedly the dollar sign — you know, the S with the two lines through it? — that came from the Spanish coat of arms, which showed the Pillars of Hercules with a banner curling between them.'

Great, Piper thought. Jason finally gets along with Annabeth, and her brainiac tendencies start rubbing off on him.

'Anything helpful?' she asked.

'Wait. Here's a tiny reference to Achelous: *This river god fought Hercules for the hand of the beautiful Deianira. During the struggle, Hercules broke off one of the river god's horns, which became the first cornucopia.*'

'Corn of what?'

'It's that Thanksgiving decoration,' Jason said. 'The horn with all the goodies spilling out? We have some in the mess hall at Camp Jupiter. I didn't know the original one was actually some guy's horn.'

'And we're supposed to take his other one,' Piper said. 'I'm guessing that won't be so easy. Who was Deianira?'

'Hercules married her,' Jason said. 'I think . . . doesn't say here. But I think something bad happened to her.'

Piper remembered what Hercules had told them: his first family dead, his second wife dead after being tricked into poisoning him. She was liking this challenge less and less.

They trudged across a ridge between two hills, trying to stay in the shade, but Piper was already soaked with perspiration. The mosquitoes left welts on her ankles, arms and neck, so she probably looked like a smallpox victim.

She'd finally got some alone time with Jason and *this* was how they spent it.

She was irritated with Jason for having mentioned Hera, but she knew she shouldn't blame him. Maybe she was just irritated with him in general. Ever since Camp Jupiter, she'd been carrying around a lot of worry and resentment.

She wondered what Hercules had wanted to tell her about the sons of Zeus. They couldn't be trusted? They were under too much pressure? Piper tried to imagine Jason becoming a god when he died, standing on some beach guarding the gates to an ocean long after Piper and everyone else he knew in his mortal life were dead.

She wondered if Hercules had ever been as positive as Jason – more upbeat, confident, quick to comfort. It was hard to picture.

As they hiked down into the next valley, Piper wondered

what was happening back on the *Argo II*. She was tempted to send an Iris-message, but Hercules had warned them not to contact their friends. She hoped Annabeth could guess what was going on and didn't try to send another party ashore. Piper wasn't sure what Hercules would do if he were bothered further. She imagined Coach Hedge getting impatient and aiming a ballista at the man in purple, or eidolons possessing the crew and forcing them to commit suicide-by-Hercules.

Piper shuddered. She didn't know what time it was, but the sun was already starting to sink. How had the day passed so quickly? She would have welcomed sundown for the cooler temperatures, except it was also their deadline. A cool night breeze wouldn't mean much if they were dead. Besides, tomorrow was 1 July, the Kalends of July. If their information was correct, it would be Nico di Angelo's last day of life, and the day Rome was destroyed.

'Stop,' Jason said.

Piper wasn't sure what was wrong. Then she realized she could hear running water up ahead. They crept through the trees and found themselves on the bank of a river. It was maybe forty feet wide but only a few inches deep, a silver sheet of water racing over a smooth bed of stones. A few yards downstream, the rapids plunged into a dark blue swimming hole.

Something about the river bothered her. The cicadas in the trees had gone quiet. No birds were chirping. It was as if the water was giving a lecture and would only allow its own voice.

But the more Piper listened the more inviting the river seemed. She wanted to take a drink. Maybe she should take off her shoes. Her feet could really use a soak. And that swimming hole . . . it would be so nice to jump in with Jason and relax in the shade of the trees, floating in the nice cool water. So romantic.

Piper shook herself. These thoughts weren't hers. Something was wrong. It almost felt like the river was charmspeaking.

Jason sat on a rock and started taking off his shoes. He grinned at the swimming hole like he couldn't wait to get in.

'Cut it out!' Piper yelled at the river.

Jason looked startled. 'Cut what out?'

'Not you,' Piper said. 'Him.'

She felt silly pointing at the water, but she was certain it was working some sort of magic, swaying their feelings.

Just when she thought she had lost it and Jason would tell her so, the river spoke: *Forgive me. Singing is one of the few pleasures I have left.*

A figure emerged from the swimming hole as if rising on an elevator.

Piper's shoulders tensed. It was the creature she'd seen in her knife blade, the bull with the human face. His skin was as blue as the water. His hooves levitated on the river's surface. At the top of his bovine neck was the head of a man with short curly black hair, a beard done in ringlets Ancient Greek style, deep, mournful eyes behind bifocal glasses and a mouth that seemed set in a permanent pout. Sprouting from the left side of his head was a single bull's horn – a curved black-and-white one like warriors might turn into drinking cups. The imbalance made his head tilt to the left, so that he looked like he was trying to get water out of his ear.

'Hello,' he said sadly. 'Come to kill me, I suppose.'

Jason put his shoes back on and stood slowly. 'Um, well –'

'No!' Piper intervened. 'I'm sorry. This is embarrassing. We didn't want to bother you, but Hercules sent us.'

'Hercules!' The bull-man sighed. His hooves pawed the water as if ready to charge. 'To me, he'll always be Heracles. That's his Greek name, you know: *the glory of Hera*.'

'Funny name,' Jason said. 'Since he hates her.'

'Indeed,' the bull-man said. 'Perhaps that's why he didn't protest when the Romans renamed him Hercules. Of course, that's the name most people know him by . . . his *brand*, if you will. Hercules is nothing if not image-conscious.'

The bull-man spoke with bitterness but familiarity, as if Hercules were an old friend who had lost his way.

'You're Achelous?' Piper asked.

The bull-man bent his front legs and lowered his head in a bow, which Piper found both sweet and a little sad. 'At your service. River god extraordinaire. Once the spirit of the mightiest river in Greece. Now sentenced to dwell here, on the opposite side of the island from my old enemy. Oh, the gods are cruel! But whether they put us so close together to punish me or Hercules I have never been sure.'

Piper wasn't sure what he meant, but the background noise of the river was invading her mind again – reminding her how hot and thirsty she felt, how pleasant a nice swim would be. She tried to focus.

'I'm Piper,' she said. 'This is Jason. We don't want to fight. It's just that Heracles – Hercules – whoever he is, got mad at us and sent us here.'

She explained about their quest to the ancient lands to stop the giants from waking Gaia. She described how their team of Greeks and Romans had come together, and how Hercules had thrown a temper tantrum when he found out Hera was behind it.

Achelous kept tipping his head to the left, so Piper wasn't sure if he was dozing off or dealing with one-horn fatigue.

When she was done, Achelous regarded her as if she were developing a regrettable skin rash. 'Ah, my dear . . . the legends are true, you know. The spirits, the water cannibals.'

Piper had to fight back a whimper. She hadn't told Achelous *anything* about that. 'H-how –?'

'River gods know many things,' he said. 'Alas, you are focusing on the wrong story. If you had made it to Rome, the story of the flood would have served you better.'

'Piper?' Jason asked. 'What's he talking about?'

Her thoughts were suddenly as jumbled as kaleidoscope glass. *The story of the flood . . . If you had made it to Rome.*

'I – I'm not sure,' she said, though the mention of a flood story rang a distant bell. 'Achelous, I don't understand –'

'No, you don't,' the river god sympathized. 'Poor thing. Another girl stuck with a son of Zeus.'

'Wait a minute,' Jason said. 'It's Jupiter, actually. And how does that make her a *poor thing*?'

Achelous ignored him. 'My girl, do you know the cause of my fight with Hercules?'

'It was over a woman,' Piper recalled. 'Deianira?'

'Yes.' Achelous heaved a sigh. 'And do you know what happened to her?'

'Uh . . .' Piper glanced at Jason.

He took out his guidebook and began flipping through pages. 'It doesn't really –'

Achelous snorted indignantly. 'What is *that*?'

Jason blinked. 'Just . . . *The Hercules Guide to Mare Nostrum*. He gave us the guidebook so –'

'That is *not* a book,' Achelous insisted. 'He gave you that just to get under my skin, didn't he? He knows I hate those things.'

'You hate . . . books?' Piper asked.

'Bah!' Achelous's face flushed, turning his blue skin aubergine purple. 'That's *not* a book.'

He pawed the water. A scroll shot from the river like a miniature rocket and landed in front of him. He nudged it open with his hooves. The weathered yellow parchment unfurled, covered with faded Latin script and elaborate hand-drawn pictures.

'*This* is a book!' Achelous said. 'Oh, the smell of sheepskin! The elegant feel of the scroll unrolling beneath my hooves. You simply can't duplicate it in something like *that*.'

He nodded indignantly at the guidebook in Jason's hand. 'You young folks today and your newfangled gadgets. Bound pages. Little compact squares of text that are not hoof-friendly. That's a *bound* book, a b-book, if you must. But it's not a traditional book. It'll never replace the good old-fashioned scroll!'

'Um, I'll just put this away now.' Jason slipped the guidebook in his back pocket the way he might holster a dangerous weapon.

Achelous seemed to calm down a little, which was a relief to Piper. She didn't need to get run over by a one-horned bull with a scroll obsession.

'Now,' Achelous said, tapping a picture on his scroll. 'This is Deianira.'

Piper knelt down to look. The hand-painted portrait was small, but she could tell the woman had been very beautiful, with long dark hair, dark eyes and a playful smile that probably drove guys crazy.

'Princess of Calydon,' the river god said mournfully. 'She was promised to me, until Hercules butted in. He insisted on combat.'

'And he broke off your horn?' Jason guessed.

'Yes,' Achelous said. 'I could never forgive him for that. Horribly uncomfortable, having only one horn. But the situation was worse for poor Deianira. She could have had a long, happy life married to me.'

'A man-headed bull,' Piper said, 'who lives in a river.'

'Exactly,' Achelous agreed. 'It seems impossible she would refuse, eh? Instead, she went off with Hercules. She picked the handsome, flashy hero over the good, faithful husband who would have treated her well. What happened next? Well, she should have known. Hercules was much too wrapped up in his own problems to be a good husband. He had already murdered one wife, you know. Hera cursed him, so he flew into a rage and killed his entire family. Horrible business. That's why he had to do those twelve labours as penance.'

Piper felt appalled. 'Wait . . . Hera *made* him crazy and *Hercules* had to do the penance?'

Achelous shrugged. 'The Olympians never seem to pay for their crimes. And Hera has always hated the sons of Zeus . . . or Jupiter.' He glanced distrustfully at Jason. 'At any rate, my poor Deianira had a tragic end. She became jealous of Hercules's many affairs. He gallivanted all over the world, you see, just like his father, Zeus, flirting with every woman he met. Finally Deianira got so desperate she listened to bad advice. A crafty centaur named Nessus told her that if she wanted Hercules to be faithful forever she should spread some centaur blood on the inside of Hercules's favourite shirt. Unfortunately Nessus was lying because he wanted revenge on Hercules. Deianira followed his instructions, but instead of making Hercules a faithful husband –'

'Centaur blood is like acid,' Jason said.

'Yes,' Achelous said. 'Hercules died a painful death. When Deianira realized what she'd done, she . . .' The river god drew a line across his neck.

'That's awful,' Piper said.

'And the moral, my dear?' Achelous said. 'Beware the sons of Zeus.'

Piper couldn't look at her boyfriend. She wasn't sure she could mask the uneasiness in her eyes. Jason would never be like Hercules. But the story played into all her fears. Hera had manipulated their relationship, just as she had manipulated Hercules. Piper wanted to believe that Jason could never go into a murderous frenzy like Hercules had. Then again, only four days ago he had been controlled by an eidolon and almost killed Percy Jackson.

'Hercules is a god now,' Achelous said. 'He married Hebe, the youth goddess, but still he is rarely at home. He dwells here on this island, guarding those silly pillars. He says Zeus *makes* him do this, but I think he prefers being here to Mount Olympus, nursing his bitterness and mourning his mortal life. My presence reminds him of his failures – especially the woman who finally killed him. And *his* presence reminds me of poor Deianira, who could have been my wife.'

The bull-man tapped the scroll, which rolled itself up and sank into the water.

'Hercules wants my other horn in order to humiliate me,' Achelous said. 'Perhaps it would make him feel better about himself, knowing that I'm miserable, too. Besides, the horn would become a cornucopia. Good food and drink would flow from it, just as my power causes the river to flow. No doubt Hercules would keep the cornucopia for himself. It would be a tragedy and a waste.'

Piper suspected the noise of the river and the drowsy sound of Achelous's voice were still affecting her thoughts, but she couldn't help agreeing with the river god. She was starting to hate Hercules. This poor bull-man seemed so sad and lonely.

Jason stirred. 'I'm sorry, Achelous. Honestly, you've got a bum deal. But maybe . . . well, without the other horn, you might not be so lopsided. It might feel better.'

'Jason!' Piper protested.

Jason held up his hands. 'Just a thought. Besides, I don't

see that we have many choices. If Hercules doesn't get that horn, he'll kill us and our friends.'

'He's right,' Achelous said. 'You have no choice. Which is why I hope you'll forgive me.'

Piper frowned. The river god sounded so heartbroken she wanted to pat his head. 'Forgive you for what?'

'I have no choice either,' Achelous said. 'I have to stop you.'

The river exploded, and a wall of water crashed over Piper.

XXVIII

PIPER

THE CURRENT GRABBED HER LIKE A FIST and pulled her into the deep. Struggling was useless. She clamped her mouth shut, forcing herself not to inhale, but she could barely keep from panicking. She couldn't see anything but a torrent of bubbles. She could only hear her own thrashing and the dull roar of the rapids.

She'd just about decided this was how she would die: drowning in a swimming hole on an island that didn't exist. Then, as suddenly as she'd been pulled under, she was thrust to the surface. She found herself at the centre of a whirlpool, able to breathe but unable to break free.

A few yards away, Jason broke the surface and gasped, his sword in one hand. He swung wildly, but there was nothing to attack.

Twenty feet to Piper's right, Achelous rose from the water. 'I'm really sorry about this,' he said.

Jason lunged towards him, summoning the winds to lift

him out of the river, but Achelous was quicker and more powerful. A curl of water slammed into Jason and sent him under once more.

'Stop it!' Piper screamed.

Using charmspeak wasn't easy when she was floundering in a whirlpool, but she got Achelous's attention.

'I'm afraid I can't stop,' said the river god. 'I can't let Hercules have my other horn. It would be mortifying.'

'There's another way!' Piper said. 'You don't have to kill us!'

Jason clawed his way to the surface again. A miniature storm cloud formed over his head. Thunder boomed.

'None of that, son of Jupiter,' Achelous chided. 'If you call lightning, you'll just electrocute your girlfriend.'

The water pulled Jason under again.

'Let him go!' Piper charged her voice with all the persuasiveness she could muster. 'I promise I won't let Hercules get the horn!'

Achelous hesitated. He cantered over to her, his head tilting to the left. 'I believe you mean that.'

'I do!' Piper promised. 'Hercules is despicable. But, please, first let my friend go.'

The water churned where Jason had gone under. Piper wanted to scream. How much longer could he hold his breath?

Achelous looked down at her through his bifocals. His expression softened. 'I see. You would be my Deianira. You would be my bride to compensate for my loss.'

'What?' Piper wasn't sure if she'd heard him right. The

whirlpool was literally making her head spin. 'Uh, actually I was thinking –'

'Oh, I understand,' Achelous said. 'You were too modest to suggest this in front of your boyfriend. You are right, of course. I would treat you much better than a son of Zeus would. I could make things right after all these centuries. I could not save Deianira, but I could save you.'

Had it been thirty seconds now? A minute? Jason couldn't hold out much longer.

'You would have to let your friends die,' Achelous continued. 'Hercules would be angry, but I can protect you from him. We could be quite happy together. Let's start by letting that Jason fellow drown, eh?'

Piper could barely hold it together, but she *had* to concentrate. She masked her fear and her anger. She was a child of Aphrodite. She had to use the tools she was given.

She smiled as sweetly as she could and raised her arms. 'Lift me up, please.'

Achelous's face brightened. He grabbed Piper's hands and pulled her out of the whirlpool.

She'd never ridden a bull before, but she'd practised bareback pegasus riding at Camp Half-Blood, and she remembered what to do. She used her momentum, swinging one leg over Achelous's back. Then she locked her ankles around his neck, wrapped one arm around his throat and drew her knife with the other. She pressed the blade under the river god's chin.

'Let – Jason – go.' She put all her force into the command. 'Now!'

Piper realized there were many flaws in her plan. The river god might simply dissolve into water. Or he could pull her under and wait for her to drown. But apparently her charmspeak worked. Or maybe Achelous was just too surprised to think straight. He probably wasn't used to pretty girls threatening to cut his throat.

Jason shot out of the water like a human cannonball. He broke through the branches of an olive tree and tumbled onto the grass. That couldn't have felt good, but he struggled to his feet, gasping and coughing. He raised his sword, and the dark clouds thickened over the river.

Piper shot him a warning look: *Not yet.* She still had to get out of this river without drowning or getting electrocuted.

Achelous arched his back as if contemplating a trick. Piper pressed the knife harder against his throat.

'Be a good bull,' she warned.

'You promised,' Achelous said through gritted teeth. 'You promised Hercules wouldn't get my horn.'

'And he won't,' Piper said. 'But I will.'

She raised her knife and slashed off the god's horn. The Celestial bronze cut through the base like it was wet clay. Achelous bellowed in rage. Before he could recover, Piper stood up on his back. With the horn in one hand and her dagger in the other, she leaped for the shore.

'Jason!' she yelled.

Thank the gods, he understood. A gust of wind caught her and carried her safely over the bank. Piper hit the ground rolling as the hairs on her neck stood up. A metallic smell filled the air. She turned towards the river in time to be blinded.

BOOM! Lightning stirred the water into a boiling cauldron, steaming and hissing with electricity. Piper blinked the yellow spots out of her eyes as the god Achelous wailed and dissolved beneath the surface. His horrified expression seemed to be asking: *How could you?*

'Jason, run!' She was still dizzy and sick with fear, but she and Jason crashed through the woods.

As she climbed the hill, clasping the bull's horn to her chest, Piper realized she was sobbing – though she wasn't sure if it was from fear, or relief, or shame for what she'd done to the old river god.

They didn't slow down until they reached the crest of the hill.

Piper felt silly, but she kept breaking down and crying as she told Jason what had happened while he was struggling underwater.

'Piper, you had no choice.' He put his hand on her shoulder. 'You saved my life.'

She wiped her eyes and tried to control herself. The sun was nearing the horizon. They had to get back to Hercules quickly, or their friends would die.

'Achelous forced your hand,' Jason continued. 'Besides, I doubt that lightning bolt killed him. He's an ancient god. You'd have to destroy his river to destroy him. And he can live without a horn. If you had to lie about not giving it to Hercules, well –'

'I wasn't lying.'

Jason stared at her. 'Pipes . . . we don't have a choice. Hercules will kill –'

'Hercules doesn't deserve this.' Piper wasn't sure where this rage was coming from, but she had never felt more certain of anything in her life.

Hercules was a bitter, selfish jerk. He'd hurt too many people, and he wanted to keep on hurting them. Maybe he'd had some bad breaks. Maybe the gods had kicked him around. But that didn't excuse it. A hero couldn't control the gods, but he should be able to control himself.

Jason would never be like that. He would never blame others for his problems or make a grudge more important than doing the right thing.

Piper was not going to repeat Deianira's story. She wasn't going to go along with what Hercules wanted just because he was handsome and strong and scary. He couldn't get his way this time – not after threatening their lives and sending them to make Achelous miserable for the sake of spiting Hera. Hercules didn't deserve a horn of plenty. Piper was going to put him in his place.

'I have a plan,' she said.

She told Jason what to do. She didn't even realize she was using charmspeak until his eyes glazed over.

'Whatever you say,' he promised. Then he blinked a few times. 'We're going to die, but I'm in.'

Hercules was waiting right where they'd left him. He was staring at the *Argo II*, docked between the pillars as the sun set behind it. The ship looked okay, but Piper's plan had started to feel insane to her.

Too late to reconsider. She'd already sent an Iris-message to

Leo. Jason was prepared. And, seeing Hercules again, she felt more certain than ever she couldn't give him what he wanted.

Hercules didn't exactly brighten when he saw Piper carrying the bull's horn, but his scowl lines lessened.

'Good,' he said. 'You got it. In that case, you are free to go.'

Piper glanced at Jason. 'You heard him. He gave us permission.' She turned back to the god. 'That means our ship will be able to pass into the Mediterranean?'

'Yes, yes.' Hercules snapped his fingers. 'Now, the horn.'

'No,' Piper said.

The god frowned. 'Excuse me?'

She raised the cornucopia. Since she'd cut it from Achelous's head, the horn had hollowed out, becoming smooth and dark on the inside. It didn't appear magical, but Piper was counting on its power.

'Achelous was right,' she said. 'You're *his* curse as much as he is yours. You're a sorry excuse for a hero.'

Hercules stared at her as if she was speaking in Japanese. 'You realize I could kill you with a flick of my finger,' he said. 'I could throw my club at your ship and cut straight through its hull. I could –'

'You could shut up,' Jason said. He drew his sword. 'Maybe Zeus *is* different from Jupiter. Because I wouldn't put up with any brother who acts like you.'

The veins on Hercules's neck turned as purple as his robes. 'You would not be the first demigod I've killed.'

'Jason is better than you,' Piper said. 'But don't worry. We're not going to fight you. We're going to leave this island with the horn. You don't deserve it as a prize. I'm going to keep it, to remind me of what *not* to be like as a demigod, and to remind me of poor Achelous and Deianira.'

The god's nostrils flared. 'Do *not* mention that name! You can't seriously think I'm worried about your puny boyfriend. No one is stronger than me.'

'I didn't say stronger,' Piper corrected. 'I said he's *better*.'

Piper pointed the mouth of the horn at Hercules. She let go of the resentment and doubt and anger she'd been harbouring since Camp Jupiter. She concentrated on all the good things she'd shared with Jason Grace: soaring upward in the Grand Canyon, walking on the beach at Camp Half-Blood, holding hands at the sing-along and watching the stars, sitting by the strawberry fields together on lazy afternoons and listening to the satyrs play their pipes.

She thought about a future when the giants had been defeated, Gaia was asleep and they would live happily together – no jealousy, no monsters left to battle. She filled her heart with those thoughts, and she felt the cornucopia grow warm.

The horn blasted forth a flood of food as powerful as Achelous's river. A torrent of fresh fruit, baked goods and smoked hams completely buried Hercules. Piper didn't understand how all that stuff could fit through the entrance of the horn, but she thought the hams were especially appropriate.

When it had spewed out enough goodies to fill a house, the horn shut itself off. Piper heard Hercules shrieking and struggling somewhere underneath. Apparently even the strongest god in the world could be caught off guard when buried under fresh produce.

'Go!' she told Jason, who'd forgotten his part of the plan and was staring in amazement at the fruit pile. 'Go!'

He grabbed Piper's waist and summoned the wind. They shot away from the island so quickly that Piper almost got whiplash, but it wasn't a second too soon.

As the island retreated from view, Hercules's head broke above the mound of goodies. Half a coconut was stuck on his noggin like a war helmet. 'Kill!' he bellowed, like he'd had a lot of practice saying it.

Jason touched down on the deck of the *Argo II*. Thankfully, Leo had done his part. The ship's oars were already in aerial mode. The anchor was up. Jason summoned a gale so strong it pushed them into the sky, while Percy sent a ten-foot-tall wave against the shore, knocking Hercules down a second time, in a cascade of seawater and pineapples.

By the time the god regained his feet and started lobbing coconuts at them from far below, the *Argo II* was already sailing through the clouds above the Mediterranean.

XXIX

PERCY

PERCY WAS NOT FEELING THE LOVE.

Bad enough he'd been run out of Atlanta by evil sea gods. Then he had failed to stop a giant shrimp attack on the *Argo II*. Then the ichthyocentaurs, Chiron's brothers, hadn't even wanted to meet him.

After all that, they had arrived at the Pillars of Hercules, and Percy had to stay aboard ship while Jason the Big Shot visited his half brother, Hercules, the most famous demigod of all time, and Percy didn't get to meet him either.

Okay, sure, from what Piper said afterwards, Hercules was a jerk, but still . . . Percy was getting kind of tired of staying aboard ship and pacing the deck.

The open sea was supposed to be *his* territory. Percy was supposed to step up, take charge and keep everybody safe. Instead, all the way across the Atlantic, he'd done pretty much nothing except make small talk with sharks and listen to Coach Hedge sing TV theme songs.

To make matters worse, Annabeth had been distant ever since they had left Charleston. She spent most of her time in her cabin, studying the bronze map she'd retrieved from Fort Sumter, or looking up information on Daedalus's laptop.

Whenever Percy stopped by to see her, she was so lost in thought that the conversation went something like this:

Percy: 'Hey, how's it going?'

Annabeth: 'Uh, no thanks.'

Percy: 'Okay . . . have you eaten anything today?'

Annabeth: 'I think Leo is on duty. Ask him.'

Percy: 'So, my hair is on fire.'

Annabeth: 'Okay. In a while.'

She got like this sometimes. It was one of the challenges of dating an Athena girl. Still, Percy wondered what he had to do to get her attention. He was worried about her after her encounter with the spiders at Fort Sumter, and he didn't know how to help her, especially if she shut him out.

After leaving the Pillars of Hercules – unscathed except for a few coconuts lodged in the hull's bronze plating – the ship travelled by air for a few hundred miles.

Percy hoped the ancient lands wouldn't be as bad as they'd heard. But it was almost like a commercial: *You'll notice the difference immediately!*

Several times an hour, something attacked the ship. A flock of flesh-eating Stymphalian birds swooped out of the night sky, and Festus torched them. Storm spirits swirled around the mast, and Jason blasted them with lightning. While Coach Hedge was having dinner on the foredeck, a wild pegasus appeared from nowhere, stampeded over the coach's enchiladas and flew off again, leaving cheesy hoof prints all across the deck.

'What was *that* for?' the coach demanded.

The sight of the pegasus made Percy wish Blackjack were here. He hadn't seen his friend in days. Tempest and Arion also hadn't shown themselves. Maybe they didn't want to venture into the Mediterranean. If so, Percy couldn't blame them.

Finally around midnight, after the ninth or tenth aerial attack, Jason turned to him. 'How about you get some sleep? I'll keep blasting stuff out of the sky as long as I can. Then we can go by sea for a while, and you can take point.'

Percy wasn't sure that he'd be able to sleep with the boat rocking through the clouds as it was shaken by angry wind spirits, but Jason's idea made sense. He went belowdecks and crashed on his bunk.

His nightmares, of course, were anything but restful.

He dreamed he was in a dark cavern. He could only see a few feet in front of him, but the space must have been vast. Water dripped from somewhere nearby, and the sound echoed off distant walls. The way the air moved made Percy suspect the cave's ceiling was far, far above.

He heard heavy footsteps, and the twin giants Ephialtes and Otis shuffled out of the gloom. Percy could distinguish them only by their hair – Ephialtes had the green locks braided with silver and gold coins; Otis had the purple ponytail braided with . . . were those firecrackers?

Otherwise they were dressed identically, and their outfits definitely belonged in a nightmare. They wore matching white slacks and gold buccaneer shirts with V-necks that showed way too much chest hair. A dozen sheathed daggers lined their rhinestone belts. Their shoes were open-toed sandals, proving that – yes, indeed – they had snakes for feet. The straps wrapped around the serpents' necks. Their heads curled up where the toes should be. The snakes flicked their tongues excitedly and turned their gold eyes in every direction, like dogs looking out of the window of a car. Maybe it had been a long time since they'd had shoes with a view.

The giants stood in front of Percy, but they paid him no attention. Instead, they gazed up into the darkness.

'We're here,' Ephialtes announced. Despite his booming voice, his words dissipated in the cavern, echoing until they sounded small and insignificant.

Far above, something answered, 'Yes. I can see that. Those outfits are hard to miss.'

The voice made Percy's stomach drop about six inches. It sounded vaguely female, but not at all human. Each word was a garbled hiss in multiple tones, as if a swarm of African killer bees had learned to speak English in unison.

It wasn't Gaia. Percy was sure of that. But, whatever it was, the twin giants became nervous. They shifted on their snakes and bobbed their heads respectfully.

'Of course, Your Ladyship,' Ephialtes said. 'We bring news of –'

'Why are you dressed like that?' asked the thing in the dark. She didn't seem to be coming any closer, which was fine with Percy.

Ephialtes shot his brother an irritated look. 'My brother

was supposed to wear something different. Unfortunately –'

'You said *I* was the knife thrower today,' Otis protested.

'I said *I* was the knife thrower! You were supposed to be the magician! Ah, forgive me, Your Ladyship. You don't want to hear us arguing. We came as you requested, to bring you news. The ship is approaching.'

Her Ladyship, whatever she was, made a series of violent hisses like a tyre being slashed repeatedly. With a shudder, Percy realized she was laughing.

'How long?' she asked.

'They should land in Rome shortly after daybreak, I think,' Ephialtes said. 'Of course, they'll have to get past the golden boy.'

He sneered, as if the *golden boy* was not his favourite person.

'I hope they arrive safely,' Her Ladyship said. 'It would spoil our fun to have them captured too soon. Are your preparations made?'

'Yes, Your Ladyship.' Otis stepped forward, and the cavern trembled. A crack appeared under Otis's left snake.

'Careful, you dolt!' Her Ladyship snarled. 'Do you want to return to Tartarus the hard way?'

Otis scrambled back, his face slack with terror. Percy realized that the floor, which looked like solid stone, was more like the glacier he'd walked on in Alaska – in some places solid, in other places . . . not so much. He was glad he weighed nothing in his dreams.

'There is little left holding this place together,' Her Ladyship cautioned. 'Except, of course, my own skill. Centuries of Athena's rage can only be contained so well, and the great Earth Mother churns below us in her sleep. Between those two forces, well . . . my nest has quite eroded. We must hope this child of Athena proves to be a worthy victim. She may be my last plaything.'

Ephialtes gulped. He kept his eyes on the crack in the floor. 'Soon it will not matter, Your Ladyship. Gaia will rise, and we all will be rewarded. You will no longer have to guard this place or keep your works hidden.'

'Perhaps,' said the voice in the dark. 'But I will miss the sweetness of my revenge. We have worked well together over the centuries, have we not?'

The twins bowed. The coins glittered in Ephialtes's hair, and Percy realized with nauseating certainty that some of them were silver drachma, exactly like the one Annabeth had got from her mom.

Annabeth had told him that in each generation a few children of Athena were sent on the quest to recover the missing Parthenon statue. None had ever succeeded.

We have worked well together over the centuries . . .

The giant Ephialtes had centuries' worth of coins in his braids – hundreds of trophies. Percy pictured Annabeth standing in this dark place alone. He imagined the giant taking that coin she carried and adding it to his collection. Percy wanted to draw his sword and give the giant a haircut starting at the neck, but he was powerless to act. He could only watch.

'Uh, Your Ladyship,' Ephialtes said nervously. 'I would remind you that Gaia wishes the girl to be taken alive. You can torment her. Drive her insane. Whatever you wish, of course. But her blood must be spilled on the ancient stones.'

Her Ladyship hissed. 'Others could be used for that purpose.'

'Y-yes,' Ephialtes said. 'But *this* girl is preferred. And the boy – the son of Poseidon. You can see why those two would be most suited for the task.'

Percy wasn't sure what that meant, but he wanted to crack the floor and send these stupid gold-shirted twins down to oblivion. He'd never let Gaia spill his blood for any task – and there was *no way* he'd let anyone hurt Annabeth.

'We will see,' Her Ladyship grumbled. 'Leave me now. Tend to your own preparations. You will have your spectacle. And I . . . I will work in darkness.'

The dream dissolved, and Percy woke with a start.

Jason was knocking at his open doorway.

'We've set down in the water,' he said, looking utterly exhausted. 'Your turn.'

Percy didn't want to, but he woke Annabeth. He figured even Coach Hedge wouldn't mind their talking after curfew if it meant giving her information that might save her life.

They stood on deck, alone except for Leo, who was still manning the helm. The guy must have been shattered, but he refused to go to sleep.

'I don't want any more Shrimpzilla surprises,' he insisted.

They'd all tried to convince Leo that the skolopendra attack hadn't been entirely his fault, but he wouldn't listen. Percy knew how he felt. Not forgiving himself for mistakes was one of Percy's biggest talents.

It was about four in the morning. The weather was miserable. The fog was so thick Percy couldn't see Festus at the end of the prow, and warm drizzle hung in the air like a bead curtain. As they sailed into twenty-foot swells, the sea heaving underneath them, Percy could hear poor Hazel down in her cabin . . . also heaving.

Despite all that, Percy was grateful to be back on the water. He preferred it to flying through storm clouds and being attacked by man-eating birds and enchilada-trampling pegasi.

He stood with Annabeth at the forward rail while he told her about his dream.

Percy wasn't sure how she'd take the news. Her reaction was even more troubling than he anticipated: she didn't seem surprised.

She peered into the fog. 'Percy, you have to promise me something. Don't tell the others about this dream.'

'Don't *what*? Annabeth –'

'What you saw was about the Mark of Athena,' she said. 'It won't help the others to know. It'll only make them worry, and it'll make it harder for me to go off on my own.'

'Annabeth, you can't be serious. That thing in the dark, the big chamber with the crumbling floor –'

'I know.' Her face looked unnaturally pale, and Percy suspected it wasn't just the fog. 'But I have to do this alone.'

Percy swallowed back his anger. He wasn't sure if he was mad at Annabeth, or his dream, or the entire Greek/Roman world that had endured and shaped human history for five thousand years with one goal in mind: to make Percy Jackson's life suck as much as possible.

'You know what's in that cavern,' he guessed. 'Does it have to do with spiders?'

'Yes,' she said in a small voice.

'Then how can you even . . .?' He made himself stop.

Once Annabeth had made up her mind, arguing with her wouldn't do any good. He remembered the night three and a half years ago, when they'd saved Nico and Bianca di Angelo in Maine. Annabeth had been captured by the Titan Atlas. For a while, Percy wasn't sure if she was alive or dead. He'd travelled across the country to save her from the Titan. It had been the hardest few days of his life – not just the monsters and the fighting but the worry.

How could he *intentionally* let her go now, knowing she was heading into something even more dangerous?

Then it dawned on him: the way he had felt back then, for a few days, was probably how Annabeth had felt for the six months he had been missing with amnesia.

That made him feel guilty, and a little bit selfish, to be standing here arguing with her. She *had* to go on this quest. The fate of the world might depend on it. But part of him wanted to say: *Forget the world.* He didn't want to be without her.

Percy stared into the fog. He couldn't see anything around them, but he had perfect bearings at sea. He knew their exact latitude and longitude. He knew the depth of the ocean and which way the currents were flowing. He knew the ship's speed, and could sense no rocks, sandbars or other natural dangers in their path. Still, being blind was unsettling.

They hadn't been attacked since they had touched the water, but the sea seemed different. Percy had been in the Atlantic, the Pacific, even the Gulf of Alaska, but this sea felt more ancient and powerful. Percy could sense its layers swirling below him. Every Greek or Roman hero had sailed these waters – from Hercules to Aeneas. Monsters still dwelt in the depths, so deeply wrapped in the Mist that they slept most of the time, but Percy could feel them stirring, responding to the Celestial bronze hull of a Greek trireme and the presence of demigod blood.

They are back, the monsters seemed to say. *Finally, fresh blood.*

'We're not far from the Italian coast,' Percy said, mostly to break the silence. 'Maybe a hundred nautical miles to the mouth of the Tiber.'

'Good,' Annabeth said. 'By daybreak, we should –'

'Stop.' Percy's skin felt washed with ice. 'We have to stop.'

'Why?' Annabeth asked.

'Leo, stop!' he yelled.

Too late. The other boat appeared out of the fog and rammed them head-on. In that split second, Percy registered random details: another trireme; black sails painted with a gorgon's head; hulking warriors, not quite human, crowded at the front of the boat in Greek armour, swords and spears ready; and a bronze ram at water level, slamming against the hull of the *Argo II*.

Annabeth and Percy were almost thrown overboard.

Festus blew fire, sending a dozen very surprised warriors screaming and diving into the sea, but more swarmed aboard the *Argo II*. Grappling lines wrapped around the rails and the mast, digging iron claws into the hull's planks.

By the time Percy had recovered his wits, the enemy was everywhere. He couldn't see well through the fog and the dark, but the invaders seemed to be humanlike dolphins, or dolphinlike humans. Some had grey snouts. Others held their swords in stunted flippers. Some waddled on legs partially fused together, while others had flippers for feet, which reminded Percy of clown shoes.

Leo sounded the alarm bell. He made a dash for the nearest ballista but went down under a pile of chattering dolphin warriors.

Annabeth and Percy stood back to back, as they'd done many times before, their weapons drawn. Percy tried to summon the waves, hoping he could push the ships apart or even capsize the enemy vessel, but nothing happened. It almost felt like something was pushing against his will, wresting the sea from his control.

He raised Riptide, ready to fight, but they were hopelessly outnumbered. Several dozen warriors lowered their spears and made a ring around them, wisely keeping out of striking distance of Percy's sword. The dolphin-men opened their snouts and made whistling, popping noises. Percy had never considered just how vicious dolphin teeth looked.

He tried to think. Maybe he could break out of the

circle and destroy a few invaders, but not without the others skewering him and Annabeth.

At least the warriors didn't seem interested in killing them immediately. They kept Percy and Annabeth contained while more of their comrades flooded belowdecks and secured the hull. Percy could hear them breaking down the cabin doors, scuffling with his friends. Even if the other demigods hadn't been fast asleep, they wouldn't have stood a chance against so many.

Leo was dragged across the deck, half-conscious and groaning, and dumped on a pile of ropes. Below, the sounds of fighting tapered off. Either the others had been subdued or . . . or Percy refused to think about it.

On one side of the ring of spears, the dolphin warriors parted to let someone through. He appeared to be fully human, but, from the way the dolphins fell back before him, he was clearly the leader. He was dressed in Greek combat armour – sandals, kilt and greaves, a breastplate decorated with elaborate sea-monster designs – and everything he wore was gold. Even his sword, a Greek blade like Riptide, was gold instead of bronze.

The golden boy, Percy thought, remembering his dream. *They'll have to get past the golden boy.*

What really made Percy nervous was the guy's helmet. His visor was a full face mask fashioned like a gorgon's head – curved tusks, horrible features pinched into a snarl and golden snake hair curling around the face. Percy had met gorgons before. The likeness was good – a little too good for his taste.

Annabeth turned so she was shoulder to shoulder with Percy. He wanted to put his arm around her protectively, but he doubted she'd appreciate the gesture, and he didn't want to give this golden guy any indication that Annabeth was his girlfriend. No sense giving the enemy more leverage than they already had.

'Who are you?' Percy demanded. 'What do you want?'

The golden warrior chuckled. With a flick of his blade, faster than Percy could follow, he smacked Riptide out of Percy's hand and sent it flying into the sea.

He might as well have thrown Percy's lungs into the sea, because suddenly Percy couldn't breathe. He'd never been disarmed so easily.

'Hello, brother.' The golden warrior's voice was rich and velvety, with an exotic accent – Middle Eastern, maybe – that seemed vaguely familiar. 'Always happy to rob a fellow son of Poseidon. I am Chrysaor, the Golden Sword. As for what I want . . .' He turned his metal mask towards Annabeth. 'Well, that's easy. I want everything you have.'

XXX

PERCY

PERCY'S HEART DID JUMPING JACKS while Chrysaor walked back and forth, inspecting them like prized cattle. A dozen of his dolphin-man warriors stayed in a ring around them, spears levelled at Percy's chest, while dozens more ransacked the ship, banging and crashing around belowdecks. One carried a box of ambrosia up the stairs. Another carried an armful of ballista bolts and a crate of Greek fire.

'Careful with that!' Annabeth warned. 'It'll blow up both our ships.'

'Ha!' Chrysaor said. 'We know all about Greek fire, girl. Don't worry. We've been looting and pillaging ships on the Mare Nostrum for aeons.'

'Your accent sounds familiar,' Percy said. 'Have we met?'

'I haven't had the pleasure.' Chrysaor's golden gorgon mask snarled at him, though it was impossible to tell what his real expression might be underneath. 'But I've heard all about you,

Percy Jackson. Oh, yes, the young man who saved Olympus. And his faithful sidekick, Annabeth Chase.'

'I'm nobody's sidekick,' Annabeth growled. 'And, Percy, his accent sounds familiar because he sounds like his mother. We killed her in New Jersey.'

Percy frowned. 'I'm pretty sure that accent isn't New Jersey. Who's his –? Oh.'

It all fell into place. Aunty Em's Garden Gnome Emporium – the lair of Medusa. She'd talked with that same accent, at least until Percy had cut off her head.

'*Medusa* is your mom?' he asked. 'Dude, that sucks for you.'

Judging from the sound in Chrysaor's throat, he was now snarling under the mask, too.

'You are as arrogant as the *first* Perseus,' Chrysaor said. 'But, yes, Percy Jackson. Poseidon was my father. Medusa was my mother. After Medusa was changed into a monster by that so-called goddess of wisdom . . .' The golden mask turned on Annabeth. 'That would be *your* mother, I believe . . . Medusa's two children were trapped inside her, unable to be born. When the original Perseus cut off Medusa's head –'

'Two children sprang out,' Annabeth remembered. 'Pegasus and you.'

Percy blinked. 'So your brother is a winged horse. But you're also my half brother, which means all the flying horses in the world are my . . . You know what? Let's forget it.'

He'd learned years ago it was better not to dwell too much on who was related to whom on the godly side of things. After Tyson the Cyclops adopted him as a brother, Percy decided that that was about as far as he wanted to extend the family.

'But if you're Medusa's kid,' he said, 'why haven't I ever heard of you?'

Chrysaor sighed in exasperation. 'When your brother is Pegasus, you get used to being forgotten. Oh, look, a winged horse! Does anyone care about me? No!' He raised the tip of his blade to Percy's eyes. 'But don't underestimate me. My name means the Golden Sword for a reason.'

'Imperial gold?' Percy guessed.

'Bah! *Enchanted* gold, yes. Later on, the Romans called it Imperial gold, but I was the first to ever wield such a blade. I should have been the most famous hero of all time! Since the legend-tellers decided to ignore me, I became a villain instead. I resolved to put my heritage to use. As the son of Medusa, I would inspire terror. As the son of Poseidon, I would rule the seas!'

'You became a pirate,' Annabeth summed up.

Chrysaor spread his arms, which was fine with Percy since it got the sword point away from his eyes.

'The *best* pirate,' Chrysaor said. 'I've sailed these waters for centuries, waylaying any demigods foolish enough to explore the Mare Nostrum. This is my territory now. And all you have is mine.'

One of the dolphin warriors dragged Coach Hedge up from below.

'Let me go, you tuna fish!' Hedge bellowed. He tried to kick the warrior, but his hoof clanged off his captor's armour. Judging from the hoof-shaped prints in the dolphin's breastplate and helmet, the coach had already made several attempts.

'Ah, a satyr,' Chrysaor mused. 'A little old and stringy, but Cyclopes will pay well for a morsel like him. Chain him up.'

'I'm nobody's goat meat!' Hedge protested.

'Gag him as well,' Chrysaor decided.

'Why you gilded little –' Hedge's insult was cut short when the dolphin put a greasy wad of canvas in his mouth. Soon the coach was trussed like a rodeo calf and dumped with the other loot – crates of food, extra weapons, even the magical ice chest from the mess hall.

'You can't do this!' Annabeth shouted.

Chrysaor's laughter reverberated inside his gold face mask. Percy wondered if he was horribly disfigured under there, or if his gaze could petrify people the way his mother's could.

'I can do anything I want,' Chrysaor said. 'My warriors have been trained to perfection. They are vicious, cut-throat –'

'Dolphins,' Percy noted.

Chrysaor shrugged. 'Yes. So? They had some bad luck a few millennia ago, kidnapped the wrong person. Some of their crew got turned *completely* into dolphins. Others went mad. But these . . . these survived as hybrid creatures. When I found them under the sea and offered them a new life, they became my loyal crew. They fear nothing!'

One of the warriors chattered at him nervously.

'Yes, yes,' Chrysaor growled. 'They fear *one* thing, but it hardly matters. He's not here.'

An idea began tickling at the base of Percy's skull. Before

he could pursue it, more dolphin warriors climbed the stairs, hauling up the rest of his friends. Jason was unconscious. Judging from the new bruises on his face, he'd tried to fight. Hazel and Piper were bound hand and foot. Piper had a gag in her mouth, so apparently the dolphins had discovered she could charmspeak. Frank was the only one missing, though two of the dolphins had bee stings covering their faces.

Could Frank actually turn into a swarm of bees? Percy hoped so. If he was free aboard the ship somewhere, that could be an advantage, assuming Percy could figure out how to communicate with him.

'Excellent!' Chrysaor gloated. He directed his warriors to dump Jason by the crossbows. Then he examined the girls like they were Christmas presents, which made Percy grit his teeth.

'The boy is no use to me,' Chrysaor said. 'But we have an understanding with the witch Circe. She will buy the women — either as slaves or trainees, depending on their skill. But not you, lovely Annabeth.'

Annabeth recoiled. 'You are *not* taking me anywhere.'

Percy's hand crept to his pocket. His pen had appeared back in his jeans. He only needed a moment's distraction to draw his sword. Maybe, if he could take down Chrysaor quickly, his crew would panic.

He wished he knew something about Chrysaor's weaknesses. Usually Annabeth provided him with information like that, but apparently Chrysaor didn't *have* any legends, so they were both in the dark.

The golden warrior tutted. 'Oh, sadly, Annabeth, you will

not be staying with me. I would love that. But you and your friend Percy are spoken for. A certain goddess is paying a high bounty for your capture – alive, if possible, though she didn't say you had to be unharmed.'

At that moment, Piper caused the disturbance they needed. She wailed so loudly it could be heard through her gag. Then she fainted against the nearest guard, knocking him over. Hazel got the idea and crumpled to the deck, kicking her legs and thrashing like she was having a fit.

Percy drew Riptide and lashed out. The blade should have gone straight through Chrysaor's neck, but the golden warrior was unbelievably fast. He dodged and parried as the dolphin warriors backed up, guarding the other captives while giving their captain room to battle. They chattered and squeaked, egging him on, and Percy got the sinking suspicion the crew was used to this sort of entertainment. They didn't feel their leader was in any sort of danger.

Percy hadn't crossed swords with an opponent like this since . . . well, since he'd battled the war god Ares. Chrysaor was *that* good. Many of Percy's powers had got stronger over the years, but now, too late, Percy realized that swordplay wasn't one of them.

He was rusty – at least against an adversary like Chrysaor.

They battled back and forth, thrusting and parrying. Without meaning to, Percy heard the voice of Luke Castellan, his first sword-fighting mentor at Camp Half-Blood, throwing out suggestions. But it didn't help.

The golden gorgon mask was too unnerving. The warm

fog, the slick deck boards, the chattering of the warriors – none of it helped. And, in the corner of his eye, Percy could see one of the dolphin-men holding a knife at Annabeth's throat in case she tried anything tricky.

He feinted and thrust at Chrysaor's gut, but Chrysaor anticipated the move. He knocked Percy's sword out of his hand again, and once more Riptide flew into the sea.

Chrysaor laughed easily. He wasn't even winded. He pressed the tip of his golden sword against Percy's sternum.

'A good try,' said the pirate. 'But now you'll be chained and transported to Gaia's minions. They are quite eager to spill your blood and wake the goddess.'

PERCY

NOTHING LIKE TOTAL FAILURE TO GENERATE great ideas.

As Percy stood there, disarmed and outmatched, the plan formed in his head. He was so used to Annabeth providing Greek legend information that he was kind of stunned to actually remember something useful, but he *had* to act fast. He couldn't let anything happen to his friends. He wasn't going to lose Annabeth – not again.

Chrysaor couldn't be beaten. At least not in single combat. But without his crew . . . maybe then he could be overwhelmed if enough demigods attacked him at once.

How to deal with Chrysaor's crew? Percy put the pieces together: the pirates had been turned into dolphin-men millennia ago when they had kidnapped the wrong person. Percy *knew* that story. Heck, the wrong person in question had threatened to turn *him* into a dolphin. And when Chrysaor said the crew wasn't afraid of anything, one of the dolphins had nervously corrected him. *Yes,* Chrysaor said. *But he's not here.*

Percy glanced towards the stern and spotted Frank, in human form, peeking out from behind a ballista, waiting. Percy resisted the urge to smile. The big guy claimed to be clumsy and useless, but he always seemed to be in exactly the right place when Percy needed him.

The girls . . . Frank . . . the ice chest.

It was a crazy idea. But, as usual, that's all Percy had.

'Fine!' Percy shouted, so loudly that he got everyone's attention. 'Take us away, if our captain will let you.'

Chrysaor turned his golden mask. 'What captain? My men searched the ship. There is no one else.'

Percy raised his hands dramatically. 'The god appears only when he wishes. But he is our leader. He runs our camp for demigods. Doesn't he, Annabeth?'

Annabeth was quick. 'Yes!' She nodded enthusiastically. 'Mr D! The great Dionysus!'

A ripple of uneasiness passed through the dolphin-men. One dropped his sword.

'Stand fast!' Chrysaor bellowed. 'There is no god on this ship. They are trying to scare you.'

'You should be scared!' Percy looked at the pirate crew with sympathy. 'Dionysus will be severely cranky with you for having delayed our voyage. He will punish all of us. Didn't you notice the girls falling into the wine god's madness?'

Hazel and Piper had stopped the shaking fits. They were sitting on the deck, staring at Percy, but when he glared at them pointedly they started hamming it up again, trembling and flopping around like fish. The dolphin-men fell over themselves trying to get away from their captives.

'Fakes!' Chrysaor roared. 'Shut up, Percy Jackson. Your camp director is not here. He was recalled to Olympus. This is common knowledge.'

'So you admit Dionysus is our director!' Percy said.

'He *was*,' Chrysaor corrected. 'Everyone knows that.'

Percy gestured at the golden warrior like he'd just betrayed himself. 'You see? We are doomed. If you don't believe me, let's check the ice chest!'

Percy stormed over to the magical cooler. No one tried to stop him. He knocked open the lid and rummaged through the ice. There had to be one. Please. He was rewarded with a silver-and-red can of soda. He brandished it at the dolphin warriors as if spraying them with bug repellent.

'Behold!' Percy shouted. 'The god's chosen beverage. Tremble before the horror of Diet Coke!'

The dolphin-men began to panic. They were on the edge of retreat. Percy could feel it.

'The god will take your ship,' Percy warned. 'He will finish your transformation into dolphins, or make you insane, or transform you into insane dolphins! Your only hope is to swim away now, quickly!'

'Ridiculous!' Chrysaor's voice turned shrill. He didn't seem sure where to level his sword – at Percy or his own crew.

'Save yourselves!' Percy warned. 'It is too late for us!'

Then he gasped and pointed to the spot where Frank was hiding. 'Oh, no! Frank is turning into a crazy dolphin!'

Nothing happened.

'I *said*,' Percy repeated, 'Frank is turning into a crazy dolphin!'

Frank stumbled out of nowhere, making a big show of grabbing his throat. 'Oh, no,' he said, like he was reading from a teleprompter. 'I am turning into a crazy dolphin.'

He began to change, his nose elongating into a snout, his skin becoming sleek and grey. He fell to the deck as a dolphin, his tail thumping against the boards.

The pirate crew disbanded in terror, chattering and clicking as they dropped their weapons, forgot the captives, ignored Chrysaor's orders and jumped overboard. In the confusion, Annabeth moved quickly to cut the bonds on Hazel, Piper and Coach Hedge.

Within seconds, Chrysaor was alone and surrounded. Percy and his friends had no weapons except for Annabeth's knife and Hedge's hooves, but the murderous looks on their faces evidently convinced the golden warrior he was doomed.

He backed to the edge of the rail.

'This isn't over, Jackson,' Chrysaor growled. 'I will have my revenge –'

His words were cut short by Frank, who had changed form again. An eight-hundred-pound grizzly bear can definitely break up a conversation. He sideswiped Chrysaor and raked the golden mask off his helmet. Chrysaor screamed, instantly covering his face with his arms and tumbling into the water.

They ran to the rail. Chrysaor had disappeared. Percy thought about chasing him, but he didn't know these waters, and he didn't want to confront that guy alone again.

'That was brilliant!' Annabeth kissed him, which made him feel a little better.

'It was desperate,' Percy corrected. 'And we need to get rid of this pirate trireme.'

'Burn it?' Annabeth asked.

Percy looked at the Diet Coke in his hand. 'No. I've got another idea.'

It took them longer than Percy wanted. As they worked, he kept glancing at the sea, waiting for Chrysaor and his pirate dolphins to return, but they didn't.

Leo got back on his feet, thanks to a little nectar. Piper tended to Jason's wounds, but he wasn't as badly hurt as he looked. Mostly he was just ashamed that he'd been overpowered again, which Percy could relate to.

They returned all their own supplies to the proper places and tidied up from the invasion while Coach Hedge had a field day on the enemy ship, breaking everything he could find with his baseball bat.

When he was done, Percy loaded the enemy's weapons back on the pirate ship. Their storeroom was full of treasure, but Percy insisted that they touch none of it.

'I can sense about six million dollars' worth of gold aboard,' Hazel said. 'Plus diamonds, rubies –'

'Six m-million?' Frank stammered. 'Canadian dollars or American?'

'Leave it,' Percy said. 'It's part of the tribute.'

'Tribute?' Hazel asked.

'Oh.' Piper nodded. 'Kansas.'

Jason grinned. He'd been there too when they'd met the wine god. 'Crazy. But I like it.'

Finally Percy went aboard the pirate ship and opened the flood valves. He asked Leo to drill a few extra holes in the bottom of the hull with his power tools, and Leo was happy to oblige.

The crew of the *Argo II* assembled at the rail and cut the grappling lines. Piper brought out her new horn of plenty and, on Percy's direction, willed it to spew Diet Coke, which came out with the strength of a fire hose, dousing the enemy deck. Percy thought it would take hours, but the ship sank remarkably fast, filling with Diet Coke and seawater.

'Dionysus,' Percy called, holding up Chrysaor's golden mask. 'Or Bacchus – whatever. You made this victory possible, even if you weren't here. Your enemies trembled at your name . . . or your Diet Coke, or something. So, yeah, thank you.'

The words were hard to get out, but Percy managed not to gag. 'We give this ship to you as tribute. We hope you like it.'

'Six million in gold,' Leo muttered. 'He'd *better* like it.'

'Shh,' Hazel scolded. 'Precious metal isn't all that great. Believe me.'

Percy threw the golden mask aboard the vessel, which was now sinking even faster, brown fizzy liquid spewing out of the trireme's oar slots and bubbling from the cargo hold, turning the sea frothy brown.

Percy summoned a wave, and the enemy ship was swamped. Leo steered the *Argo II* away as the pirate vessel disappeared underwater.

'Isn't that polluting?' Piper asked.

'I wouldn't worry,' Jason told her. 'If Bacchus likes it, the ship should vanish.'

Percy didn't know if that would happen, but he felt like he'd done all he could. He had no faith that Dionysus would hear them or care, much less help them in their battle against the twin giants, but he had to try.

As the *Argo II* headed east into the fog, Percy decided at least one good thing had come out of his sword fight with Chrysaor. He was feeling humble – even humble enough to pay tribute to the wine dude.

After their bout with the pirates, they decided to fly the rest of the way to Rome. Jason insisted he was well enough to take sentry duty, along with Coach Hedge, who was still so charged with adrenalin that every time the ship hit turbulence he swung his bat and yelled, 'Die!'

They had a couple of hours before daybreak, so Jason suggested Percy try to get a few more hours of sleep.

'It's fine, man,' Jason said. 'Give somebody else a chance to save the ship, huh?'

Percy agreed, though once in his cabin he had trouble falling asleep.

He stared at the bronze lantern swaying from the ceiling and thought about how easily Chrysaor had beaten him at swordplay. The golden warrior could've killed him without breaking a sweat. He'd only kept Percy alive because someone else wanted to pay for the privilege of killing him later.

Percy felt like an arrow had slipped through a chink in his armour – as if he still had the blessing of Achilles and someone had found his weak spot. The older he got, the longer he survived as a half-blood, the more his friends looked up to him. They depended on him and relied on his powers. Even the Romans had raised him on a shield and made him praetor, and he'd only known them for a couple of weeks.

But Percy didn't *feel* powerful. The more heroic stuff he did, the more he realized how limited he was. He felt like a fraud. *I'm not as great as you think*, he wanted to warn his friends. His failures, like tonight, seemed to prove it. Maybe that's why he had started to fear suffocation. It wasn't so much drowning in the earth or the sea but the feeling that he was sinking into too many expectations, literally getting in over his head.

Wow . . . when he started having thoughts like that, he *knew* he'd been spending too much time with Annabeth.

Athena had once told Percy his fatal flaw: he was supposedly too loyal to his friends. He couldn't see the big picture. He would save a friend even if it meant destroying the world.

At the time, Percy had shrugged this off. How could loyalty be a bad thing? Besides, things had worked out okay against the Titans. He'd saved his friends *and* beaten Kronos.

Now, though, he started to wonder. He would gladly throw himself at any monster, god or giant to keep his friends from being hurt. But what if he wasn't up to the task? What if someone *else* had to do it? That was *very* hard for him to admit. He even had trouble with simple things like letting Jason take a turn at watch. He didn't want to rely on someone else to protect him, someone who could get hurt on his account.

Percy's mom had done that for him. She'd stayed in a bad relationship with a gross mortal guy because she thought it would save Percy from monsters. Grover, his best friend, had protected Percy for almost a year before Percy even realized he was a demigod, and Grover had almost been killed by the Minotaur.

Percy wasn't a kid any more. He didn't want anybody he loved taking a risk for him. He *had* to be strong enough to be the protector himself. But now he was supposed to let Annabeth go off on her own to follow the Mark of Athena, knowing she might die. If it came to a choice – save Annabeth or let the quest succeed – could Percy really choose the quest?

Exhaustion finally overtook him. He fell asleep, and in his nightmare the rumble of thunder became the laughter of the earth goddess Gaia.

Percy dreamed he was standing on the front porch of the Big House at Camp Half-Blood. The sleeping face of Gaia appeared on the side of Half-Blood Hill – her massive features formed from the shadows on the grassy slopes. Her lips didn't move, but her voice echoed across the valley.

So this is your home, Gaia murmured. *Take a last look, Percy Jackson. You should have returned here. At least then you could have died with your comrades when the Romans invaded. Now your blood will be spilled far from home, on the ancient stones, and I will rise.*

The ground shook. At the top of Half-Blood Hill, Thalia's

pine tree burst into flames. Disruption rolled across the valley – grass turning to sand, forest crumbling to dust. The river and the canoe lake dried up. The cabins and the Big House burned to ashes. When the tremor stopped, Camp Half-Blood looked like a wasteland after an atomic blast. The only thing left was the porch where Percy stood.

Next to him, the dust swirled and solidified into the figure of a woman. Her eyes were closed, as if she were sleepwalking. Her robes were forest green, dappled with gold and white like sunlight shifting through branches. Her hair was as black as tilled soil. Her face was beautiful, but even with a dreamy smile on her lips she seemed cold and distant. Percy got the feeling she could watch demigods die or cities burn and that smile wouldn't waver.

'When I reclaim the earth,' Gaia said, 'I will leave this spot barren forever, to remind me of your kind and how utterly powerless they were to stop me. It doesn't matter *when* you fall, my sweet little pawn – to Phorcys or Chrysaor or my dear twins. You *will* fall, and I will be there to devour you. Your only choice now . . . will you fall alone? Come to me willingly; bring the girl. Perhaps I will spare this place you love. Otherwise . . .'

Gaia opened her eyes. They swirled in green and black, as deep as the crust of the earth. Gaia saw everything. Her patience was infinite. She was slow to wake, but once she arose her power was unstoppable.

Percy's skin tingled. His hands went numb. He looked down and realized he was crumbling to dust, like all the monsters he'd ever defeated.

'Enjoy Tartarus, my little pawn,' Gaia purred.

A metallic *CLANG-CLANG-CLANG* jolted Percy out of his dream. His eyes shot open. He realized he'd just heard the landing gear being lowered.

There was a knock on his door, and Jason poked his head in. The bruises on his face had faded. His blue eyes glittered with excitement.

'Hey, man,' he said. 'We're descending over Rome. You really should see this.'

The sky was brilliant blue, as if the stormy weather had never happened. The sun rose over the distant hills, so everything below them shone and sparkled like the entire city of Rome had just come out of the car wash.

Percy had seen big cities before. He was from New York, after all. But the sheer vastness of Rome grabbed him by the throat and made it hard to breathe. The city seemed to have no regard for the limits of geography. It spread through hills and valleys, jumped over the Tiber with dozens of bridges, and just kept sprawling to the horizon. Streets and alleys zigzagged with no rhyme or reason through quilts of neighbourhoods. Glass office buildings stood next to excavation sites. A cathedral stood next to a line of Roman columns, which stood next to a modern football stadium. In some neighbourhoods, old stucco villas with red-tiled roofs crowded the cobblestone streets, so that if Percy concentrated just on those areas he could imagine he was back in ancient times. Everywhere he looked, there were wide piazzas and traffic-clogged streets. Parks cut across the city with a crazy collection of palm trees, pines, junipers and olive trees, as if Rome couldn't decide what part of the world it belonged to – or maybe it just believed all the world still belonged to *Rome*.

It was as if the city knew about Percy's dream of Gaia. It knew that the earth goddess intended on razing all human civilization, and this city, which had stood for thousands of years, was saying back to her: *You wanna dissolve this city, Dirt Face? Give it a shot.*

In other words, it was the Coach Hedge of mortal cities – only taller.

'We're setting down in that park,' Leo announced, pointing to a wide green space dotted with palm trees. 'Let's hope the Mist makes us look like a large pigeon or something.'

Percy wished Jason's sister, Thalia, were here. She'd always had a way of bending the Mist to make people see what she wanted. Percy had never been very good at that. He just kept thinking, *Don't look at me*, and hoped the Romans below would fail to notice the giant bronze trireme descending on their city in the middle of morning rush hour.

It seemed to work. Percy didn't notice any cars veering off the road or Romans pointing to the sky and screaming, 'Aliens!' The *Argo II* set down in the grassy field and the oars retracted.

The noise of traffic was all around them, but the park itself was peaceful and deserted. To their left, a green lawn sloped towards a line of woods. An old villa nestled in the shade of some weird-looking pine trees with thin curvy trunks that shot up thirty or forty feet, then sprouted into puffy canopies. They reminded Percy of trees in those Dr Seuss books his mom used to read him when he was little.

To their right, snaking along the top of a hill, was a long brick wall with notches at the top for archers – maybe a mediaeval defensive line, maybe Ancient Roman. Percy wasn't sure.

To the north, about a mile away through the folds of the city, the top of the Colosseum rose above the rooftops, looking just like it did in travel photos. That's when Percy's legs started shaking. He was actually here. He'd thought his trip to Alaska had been pretty exotic, but now he was in the heart of the old Roman Empire, enemy territory for a Greek demigod. In a way, this place had shaped his life as much as New York.

Jason pointed to the base of the archers' wall, where steps led down into some kind of tunnel.

'I think I know where we are,' he said. 'That's the Tomb of the Scipios.'

Percy frowned. 'Scipio . . . Reyna's pegasus?'

'No,' Annabeth put in. 'They were a noble Roman family, and . . . wow, this place is amazing.'

Jason nodded. 'I've studied maps of Rome before. I've always wanted to come here, but . . .'

Nobody bothered finishing that sentence. Looking at his friends' faces, Percy could tell they were just as much in awe as he was. They'd made it. They'd landed in Rome – *the* Rome.

'Plans?' Hazel asked. 'Nico has until sunset – at best. And this entire city is supposedly getting destroyed today.'

Percy shook himself out of his daze. 'You're right.

Annabeth . . . did you zero in on that spot from your bronze map?'

Her grey eyes turned extra thunderstorm dark, which Percy could interpret just fine: *Remember what I said, buddy. Keep that dream to yourself.*

'Yes,' she said carefully. 'It's on the Tiber River. I think I can find it, but I should –'

'Take me along,' Percy finished. 'Yeah, you're right.'

Annabeth glared daggers at him. 'That's not –'

'Safe,' he supplied. 'One demigod walking through Rome alone. I'll go with you as far as the Tiber. We can use that letter of introduction, hopefully meet the river god Tiberinus. Maybe he can give you some help or advice. Then you can go on alone from there.'

They had a silent staring contest, but Percy didn't back down. When he and Annabeth had started dating, his mother had drummed it into his head: *It's good manners to walk your date to the door.* If that were true, it *had* to be good manners to walk her to the start of her epic solo death quest.

'Fine,' Annabeth muttered. 'Hazel, now that we're in Rome, do you think you can pinpoint Nico's location?'

Hazel blinked, as if coming out of a trance from watching the *Percy/Annabeth Show*. 'Um . . . hopefully, if I get close enough. I'll have to walk around the city. Frank, would you come with me?'

Frank beamed. 'Absolutely.'

'And, uh . . . Leo,' Hazel added. 'It might be a good idea if you came along, too. The fish-centaurs said we'd need your help with something mechanical.'

'Yeah,' Leo said, 'no problem.'

Frank's smile turned into something more like Chrysaor's mask.

Percy was no genius when it came to relationships, but even he could feel the tension among those three. Ever since they'd been knocked into the Atlantic, they hadn't acted quite the same. It wasn't just the two guys competing for Hazel. It was like the three of them were locked together, acting out some kind of murder mystery, but they hadn't yet discovered which of them was the victim.

Piper drew her knife and set it on the rail. 'Jason and I can watch the ship for now. I'll see what Katoptris can show me. But, Hazel, if you guys get a fix on Nico's location, don't go in there by yourselves. Come back and get us. It'll take all of us to fight the giants.'

She didn't say the obvious: even all of them together wouldn't be enough, unless they had a god on their side. Percy decided not to bring that up.

'Good idea,' Percy said. 'How about we plan to meet back here at . . . what?'

'Three this afternoon?' Jason suggested. 'That's probably the latest we could rendezvous and still hope to fight the giants and save Nico. If something happens to change the plan, try to send an Iris-message.'

The others nodded in agreement, but Percy noticed several of them glancing at Annabeth. Another thing no one wanted to say: Annabeth would be on a different schedule. She might be back at three, or much later, or never. But she would be on her own, searching for the Athena Parthenos.

Coach Hedge grunted. 'That'll give me time to eat the coconuts – I mean dig the coconuts out of our hull. Percy, Annabeth . . . I don't like you two going off on your own. Just remember: *behave*. If I hear about any funny business, I will ground you until the Styx freezes over.'

The idea of getting grounded when they were about to risk their lives was so ridiculous Percy couldn't help smiling.

'We'll be back soon,' he promised. He looked around at his friends, trying not to feel like this was the last time they'd ever be together. 'Good luck, everyone.'

Leo lowered the gangplank, and Percy and Annabeth were first off the ship.

XXXII

PERCY

UNDER DIFFERENT CIRCUMSTANCES, WANDERING THROUGH
Rome with Annabeth would have been pretty awesome.
They held hands as they navigated the winding streets,
dodging cars and crazy Vespa drivers, squeezing through
mobs of tourists and wading through oceans of pigeons. The
day warmed up quickly. Once they got away from the car
exhaust on the main roads, the air smelled of baking bread
and freshly cut flowers.

They aimed for the Colosseum because that was an
easy landmark, but getting there proved harder than Percy
anticipated. As big and confusing as the city had looked from
above, it was even more so on the ground. Several times they
got lost on dead-end streets. They found beautiful fountains
and huge monuments by accident.

Annabeth commented on the architecture, but Percy kept
his eyes open for other things. Once he spotted a glowing
purple ghost – a Lar – glaring at them from the window of

an apartment building. Another time he saw a white-robed woman – maybe a nymph or a goddess – holding a wicked-looking knife, slipping between ruined columns in a public park. Nothing attacked them, but Percy felt like they were being watched, and the watchers were not friendly.

Finally they reached the Colosseum, where a dozen guys in cheap gladiator costumes were scuffling with the police – plastic swords versus batons. Percy wasn't sure what that was about, but he and Annabeth decided to keep walking. Sometimes mortals were even stranger than monsters.

They made their way west, stopping every once in a while to ask directions to the river. Percy hadn't considered that – duh – people in Italy spoke Italian, while he did not. As it turned out, though, that wasn't much of a problem. The few times someone approached them on the street and asked a question, Percy just looked at them in confusion, and they switched to English.

Next discovery: the Italians used euros, and Percy didn't have any. He regretted this as soon as he found a tourist shop that sold sodas. By then it was almost noon, getting really hot, and Percy was starting to wish he had a trireme filled with Diet Coke.

Annabeth solved the problem. She dug around in her backpack, brought out Daedalus's laptop and typed in a few commands. A plastic card ejected from a slot in the side.

Annabeth waved it triumphantly. 'International credit card. For emergencies.'

Percy stared at her in amazement. 'How did you –? No. Never mind. I don't want to know. Just keep being awesome.'

The sodas helped, but they were still hot and tired by the time they arrived at the Tiber River. The shore was edged with a stone embankment. A chaotic assortment of warehouses, apartments, stores and cafés crowded the riverfront.

The Tiber itself was wide, lazy and caramel-coloured. A few tall cypress trees hung over the banks. The nearest bridge looked fairly new, made from iron girders, but right next to it stood a crumbling line of stone arches that stopped halfway across the river – ruins that might've been left over from the days of the Caesars.

'This is it.' Annabeth pointed at the old stone bridge. 'I recognize that from the map. But what do we do now?'

Percy was glad she had said *we*. He didn't want to leave her yet. In fact, he wasn't sure he could make himself do it when the time came. Gaia's words came back to him: *Will you fall alone?*

He stared at the river, wondering how they could make contact with the god Tiberinus. He didn't really want to jump in. The Tiber didn't look much cleaner than the East River back home, where he'd had too many encounters with grouchy river spirits.

He gestured to a nearby café with tables overlooking the water. 'It's about lunchtime. How about we try your credit card again?'

Even though it was noon, the place was empty. They picked a table outside by the river, and a waiter hurried over. He looked a bit surprised to see them – especially when they said they wanted lunch.

'American?' he asked, with a pained smile.

'Yes,' Annabeth said.

'And I'd love a pizza,' Percy said.

The waiter looked like he was trying to swallow a euro coin. 'Of course you would, *signor*. And let me guess: a Coca-Cola? With ice?'

'Awesome,' Percy said. He didn't understand why the guy was giving him such a sour face. It wasn't like Percy had asked for a *blue* Coke.

Annabeth ordered a panini and some fizzy water. After the waiter left, she smiled at Percy. 'I think Italians eat a lot later in the day. They don't put ice in their drinks. And they only do pizza for tourists.'

'Oh.' Percy shrugged. 'The best Italian food, and they don't even eat it?'

'I wouldn't say that in front of the waiter.'

They held hands across the table. Percy was content just to look at Annabeth in the sunlight. It always made her hair so bright and warm. Her eyes took on the colours of the sky and the cobblestones, alternately brown or blue.

He wondered if he should tell Annabeth his dream about Gaia destroying Camp Half-Blood. He decided against it. She didn't need anything else to worry about – not with what she was facing.

But it made him wonder . . . What would have happened if they hadn't scared off Chrysaor's pirates? Percy and Annabeth would've been put in chains and taken to Gaia's minions. Their blood would have been spilled on ancient stones. Percy guessed that meant they would've been taken to Greece for some big horrible sacrifice. But Annabeth and he had been in plenty of bad situations together. They could've figured out an escape plan, saved the day . . . and Annabeth wouldn't be facing this solo quest in Rome.

It doesn't matter when you fall, Gaia had said.

Percy knew it was a horrible wish, but he almost regretted that they hadn't been captured at sea. At least Annabeth and he would've been together.

'You shouldn't feel ashamed,' Annabeth said. 'You're thinking about Chrysaor, aren't you? Swords can't solve every problem. You saved us in the end.'

In spite of himself, Percy smiled. 'How do you *do* that? You always know what I'm thinking.'

'I know you,' she said.

And you like me anyway? Percy wanted to ask, but he held it back.

'Percy,' she said, 'you can't carry the weight of this whole quest. It's impossible. That's why there are seven of us. And you'll have to let me search for the Athena Parthenos on my own.'

'I missed you,' he confessed. 'For months. A huge chunk of our lives was taken away. If I lost you again –'

Lunch arrived. The waiter looked much calmer. Having accepted the fact that they were clueless Americans, he had apparently decided to forgive them and treat them politely.

'It is a beautiful view,' he said, nodding towards the river. 'Enjoy, please.'

Once he left, they ate in silence. The pizza was a bland, doughy square with not a lot of cheese. Maybe, Percy thought, that's why Romans didn't eat it. Poor Romans.

'You'll have to trust me,' Annabeth said. Percy almost thought she was talking to her sandwich, because she didn't meet his eyes. 'You've got to believe I'll come back.'

He swallowed another bite. 'I believe in *you*. That's not the problem. But come back from *where*?'

The sound of a Vespa interrupted them. Percy looked along the riverfront and did a double take. The motor scooter was an old-fashioned model: big and baby blue. The driver was a guy in a silky grey suit. Behind him sat a younger woman with a headscarf, her hands around the man's waist. They weaved between café tables and puttered to a stop next to Percy and Annabeth.

'Why, hello,' the man said. His voice was deep, almost croaky, like a movie actor's. His hair was short and greased back from his craggy face. He was handsome in a 1950s dad-on-television way. Even his clothes seemed old-fashioned. When he stepped off his bike, the waistline of his slacks was way higher than normal, but somehow he still managed to look manly and stylish and not like a total goober. Percy had trouble guessing his age – maybe thirty-something, though the man's fashion and manner seemed grandfatherish.

The woman slid off the bike. 'We've had the most *lovely* morning,' she said breathlessly.

She looked about twenty-one, also dressed in an old-fashioned style. Her ankle-length marigold skirt and white blouse were pinched together with a large leather belt, giving her the narrowest waist Percy had ever seen. When she removed her scarf, her short wavy black hair bounced into perfect shape. She had dark playful eyes and a brilliant smile.

Percy had seen naiads that looked less pixieish than this lady.

Annabeth's sandwich fell out of her hands. 'Oh, gods. How – how . . .?'

She seemed so stunned that Percy figured he ought to know these two.

'You guys *do* look familiar,' he decided. He thought he might have seen their faces on television. It seemed like they were from an old show, but that couldn't be right. They hadn't aged at all. Nevertheless, he pointed at the guy and took a guess. 'Are you that guy on *Mad Men*?'

'Percy!' Annabeth looked horrified.

'What?' he protested. 'I don't watch a lot of TV.'

'That's Gregory Peck!' Annabeth's eyes were wide, and her mouth kept falling open. 'And . . . oh *gods*! Audrey Hepburn! I *know* this movie. *Roman Holiday*. But that was from the 1950s. How –?'

'Oh, my dear!' The woman twirled like an air spirit and sat down at their table. 'I'm afraid you've mistaken me for someone else! My name is Rhea Silvia. I was the mother to Romulus and Remus, *thousands* of years ago. But you're so kind to think I look as young as the 1950s. And this is my husband . . .'

'Tiberinus,' said Gregory Peck, thrusting out his hand to Percy in a manly way. 'God of the River Tiber.'

Percy shook his hand. The guy smelled of aftershave. Of course, if Percy were the Tiber River, he'd probably want to mask the smell with cologne too.

'Uh, hi,' Percy said. 'Do you two always look like American movie stars?'

'Do we?' Tiberinus frowned and studied his clothes. 'I'm not sure, actually. The migration of Western civilization goes both ways, you know. Rome affected the world, but the world also affects Rome. There *does* seem to be a lot of American influence lately. I've rather lost track over the centuries.'

'Okay,' Percy said. 'But . . . you're here to help?'

'My naiads told me you two were here.' Tiberinus cast his dark eyes towards Annabeth. 'You have the map, my dear? And your letter of introduction?'

'Uh . . .' Annabeth handed him the letter and the disc of bronze. She was staring at the river god so intently Percy started to feel jealous.

'S-so . . .' she stammered, 'you've helped other children of Athena with this quest?'

'Oh, my dear!' The pretty lady, Rhea Silvia, put her hand on Annabeth's shoulder. 'Tiberinus is *ever* so helpful. He saved my children Romulus and Remus, you know, and brought them to the wolf goddess Lupa. Later, when that old king Numen tried to kill me, Tiberinus took pity on me and made me his wife. I've been ruling the river kingdom at his side ever since. He's just dreamy!'

'Thank you, my dear,' Tiberinus said with a wry smile. 'And, yes, Annabeth Chase, I've helped many of your siblings . . . to at least begin their journey safely. A shame all of them died painfully later on. Well, your documents seem in order. We should get going. The Mark of Athena awaits!'

Percy gripped Annabeth's hand – probably a little too tight. 'Tiberinus, let me go with her. Just a little further.'

Rhea Silvia laughed sweetly. 'But you can't, silly boy.

You must return to your ship and gather your other friends. Confront the giants! The way will appear in your friend Piper's knife. Annabeth has a different path. She must walk alone.'

'Indeed,' Tiberinus said. 'Annabeth must face the guardian of the shrine by herself. It is the only way. And, Percy Jackson, you have less time than you realize to rescue your friend in the jar. You must hurry.'

Percy's pizza felt like a cement lump in his stomach. 'But –'

'It's all right, Percy.' Annabeth squeezed his hand. 'I need to do this.'

He started to protest. Her expression stopped him. She was terrified but doing her best to hide it – for his sake. If he tried to argue, he would only make things harder for her. Or, worse, he might convince her to stay. Then she would have to live with the knowledge that she'd backed down from her biggest challenge . . . assuming that they survived at all, with Rome about to get levelled and Gaia about to rise and destroy the world. The Athena statue held the key to defeating the giants. Percy didn't know why or how, but Annabeth was the only one who could find it.

'You're right,' he said, forcing out the words. 'Be safe.'

Rhea Silvia giggled like it was a ridiculous comment. 'Safe? Not at all! But necessary. Come, Annabeth, my dear. We will show you where your path starts. After that, you're on your own.'

Annabeth kissed Percy. She hesitated, like she was wondering what else to say. Then she shouldered her backpack and climbed on the back of the scooter.

Percy hated it. He would've preferred to fight any monster in the world. He would've preferred a rematch with Chrysaor. But he forced himself to stay in his chair and watch as Annabeth motored off through the streets of Rome with Gregory Peck and Audrey Hepburn.

XXXIII

ANNABETH

ANNABETH FIGURED IT COULD'VE BEEN WORSE. If she had to go on a horrifying solo quest, at least she'd been able to have lunch with Percy on the banks of the Tiber first. Now she got to take a scooter ride with Gregory Peck.

She only knew about that old movie because of her dad. Over the past few years, since the two of them had made up, they'd spent more time together, and she had learned that her dad had a sappy side. Sure, he liked military history, weapons and biplanes, but he also loved old films, especially romantic comedies from the 1940s and 50s. *Roman Holiday* was one of his favourites. He'd made Annabeth watch it.

She thought the plot was silly – a princess escapes her minders and falls in love with an American journalist in Rome – but she suspected her dad liked it because it reminded him of his own romance with the goddess Athena: another impossible pairing that couldn't end happily. Her dad was nothing like Gregory Peck. Athena certainly wasn't anything like Audrey Hepburn. But Annabeth knew that people saw what they wanted to see. They didn't need the Mist to warp their perceptions.

As the baby-blue scooter zipped through the streets of Rome, the goddess Rhea Silvia gave Annabeth a running commentary on how the city had changed over the centuries.

'The Sublician Bridge was over there,' she said, pointing to a bend in the Tiber. 'You know, where Horatius and his two friends defended the city from an invading army? Now, *there* was a brave Roman!'

'And look, dear,' Tiberinus added, 'that's the place where Romulus and Remus washed ashore.'

He seemed to be talking about a spot on the riverside where some ducks were making a nest out of torn-up plastic bags and candy wrappers.

'Ah, yes,' Rhea Silvia sighed happily. 'You were so kind to flood yourself and wash my babies ashore for the wolves to find.'

'It was nothing,' Tiberinus said.

Annabeth felt light-headed. The river god was talking about something that had happened thousands of years ago, when this area was nothing but marshes and maybe some shacks. Tiberinus saved two babies, one of whom went on to found the world's greatest empire. *It was nothing.*

Rhea Silvia pointed out a large modern apartment building. 'That used to be a temple to Venus. Then it was a church. Then a palace. Then an apartment building. It burned down three times. Now it's an apartment building again. And that spot right there –'

'Please,' Annabeth said. 'You're making me dizzy.'

Rhea Silvia laughed. 'I'm sorry, dear. Layers upon layers of history here, but it's nothing compared to Greece. Athens was old when Rome was a collection of mud huts. You'll see, if you survive.'

'Not helping,' Annabeth muttered.

'Here we are,' Tiberinus announced. He pulled over in front of a large marble building, the facade covered in city grime but still beautiful. Ornate carvings of Roman gods decorated the roofline. The massive entrance was barred with iron gates, heavily padlocked.

'I'm going in there?' Annabeth wished she'd brought Leo, or at least borrowed some wire cutters from his tool belt.

Rhea Silvia covered her mouth and giggled. 'No, my dear. Not *in* it. *Under* it.'

Tiberinus pointed to a set of stone steps on the side of the building – the sort that would have led to a basement apartment if this place were in Manhattan.

'Rome is chaotic above ground,' Tiberinus said, 'but that's nothing compared to *below* ground. You must descend into the buried city, Annabeth Chase. Find the altar of the foreign god. The failures of your predecessors will guide you. After that . . . I do not know.'

Annabeth's backpack felt heavy on her shoulders. She'd been studying the bronze map for days now, scouring Daedalus's laptop for information. Unfortunately, the few things she had learned made this quest seem even more impossible. 'My siblings . . . none of them made it all the way to the shrine, did they.'

Tiberinus shook his head. 'But you know what prize awaits, if you can liberate it.'

'Yes,' Annabeth said.

'It could bring peace to the children of Greece and Rome,' Rhea Silvia said. 'It could change the course of the coming war.'

'If I live,' Annabeth said.

Tiberinus nodded sadly. 'Because you also understand the guardian you must face?'

Annabeth remembered the spiders at Fort Sumter and the dream Percy had described – the hissing voice in the dark. 'Yes.'

Rhea Silvia looked at her husband. 'She is brave. Perhaps she is stronger than the others.'

'I hope so,' said the river god. 'Goodbye, Annabeth Chase. And good luck.'

Rhea Silvia beamed. 'We have such a lovely afternoon planned! Off to shop!'

Gregory Peck and Audrey Hepburn sped off on their baby-blue motorbike. Then Annabeth turned and descended the steps alone.

She'd been underground plenty of times.

But halfway down the steps she realized just how long it had been since she'd adventured by herself. She froze.

Gods . . . she hadn't done something like this since she was a *kid*. After running away from home, she'd spent a few weeks surviving on her own, living in alleyways and hiding from monsters until Thalia and Luke took her under their wing. Then, once she'd arrived at Camp Half-Blood, she'd lived there until she was twelve. After that, all her quests had been with Percy or her other friends.

The last time she had felt this scared and alone, she'd been seven years old. She remembered the day Thalia, Luke and she had wandered into a Cyclopes' lair in Brooklyn. Thalia and Luke had been captured, and Annabeth had had to cut them free. She still remembered shivering in a dark corner of that dilapidated mansion, listening to the Cyclopes mimicking her friends' voices, trying to trick her into coming out into the open.

What if *this* is a trick, too? she wondered. What if those other children of Athena died because Tiberinus and Rhea Silvia led them into a trap? Would Gregory Peck and Audrey Hepburn do something like that?

She forced herself to keep going. She had no choice. If the Athena Parthenos was really down here, it could decide the fate of the war. More importantly, it could help her mom. Athena *needed* her.

At the bottom of the steps she reached an old wooden door with an iron pull-ring. Above the ring was a metal plate with a keyhole. Annabeth started considering ways to pick the lock, but, as soon as she touched the pull ring, a fiery shape burned in the middle of the door: the silhouette of Athena's owl. Smoke plumed from the keyhole. The door swung inwards.

Annabeth looked up one last time. At the top of the stairwell, the sky was a square of brilliant blue. Mortals would be enjoying the warm afternoon. Couples would be holding hands at the cafés. Tourists would be bustling through the shops and museums. Regular Romans would be going about their daily business, probably not considering the thousands of years of history under their feet, and definitely unaware of the spirits, gods and monsters that still dwelt here, or the fact that their city might be destroyed today unless a certain group of demigods succeeded in stopping the giants.

Annabeth stepped through the doorway.

She found herself in a basement that was an architectural cyborg. Ancient brick walls were crisscrossed with modern electrical cables and plumbing. The ceiling was held up with a combination of steel scaffolding and old granite Roman columns.

The front half of the basement was stacked with crates. Out of curiosity, Annabeth opened a few. Some were packed with multicoloured spools of string – like for kites or arts-and-crafts projects. Other crates were full of cheap plastic gladiator swords. Maybe at one point this had been a storage area for a tourist shop.

In the back of the basement, the floor had been excavated, revealing another set of steps – these of white stone – leading still deeper underground.

Annabeth crept to the edge. Even with the glow cast by her dagger, it was too dark to see below. She rested her hand on the wall and found a light switch.

She flipped it. Glaring white fluorescent bulbs illuminated the stairs. Below, she saw a mosaic floor decorated with deer and fauns – maybe a room from an Ancient Roman villa, just stashed away under this modern basement along with the crates of string and plastic swords.

She climbed down. The room was about twenty feet square. The walls had once been brightly painted, but most of the frescoes had peeled or faded. The only exit was a hole dug in one corner of the floor where the mosaic had been pulled up. Annabeth crouched next to the opening. It dropped straight down into a larger cavern, but Annabeth couldn't see the bottom.

She heard running water maybe thirty or forty feet below. The air didn't smell like a sewer – just old and musty, and slightly sweet, like mouldering flowers. Perhaps it was an old water line from the aqueducts. There was no way down.

'I'm not jumping,' she muttered to herself.

As if in reply, something glowed in the darkness. The Mark of Athena blazed to life at the bottom of the cavern, revealing glistening brickwork along a subterranean canal forty feet below. The fiery owl seemed to be taunting her: *Well, this is the way, kid. So you'd better figure something out.*

Annabeth considered her options. Too dangerous to jump. No ladders or ropes. She thought about borrowing some metal scaffolding from above to use as a fire pole, but it was all bolted in place. Besides, she didn't want to cause the building to collapse on top of her.

Frustration crawled through her like an army of termites. She had spent her life watching other demigods gain amazing powers. Percy could control water. If he were here, he could raise the water level and simply float down. Hazel, from what she had said, could find her way underground with flawless accuracy and even create or change the course of tunnels. She could easily make a new path. Leo would pull just the right tools from his belt and build something to do the job. Frank could turn into a bird. Jason could simply control the wind and float down. Even Piper with her charmspeak . . . she could have convinced Tiberinus and Rhea Silvia to be a little more helpful.

What did Annabeth have? A bronze dagger that did nothing special and a cursed silver coin. She had her backpack with Daedalus's laptop, a water bottle, a few pieces of ambrosia for emergencies and a box of matches – probably useless, but her dad had drilled into her head that she should always have a way to make fire.

She had no amazing powers. Even her one true magic item, her New York Yankees cap of invisibility, had stopped working, and was still back in her cabin on the *Argo II.*

You've got your intelligence, a voice said. Annabeth wondered if Athena was speaking to her, but that was probably just wishful thinking.

Intelligence . . . like Athena's favourite hero, Odysseus. He'd won the Trojan War with cleverness, not strength. He had overcome all sorts of monsters and hardships with his quick wits. That's what Athena valued.

Wisdom's daughter walks alone.

That didn't mean just without other people, Annabeth realized. It meant without any special powers.

Okay . . . so how to get down there safely and make sure she had a way to get out again if necessary?

She climbed back to the basement and stared at the open

crates. Kite string and plastic swords. The idea that came to her was so ridiculous she almost had to laugh, but it was better than nothing.

She set to work. Her hands seemed to know exactly what to do. Sometimes that happened, like when she was helping Leo with the ship's machinery or drawing architectural plans on the computer. She'd never made anything out of kite string and plastic swords, but it seemed easy, natural. Within minutes she'd used a dozen balls of string and a crateful of swords to create a makeshift rope ladder – a braided line, woven for strength yet not too thick, with swords tied at two-foot intervals to serve as hand- and footholds.

As a test, she tied one end around a support column and leaned on the rope with all her weight. The plastic swords bent under her, but they provided some extra bulk to the knots in the cord, so at least she could keep a better grip.

The ladder wouldn't win any design awards, but it might get her to the bottom of the cavern safely. First, she stuffed her backpack with the leftover spools of string. She wasn't sure why, but they were one more resource and not too heavy.

She headed back to the hole in the mosaic floor. She secured one end of her ladder to the nearest piece of scaffolding, lowered the rope into the cavern and shinned down.

XXXIV

ANNABETH

As Annabeth hung in the air, descending hand over hand with the ladder swinging wildly, she thanked Chiron for all those years of training on the climbing course at Camp Half-Blood. She'd complained loudly and often that rope climbing would never help her defeat a monster. Chiron had just smiled, like he knew this day would come.

Finally Annabeth made it to the bottom. She missed the brickwork edge and landed in the canal, but it turned out to be only a few inches deep. Freezing water soaked into her running shoes.

She held up her glowing dagger. The shallow channel ran down the middle of a brickwork tunnel. Every few yards, ceramic pipes jutted from the walls. She guessed that the pipes were drains, part of the Ancient Roman plumbing system, though it was amazing to her that a tunnel like this had survived, crowded underground with all the other centuries' worth of pipes, basements and sewers.

A sudden thought chilled her even more than the water. A few years ago, Percy and she had gone on a quest in Daedalus's labyrinth – a secret network of tunnels and rooms, heavily enchanted and trapped, which ran under all the cities of America.

When Daedalus died in the Battle of the Labyrinth, the entire maze had collapsed – or so Annabeth believed. But what if that was only in America? What if this was an older version of the labyrinth? Daedalus once told her that his maze had a life of its own. It was constantly growing and changing. Maybe the labyrinth could regenerate, like monsters. That would make sense. It was an archetypal force, as Chiron would say – something that could never really die.

If this was part of the labyrinth . . .

Annabeth decided not to dwell on that, but she also decided not to assume her directions were accurate. The labyrinth made distance meaningless. If she wasn't careful, she could walk twenty feet in the wrong direction and end up in Poland.

Just to be safe, she tied a new ball of string to the end of her rope ladder. She could unravel it behind her as she explored. An old trick, but a good one.

She debated which way to go. The tunnel seemed the same in both directions. Then, about fifty feet to her left, the Mark of Athena blazed against the wall. Annabeth could swear it was glaring at her with those big fiery eyes, as if to say, *What's your problem? Hurry up!*

She was really starting to hate that owl.

By the time she reached the spot, the image had faded and she'd run out of string on her first spool.

As she was attaching a new line, she glanced across the tunnel. There was a broken section in the brickwork, as if a sledgehammer had knocked a hole in the wall. She crossed to take a look. Sticking her dagger through the opening for light, Annabeth could see a lower chamber, long and narrow, with a mosaic floor, painted walls and benches running down either side. It was shaped sort of like a subway car.

She stuck her head into the hole, hoping nothing would bite it off. At the near end of the room was a bricked-off doorway. At the far end was a stone table, or maybe an altar.

Hmm . . . The water tunnel kept going, but Annabeth was sure this was the way. She remembered what Tiberinus had said: *Find the altar of the foreign god.* There didn't seem to be any exits from the altar room, but it was a short drop onto the bench below. She should be able to climb out again with no problem.

Still holding her string, she lowered herself down.

The room's ceiling was barrel-shaped with brick arches, but Annabeth didn't like the look of the supports. Directly above her head, on the arch nearest to the bricked-in doorway, the capstone was cracked in half. Stress fractures ran across the ceiling. The place had probably been intact for two thousand years, but she decided she'd rather not spend too much time here. With her luck, it would collapse in the next two minutes.

The floor was a long narrow mosaic with seven pictures in

a row, like a time line. At Annabeth's feet was a raven. Next was a lion. Several others looked like Roman warriors with various weapons. The rest were too damaged or covered in dust for Annabeth to make out details. The benches on either side were littered with broken pottery. The walls were painted with scenes of a banquet: a robed man with a curved cap like an ice-cream scoop, sitting next to a larger guy who radiated sunbeams. Standing around them were torchbearers and servants, and various animals like crows and lions wandered in the background. Annabeth wasn't sure what the picture represented, but it didn't remind her of any Greek legends that she knew.

At the far end of the room, the altar was elaborately carved with a frieze showing the man with the ice-cream-scoop hat holding a knife to the neck of a bull. On the altar stood a stone figure of a man sunk to his knees in rock, a dagger and a torch in his outraised hands. Again, Annabeth had no idea what those images meant.

She took one step towards the altar. Her foot went *CRUNCH*. She looked down and realized she'd just put her shoe through a human rib cage.

Annabeth swallowed back a scream. Where had *that* come from? She had glanced down only a moment before and hadn't seen any bones. Now the floor was littered with them. The rib cage was obviously old. It crumbled to dust as she removed her foot. Nearby lay a corroded bronze dagger very much like her own. Either this dead person had been carrying the weapon, or it had killed him.

She held out her blade to see in front of her. A little further down the mosaic path sprawled a more complete skeleton in the remains of an embroidered red doublet, like a man from the Renaissance. His frilled collar and skull had been badly burned, as if the guy had decided to wash his hair with a blowtorch.

Wonderful, Annabeth thought. She lifted her eyes to the altar statue, which held a dagger and a torch.

Some kind of test, Annabeth decided. These two guys had failed. Correction: not just two guys. More bones and scraps of clothing were scattered all the way to the altar. She couldn't guess how many skeletons were represented, but she was willing to bet they were all demigods from the past, children of Athena on the same quest.

'I will not be another skeleton on your floor,' she called to the statue, hoping she sounded brave.

A girl, said a watery voice, echoing through the room. *Girls are not allowed.*

A female demigod, said a second voice. *Inexcusable.*

The chamber rumbled. Dust fell from the cracked ceiling. Annabeth bolted for the hole she'd come through, but it had disappeared. Her string had been severed. She clambered up on the bench and pounded on the wall where the hole had been, hoping the hole's absence was just an illusion, but the wall felt solid.

She was trapped.

Along the benches, a dozen ghosts shimmered into existence – glowing purple men in Roman togas, like the Lares she'd seen at Camp Jupiter. They glared at her as if she'd interrupted their meeting.

She did the only thing she could. She stepped down from the bench and put her back to the bricked-in doorway. She tried to look confident, though the scowling purple ghosts and the demigod skeletons at her feet made her want to turtle into her T-shirt and scream.

'I'm a child of Athena,' she said, as boldly as she could manage.

'A Greek,' one of the ghosts said with disgust. 'That is even worse.'

At the other end of the chamber, an old-looking ghost rose with some difficulty (do ghosts have arthritis?) and stood by the altar, his dark eyes fixed on Annabeth. Her first thought was that he looked like the pope. He had a glittering robe, a pointed hat and a shepherd's crook.

'This is the cavern of Mithras,' said the old ghost. 'You have disturbed our sacred rituals. You cannot look upon our mysteries and live.'

'I don't want to look upon your mysteries,' Annabeth assured him. 'I'm following the Mark of Athena. Show me the exit, and I'll be on my way.'

Her voice sounded calm, which surprised her. She had no idea how to get out of here, but she knew she had to succeed where her siblings had failed. Her path led further on – deeper into the underground layers of Rome.

The failures of your predecessors will guide you, Tiberinus had said. *After that . . . I do not know.*

The ghosts mumbled to each other in Latin. Annabeth caught a few unkind words about female demigods and Athena.

Finally the ghost with the pope hat struck his shepherd's crook against the floor. The other Lares fell silent.

'Your Greek goddess is powerless here,' said the pope. 'Mithras is the god of Roman warriors! He is the god of the legion, the god of the empire!'

'He wasn't even Roman,' Annabeth protested. 'Wasn't he, like, Persian or something?'

'Sacrilege!' the old man yelped, banging his staff on the floor a few more times. 'Mithras protects us! I am the *pater* of this brotherhood –'

'The father,' Annabeth translated.

'Do not interrupt! As *pater*, I must protect our mysteries.'

'What mysteries?' Annabeth asked. 'A dozen dead guys in togas sitting around in a cave?'

The ghosts muttered and complained, until the *pater* got them under control with a taxicab whistle. The old guy had a good set of lungs. 'You are clearly an unbeliever. Like the others, you must die.'

The others. Annabeth made an effort not to look at the skeletons.

Her mind worked furiously, grasping for anything she knew about Mithras. He had a secret cult for warriors. He was popular in the legion. He was one of the gods who'd supplanted Athena as a war deity. Aphrodite had mentioned him during their teatime chat in Charleston. Aside from that, Annabeth had no idea. Mithras just wasn't one of the gods they talked about at Camp Half-Blood. She doubted the ghosts would wait while she whipped out Daedalus's laptop and did a search.

She scanned the floor mosaic – seven pictures in a row. She studied the ghosts and noticed all of them wore some sort of badge on their toga – a raven, or a torch, or a bow.

'You have rites of passage,' she blurted out. 'Seven levels of membership. And the top level is the *pater*.'

The ghosts let out a collective gasp. Then they all began shouting at once.

'How does she know this?' one demanded.

'The girl has gleaned our secrets!'

'Silence!' the *pater* ordered.

'But she might know about the ordeals!' another cried.

'The ordeals!' Annabeth said. 'I know about them!'

Another round of incredulous gasping.

'Ridiculous!' the *pater* yelled. 'The girl lies! Daughter of Athena, choose your way of death. If you do not choose, the god will choose for you!'

'Fire or dagger,' Annabeth guessed.

Even the *pater* looked stunned. Apparently he hadn't remembered there were victims of past punishments lying on the floor.

'How – how did you . . .?' He gulped. 'Who *are* you?'

'A child of Athena,' Annabeth said again. 'But not just any child. I am . . . uh, the *mater* in my sisterhood. The *magna mater*, in fact. There are no mysteries to me. Mithras cannot hide anything from my sight.'

'The *magna mater*!' a ghost wailed in despair. 'The big mother!'

'Kill her!' One of the ghosts charged, his hands out to strangle her, but he passed right through her.

'You're dead,' Annabeth reminded him. 'Sit down.'

The ghost looked embarrassed and took his seat.

'We do not need to kill you ourselves,' the *pater* growled. 'Mithras shall do that for us!'

The statue on the altar began to glow.

Annabeth pressed her hands against the bricked-in doorway at her back. That *had* to be the exit. The mortar was crumbling, but it was not weak enough for her to break through with brute force.

She looked desperately around the room – the cracked ceiling, the floor mosaic, the wall paintings and the carved altar. She began to talk, pulling deductions from the top of her head.

'It is no good,' she said. 'I know all. You test your initiates with fire because the torch is the symbol of Mithras. His other symbol is the dagger, which is why you can also be tested with the blade. You want to kill me, just as . . . uh, as Mithras killed the sacred bull.'

It was a total guess, but the altar showed Mithras killing a bull, so Annabeth figured it must be important. The ghosts wailed and covered their ears. Some slapped their faces as if to wake up from a bad dream.

'The big mother knows!' one said. 'It is impossible!'

Unless you look around the room, Annabeth thought, her confidence growing.

She glared at the ghost who had just spoken. He had a raven badge on his toga – the same symbol as on the floor at her feet.

'You are just a raven,' she scolded. 'That is the lowest rank. Be silent and let me speak to your *pater*.'

The ghost cringed. 'Mercy! Mercy!'

At the front of the room, the *pater* trembled – either from rage or fear, Annabeth wasn't sure which. His pope hat tilted sideways on his head like a fuel gauge dropping towards empty. 'Truly, you know much, big mother. Your wisdom is great, but that is all the more reason why you cannot leave. The weaver warned us you would come.'

'The weaver . . .' Annabeth realized with a sinking feeling what the *pater* was talking about: the thing in the dark from Percy's dream, the guardian of the shrine. This was one time she wished she *didn't* know the answer, but she tried to maintain her calm. 'The weaver fears me. She doesn't want me to follow the Mark of Athena. But you will let me pass.'

'You must choose an ordeal!' the *pater* insisted. 'Fire or dagger! Survive one, and then perhaps!'

Annabeth looked down at the bones of her siblings. *The failures of your predecessors will guide you.*

They'd all chosen one or the other: fire or dagger. Maybe they'd thought they could beat the ordeal. But they had all died. Annabeth needed a third choice.

She stared at the altar statue, which was glowing brighter by the second. She could feel its heat across the room. Her instinct was to focus on the dagger or the torch, but instead she concentrated on the statue's base. She wondered why its legs were stuck in stone. Then it occurred to her: maybe the little statue of Mithras wasn't *stuck* in the rock. Maybe he was *emerging* from the rock.

'Neither torch nor dagger,' Annabeth said firmly. 'There is a third test, which I will pass.'

'A third test?' the *pater* demanded.

'Mithras was born from rock,' Annabeth said, hoping she was right. 'He emerged fully grown from the stone, holding his dagger and torch.'

The screaming and wailing told her she had guessed correctly.

'The big mother knows all!' a ghost cried. 'That is our most closely guarded secret!'

Then maybe you shouldn't put a statue of it on your altar, Annabeth thought. But she was thankful for stupid male ghosts. If they'd let women warriors into their cult, they might have learned some common sense.

Annabeth gestured dramatically to the wall she'd come from. 'I was born from stone, just as Mithras was! Therefore, I have already passed your ordeal!'

'Bah!' the *pater* spat. 'You came from a hole in the wall! That's not the same thing.'

Okay. So apparently the *pater* wasn't a complete moron, but Annabeth remained confident. She glanced at the ceiling, and another idea came to her – all the details clicking together.

'I have control over the very stones.' She raised her arms. 'I will prove my power is greater than Mithras. With a single strike, I will bring down this chamber.'

The ghosts wailed and trembled and looked at the ceiling, but Annabeth knew they didn't see what she saw. These ghosts were warriors, not engineers. The children of Athena had many skills, and not just in combat. Annabeth had studied architecture for years. She knew this ancient chamber was on the verge of collapse. She recognized what the stress fractures in the ceiling meant, all emanating from a single point – the top of the stone arch just above her. The capstone was about to crumble, and when that happened, assuming she could time it correctly . . .

'Impossible!' the *pater* shouted. 'The weaver has paid us much tribute to destroy any children of Athena who would dare enter our shrine. We have never let her down. We cannot let you pass.'

'Then you fear my power!' Annabeth said. 'You admit that I could destroy your sacred chamber!'

The *pater* scowled. He straightened his hat uneasily. Annabeth knew she'd put him in an impossible position. He couldn't back down without looking cowardly.

'Do your worst, child of Athena,' he decided. 'No one can bring down the cavern of Mithras, especially with one strike. Especially not a girl!'

Annabeth hefted her dagger. The ceiling was low. She could reach the capstone easily, but she'd have to make her one strike count.

The doorway behind her was blocked, but in theory, if the room started to collapse, those bricks should weaken and crumble. She *should* be able to bust her way through before the entire ceiling came down – assuming, of course, that there was something behind the brick wall, not just solid earth, and assuming that Annabeth was quick enough and strong enough and lucky enough. Otherwise, she was about to be a demigod pancake.

'Well, boys,' she said. 'Looks like you chose the wrong war god.'

She struck the capstone. The Celestial bronze blade shattered it like a sugar cube. For a moment, nothing happened.

'Ha!' the *pater* gloated. 'You see? Athena has no power here!'

The room shook. A fissure ran across the length of the ceiling and the far end of the cavern collapsed, burying the altar and the *pater*. More cracks widened. Bricks fell from the arches. Ghosts screamed and ran, but they couldn't seem to pass through the walls. Apparently they were bound to this chamber even in death.

Annabeth turned. She slammed against the blocked entrance with all her might, and the bricks gave way. As the cavern of Mithras imploded behind her, she lunged into darkness and found herself falling.

XXXV

ANNABETH

ANNABETH THOUGHT SHE KNEW PAIN. She had fallen off the lava wall at Camp Half-Blood. She'd been stabbed in the arm with a poison blade on the Williamsburg Bridge. She had even held the weight of the sky on her shoulders.

But that was nothing compared to landing hard on her ankle.

She immediately knew she'd broken it. Pain like a hot steel wire jabbed its way up her leg and into her hip. The world narrowed to just her, her ankle and the agony.

She almost blacked out. Her head spun. Her breath became short and rapid.

No, she told herself. *You can't go into shock.*

She tried to breathe more slowly. She lay as still as possible until the pain subsided from absolute torture to just horrible throbbing.

Part of her wanted to howl at the world for being so unfair.

All this way, just to be stopped by something as common as a broken ankle?

She forced her emotions back down. At camp, she'd been trained to survive in all sorts of bad situations, *including* injuries like this.

She looked around her. Her dagger had skittered a few feet away. In its dim light she could make out the features of the room. She was lying on a cold floor of sandstone blocks. The ceiling was two storeys tall. The doorway through which she'd fallen was ten feet off the ground, now completely blocked with debris that had cascaded into the room, making a rockslide. Scattered around her were old pieces of lumber – some cracked and desiccated, others broken into kindling.

Stupid, she scolded herself. She'd lunged through that doorway, assuming there would be a level corridor or another room. It had never occurred to her that she'd be tumbling into space. The lumber had probably once been a staircase, long ago collapsed.

She inspected her ankle. Her foot didn't appear too strangely bent. She could feel her toes. She didn't see any blood. That was all good.

She reached out for a piece of lumber. Even that small bit of movement made her yelp.

The board crumbled in her hand. The wood might be centuries old, or even millennia. She had no way of knowing if this room was older than the shrine of Mithras, or if – like the labyrinth – the rooms were a hodge-podge from many eras thrown randomly together.

'Okay,' she said aloud, just to hear her voice. 'Think, Annabeth. Prioritize.'

She remembered a silly wilderness survival course Grover had taught her back at camp. At least it had seemed silly at the time. First step: scan your surroundings for immediate threats.

This room didn't seem to be in danger of collapsing. The rockslide had stopped. The walls were solid blocks of stone with no major cracks that she could see. The ceiling was not sagging. Good.

The only exit was on the far wall – an arched doorway that led into darkness. Between her and the doorway, a small brickwork trench cut across the floor, letting water flow through the room from left to right. Maybe plumbing from the Roman days? If the water was drinkable, that was good, too.

Piled in one corner were some broken ceramic vases, spilling out shrivelled brown clumps that might once have been fruit. Yuck. In another corner were some wooden crates that looked more intact and some wicker boxes bound with leather straps.

'So, no immediate danger,' she said to herself. 'Unless something comes barrelling out of that dark tunnel.'

She glared at the doorway, almost daring her luck to get worse. Nothing happened.

'Okay,' she said. 'Next step: take inventory.'

What could she use? She had her water bottle, and more water in that trench if she could reach it. She had her knife. Her backpack was full of colourful string (whee), her laptop, the bronze map, some matches and some ambrosia for emergencies.

Ah . . . yeah. This qualified as an emergency. She dug the godly food out of her pack and wolfed it down. As usual, it tasted like comforting memories. This time it was buttered popcorn – movie night with her dad at his place in San Francisco, no stepmom, no stepbrothers, just Annabeth and her father curled up on the sofa watching sappy old romantic comedies.

The ambrosia warmed her whole body. The pain in her leg became a dull throb. Annabeth knew she was still in major trouble. Even ambrosia couldn't heal broken bones right away. It might speed up the process, but, best-case scenario, she wouldn't be able to put any weight on her foot for a day or more.

She tried to reach her knife, but it was too far away. She scooted in that direction. Pain flared again, like nails were piercing her foot. Her face beaded with sweat, but after one more scoot she managed to reach the dagger.

She felt better holding it – not just for light and protection, but also because it was so familiar.

What next? Grover's survival class had mentioned something about staying put and waiting for rescue, but that wasn't going to happen. Even if Percy somehow managed to trace her steps, the cavern of Mithras had collapsed.

She could try contacting someone with Daedalus's laptop, but she doubted she could get a signal down here. Besides, who would she call? She couldn't text anyone who was close enough to help. Demigods never carried cell phones, because their signals attracted too much monstrous attention, and none of her friends would be sitting around checking their e-mail.

An Iris-message? She had water, but she doubted that she could make enough light for a rainbow. The only coin she had was her silver Athenian drachma, which didn't make a great tribute.

There was another problem with calling for help: this was supposed to be a solo quest. If Annabeth did get rescued, she'd be admitting defeat. Something told her that the Mark of Athena would no longer guide her. She could wander down here forever, and she'd never find the Athena Parthenos.

So . . . no good staying put and waiting for help. Which meant she had to find a way to keep going on her own.

She opened her water bottle and drank. She hadn't realized how thirsty she was. When the bottle was empty, she crawled to the gutter and refilled it.

The water was cold and moving swiftly – good signs that it might be safe to drink. She filled her bottle, then cupped some water in her hands and splashed her face. Immediately she felt more alert. She washed off and cleaned her scrapes as best she could.

Annabeth sat up and glared at her ankle.

'You *had* to break,' she scolded it.

The ankle did not reply.

She'd have to immobilize it in some sort of cast. That was the only way she'd be able to move.

Hmm . . .

She raised her dagger and inspected the room again in its

bronze light. Now that she was closer to the open doorway, she liked it even less. It led into a dark silent corridor. The air wafting out smelled sickly sweet and somehow evil. Unfortunately, Annabeth didn't see any other way she could go.

With a lot of gasping and blinking back tears, she crawled over to the wreckage of the stairs. She found two planks that were in fairly good shape and long enough for a splint. Then she scooted over to the wicker boxes and used her knife to cut off the leather straps.

While she was psyching herself up to immobilize her ankle, she noticed some faded words on one of the wooden crates: HERMES EXPRESS.

Annabeth scooted excitedly towards the box.

She had no idea what it was doing here, but Hermes delivered all sorts of useful stuff to gods, spirits and even demigods. Maybe he'd dropped this care package here years ago to help demigods like her with this quest.

She prised it open and pulled out several sheets of bubble wrap, but whatever had been inside was gone.

'Hermes!' she protested.

She stared glumly at the bubble wrap. Then her mind kicked into gear, and she realized the wrapping *was* a gift. 'Oh . . . that's perfect!'

Annabeth covered her broken ankle in a bubble-wrap cast. She set it with the lumber splints and tied it all together with the leather straps.

Once before, in first-aid practice, she'd splinted a fake broken leg for another camper, but she'd never imagined she'd have to make a splint for herself.

It was hard, painful work, but finally it was done. She searched the wreckage of the stairs until she found part of the railing – a narrow board about four feet long that could serve as a crutch. She put her back against the wall, got her good leg ready and hauled herself up.

'Whoa.' Black spots danced in her eyes, but she stayed upright.

'Next time,' she muttered to the dark room, 'just let me fight a monster. Much easier.'

Above the open doorway, the Mark of Athena blazed to life against the arch.

The fiery owl seemed to be watching her expectantly, as if to say: *About time. Oh, you want monsters? Right this way!*

Annabeth wondered if that burning mark was based on a real sacred owl. If so, when she survived, she was going to find that owl and punch it in the face.

That thought lifted her spirits. She made it across the trench and hobbled slowly into the corridor.

XXXVI

ANNABETH

THE TUNNEL RAN STRAIGHT AND SMOOTH, but after her fall Annabeth decided to take no chances. She used the wall for support and tapped the floor in front of her with her crutch to make sure there were no traps.

As she walked, the sickly sweet smell got stronger and set her nerves on edge. The sound of running water faded behind her. In its place came a dry chorus of whispers like a million tiny voices. They seemed to be coming from inside the walls, and they were getting louder.

Annabeth tried to speed up, but she couldn't go much faster without losing her balance or jarring her broken ankle. She hobbled onward, convinced that something was following her. The small voices were massing together, getting closer.

She touched the wall, and her hand came back covered in cobwebs.

She yelped, then cursed herself for making a sound.

It's only a web, she told herself. But that didn't stop the roaring in her ears.

She'd expected spiders. She knew what was ahead: *The weaver. Her Ladyship. The voice in the dark.* But the webs made her realize how close she was.

Her hand trembled as she wiped it on the stones. What had she been thinking? She couldn't do this quest alone.

Too late, she told herself. Just keep going.

She made her way down the corridor one painful step at a time. The whispering sounds got louder behind her until they sounded like millions of dried leaves swirling in the wind. The cobwebs became thicker, filling the tunnel. Soon she was pushing them out of her face, ripping through gauzy curtains that covered her like Silly String.

Her heart wanted to break out of her chest and run. She stumbled ahead more recklessly, trying to ignore the pain in her ankle.

Finally the corridor ended in a doorway filled waist-high with old lumber. It looked as if someone had tried to barricade the opening. That didn't bode well, but Annabeth used her crutch to push away the boards as best she could. She crawled over the remaining pile, getting a few dozen splinters in her free hand.

On the other side of the barricade was a chamber the size of a basketball court. The floor was done in Roman mosaics. The remains of tapestries hung from the walls. Two unlit torches sat in wall sconces on either side of the doorway, both covered in cobwebs.

At the far end of the room, the Mark of Athena burned over another doorway. Unfortunately, between Annabeth and that exit, the floor was bisected by a chasm fifty feet across. Spanning the pit were two parallel wooden beams, too far apart for both feet, but each too narrow to walk on unless Annabeth was an acrobat, which she wasn't, and didn't have a broken ankle, which she did.

The corridor she'd come from was filled with hissing noises. Cobwebs trembled and danced as the first of the spiders appeared: no larger than gumdrops, but plump and black, skittering over the walls and the floor.

What kind of spiders? Annabeth had no idea. She only knew they were coming for her, and she only had seconds to figure out a plan.

Annabeth wanted to sob. She wanted someone, *anyone*, to be here for her. She wanted Leo with his fire skills, or Jason with his lightning, or Hazel to collapse the tunnel. Most of all she wanted Percy. She always felt braver when Percy was with her.

I am not going to die here, she told herself. I'm going to see Percy again.

The first spiders were almost to the door. Behind them came the bulk of the army – a black sea of creepy-crawlies.

Annabeth hobbled to one of the wall sconces and snatched up the torch. The end was coated in pitch for easy lighting. Her fingers felt like lead, but she rummaged through her backpack and found the matches. She struck one and set the torch ablaze.

She thrust it into the barricade. The old dry wood caught immediately. Flames leaped to the cobwebs and roared down the corridor in a flash fire, roasting spiders by the thousands.

Annabeth stepped back from her bonfire. She'd bought herself some time, but she doubted that she'd killed all the spiders. They would regroup and swarm again as soon as the fire died.

She stepped to the edge of the chasm.

She shone her light into the pit, but she couldn't see the bottom. Jumping in would be suicide. She could try to cross one of the bars hand over hand, but she didn't trust her arm strength, and she didn't see how she would be able to haul herself up with a full backpack and a broken ankle once she reached the other side.

She crouched and studied the beams. Each had a set of iron eye hooks along the inside, set at one-foot intervals. Maybe the rails had been the sides of a bridge and the middle planks had been removed or destroyed. But eye hooks? Those weren't for supporting planks. More like . . .

She glanced at the walls. The same kind of hooks had been used to hang the shredded tapestries.

She realized the planks weren't meant as a bridge. They were some kind of loom.

Annabeth threw her flaming torch to the other side of the chasm. She had no faith her plan would work, but she pulled all the string out of her backpack and began weaving between the beams, stringing a cat's cradle pattern back and forth from eye hook to eye hook, doubling and tripling the line.

Her hands moved with blazing speed. She stopped

thinking about the task and just did it, looping and tying off lines, slowly extending her woven net over the pit.

She forgot the pain in her leg and the fiery barricade guttering out behind her. She inched over the chasm. The weaving held her weight. Before she knew it, she was halfway across.

How had she learned to do this?

It's Athena, she told herself. My mother's skill with useful crafts. Weaving had never seemed particularly useful to Annabeth – until now.

She glanced behind her. The barricade fire was dying. A few spiders crawled in around the edges of the doorway.

Desperately she continued weaving, and finally she made it across. She snatched up the torch and thrust it into her woven bridge. Flames raced along the string. Even the beams caught fire as if they'd been pre-soaked in oil.

For a moment, the bridge burned in a clear pattern – a fiery row of identical owls. Had Annabeth really woven them into the string, or was it some kind of magic? She didn't know, but, as the spiders began to cross, the beams crumbled and collapsed into the pit.

Annabeth held her breath. She didn't see any reason why the spiders couldn't reach her by climbing the walls or the ceiling. If they started to do that, she'd have to run for it, and she was pretty sure she couldn't move fast enough.

For some reason, the spiders didn't follow. They massed at the edge of the pit – a seething black carpet of creepiness. Then they dispersed, flooding back into the burnt corridor, almost as if Annabeth was no longer interesting.

'Or I passed a test,' she said aloud.

Her torch sputtered out, leaving her with only the light of her dagger. She realized that she'd left her makeshift crutch on the other side of the chasm.

She felt exhausted and out of tricks, but her mind was clear. Her panic seemed to have burned up along with that woven bridge.

The weaver, she thought. I must be close. At least I know what's ahead.

She made her way down the next corridor, hopping to keep the weight off her bad foot.

She didn't have far to go.

After twenty feet, the tunnel opened into a cavern as large as a cathedral, so majestic that Annabeth had trouble processing everything she saw. She guessed that this was the room from Percy's dream, but it wasn't dark. Bronze braziers of magical light, like the gods used on Mount Olympus, glowed around the circumference of the room, interspersed with gorgeous tapestries. The stone floor was webbed with fissures like a sheet of ice. The ceiling was so high it was lost in the gloom and layers upon layers of spiderwebs.

Strands of silk as thick as pillars ran from the ceiling all over the room, anchoring the walls and the floor like the cables of a suspension bridge.

Webs also surrounded the centrepiece of the shrine, which was so intimidating that Annabeth had trouble raising her eyes to look at it. Looming over her was a forty-foot-tall statue of Athena, with luminous ivory skin and a dress of gold. In her outstretched hand, Athena held a statue of Nike, the winged victory goddess – a statue that looked tiny from here, but was probably as tall as a real person. Athena's other hand rested on a shield as big as a billboard, with a sculpted snake peeking out from behind, as if Athena was protecting it.

The goddess's face was serene and kindly . . . and it *looked* like Athena. Annabeth had seen many statues that didn't resemble her mom at all, but this giant version, made thousands of years ago, made her think that the artist must have met Athena in person. He had captured her perfectly.

'Athena Parthenos,' Annabeth murmured. 'It's really here.'

All her life, she had wanted to visit the Parthenon. Now she was seeing the main attraction that *used* to be there – and she was the first child of Athena to do so in millennia.

She realized her mouth was hanging open. She forced herself to swallow. Annabeth could have stood there all day looking at the statue, but she had only accomplished half her mission. She had found the Athena Parthenos. Now, how could she rescue it from this cavern?

Strands of web covered it like a gauze pavilion. Annabeth suspected that without those webs the statue would have fallen through the weakened floor long ago. As she stepped into the room, she could see that the cracks below were so wide, she could have lost her foot in them. Beneath the cracks, she saw nothing but empty darkness.

A chill washed over her. Where was the guardian? How could Annabeth free the statue without collapsing the floor? She couldn't very well shove the Athena Parthenos down the corridor that she'd come from.

She scanned the chamber, hoping to see something that

might help. Her eyes wandered over the tapestries, which were heart-wrenchingly beautiful. One showed a pastoral scene so three-dimensional it could've been a window. Another tapestry showed the gods battling the giants. Annabeth saw a landscape of the Underworld. Next to it was the skyline of modern Rome. And in the tapestry to her left . . .

She caught her breath. It was a portrait of two demigods kissing underwater: Annabeth and Percy, the day their friends had thrown them into the canoe lake at camp. It was so lifelike that she wondered if the weaver had been there, lurking in the lake with a waterproof camera.

'How is that possible?' she murmured.

Above her in the gloom, a voice spoke. 'For ages I have known that you would come, my sweet.'

Annabeth shuddered. Suddenly she was seven years old again, hiding under her covers, waiting for the spiders to attack her in the night. The voice sounded just as Percy had described: an angry buzz in multiple tones, female but not human.

In the webs above the statue, something moved – something dark and large.

'I have seen you in my dreams,' the voice said, sickly sweet and evil, like the smell in the corridors. 'I had to make sure you were worthy, the *only* child of Athena clever enough to pass my tests and reach this place alive. Indeed, you are her most talented child. This will make your death so much more painful to my old enemy when you *fail utterly*.'

The pain in Annabeth's ankle was nothing compared to the icy acid now filling her veins. She wanted to run. She wanted to plead for mercy. But she couldn't show weakness – not now.

'You're Arachne,' she called out. 'The weaver who was turned into a spider.'

The figure descended, becoming clearer and more horrible. 'Cursed by your mother,' she said. 'Scorned by all and made into a hideous thing . . . because *I* was the better weaver.'

'But you lost the contest,' Annabeth said.

'That's the story written by the winner!' cried Arachne. 'Look on my work! See for yourself!'

Annabeth didn't have to. The tapestries were the best she'd ever seen – better than the witch Circe's work, and, yes, even better than some weavings she'd seen on Mount Olympus. She wondered if her mother truly *had* lost – if she'd hidden Arachne away and rewritten the truth. But right now it didn't matter.

'You've been guarding this statue since the ancient times,' Annabeth guessed. 'But it doesn't belong here. I'm taking it back.'

'Ha,' Arachne said.

Even Annabeth had to admit her threat sounded ridiculous. How could one girl in a bubble-wrap ankle cast remove this huge statue from its underground chamber?

'I'm afraid you would have to defeat me first, my sweet,' Arachne said. 'And, alas, that is impossible.'

The creature appeared from the curtains of webbing, and Annabeth realized that her quest was hopeless. She was about to die.

Arachne had the body of a giant black widow, with a hairy

red hourglass mark on the underside of her abdomen and a pair of oozing spinnerets. Her eight spindly legs were lined with curved barbs as big as Annabeth's dagger. If the spider came any closer, her sweet stench alone would have been enough to make Annabeth faint. But the most horrible part was her misshapen face.

She might once have been a beautiful woman. Now black mandibles protruded from her mouth like tusks. Her other teeth had grown into thin white needles. Fine dark whiskers dotted her cheeks. Her eyes were large, lidless and pure black, with two smaller eyes sticking out of her temples.

The creature made a violent *rip-rip-rip* sound that might have been laughter.

'Now I will feast on you, my sweet,' Arachne said. 'But do not fear. I will make a beautiful tapestry depicting your death.'

XXXVII

LEO

LEO WISHED HE WASN'T SO GOOD.

Really, sometimes it was just embarrassing. If he hadn't had such an eye for mechanical stuff, they might never have found the secret chute, got lost in the underground and been attacked by metal dudes. But he just couldn't help himself.

Part of it was Hazel's fault. For a girl with super underground senses, she wasn't much good in Rome. She kept leading them around and around the city, getting dizzy and doubling back.

'Sorry,' she said. 'It's just . . . there's so much underground here, so many layers that it's overwhelming. Like standing in the middle of an orchestra and trying to concentrate on a single instrument. I'm going deaf.'

As a result, they got a tour of Rome. Frank seemed happy to plod along like a big sheepdog (hmm, Leo wondered if he could turn into one of those, or even better: a horse that Leo could ride). But Leo started to get impatient. His feet were sore, the day was sunny and hot, and the streets were choked with tourists.

The Forum was okay, but it was mostly ruins overgrown with bushes and trees. It took a lot of imagination to see it as the bustling centre of Ancient Rome. Leo could only manage it because he'd seen New Rome in California.

They passed big churches, freestanding arches, clothing stores and fast-food restaurants. One statue of some Ancient Roman dude seemed to be pointing to a nearby McDonald's.

On the wider streets, the car traffic was absolutely nuts – man, Leo thought people in *Houston* drove crazy – but they spent most of their time weaving through small alleys, coming across fountains and little cafés where Leo was not allowed to rest.

'I never thought I'd get to see Rome,' Hazel said. 'When I was alive, I mean the first time, Mussolini was in charge. We were at war.'

'Mussolini?' Leo frowned. 'Wasn't he like BFFs with Hitler?'

Hazel stared at him like he was an alien. 'BFFs?'

'Never mind.'

'I'd love to see the Trevi Fountain,' she said.

'There's a fountain on every block,' Leo grumbled.

'Or the Spanish Steps,' Hazel said.

'Why would you come to Italy to see Spanish steps?' Leo asked. 'That's like going to China for Mexican food, isn't it?'

'You're hopeless,' Hazel complained.

'So I've been told.'

She turned to Frank and grabbed his hand, as if Leo had ceased to exist. 'Come on. I think we should go this way.'

Frank gave Leo a confused smile – like he couldn't decide whether to gloat or to thank Leo for being a doofus – but he cheerfully let Hazel drag him along.

After walking forever, Hazel stopped in front of a church. At least, Leo assumed it was a church. The main section had a big domed roof. The entrance had a triangular roof, typical Roman columns and an inscription across the top: M. AGRIPPA something or other.

'Latin for *Get a grip*?' Leo speculated.

'This is our best bet.' Hazel sounded more certain than she had all day. 'There should be a secret passage somewhere inside.'

Tour groups milled around the steps. Guides held up coloured placards with different numbers and lectured in dozens of languages like they were playing some kind of international bingo.

Leo listened to the Spanish tour guide for a few seconds, and then he reported to his friends, 'This is the Pantheon. It was originally built by Marcus Agrippa as a temple to the gods. After it burned down, Emperor Hadrian rebuilt it, and it's been standing for two thousand years. It's one of the best-preserved Roman buildings in the world.'

Frank and Hazel stared at him.

'How did you know that?' Hazel asked.

'I'm naturally brilliant.'

'Centaur poop,' Frank said. 'He eavesdropped on a tour group.'

Leo grinned. 'Maybe. Come on. Let's go find that secret passage. I hope this place has air conditioning.'

Of course, no AC.

On the bright side, there were no lines and no admission fee, so they just muscled their way past the tour groups and walked on in.

The interior was pretty impressive, considering it had been constructed two thousand years ago. The marble floor was patterned with squares and circles like a Roman tic-tac-toe game. The main space was one huge chamber with a circular rotunda, sort of like a capitol building back in the States. Lining the walls were different shrines and statues and tombs and stuff. But the real eye-catcher was the dome overhead. All the light in the building came from one circular opening right at the top. A beam of sunlight slanted into the rotunda and glowed on the floor, like Zeus was up there with a magnifying glass, trying to fry puny humans.

Leo was no architect like Annabeth, but he could appreciate the engineering. The Romans had made the dome out of big stone panels, but they'd hollowed out each panel in a square-within-square pattern. It looked cool. Leo figured it also made the dome lighter and easier to support.

He didn't mention that to his friends. He doubted they would care, but if Annabeth were here she would've spent the whole day talking about it. Thinking about that made Leo wonder how she was doing on her Mark of Athena expedition. Leo never thought he'd feel this way, but he was worried about that scary blonde girl.

Hazel stopped in the middle of the room and turned in a circle. 'This is amazing. In the old days, the children of Vulcan would come here in secret to consecrate demigod weapons. This is where Imperial gold was enchanted.'

Leo wondered how that worked. He imagined a bunch of demigods in dark robes trying to quietly roll a scorpion ballista through the front doors.

'But we're not here because of that,' he guessed.

'No,' Hazel said. 'There's an entrance – a tunnel that will lead us towards Nico. I can sense it close by. I'm not sure where.'

Frank grunted. 'If this building is two thousand years old, it makes sense there could be some kind of secret passage left over from the Roman days.'

That's when Leo made his mistake of simply being too good.

He scanned the temple's interior, thinking: *If I were designing a secret passage, where would I put it?*

He could sometimes figure out how a machine worked by putting his hand on it. He'd learned to fly a helicopter that way. He'd fixed Festus the dragon that way (before Festus crashed and burned). Once he'd even reprogrammed the electronic billboards in Times Square to read: ALL DA LADIES LUV LEO . . . accidentally, of course.

Now he tried to sense the workings of this ancient building. He turned towards a red marble altar-looking thing with a statue of the Virgin Mary on the top. 'Over there,' he said.

He marched confidently to the shrine. It was shaped sort

of like a fireplace, with an arched recess at the bottom. The mantel was inscribed with a name, like a tomb.

'The passage is around here,' he said. 'This guy's final resting place is in the way. Raphael somebody?'

'Famous painter, I think,' Hazel said.

Leo shrugged. He had a cousin named Raphael, and he didn't think much of the name. He wondered if he could produce a stick of dynamite from his tool belt and do a little discreet demolition, but he figured the caretakers of this place probably wouldn't approve.

'Hold on . . .' Leo looked around to make sure they weren't being watched.

Most of the tour groups were gawking at the dome, but one trio made Leo uneasy. About fifty feet away, some overweight middle-aged dudes with American accents were conversing loudly, complaining to each other about the heat. They looked like manatees stuffed into beach clothes – sandals, walking shorts, touristy T-shirts and floppy hats. Their legs were big and pasty and covered with spider veins. The guys acted extremely bored, and Leo wondered why they were hanging around.

They weren't watching him. Leo wasn't sure why they made him nervous. Maybe he just didn't like manatees.

Forget them, Leo told himself.

He slipped around the side of the tomb. He ran his hand down the back of a Roman column, all the way to the base. Right at the bottom, a series of lines had been etched into the marble – Roman numerals.

'Heh,' Leo said. 'Not very elegant, but effective.'

'What is?' Frank asked.

'The combination for a lock.' He felt around the back of the column some more and discovered a square hole about the size of an electrical socket. 'The lock face itself has been ripped out – probably vandalized sometime in the last few centuries. But I should be able to control the mechanism inside, if I can . . .'

Leo placed his hand on the marble floor. He could sense old bronze gears under the surface of the stone. Regular bronze would have corroded and become unusable long ago, but these were Celestial bronze – the handiwork of a demigod. With a little willpower, Leo urged them to move, using the Roman numerals to guide him. The cylinders turned – *click, click, click.* Then *click, click.*

On the floor next to the wall, one section of marble tile slid under another, revealing a dark square opening barely large enough to wiggle through.

'Romans must've been small.' Leo looked at Frank appraisingly. 'You'll need to change into something thinner to get through here.'

'That's not nice!' Hazel chided.

'What? Just saying –'

'Don't worry about it,' Frank mumbled. 'We should go get the others before we explore. That's what Piper said.'

'They're halfway across the city,' Leo reminded him. 'Besides, uh, I'm not sure I can close this hatch again. The gears are pretty old.'

'Great,' Frank said. 'How do we know it's safe down there?'

Hazel knelt. She put her hand over the opening as if checking the temperature. 'There's nothing alive . . . at least not for several hundred feet. The tunnel slants down, then levels out and goes south, more or less. I don't sense any traps . . .'

'How can you tell all that?' Leo asked.

She shrugged. 'Same way you can pick locks on marble columns, I guess. I'm glad you're not into robbing banks.'

'Oh . . . bank vaults,' Leo said. 'Never thought about that.'

'Forget I said anything.' Hazel sighed. 'Look, it's not three o'clock yet. We can at least do a little exploring, try to pinpoint Nico's location before we contact the others. You two stay here until I call for you. I want to check things out, make sure the tunnel is structurally sound. I'll be able to tell more once I'm underground.'

Frank scowled. 'We can't let you go by yourself. You could get hurt.'

'Frank, I can take care of myself,' she said. 'Underground is my speciality. It's safest for all of us if I go first.'

'Unless Frank wants to turn into a mole,' Leo suggested. 'Or a prairie dog. Those things are awesome.'

'Shut up,' Frank mumbled.

'Or a badger.'

Frank jabbed a finger at Leo's face. 'Valdez, I swear –'

'Both of you, be quiet,' Hazel scolded. 'I'll be back soon. Give me ten minutes. If you don't hear from me by then . . . Never mind. I'll be fine. Just try not to kill each other while I'm down there.'

She dropped down the hole. Leo and Frank blocked her from view as best they could. They stood shoulder to shoulder, trying to look casual, like it was completely natural for two teenaged guys to hang around Raphael's tomb.

Tour groups came and went. Most ignored Leo and Frank. A few people glanced at them apprehensively and kept walking. Maybe the tourists thought they would ask for tips. For some reason, Leo could unnerve people when he grinned.

The three American manatees were still hanging out in the middle of the room. One of them wore a T-shirt that said ROMA, as if he'd forget which city he was in if he didn't wear it. Every once in a while, he would glance over at Leo and Frank like he found their presence distasteful.

Something about that dude bothered Leo. He wished Hazel would hurry up.

'She talked to me earlier,' Frank said abruptly. 'Hazel told me you figured out about my lifeline.'

Leo stirred. He'd almost forgotten Frank was standing next to him.

'Your lifeline . . . oh, the burning stick. Right.' Leo resisted the urge to set his hand ablaze and yell: *Bwah ha ha!* The idea was sort of funny, but he wasn't that cruel.

'Look, man,' he said. 'It's cool. I'd never do anything to put you in danger. We're on the same team.'

Frank fiddled with his centurion badge. 'I always knew fire could kill me, but since my grandmother's mansion burned down in Vancouver . . . it seems a lot more *real*.'

Leo nodded. He felt sympathy for Frank, but the guy didn't make it easy when he talked about his family mansion.

Sort of like saying, *I crashed my Lamborghini*, and waiting for people to say, *Oh, you poor baby!*

Of course Leo didn't tell him that. 'Your grandmother – did she die in that fire? You didn't say.'

'I – I don't know. She was sick and pretty old. She said she would die in her own time, in her own way. But I think she made it out of the fire. I saw this bird flying up from the flames.'

Leo thought about that. 'So your whole family has the shape-changing thing?'

'I guess,' Frank said. 'My mom did. Grandmother thought that's what got her killed in Afghanistan, in the war. Mom tried to help some of her buddies, and . . . I don't know exactly what happened. There was a firebomb.'

Leo winced with sympathy. 'So we both lost our moms to fire.'

He hadn't been planning on it, but he told Frank the whole story of the night at the workshop when Gaia had appeared to him and his mother had died.

Frank's eyes got watery. 'I never like it when people tell me, *Sorry about your mom*.'

'It never feels genuine,' Leo agreed.

'But I'm sorry about your mom.'

'Thanks.'

No sign of Hazel. The American tourists were still milling around the Pantheon. They seemed to be circling closer, like they were trying to sneak up on Raphael's tomb without it noticing.

'Back at Camp Jupiter,' Frank said, 'our cabin Lar, Reticulus, told me I have more power than most demigods, being a son of Mars, plus having the shape-changing ability from my mom's side. He said that's why my life is tied to a burning stick. It's such a huge weakness that it kind of balances things out.'

Leo remembered his conversation with Nemesis the revenge goddess at the Great Salt Lake. She'd said something similar about wanting the scales to balance. *Good luck is a sham. True success requires sacrifice.*

Her fortune cookie was still in Leo's tool belt, waiting to be opened. *Soon you will face a problem you cannot solve, though I could help you . . . for a price.*

Leo wished he could pluck that memory out of his head and shove it in his tool belt. It was taking up too much space. 'We've all got weaknesses,' he said. 'Me, for instance. I'm tragically funny and good-looking.'

Frank snorted. 'You might have weaknesses. But your life doesn't depend on a piece of firewood.'

'No,' Leo admitted. He started thinking: if Frank's problem were *his* problem, how would he solve it? Almost every design flaw could be fixed. 'I wonder . . .'

He looked across the room and faltered. The three American tourists were coming their way; no more circling or sneaking. They were making a straight line for Raphael's tomb, and all three were glaring at Leo.

'Uh, Frank?' Leo asked. 'Has it been ten minutes yet?'

Frank followed his gaze. The Americans' faces were angry

and confused, like they were sleepwalking through a very annoying nightmare.

'*Leo Valdez*,' called the guy in the ROMA shirt. His voice had changed. It was hollow and metallic. He spoke English as if it was a second language. '*We meet again.*'

All three tourists blinked, and their eyes turned solid gold.

Frank yelped. 'Eidolons!'

The manatees clenched their beefy fists. Normally, Leo wouldn't have worried about getting murdered by overweight guys in floppy hats, but he suspected the eidolons were dangerous even in those bodies, especially since the spirits wouldn't care whether their hosts survived or not.

'They can't fit down the hole,' Leo said.

'Right,' Frank said. 'Underground is sounding really good.'

He turned into a snake and slithered over the edge. Leo jumped in after him while the spirits began to wail above, '*Valdez! Kill Valdez!*'

XXXVIII

LEO

ONE PROBLEM SOLVED: THE HATCH ABOVE THEM closed automatically, cutting off their pursuers. It also cut off all light, but Leo and Frank could deal with that. Leo just hoped they didn't need to get out the same way they came in. He wasn't sure he could open the tile from underneath.

At least the possessed manatee dudes were on the other side. Over Leo's head, the marble floor shuddered, like fat touristy feet were kicking it.

Frank must have turned back to human form. Leo could hear him wheezing in the dark.

'What now?' Frank asked.

'Okay, don't freak,' Leo said. 'I'm going to summon a little fire, just so we can see.'

'Thanks for the warning.'

Leo's index finger blazed like a birthday candle. In front of them stretched a stone tunnel with a low ceiling. Just as

Hazel had predicted, it slanted down, then levelled out and went south.

'Well,' Leo said. 'It only goes in one direction.'

'Let's find Hazel,' Frank said.

Leo had no argument with that suggestion. They made their way down the corridor, Leo going first with the fire. He was glad to have Frank at his back, big and strong and able to turn into scary animals in case those possessed tourists somehow broke through the hatch, squeezed inside and followed them. He wondered if the eidolons might just leave those bodies behind, seep underground and possess one of them instead.

Oh, there's my happy thought for the day! Leo scolded himself.

After a hundred feet or so, they turned a corner and found Hazel. In the light of her golden cavalry sword, she was examining a door. She was so engrossed she didn't notice them until Leo said, 'Hi.'

Hazel whirled, trying to swing her *spatha*. Fortunately for Leo's face, the blade was too long to wield in the corridor.

'What are you doing here?' Hazel demanded.

Leo gulped. 'Sorry. We ran into some angry tourists.' He told her what had happened.

She hissed in frustration. 'I hate eidolons. I thought Piper made them promise to stay away.'

'Oh . . .' Frank said, like he'd just had his own daily happy thought. 'Piper made them promise to stay off the ship and not possess any of *us*. But if they followed us, and used other bodies to attack us, then they're not technically breaking their vow . . .'

'Great,' Leo muttered. 'Eidolons who are also lawyers. Now I *really* want to kill them.'

'Okay, forget them for now,' Hazel said. 'This door is giving me fits. Leo, can you try your skill with the lock?'

Leo cracked his knuckles. 'Stand aside for the master, please.'

The door was interesting, much more complicated than the Roman-numeral combination lock above. The entire door was coated in Imperial gold. A mechanical sphere about the size of a bowling ball was embedded in the centre. The sphere was constructed from five concentric rings, each inscribed with zodiac symbols – the bull, the scorpion, et cetera – and seemingly random numbers and letters.

'These letters are Greek,' Leo said in surprise.

'Well, lots of Romans spoke Greek,' Hazel said.

'I guess,' Leo said. 'But this workmanship . . . no offence to you Camp Jupiter types, but this is too complicated to be Roman.'

Frank snorted. 'Whereas you Greeks just *love* making things complicated.'

'Hey,' Leo protested. 'All I'm saying is this machinery is delicate, sophisticated. It reminds me of . . .' Leo stared at the sphere, trying to recall where he'd read or heard about a similar ancient machine. 'It's a more advanced sort of lock,' he decided. 'You line up the symbols on the different rings in the right order, and that opens the door.'

'But what's the right order?' Hazel asked.

'Good question. Greek spheres . . . astronomy, geometry . . .'

Leo got a warm feeling inside. 'Oh, no way. I wonder . . . What's the value of pi?'

Frank frowned. 'What kind of pie?'

'He means the number,' Hazel guessed. 'I learned that in maths class once, but –'

'It's used to measure circles,' Leo said. 'This sphere, if it's made by the guy I'm thinking of . . .'

Hazel and Frank both stared at him blankly.

'Never mind,' Leo said. 'I'm pretty sure pi is, uh, 3.1415 blah blah blah. The number goes on forever, but the sphere has only five rings, so that should be enough, if I'm right.'

'And if you're not?' Frank asked.

'Well, then, Leo fall down, go boom. Let's find out!'

He turned the rings, starting on the outside and moving in. He ignored the zodiac signs and letters, lining up the correct numbers so they made the value of pi. Nothing happened.

'I'm stupid,' Leo mumbled. 'Pi would expand outwards, because it's infinite.'

He reversed the order of the numbers, starting in the centre and working towards the edge. When he aligned the last ring, something inside the sphere clicked. The door swung open.

Leo beamed at his friends. 'That, good people, is how we do things in Leo World. Come on in!'

'I hate Leo World,' Frank muttered.

Hazel laughed.

Inside was enough cool stuff to keep Leo busy for years. The room was about the size of the forge back at Camp Half-Blood, with bronze-topped worktables along the walls and baskets full of ancient metalworking tools. Dozens of bronze and gold spheres like steampunk basketballs sat around in various stages of disassembly. Loose gears and wiring littered the floor. Thick metal cables ran from each table towards the back of the room, where there was an enclosed loft like a theatre's sound booth. Stairs led up to the booth on either side. All the cables seemed to run into it. Next to the stairs on the left, a row of cubbyholes was filled with leather cylinders – probably ancient scroll cases.

Leo was about to head towards the tables when he glanced to his left and nearly jumped out of his shoes. Flanking the doorway were two armoured manikins – like skeletal scarecrows made from bronze pipes, outfitted with full suits of Roman armour, shield and sword.

'Dude.' Leo walked up to one. 'These would be *awesome* if they worked.'

Frank edged away from the manikins. 'Those things are going to come alive and attack us, aren't they?'

Leo laughed. 'Not a chance. They aren't complete.' He tapped the nearest manikin's neck, where loose copper wires sprouted from underneath its breastplate. 'Look, the head's wiring has been disconnected. And here, at the elbow, the pulley system for this joint is out of alignment. My guess? The Romans were trying to duplicate a Greek design, but they didn't have the skill.'

Hazel arched her eyebrows. 'The Romans weren't good enough at being *complicated*, I suppose.'

'Or delicate,' Frank added. 'Or sophisticated.'

'Hey, I just call it like I see it.' Leo jiggled the manikin's head, making it nod like it was agreeing with him. 'Still . . . a pretty impressive try. I've heard legends that the Romans confiscated the writings of Archimedes, but –'

'Archimedes?' Hazel looked baffled. 'Wasn't he an ancient mathematician or something?'

Leo laughed. 'He was a lot more than that. He was only the most famous son of Hephaestus who ever lived.'

Frank scratched his ear. 'I've heard his name before, but how can you be sure this manikin is his design?'

'It has to be!' Leo said. 'Look, I've read all about Archimedes. He's a hero to Cabin Nine. The dude was Greek, right? He lived in one of the Greek colonies in southern Italy, back before Rome got all huge and took over. Finally the Romans moved in and destroyed his city. The Roman general wanted to spare Archimedes, because he was so valuable – sort of like the Einstein of the ancient world – but some stupid Roman soldier killed him.'

'There you go again,' Hazel muttered. '*Stupid* and *Roman* don't always go together, Leo.'

Frank grunted agreement. 'How do you know all this, anyway?' he demanded. 'Is there a Spanish tour guide around here?'

'No, man,' Leo said. 'You can't be a demigod who's into building stuff and not know about Archimedes. The guy was *seriously* elite. He calculated the value of pi. He did all this maths stuff we still use for engineering. He invented a hydraulic screw that could move water through pipes.'

Hazel scowled. 'A hydraulic screw. Excuse me for not knowing about *that* awesome achievement.'

'He also built a death ray made of mirrors that could burn enemy ships,' Leo said. 'Is that awesome enough for you?'

'I saw something about that on TV,' Frank admitted. 'They proved it didn't work.'

'Ah, that's just because modern mortals don't know how to use Celestial bronze,' Leo said. '*That's* the key. Archimedes also invented a massive claw that could swing on a crane and pluck enemy ships out of the water.'

'Okay, that's cool,' Frank admitted. 'I love grabber-arm games.'

'Well, there you go,' Leo said. 'Anyway, all his inventions weren't enough. The Romans destroyed his city. Archimedes was killed. According to legends, the Roman general was a big fan of his work, so he raided Archimedes's workshop and carted a bunch of souvenirs back to Rome. They disappeared from history, except . . .' Leo waved his hands at the stuff on the tables. 'Here they are.'

'Metal basketballs?' Hazel asked.

Leo couldn't believe that they didn't appreciate what they were looking at, but he tried to contain his irritation. 'Guys, Archimedes constructed *spheres*. The Romans couldn't figure them out. They thought they were just for telling time or following constellations, because they were covered with pictures of stars and planets. But that's like finding a rifle and thinking it's a walking stick.'

'Leo, the Romans were top-notch engineers,' Hazel reminded him. 'They built aqueducts, roads –'

'Siege weapons,' Frank added. 'Public sanitation.'

'Yeah, fine,' Leo said. 'But Archimedes was in a class by

himself. His spheres could do all sorts of things, only nobody is sure . . .'

Suddenly Leo got an idea so incredible that his nose burst into flames. He patted it out as quickly as possible. Man, it was *embarrassing* when that happened.

He ran to the row of cubbyholes and examined the markings on the scroll cases. 'Oh, gods. This is it!'

He gingerly lifted out one of the scrolls. He wasn't great at Ancient Greek, but he could tell the inscription on the case read *On Building Spheres*.

'Guys, this is the lost book!' His hands were shaking. 'Archimedes wrote this, describing his construction methods, but all the copies were lost in ancient times. If I can translate this . . .'

The possibilities were endless. For Leo, the quest had now totally taken on a new dimension. Leo had to get the spheres and scrolls safely out of here. He had to protect this stuff until he could get it back to Bunker 9 and study it.

'The secrets of Archimedes,' he murmured. 'Guys, this is bigger than Daedalus's laptop. If there's a Roman attack on Camp Half-Blood, these secrets could save the camp. They might even give us an edge over Gaia and the giants!'

Hazel and Frank glanced at each other sceptically.

'Okay,' Hazel said. 'We didn't come here for a scroll, but I guess we can take it with us.'

'Assuming,' Frank added, 'that you don't mind sharing its secrets with us stupid uncomplicated Romans.'

'What?' Leo stared at him blankly. 'No. Look, I didn't

mean to insult – Ah, never mind. The point is this is good news!'

For the first time in days, Leo felt really hopeful.

Naturally, that's when everything went wrong.

On the table next to Hazel and Frank, one of the orbs clicked and whirred. A row of spindly legs extended from its equator. The orb stood, and two bronze cables shot out of the top, hitting Hazel and Frank like Taser wires. Leo's friends both crumpled to the floor.

Leo lunged to help them, but the two armoured manikins that couldn't possibly move *did* move. They drew their swords and stepped towards Leo.

The one on the left turned its crooked helmet, which was shaped like a wolf's head. Despite the fact that it had no face or mouth, a familiar hollow voice spoke from behind its visor.

'*You cannot escape us, Leo Valdez,*' it said. '*We do not like possessing machines, but they are better than tourists. You will not leave here alive.*'

XXXIX

LEO

LEO AGREED WITH NEMESIS ABOUT ONE THING: good luck was a sham. At least when it came to Leo's luck.

Last winter he had watched in horror while a family of Cyclopes prepared to roast Jason and Piper with hot sauce. He'd schemed his way out of that one and saved his friends all by himself, but at least he'd had time to think.

Now, not so much. Hazel and Frank had been knocked out by the tendrils of a possessed steampunk bowling ball. Two suits of armour with bad attitudes were about to kill him.

Leo couldn't blast them with fire. Suits of armour wouldn't be hurt by that. Besides, Hazel and Frank were too close. He didn't want to burn them, or accidentally hit the piece of firewood that controlled Frank's life.

On Leo's right, the suit of armour with a lion's head helmet creaked its wiry neck and regarded Hazel and Frank, who were still lying unconscious.

'*A male and female demigod*,' said Lion Head. '*These will do, if the others die.'* Its hollow face mask turned back to Leo. *'We do not need you, Leo Valdez.'*

'Oh, hey!' Leo tried for a winning smile. 'You always need Leo Valdez!'

He spread his hands and hoped he looked confident and useful, not desperate and terrified. He wondered if it was too late to write TEAM LEO on his shirt.

Sadly, the suits of armour were not as easily swayed as the Narcissus Fan Club had been.

The one with the wolf-headed helmet snarled, *'I have been in your mind, Leo. I helped you start the war.'*

Leo's smile crumbled. He took a step back. 'That was you?'

Now he understood why those tourists had bothered him right away and why this thing's voice sounded so familiar. He'd heard it in his mind.

'You made me fire that ballista?' Leo demanded. 'You call that *helping*?'

'I know how you think,' said Wolf Head. *'I know your limits. You are small and alone. You need friends to protect you. Without them, you are unable to withstand me. I vowed not to possess you again, but I can still kill you.'*

The armoured dudes stepped forward. The points of their swords hovered a few inches from Leo's face.

Leo's fear suddenly made way for a whole lot of anger. This eidolon in the wolf helmet had shamed him, controlled him and made him attack New Rome. It had endangered his friends and botched their quest.

Leo glanced at the dormant spheres on the worktables.

He considered his tool belt. He thought about the loft behind him – the area that looked like a sound booth. Presto: *Operation Junk Pile* was born.

'First: you don't know me,' he told Wolf Head. 'And second: bye.'

He lunged for the stairs and bounded to the top. The suits of armour were scary, but they were not fast. As Leo suspected, the loft had doors on either side – folding metal gates. The operators would've wanted protection in case their creations went haywire . . . like now. Leo slammed both gates shut and summoned fire to his hands, fusing the locks.

The suits of armour closed in on either side. They rattled the gates, hacking at them with their swords.

'*This is foolish,*' said Lion Head. '*You only delay your death.*'

'Delaying death is one of my favourite hobbies.' Leo scanned his new home. Overlooking the workshop was a single table like a control board. It was crowded with junk, and most of it Leo dismissed immediately: a diagram for a human catapult that would never work; a strange black sword (Leo was no good with swords); a large bronze mirror (Leo's reflection looked terrible); and a set of tools that someone had broken, either in frustration or clumsiness.

He focused on the main project. In the centre of the table, someone had disassembled an Archimedes sphere. Gears, springs, levers and rods were littered around it. All the bronze cables to the room below were connected to a metal plate under the sphere. Leo could sense the Celestial bronze running through the workshop like arteries from a heart – ready to conduct magical energy from this spot.

'One basketball to rule them all,' Leo muttered.

This sphere was a master regulator. He was standing at Ancient Roman mission control.

'*Leo Valdez!*' the spirit howled. '*Open this gate or I will kill you!*'

'A fair and generous offer!' Leo said, his eyes still on the sphere. 'Just let me finish this. A last request, all right?'

That must have confused the spirits, because they momentarily stopped hacking at the bars.

Leo's hands flew over the sphere, reassembling its missing pieces. Why did the stupid Romans have to take apart such a beautiful machine? They had killed Archimedes, stolen his stuff, then messed with a piece of equipment they could never understand. On the other hand, at least they'd had the sense to lock it away for two thousand years so that Leo could retrieve it.

The eidolons started pounding on the gates again.

'Who is it?' Leo called.

'*Valdez!*' Wolf Head bellowed.

'Valdez who?' Leo asked.

Eventually the eidolons would realize they couldn't get in. Then, if Wolf Head truly knew Leo's mind, he would decide there were other ways to force his cooperation. Leo had to work faster.

He connected the gears, got one wrong and had to start again. Hephaestus's Hand Grenades, this was hard!

Finally he got the last spring in place. The ham-fisted Romans had almost ruined the tension adjuster, but Leo pulled a set of watchmaker's tools from his belt and did some final calibrations. Archimedes was a genius – assuming this thing actually worked.

He wound the starter coil. The gears began to turn. Leo closed the top of the sphere and studied its concentric circles – similar to the ones on the workshop door.

'*Valdez!*' Wolf Head pounded on the gate. '*Our third comrade will kill your friends!*'

Leo cursed under his breath. *Our third comrade.* He glanced down at the spindly-legged Taser ball that had knocked out Hazel and Frank. He had figured eidolon number three was hiding inside that thing. But Leo still had to deduce the right sequence to activate this control sphere.

'Yeah, okay,' he called. 'You got me. Just . . . just a sec.'

'*No more seconds!*' Wolf Head shouted. '*Open this gate now, or they die.*'

The possessed Taser ball lashed out with its tendrils and sent another shock through Hazel and Frank. Their unconscious bodies flinched. That kind of electricity might have stopped their hearts.

Leo held back tears. This was too hard. He couldn't do it.

He stared at the face of the sphere – seven rings, each one covered with tiny Greek letters, numbers and zodiac signs. The answer wouldn't be pi. Archimedes would never do the same thing twice. Besides, just by putting his hand on the sphere Leo could feel that the sequence had been generated randomly. It was something only Archimedes would know.

Supposedly, Archimedes's last words had been: *Don't disturb my circles.*

No one knew what that meant, but Leo could apply it to this sphere. The lock was much too complicated. Maybe if Leo had a few years, he could decipher the markings and figure out the right combination, but he didn't even have a few seconds.

He was out of time. Out of luck. And his friends were going to die.

A problem you cannot solve, said a voice in his mind.

Nemesis . . . she'd told him to expect this moment. Leo thrust his hand in his pocket and brought out the fortune cookie. The goddess had warned him of a great price for her help – as great as losing an eye. But, if he didn't try, his friends would die.

'I need the access code for this sphere,' he said.

He broke open the cookie.

LEO

LEO UNFURLED THE LITTLE STRIP OF PAPER. IT READ:

THAT'S YOUR REQUEST? SERIOUSLY? (OVER)

On the back, the paper said:

YOUR LUCKY NUMBERS ARE: TWELVE, JUPITER, ORION, DELTA, THREE, THETA, OMEGA. (WREAK VENGEANCE UPON GAIA, LEO VALDEZ.)

With trembling fingers, Leo turned the rings.

Outside the gates, Wolf Head growled in frustration. '*If friends do not matter to you, perhaps you need more incentive. Perhaps I should destroy these scrolls instead – priceless works by Archimedes!*'

The last ring clicked into place. The sphere hummed with power. Leo ran his hands along the surface, sensing tiny buttons and levers awaiting his commands.

Magical and electrical pulses coursed via the Celestial bronze cables and surged through the entire room.

Leo had never played a musical instrument, but he imagined it must be like this – knowing each key or note so well that you didn't really think about what your hands were doing. You just concentrated on the kind of sound you wanted to create.

He started small. He focused on one reasonably intact gold sphere down in the main room. The gold sphere shuddered. It grew a tripod of legs and clattered over to the Taser ball. A tiny circular saw popped out of the gold sphere's head, and it began cutting into Taser ball's brain.

Leo tried to activate another orb. This one burst in a small mushroom cloud of bronze dust and smoke.

'Oops,' he muttered. 'Sorry, Archimedes.'

'*What are you doing?*' Wolf Head demanded. '*Stop your foolishness and surrender!*'

'Oh, yes, I surrender!' Leo said. 'I'm totally surrendering!'

He tried to take control of a third orb. That one broke, too. Leo felt bad about ruining all these ancient inventions, but this was life or death. Frank had accused him of caring more for machines than people, but, if it came down to saving old spheres or his friends, there was no choice.

The fourth try went better. A ruby-encrusted orb popped its top and helicopter blades unfolded. Leo was glad Buford the table wasn't here – he would've fallen in love. The ruby orb spun into the air and sailed straight for the cubbyholes. Thin golden arms extended from its middle and snapped up the precious scroll cases.

'*Enough!*' Wolf Head yelled. '*I will destroy the –*'

He turned in time to see the ruby sphere take off with the scrolls. It zipped across the room and hovered in the far corner.

'*What?!*' Wolf Head cried. '*Kill the prisoners!*'

He must have been talking to the Taser ball. Unfortunately, Taser Ball was in no shape to comply. Leo's gold sphere was sitting on top of its sawed-open head, picking through its gears and wires like it was scooping out a pumpkin.

Thank the gods, Hazel and Frank began to stir.

'*Bah!*' Wolf Head gestured to Lion Head at the opposite gate. '*Come! We will destroy the demigods ourselves.*'

'I don't think so, guys.' Leo turned towards Lion Head. His hands worked the control sphere, and he felt a shock travel through the floor.

Lion Head shuddered and lowered his sword.

Leo grinned. 'You're in Leo World, now.'

Lion Head turned and stormed down the stairs. Instead of advancing on Hazel and Leo, he marched up the opposite stairs and faced his comrade.

'*What are you doing?*' Wolf Head demanded. '*We have to –*'

BLONG!

Lion Head slammed his shield into Wolf Head's chest. He smashed the pommel of his sword into his comrade's helmet, so Wolf Head became Flat, Deformed, Not Very Happy Wolf Head.

'*Stop that!*' Wolf Head demanded.

'*I cannot!*' Lion Head wailed.

Leo was getting the hang of it now. He commanded both

suits of armour to drop their swords and shields and slap each other repeatedly.

'*Valdez!*' called Wolf Head in a warbling voice. '*You will die for this!*'

'Yeah,' Leo called out. 'Who's possessing who now, Casper?'

The machine men tumbled down the stairs, and Leo forced them to jitterbug like 1920s flappers. Their joints began smoking. The other spheres around the room began to pop. Too much energy was surging through the ancient system. The control sphere in Leo's hand grew uncomfortably warm.

'Frank, Hazel!' Leo shouted. 'Take cover!'

His friends were still dazed, staring in amazement at the jitterbugging metal guys, but they got his warning. Frank pulled Hazel under the nearest table and shielded her with his body.

One last twist of the sphere, and Leo sent a massive jolt through the system. The armoured warriors blew apart. Rods, pistons and bronze shards flew everywhere. On all the tables, spheres popped like hot soda cans. Leo's gold sphere froze. His flying ruby orb dropped to the floor with the scroll cases.

The room was suddenly quiet except for a few random sparks and sizzles. The air smelled like burning car engines. Leo raced down the stairs and found Frank and Hazel safe under their table. He had never been so happy to see those two hugging.

'You're alive!' he said.

Hazel's left eye twitched, maybe from the Taser shock. Otherwise she looked okay. 'Uh, what exactly happened?'

'Archimedes came through!' Leo said. 'Just enough power left in those old machines for one final show. Once I had the access code, it was easy.'

He patted the control sphere, which was steaming in a bad way. Leo didn't know if it could be fixed, but at the moment he was too relieved to care.

'The eidolons,' Frank said. 'Are they gone?'

Leo grinned. 'My last command overloaded their kill switches – basically locked down all their circuits and melted their cores.'

'In English?' Frank asked.

'I trapped the eidolons inside the wiring,' Leo said. 'Then I melted them. They won't be bothering anyone again.'

Leo helped his friends to their feet.

'You saved us,' Frank said.

'Don't sound so surprised.' Leo glanced around the destroyed workshop. 'Too bad all this stuff got wrecked, but at least I salvaged the scrolls. If I can get them back to Camp Half-Blood, maybe I can learn how to recreate Archimedes's inventions.'

Hazel rubbed the side of her head. 'But I don't understand. Where is Nico? That tunnel was supposed to lead us to Nico.'

Leo had almost forgotten why they'd come down here in the first place. Nico obviously wasn't here. The place was a dead end. So why . . .?

'Oh.' He felt like there was a buzz-saw sphere on his own head, pulling out his wires and gears. 'Hazel, how exactly were you tracking Nico? I mean, could you just sense him nearby because he was your brother?'

She frowned, still looking a bit wobbly from her electric shock treatment. 'Not – not totally. Sometimes I can tell when he's close, but, like I said, Rome is so confusing, so much interference because of all the tunnels and caves –'

'You tracked him with your metal-finding senses,' Leo guessed. 'His sword?'

She blinked. 'How did you know?'

'You'd better come here.' He led Hazel and Frank up to the control room and pointed to the black sword.

'Oh. Oh, no.' Hazel would've collapsed if Frank hadn't caught her. 'But that's impossible! Nico's sword was with him in the bronze jar. Percy *saw* it in his dream!'

'Either the dream was wrong,' Leo said, 'or the giants moved the sword here as a decoy.'

'So this was a trap,' Frank said. 'We were lured here.'

'But *why*?' Hazel cried. 'Where's my brother?'

A hissing sound filled the control booth. At first, Leo thought the eidolons were back. Then he realized the bronze mirror on the table was steaming.

Ah, my poor demigods. The sleeping face of Gaia appeared in the mirror. As usual, she spoke without moving her mouth, which could only have been creepier if she'd had a ventriloquism puppet. Leo hated those things.

You had your choice, Gaia said. Her voice echoed through the room. It seemed to be coming not just from the mirror but from the stone walls as well.

Leo realized she was all around them. Of course. They were in the earth. They'd gone to all the trouble of building the *Argo II* so they could travel by sea and air, and they'd ended up in the earth anyway.

I offered salvation to all of you, Gaia said. *You could have turned back. Now it is too late. You've come to the ancient lands where I am strongest – where I will wake.*

Leo pulled a hammer from his tool belt. He whacked the mirror. Being metal, it just quivered like a tea tray, but it felt good to smash Gaia in the nose.

'In case you haven't noticed, Dirt Face,' he said, 'your little ambush failed. Your three eidolons got melted in bronze, and we're fine.'

Gaia laughed softly. *Oh, my sweet Leo. You three have been separated from your friends. That was the whole point.*

The workshop door slammed shut.

You are trapped in my embrace, Gaia said. *Meanwhile, Annabeth Chase faces her death alone, terrified and crippled, at the hands of her mother's greatest enemy.*

The image in the mirror changed. Leo saw Annabeth sprawled on the floor of a dark cavern, holding up her bronze knife as if warding off a monster. Her face was gaunt. Her leg was wrapped up in some sort of splint. Leo couldn't see what she was looking at, but it was obviously something horrible. He wanted to believe the image was a lie, but he had a bad feeling it was real, and it was happening right now.

The others, Gaia said, *Jason Grace, Piper McLean and my dear friend Percy Jackson – they will perish within minutes.*

The scene changed again. Percy was holding Riptide,

leading Jason and Piper down a spiral staircase into the darkness.

Their powers will betray them, Gaia said. *They will die in their own elements. I almost hoped they would survive. They would have made a better sacrifice. But alas, Hazel and Frank, you will have to do. My minions will collect you shortly and bring you to the ancient place. Your blood will awaken me at last. Until then, I will allow you to watch your friends perish. Please . . . enjoy this last glimpse of your failed quest.*

Leo couldn't stand it. His hand glowed white hot. Hazel and Frank scrambled back as he pressed his palm against the mirror and melted it into a puddle of bronze goo.

The voice of Gaia went silent. Leo could only hear the roar of blood in his ears. He took a shaky breath.

'Sorry,' he told his friends. 'She was getting annoying.'

'What do we do?' Frank asked. 'We have to get out and help the others.'

Leo scanned the workshop, now littered with smoking pieces of broken spheres. His friends still needed him. This was still his show. As long as he had his tool belt, Leo Valdez wasn't going to sit around helplessly watching the Demigod Death Channel.

'I've got an idea,' he said. 'But it's going to take all three of us.'

He started telling them the plan.

XLI

PIPER

PIPER TRIED TO MAKE THE BEST OF THE SITUATION.

Once she and Jason had got tired of pacing the deck, listening to Coach Hedge sing 'Old MacDonald' (with weapons instead of animals), they decided to have a picnic in the park.

Hedge grudgingly agreed. 'Stay where I can see you.'

'What are we, kids?' Jason asked.

Hedge snorted. 'Kids are baby goats. They're cute, and they have redeeming social value. You are definitely not kids.'

They spread their blanket under a willow tree next to a pond. Piper turned over her cornucopia and spilled out an entire meal – neatly wrapped sandwiches, canned drinks, fresh fruit and (for some reason) a birthday cake with purple icing and candles already lit.

She frowned. 'Is it someone's birthday?'

Jason winced. 'I wasn't going to say anything.'

'Jason!'

'There's too much going on,' he said. 'And honestly . . . before last month I didn't even know when my birthday *was*. Thalia told me the last time she was at camp.'

Piper wondered what that would be like – not even knowing the day you were born. Jason had been given to Lupa the wolf when he was only two years old. He'd never really known his mortal mom. He'd only been reunited with his sister last winter.

'July first,' Piper said. 'The Kalends of July.'

'Yeah.' Jason smirked. 'The Romans would find that auspicious – the first day of the month named for Julius Caesar. Juno's sacred day. Yippee.'

Piper didn't want to push it or make a celebration if he didn't feel like celebrating.

'Sixteen?' she asked.

He nodded. 'Oh, boy. I can get my driver's licence.'

Piper laughed. Jason had killed so many monsters and saved the world so many times that the idea of him sweating a driving test seemed ridiculous. She pictured him behind the wheel of some old Lincoln with a STUDENT DRIVER sign on top and a grumpy teacher in the passenger seat with an emergency brake pedal.

'Well?' she urged. 'Blow out the candles.'

Jason did. Piper wondered if he'd made a wish – hopefully that he and Piper would survive this quest and stay together forever. She decided not to ask him. She didn't want to jinx that wish, and she definitely didn't want to find out that he'd wished for something different.

Since they'd left the Pillars of Hercules yesterday

evening, Jason had seemed distracted. Piper couldn't blame him. Hercules had been a pretty huge disappointment as a big brother, and the old river god Achelous had said some unflattering things about the sons of Jupiter.

Piper stared at the cornucopia. She wondered if Achelous was getting used to having no horns at all. She hoped so. Sure, he had tried to kill them, but Piper still felt bad for the old god. She didn't understand how such a lonely, depressed spirit could produce a horn of plenty that shot out pineapples and birthday cakes. Could it be that the cornucopia had drained all the goodness out of him? Maybe now that the horn was gone, Achelous would be able to fill up with some happiness and keep it for himself.

She also kept thinking about Achelous's advice: *If you had made it to Rome, the story of the flood would have served you better.* She knew the story he was talking about. She just didn't understand how it would help.

Jason plucked an extinguished candle from his cake. 'I've been thinking.'

That snapped Piper back to the present. Coming from your boyfriend, *I've been thinking* was kind of a scary line.

'About?' she asked.

'Camp Jupiter,' he said. 'All the years I trained there. We were always pushing teamwork, working as a unit. I thought I understood what that meant. But honestly? I was always the leader. Even when I was younger –'

'The son of Jupiter,' Piper said. 'Most powerful kid in the legion. You were the star.'

Jason looked uncomfortable, but he didn't deny it. 'Being

in this crew of seven . . . I'm not sure what to do. I'm not used to being one of so many, well, equals. I feel like I'm failing.'

Piper took his hand. 'You're *not* failing.'

'It sure felt that way when Chrysaor attacked,' Jason said. 'I've spent most of this trip knocked out and helpless.'

'Come on,' she chided. 'Being a hero doesn't mean you're invincible. It just means that you're brave enough to stand up and do what's needed.'

'And if I don't *know* what's needed?'

'That's what your friends are for. We've all got different strengths. Together, we'll figure it out.'

Jason studied her. Piper wasn't sure that he bought what she was saying, but she was glad he could confide in her. She liked it that he had a little self-doubt. He didn't succeed all the time. He didn't think the universe owed him an apology whenever something went wrong – unlike another son of the sky god she'd recently met.

'Hercules was a jerk,' he said, as if reading her thoughts. 'I never want to be like that. But I wouldn't have had the courage to stand up to him without you taking the lead. You were the hero that time.'

'We can take turns,' she suggested.

'I don't deserve you.'

'You're not allowed to say that.'

'Why not?'

'It's a break-up line. Unless you're breaking up –'

Jason leaned over and kissed her. The colours of the Roman afternoon suddenly seemed sharper, as if the world had switched to high definition.

'No break-ups,' he promised. 'I may have busted my head a few times, but I'm not *that* stupid.'

'Good,' she said. 'Now, about that cake –'

Her voice faltered. Percy Jackson was running towards them, and Piper could tell from his expression that he brought bad news.

They gathered on deck so that Coach Hedge could hear the story. When Percy was done, Piper still couldn't believe it.

'So Annabeth was kidnapped on a motor scooter,' she summed up, 'by Gregory Peck and Audrey Hepburn.'

'Not kidnapped, exactly,' Percy said. 'But I've got this bad feeling . . .' He took a deep breath, like he was trying hard not to freak out. 'Anyway, she's – she's gone. Maybe I shouldn't have let her, but –'

'You had to,' Piper said. 'You knew she had to go alone. Besides, Annabeth is tough and smart. She'll be fine.'

Piper put some charmspeak in her voice, which maybe wasn't cool, but Percy needed to be able to focus. If they went into battle, Annabeth wouldn't want him getting hurt because he was too distracted about her.

His shoulders relaxed a little. 'Maybe you're right. Anyway, Gregory – I mean Tiberinus – said we had less time to rescue Nico than we thought. Hazel and the guys aren't back yet?'

Piper checked the time on the helm control. She hadn't realized how late it was getting. 'It's two in the afternoon. We said three o'clock for a rendezvous.'

'At the latest,' Jason said.

Percy pointed at Piper's dagger. 'Tiberinus said you could find Nico's location . . . you know, with that.'

Piper bit her lip. The last thing she wanted to do was check Katoptris for more terrifying images.

'I've tried,' she said. 'The dagger doesn't always show what I want to see. In fact, it hardly *ever* does.'

'Please,' Percy said. 'Try again.'

He pleaded with those sea-green eyes, like a cute baby seal that needed help. Piper wondered how Annabeth ever won an argument with this guy.

'Fine,' she sighed, and drew her dagger.

'While you're at it,' said Coach Hedge, 'see if you can get the latest baseball scores. Italians don't cover baseball worth beans.'

'Shh.' Piper studied the bronze blade. The light shimmered. She saw a loft apartment filled with Roman demigods. A dozen of them stood around a dining table as Octavian talked and pointed to a big map. Reyna paced next to the windows, gazing down at Central Park.

'That's not good,' Jason muttered. 'They've already set up a forward base in Manhattan.'

'And that map shows Long Island,' Percy said.

'They're scouting the territory,' Jason guessed. 'Discussing invasion routes.'

Piper did *not* want to see that. She concentrated harder. Light rippled across the blade. She saw ruins – a few crumbling walls, a single column, a stone floor covered with moss and dead vines – all clustered on a grassy hillside dotted with pine trees.

'I was just there,' Percy said. 'That's in the old Forum.'

The view zoomed in. On one side of the stone floor, a set of stairs had been excavated, leading down to a modern iron gate with a padlock. The blade's image zoomed straight through the doorway, down a spiral stairwell and into a dark, cylindrical chamber like the inside of a grain silo.

Piper dropped the blade.

'What's wrong?' Jason asked. 'It was showing us something.'

Piper felt like the boat was back on the ocean, rocking under her feet. 'We can't go there.'

Percy frowned. 'Piper, Nico is dying. We've got to find him. Not to mention, Rome is about to get destroyed.'

Her voice wouldn't work. She'd kept that vision of the circular room to herself for so long that now she found it impossible to talk about. She had a horrible feeling that explaining it to Percy and Jason wouldn't change anything. She couldn't stop what was about to happen.

She picked up the knife again. Its hilt seemed colder than usual.

She forced herself to look at the blade. She saw two giants in gladiator armour sitting on oversized praetors' chairs. The giants toasted each other with golden goblets as if they'd just won an important fight. Between them stood a large bronze jar.

The vision zoomed in again. Inside the jar, Nico di Angelo was curled in a ball, no longer moving, all the pomegranate seeds eaten.

'We're too late,' Jason said.

'No,' Percy said. 'No, I can't believe that. Maybe he's gone into a deeper trance to buy time. We have to hurry.'

The blade's surface went dark. Piper slipped it back into its sheath, trying to keep her hands from shaking. She hoped that Percy was right and Nico was still alive. On the other hand, she didn't see how that image connected with the vision of the drowning room. Maybe the giants were toasting each other because she and Percy and Jason were dead.

'We should wait for the others,' she said. 'Hazel, Frank and Leo should be back soon.'

'We can't wait,' Percy insisted.

Coach Hedge grunted. 'It's just two giants. If you guys want, I can take them.'

'Uh, Coach,' Jason said, 'that's a great offer, but we need you to man the ship – or *goat* the ship. Whatever.'

Hedge scowled. 'And let you three have all the fun?'

Percy gripped the satyr's arm. 'Hazel and the others need you here. When they get back, they'll need your leadership. You're their rock.'

'Yeah.' Jason managed to keep a straight face. 'Leo always says you're his rock. You can tell them where we've gone and bring the ship around to meet us at the Forum.'

'And here.' Piper unstrapped Katoptris and put it in Coach Hedge's hands.

The satyr's eyes widened. A demigod was never supposed to leave her weapon behind, but Piper was fed up with evil visions. She'd rather face her death without any more previews.

'Keep an eye on us with the blade,' she suggested. 'And you can check the baseball scores.'

That sealed the deal. Hedge nodded grimly, prepared to do his part for the quest.

'All right,' he said. 'But if any giants come this way –'

'Feel free to blast them,' Jason said.

'What about annoying tourists?'

'No,' they all said in unison.

'Bah. Fine. Just don't take too long, or I'm coming after you with ballistae blazing.'

XLII

PIPER

FINDING THE PLACE WAS EASY. Percy led them right to it, on an abandoned stretch of hillside overlooking the ruined Forum.

Getting in was easy, too. Jason's gold sword cut through the padlock, and the metal gate creaked open. No mortals saw them. No alarms went off. Stone steps spiralled down into the gloom.

'I'll go first,' Jason said.

'No!' Piper yelped.

Both boys turned towards her.

'Pipes, what is it?' Jason asked. 'That image in the blade . . . you've seen it before, haven't you?'

She nodded, her eyes stinging. 'I didn't know how to tell you. I saw the room down there filling with water. I saw the three of us drowning.'

Jason and Percy both frowned.

'I can't drown,' Percy said, though he sounded like he was asking a question.

'Maybe the future has changed,' Jason speculated. 'In the image you showed us just now, there wasn't any water.'

Piper wished he was right, but she suspected they wouldn't be so lucky.

'Look,' Percy said. 'I'll check it out first. It's fine. Be right back.'

Before Piper could object, he disappeared down the stairwell.

She counted silently as they waited for him to come back. Somewhere around thirty-five, she heard his footsteps and he appeared at the top, looking more baffled than relieved.

'Good news: no water,' he said. 'Bad news: I don't see any exits down there. And, uh, weird news: well, you should see this . . .'

They descended cautiously. Percy took the lead, with Riptide drawn. Piper followed, and Jason walked behind her, guarding their backs. The stairwell was a cramped corkscrew of masonry, no more than six feet in diameter. Even though Percy had given the 'all clear', Piper kept her eyes open for traps. With every turn of the stairs, she anticipated an ambush. She had no weapon, just the cornucopia on a leather cord over her shoulder. If worse came to worst, the boys' swords wouldn't do much good in such close quarters. Maybe Piper could shoot their enemies with high-velocity smoked hams.

As they wound their way underground, Piper saw old graffiti gouged into the stones: Roman numerals, names and phrases in Italian. That meant other people had been down here more recently than the Roman Empire, but Piper wasn't reassured. If monsters were below, they'd ignore mortals, waiting for some nice juicy demigods to come along.

Finally, they reached the bottom.

Percy turned. 'Watch this last step.'

He jumped to the floor of the cylindrical room, which was five feet lower than the stairwell. Why would someone design a set of stairs like that? Piper had no idea. Maybe the room and the stairwell had been built during different time periods.

She wanted to turn and exit, but she couldn't do that with Jason behind her, and she couldn't just leave Percy down there. She clambered down, and Jason followed.

The room was just like she'd seen it in Katoptris's blade, except there was no water. The curved walls had once been painted with frescoes, which were now faded to eggshell white with only flecks of colour. The domed ceiling was about fifty feet above.

Around the back side of the room, opposite the stairwell, nine alcoves were carved into the wall. Each niche was about five feet off the floor and big enough for a human-sized statue, but each was empty.

The air felt cold and dry. As Percy had said, there were no other exits.

'All right.' Percy raised his eyebrows. 'Here's the weird part. Watch.'

He stepped to the middle of the room.

Instantly, green and blue light rippled across the walls. Piper heard the sound of a fountain, but there was no water.

There didn't seem to be any source of light except for Percy's and Jason's blades.

'Do you smell the ocean?' Percy asked.

Piper hadn't noticed at first. She was standing next to Percy, and he always smelled like the sea. But he was right. The scent of salt water and storm was getting stronger, like a summer hurricane approaching.

'An illusion?' she asked. All of a sudden, she felt strangely thirsty.

'I don't know,' Percy said. 'I feel like there should be water here – lots of water. But there isn't any. I've never been in a place like this.'

Jason moved to the row of niches. He touched the bottom shelf of the nearest one, which was just at his eye level. 'This stone . . . it's embedded with seashells. This is a nymphaeum.'

Piper's mouth was definitely getting drier. 'A what?'

'We have one at Camp Jupiter,' Jason said, 'on Temple Hill. It's a shrine to the nymphs.'

Piper ran her hand along the bottom of another niche. Jason was right. The alcove was studded with cowries, conches and scallops. The seashells seemed to dance in the watery light. They were ice-cold to the touch.

Piper had always thought of nymphs as friendly spirits – silly and flirtatious, generally harmless. They got along well with the children of Aphrodite. They loved to share gossip and beauty tips. This place, though, didn't feel like the canoe lake back at Camp Half-Blood, or the streams in the woods where Piper normally met nymphs. This place felt unnatural, hostile and *very* dry.

Jason stepped back and examined the row of alcoves. 'Shrines like this were all over the place in Ancient Rome. Rich people had them outside their villas to honour nymphs, to make sure the local water was always fresh. Some shrines were built around natural springs, but most were man-made.'

'So . . . no actual nymphs lived here?' Piper asked hopefully.

'Not sure,' Jason said. 'This place where we're standing would have been a pool with a fountain. A lot of times, if the nymphaeum belonged to a demigod, he or she would invite nymphs to live there. If the spirits took up residence, that was considered good luck.'

'For the owner,' Percy guessed. 'But it would also bind the nymphs to the new water source, which would be great if the fountain was in a nice sunny park with fresh water pumped in through the aqueducts –'

'But this place has been underground for centuries,' Piper guessed. 'Dry and buried. What would happen to the nymphs?'

The sound of water changed to a chorus of hissing, like ghostly snakes. The rippling light shifted from sea blue and green to purple and sickly lime. Above them, the nine niches glowed. They were no longer empty.

Standing in each was a withered old woman, so dried up and brittle they reminded Piper of mummies – except mummies didn't normally move. Their eyes were dark purple, as if the clear blue water of their life source had condensed and thickened inside them. Their fine silk dresses were now tattered and faded. Their hair had once been piled in curls, arranged with jewels in the style of Roman noblewomen, but now their locks were dishevelled and dry as straw. If water cannibals actually existed, Piper thought, this is what they looked like.

'*What would happen to the nymphs?*' said the creature in the centre niche.

She was in even worse shape than the others. Her back was hunched like the handle of a pitcher. Her skeletal hands had only the thinnest papery layer of skin. On her head, a battered wreath of golden laurels glinted in her roadkill hair.

She fixed her purple eyes on Piper. 'What an interesting question, my dear. Perhaps the nymphs would still be here, suffering, waiting for revenge.'

The next time that she got a chance, Piper swore she would melt down Katoptris and sell it for scrap metal. The stupid knife never showed her the whole story. Sure, she'd seen herself drowning. But if she'd realized that nine desiccated zombie nymphs would be waiting for her she never would've come down here.

She considered bolting for the stairs, but when she turned the doorway had disappeared. Naturally. Nothing was there now but a blank wall. Piper suspected it wasn't just an illusion. Besides, she would never make it to the opposite side of the room before the zombie nymphs could jump on them.

Jason and Percy stood to either side of her, their swords ready. Piper was glad to have them close, but she suspected their weapons wouldn't do any good. She'd seen what would happen in this room. Somehow, these things were going to defeat them.

'Who are you?' Percy demanded.

The central nymph turned her head. 'Ah . . . names. We once had names. I was Hagno, the first of the nine!'

Piper thought it was a cruel joke that a hag like her would be named *Hagno*, but she decided not to say that.

'The nine,' Jason repeated. 'The nymphs of this shrine. There were always nine niches.'

'Of course.' Hagno bared her teeth in a vicious smile. 'But we are the *original* nine, Jason Grace, the ones who attended the birth of your father.'

Jason's sword dipped. 'You mean Jupiter? You were there when he was *born*?'

'Zeus, we called him then,' Hagno said. 'Such a squealing whelp. We attended Rhea in her labour. When the baby arrived, we hid him so that his father, Kronos, would not eat him. Ah, he had lungs, that baby! It was all we could do to drown out the noise so Kronos could not find him. When Zeus grew up, we were promised eternal honours. But that was in the old country, in Greece.'

The other nymphs wailed and clawed at their niches. They seemed to be trapped in them, Piper realized, as if their feet were glued to the stone along with the decorative seashells.

'When Rome rose to power, we were invited here,' Hagno said. 'A son of Jupiter tempted us with favours. *A new home*, he promised. *Bigger and better! No down payment, an excellent neighbourhood. Rome will last forever.*'

'Forever,' the others hissed.

'We gave in to temptation,' Hagno said. 'We left our simple wells and springs on Mount Lycaeus and moved here.

For centuries, our lives were wonderful! Parties, sacrifices in our honour, new dresses and jewellery every week. All the demigods of Rome flirted with us and honoured us.'

The nymphs wailed and sighed.

'But Rome did not last,' Hagno snarled. 'The aqueducts were diverted. Our master's villa was abandoned and torn down. We were forgotten, buried under the earth, but we could not leave. Our life sources were bound to this place. Our old master never saw fit to release us. For centuries, we have withered here in the darkness, thirsty . . . so thirsty.'

The others clawed at their mouths.

Piper felt her own throat closing up.

'I'm sorry for you,' she said, trying to use charmspeak. 'That must have been terrible. But we are not your enemies. If we can help you –'

'Oh, such a sweet voice!' Hagno cried. 'Such beautiful features. I was once young like you. My voice was as soothing as a mountain stream. But do you know what happens to a nymph's mind when she is trapped in the dark, with nothing to feed on but hatred, nothing to drink but thoughts of violence? Yes, my dear. You can help us.'

Percy raised his hand. 'Uh . . . I'm the son of Poseidon. Maybe I can summon a new water source.'

'Ha!' Hagno cried, and the other eight echoed, 'Ha! Ha!'

'Indeed, son of Poseidon,' Hagno said. 'I know your father well. Ephialtes and Otis promised you would come.'

Piper put her hand on Jason's arm for balance.

'The giants,' she said. 'You're working for them?'

'They are our neighbours.' Hagno smiled. 'Their chambers lie beyond this place, where the aqueduct's water was diverted for the games. Once we have dealt with you . . . once you have *helped* us . . . the twins have promised we will never suffer again.'

Hagno turned to Jason. 'You, child of Jupiter – for the horrible betrayal of your predecessor who brought us here, you shall pay. I know the sky god's powers. I raised him as a baby! Once, we nymphs controlled the rain above our wells and springs. When I am done with you, we will have that power again. And Percy Jackson, child of the sea god . . . from you, we will take water, an endless supply of water.'

'Endless?' Percy's eyes darted from one nymph to the other. 'Uh . . . look, I don't know about *endless*. But maybe I could spare a few gallons.'

'And you, Piper McLean.' Hagno's purple eyes glistened. 'So young, so lovely, so gifted with your sweet voice. From you, we will reclaim our beauty. We have saved our last life force for this day. We are very thirsty. From you three, we shall drink!'

All nine niches glowed. The nymphs disappeared, and water poured from their alcoves – sickly dark water, like oil.

XLIII

PIPER

PIPER NEEDED A MIRACLE, not a bedtime story. But right then, standing in shock as black water poured in around her legs, she recalled the legend Achelous had mentioned – the story of the flood.

Not the Noah story, but the Cherokee version that her father used to tell her, with the dancing ghosts and the skeleton dog.

When she was little, she would cuddle next to her dad in his big recliner. She'd gaze out of the windows at the Malibu coastline, and her dad would tell her the story he'd heard from Grandpa Tom back on the rez in Oklahoma.

'This man had a dog,' her father always began.

'You can't start a story that way!' Piper protested. 'You have to say *Once upon a time*.'

Dad laughed. 'But this is a Cherokee story. They are pretty straightforward. So, anyway, this man had a dog. Every day the man took his dog to the edge of the lake to get water, and the dog would bark furiously at the lake, like he was mad at it.'

'Was he?'

'Be patient, sweetheart. Finally the man got very annoyed with his dog for barking so much, and he scolded it. "Bad dog! Stop barking at the water. It's only water!" To his surprise, the dog looked right at him and began to talk.'

'Our dog can say *Thank you*,' Piper volunteered. 'And she can bark *Out*.'

'Sort of,' her dad agreed. 'But this dog spoke entire sentences. The dog said, "One day soon, the storms will come. The waters will rise, and everyone will drown. You can save yourself and your family by building a raft, but first you will need to sacrifice me. You must throw me into the water."'

'That's terrible!' Piper said. 'I would never drown my dog!'

'The man probably said the same thing. He thought the dog was lying – I mean, once he got over the shock that his dog could talk. When he protested, the dog said, "If you don't believe me, look at the scruff of my neck. I am already dead."'

'That's sad! Why are you telling me this?'

'Because you asked me to,' her dad reminded her. And indeed, something about the story fascinated Piper. She had heard it dozens of times, but she kept thinking about it.

'Anyway,' said her dad, 'the man grabbed the dog by the scruff of its neck and saw that its skin and fur were already coming apart. Underneath was nothing but bones. The dog was a skeleton dog.'

'Gross.'

'I agree. So, with tears in his eyes, the man said goodbye to his annoying skeleton dog and tossed it into the water, where it promptly sank. The man built a raft, and when the flood came he and his family survived.'

'Without the dog.'

'Yes. Without the dog. When the rains subsided, and the raft landed, the man and his family were the only ones alive. The man heard sounds from the other side of a hill – like thousands of people laughing and dancing – but when he raced to the top, alas, down below he saw nothing except bones littering the ground – thousands of skeletons of all the people who had died in the flood. He realized the ghosts of the dead had been dancing. That was the sound he heard.'

Piper waited. 'And?'

'And, nothing. The end.'

'You can't end it that way! Why were the ghosts dancing?'

'I don't know,' Dad said. 'Your grandfather never felt the need to explain. Maybe the ghosts were happy that one family had survived. Maybe they were enjoying the afterlife. They're ghosts. Who can say?'

Piper was very unsatisfied with that. She had so many unanswered questions. Did the family ever find another dog? Obviously not all dogs drowned, because she herself had a dog.

She couldn't shake the story. She never looked at dogs the same way, wondering if one of them might be a skeleton dog. And she didn't understand why the family had to sacrifice their dog to survive. Sacrificing yourself to save your family seemed like a noble thing – a very doglike thing to do.

Now, in the nymphaeum in Rome, as the dark water rose to her waist, Piper wondered why the river god Achelous had mentioned that story.

She wished she had a raft, but she feared she was more like the skeleton dog. She was already dead.

XLIV

PIPER

THE BASIN FILLED WITH ALARMING SPEED. Piper, Jason and Percy pounded on the walls, looking for an exit, but they found nothing. They climbed into the alcoves to gain some height, but with water pouring out of each niche it was like trying to balance at the edge of a waterfall. Even as Piper stood in a niche, the water was soon up to her knees. From the floor, it was probably eight feet deep and rising fast.

'I could try lightning,' Jason said. 'Maybe blast a hole in the roof?'

'That could bring down the whole room and crush us,' Piper said.

'Or electrocute us,' Percy added.

'Not many choices,' Jason said.

'Let me search the bottom,' Percy said. 'If this place was built as a fountain, there *has* to be a way to drain the thing. You guys, check the niches for secret exits. Maybe the seashells are knobs or something.' It was a desperate idea, but Piper was glad for something to do.

Percy jumped in the water. Jason and Piper climbed from niche to niche, kicking and pounding, wiggling seashells embedded in the stone, but they had no luck.

Sooner than Piper expected, Percy broke the surface, gasping and flailing. She offered her hand, and he almost pulled her in before she could help him up.

'Couldn't breathe,' he choked. 'The water . . . not normal. Hardly made it back.'

The life force of the nymphs, Piper thought. It was so poisoned and malicious, even a son of the sea god couldn't control it.

As the water rose around her, Piper felt it affecting her, too. Her leg muscles trembled like she'd been running for miles. Her hands turned wrinkled and dry, despite being in the middle of a fountain.

The boys moved sluggishly. Jason's face was pale. He seemed to be having trouble holding his sword. Percy was drenched and shivering. His hair didn't look quite so dark, as if the colour was leaching out.

'They're taking our power,' Piper said. 'Draining us.'

'Jason,' Percy coughed, 'do the lightning.'

Jason raised his sword. The room rumbled, but no lightning appeared. The roof didn't break. Instead, a miniature rainstorm formed at the top of the chamber. Rain poured down, filling the fountain even faster, but it wasn't normal rain. The stuff was just as dark as the water in the pool. Every drop stung Piper's skin.

'Not what I wanted,' Jason said.

The water was up to their necks now. Piper could feel her strength fading. Grandpa Tom's story about the water cannibals was true. Bad nymphs would steal her life.

'We'll survive,' she murmured to herself, but she couldn't charmspeak her way out of this. Soon the poisonous water would be over their heads. They'd have to swim, and this stuff was already paralysing them.

They would drown, just like in the visions she'd seen.

Percy started pushing the water away with the back of his hand, like he was shooing a bad dog. 'Can't – can't control it!'

You will need to sacrifice me, the skeleton dog had said in the story. *You must throw me into the water.*

Piper felt like someone had grabbed the scruff of her neck and exposed the bones. She clutched her cornucopia.

'We can't fight this,' she said. 'If we hold back, that just makes us weaker.'

'What do you mean?' Jason shouted over the rain.

The water was up to their chins. Another few inches, and they'd have to swim. But the water wasn't halfway to the ceiling yet. Piper hoped that meant that they still had time.

'The horn of plenty,' she said. 'We have to overwhelm the nymphs with *fresh* water, give them more than they can use. If we can dilute this poisonous stuff –'

'Can your horn do that?' Percy struggled to keep his head above water, which was obviously a new experience for him. He looked scared out of his mind.

'Only with your help.' Piper was beginning to understand

how the horn worked. The good stuff it produced didn't come from nowhere. She'd only been able to bury Hercules in groceries when she had concentrated on all her positive experiences with Jason.

To create enough clean fresh water to fill this room, she needed to go even deeper, tap her emotions even more. Unfortunately, she was losing her ability to focus.

'I need you both to channel everything you've got into the cornucopia,' she said. 'Percy, think about the sea.'

'Salt water?'

'Doesn't matter! As long as it's clean. Jason, think about rainstorms – *much* more rain. Both of you hold the cornucopia.'

They huddled together as the water lifted them off their ledges. Piper tried to remember the safety lessons her dad had given her when they had started surfing. To help someone who's drowning, you put your arm around them from behind and kick your legs in front of you, moving backwards like you're doing the backstroke. She wasn't sure if the same strategy could work with *two* other people, but she put one arm around each boy and tried to keep them afloat as they held the cornucopia between them.

Nothing happened. The rain came down in sheets, still dark and acidic.

Piper's legs felt like lead. The rising water swirled, threatening to pull her under. She could feel her strength fading.

'No good!' Jason yelled, spitting water.

'We're getting nowhere,' Percy agreed.

'You have to work together,' Piper cried, hoping she was

right. 'Both of you think of clean water – a storm of water. Don't hold anything back. Picture all your power, all your strength leaving you.'

'That's not hard!' Percy said.

'But *force* it out!' she said. 'Offer up everything, like – like you're already dead, and your only goal is to help the nymphs. It's got to be a gift . . . a sacrifice.'

They got quiet at that word.

'Let's try again,' Jason said. 'Together.'

This time Piper bent all her concentration towards the horn of plenty as well. The nymphs wanted her youth, her life, her voice? Fine. She gave it up willingly and imagined all of her power flooding out of her.

I'm already dead, she told herself, as calm as the skeleton dog. *This is the only way.*

Clear water blasted from the horn with such force, it pushed them against the wall. The rain changed to a white torrent, so clean and cold, it made Piper gasp.

'It's working!' Jason cried.

'Too well,' Percy said. 'We're filling the room even faster!'

He was right. The water rose so quickly the roof was now only a few feet away. Piper could've reached up and touched the miniature rain clouds.

'Don't stop!' she said. 'We have to dilute the poison until the nymphs are cleansed.'

'What if they *can't* be cleansed?' Jason asked. 'They've been down here turning evil for thousands of years.'

'Just don't hold back,' Piper said. 'Give everything. Even if we go under –'

Her head hit the ceiling. The rainclouds dissipated and melted into the water. The horn of plenty kept blasting out a clean torrent.

Piper pulled Jason closer and kissed him.

'I love you,' she said.

The words just poured out of her, like the water from the cornucopia. She couldn't tell what his reaction was, because then they were underwater.

She held her breath. The current roared in her ears. Bubbles swirled around her. Light still rippled through the room, and Piper was surprised she could see it. Was the water getting clearer?

Her lungs were about to burst, but Piper poured her last energy into the cornucopia. Water continued to stream out, though there was no room for more. Would the walls crack under the pressure?

Piper's vision went dark.

She thought the roar in her ears was her own dying heartbeat. Then she realized the room was shaking. The water swirled faster. Piper felt herself sinking.

With her last strength, she kicked upward. Her head broke the surface and she gasped for breath. The cornucopia stopped. The water was draining almost as fast as it had filled the room.

With a cry of alarm, Piper realized that Percy's and Jason's faces were still underwater. She hoisted them up. Instantly, Percy gulped and began to thrash, but Jason was as lifeless as a rag doll.

Piper clung to him. She yelled his name, shook him and

slapped his face. She barely noticed when all the water had drained away and left them on the damp floor.

'Jason!' She tried desperately to think. Should she turn him on his side? Slap his back?

'Piper,' Percy said, 'I can help.'

He knelt next to her and touched Jason's forehead. Water gushed from Jason's mouth. His eyes flew open, and a clap of thunder threw Percy and Piper backwards.

When Piper's vision cleared, she saw Jason sitting up, still gasping, but the colour was coming back to his face.

'Sorry,' he coughed. 'Didn't mean to –'

Piper tackled him with a hug. She would have kissed him, but she didn't want to suffocate him.

Percy grinned. 'In case you're wondering, that was clean water in your lungs. I could make it come out with no problem.'

'Thanks, man.' Jason clasped his hand weakly. 'But I think Piper's the real hero. She saved us all.'

Yes, she did, a voice echoed through the chamber.

The niches glowed. Nine figures appeared, but they were no longer withered creatures. They were young, beautiful nymphs in shimmering blue gowns, their glossy black curls pinned up with silver and gold brooches. Their eyes were gentle shades of blue and green.

As Piper watched, eight of the nymphs dissolved into vapour and floated upward. Only the nymph in the centre remained.

'Hagno?' Piper asked.

The nymph smiled. 'Yes, my dear. I didn't think such

selflessness existed in mortals . . . especially in demigods. No offence.'

Percy got to his feet. 'How could we take offence? You just tried to drown us and suck out our lives.'

Hagno winced. 'Sorry about that. I was not myself. But you have reminded me of the sun and the rain and the streams in the meadows. Percy and Jason, thanks to you, I remembered the sea and the sky. I am cleansed. But mostly thanks to Piper. She shared something even better than clear running water.' Hagno turned to her. 'You have a good nature, Piper. And I'm a nature spirit. I know what I'm talking about.'

Hagno pointed to the other side of the room. The stairs to the surface reappeared. Directly underneath, a circular opening shimmered into existence, like a sewer pipe, just big enough to crawl through. Piper suspected this was how the water had drained out.

'You may return to the surface,' Hagno said. 'Or, if you insist, you may follow the waterway to the giants. But choose quickly, because both doors will fade soon after I am gone. That pipe connects to the old aqueduct line, which feeds both this nymphaeum and the hypogeum that the giants call home.'

'Ugh.' Percy pressed on his temples. 'Please, no more complicated words.'

'Oh, *home* is not a complicated word.' Hagno sounded completely sincere. 'I thought it was, but now you have unbound us from this place. My sisters have gone to seek new homes . . . a mountain stream, perhaps, or a lake in a meadow. I will follow them. I cannot wait to see the forests and grasslands again, and the clear running water.'

'Uh,' Percy said nervously, 'things have changed up above in the last few thousand years.'

'Nonsense,' Hagno said. 'How bad could it be? Pan would not allow nature to become tainted. I can't wait to see him, in fact.'

Percy looked like he wanted to say something, but he stopped himself.

'Good luck, Hagno,' Piper said. 'And thank you.'

The nymph smiled one last time and vaporized.

Briefly, the nymphaeum glowed with a softer light, like a full moon. Piper smelled exotic spices and blooming roses. She heard distant music and happy voices talking and laughing. She guessed she was hearing hundreds of years of parties and celebrations that had been held at this shrine in ancient times, as if the memories had been freed along with the spirits.

'What is that?' Jason asked nervously.

Piper slipped her hand into his. 'The ghosts are dancing. Come on. We'd better go meet the giants.'

PERCY

PERCY WAS TIRED OF WATER.

If he said that aloud, he would probably get kicked out of Poseidon's Junior Sea Scouts, but he didn't care.

After barely surviving the nymphaeum, he wanted to go back to the surface. He wanted to be dry and sit in the warm sunshine for a long time – preferably with Annabeth.

Unfortunately, he didn't know where Annabeth was. Frank, Hazel and Leo were missing in action. He still had to save Nico di Angelo, assuming the guy wasn't already dead. And there was that little matter of the giants destroying Rome, waking Gaia and taking over the world.

Seriously, these monsters and gods were thousands of years old. Couldn't they take a few decades off and let Percy live his life? Apparently not.

Percy took the lead as they crawled down the drainage pipe. After thirty feet, it opened into a wider tunnel. To their left, somewhere in the distance, Percy heard rumbling and creaking, like a huge machine needed oiling. He had absolutely no desire to find out what was making that sound, so he figured that must be the way to go.

Several hundred feet later, they reached a turn in the tunnel. Percy held up his hand, signalling Jason and Piper to wait. He peeked around the corner.

The corridor opened into a vast room with twenty-foot ceilings and rows of support columns. It looked like the same parking-garage-type area Percy had seen in his dreams, but now much more crowded with stuff.

The creaking and rumbling came from huge gears and pulley systems that raised and lowered sections of the floor for no apparent reason. Water flowed through open trenches (oh, great, more water), powering waterwheels that turned some of the machines. Other machines were connected to huge hamster wheels with hellhounds inside. Percy couldn't help thinking of Mrs O'Leary and how much she would hate being trapped inside one of those.

Suspended from the ceiling were cages of live animals – a lion, several zebras, a whole pack of hyenas and even an eight-headed hydra. Ancient-looking bronze and leather conveyor belts trundled along with stacks of weapons and armour, sort of like the Amazons' warehouse in Seattle, except this place was obviously much older and not as well organized.

Leo would love it, Percy thought. The whole room was like one massive, scary, unreliable machine.

'What is it?' Piper whispered.

Percy wasn't even sure how to answer. He couldn't see the

giants, so he gestured for his friends to come forward and take a look.

About twenty feet inside the doorway, a life-size wooden cut-out of a gladiator popped up from the floor. It clicked and whirred along a conveyor belt, got hooked on a rope and ascended through a slot in the roof.

Jason murmured, 'What the heck?'

They stepped inside. Percy scanned the room. There were several thousand things to look at, most of them in motion, but one good aspect of being an ADHD demigod was that Percy was comfortable with chaos. About a hundred yards away, he spotted a raised dais with two empty oversized praetor chairs. Standing between them was a bronze jar big enough to hold a person.

'Look.' He pointed it out to his friends.

Piper frowned. 'That's too easy.'

'Of course,' Percy said.

'But we have no choice,' Jason said. 'We've got to save Nico.'

'Yeah.' Percy started across the room, picking his way around conveyor belts and moving platforms.

The hellhounds in the hamster wheels paid them no attention. They were too busy running and panting, their red eyes glowing like headlights. The animals in the other cages gave them bored looks, as if to say, *I'd kill you, but it would take too much energy.*

Percy tried to watch out for traps, but *everything* here looked like a trap. He remembered how many times he'd almost died in the labyrinth a few years ago. He really wished Hazel were here so she could help with her underground skills (and of course so she could be reunited with her brother).

They jumped over a water trench and ducked under a row of caged wolves. They had made it about halfway to the bronze jar when the ceiling opened over them. A platform lowered. Standing on it like an actor, with one hand raised and his head high, was the purple-haired giant Ephialtes.

Just like Percy had seen in his dreams, the Big F was small by giant standards – about twelve feet tall – but he had tried to make up for it with his loud outfit. He'd changed out of the gladiator armour and was now wearing a Hawaiian shirt that even Dionysus would've found vulgar. It had a garish print made up of dying heroes, horrible tortures and lions eating slaves in the Colosseum. The giant's hair was braided with gold and silver coins. He had a ten-foot spear strapped to his back, which wasn't a good fashion statement with the shirt. He wore bright white jeans and leather sandals on his . . . well, not feet but curved snakeheads. The snakes flicked their tongues and writhed as if they didn't appreciate holding up the weight of a giant.

Ephialtes smiled at the demigods like he was really, really pleased to see them.

'At last!' he bellowed. 'So very happy! Honestly, I didn't think you'd make it past the nymphs, but it's so much better that you did. Much more entertaining. You're just in time for the main event!'

Jason and Piper closed ranks on either side of Percy. Having them there made him feel a little better. This giant was smaller than a lot of monsters he had faced, but something about him made Percy's skin crawl. Ephialtes's eyes danced with a crazy light.

'We're here,' Percy said, which sounded kind of obvious once he had said it. 'Let our friend go.'

'Of course!' Ephialtes said. 'Though I fear he's a bit past his expiration date. Otis, where are you?'

A stone's throw away, the floor opened, and the other giant rose on a platform.

'Otis, finally!' his brother cried with glee. 'You're not dressed the same as me! You're . . .' Ephialtes's expression turned to horror. '*What are you wearing?*'

Otis looked like the world's largest, grumpiest ballet dancer. He wore a skin-tight baby-blue leotard that Percy *really* wished left more to the imagination. The toes of his massive dancing slippers were cut away so that his snakes could protrude. A diamond tiara (Percy decided to be generous and think of it as a king's crown) was nestled in his green, firecracker-braided hair. He looked glum and miserably uncomfortable, but he managed a dancer's bow, which couldn't have been easy with snake feet and a huge spear on his back.

'Gods and Titans!' Ephialtes yelled. 'It's showtime! What are you *thinking*?'

'I didn't want to wear the gladiator outfit,' Otis complained. 'I still think a ballet would be perfect, you know, while Armageddon is going on.' He raised his eyebrows hopefully at the demigods. 'I have some extra costumes –'

'No!' Ephialtes snapped, and for once Percy was in agreement.

The purple-haired giant faced Percy. He grinned so painfully he looked like he was being electrocuted.

'Please excuse my brother,' he said. 'His stage presence is awful, and he has *no* sense of style.'

'Okay.' Percy decided not to comment on the Hawaiian shirt. 'Now, about our friend . . .'

'Oh, him,' Ephialtes sneered. 'We were going to let him finish dying in public, but he has no entertainment value. He's spent *days* curled up sleeping. What sort of spectacle is that? Otis, tip over the jar.'

Otis trudged over to the dais, stopping occasionally to do a plié. He knocked over the jar, the lid popped off and Nico di Angelo spilled out. The sight of his deathly pale face and too-skinny frame made Percy's heart stop. Percy couldn't tell whether he was alive or dead. He wanted to rush over and check, but Ephialtes stood in his way.

'Now we have to hurry,' said the Big F. 'We should go through your stage directions. The hypogeum is all set!'

Percy was ready to slice this giant in half and get out of there, but Otis was standing over Nico. If a battle started, Nico was in no condition to defend himself. Percy needed to buy him some recovery time.

Jason raised his gold *gladius*. 'We're not going to be part of any show,' he said. 'And what's a hypo— whatever-you-call-it?'

'Hypogeum!' Ephialtes said. 'You're a Roman demigod, aren't you? You should know! Ah, but I suppose if we do our job right down here in the underworks you really wouldn't know the hypogeum exists.'

'I know that word,' Piper said. 'It's the area under a

coliseum. It housed all the set pieces and machinery used to create special effects.'

Ephialtes clapped enthusiastically. 'Exactly so! Are you a student of the theatre, my girl?'

'Uh . . . my dad's an actor.'

'Wonderful!' Ephialtes turned towards his brother. 'Did you hear that, Otis?'

'Actor,' Otis murmured. 'Everybody's an actor. No one can dance.'

'Be nice!' Ephialtes scolded. 'At any rate, my girl, you're absolutely right, but *this* hypogeum is much more than the stageworks for a coliseum. You've heard that in the old days some giants were imprisoned under the earth, and from time to time they would cause earthquakes when they tried to break free? Well, we've done much better! Otis and I have been imprisoned under Rome for aeons, but we've kept busy building our very own hypogeum. Now we're ready to create the greatest spectacle Rome has ever seen – and the last!'

At Otis's feet, Nico shuddered. Percy felt like a hellhound hamster wheel somewhere in his chest had started moving again. At least Nico was alive. Now they just had to defeat the giants, preferably without destroying the city of Rome, and get out of here to find their friends.

'So!' Percy said, hoping to keep the giants' attention on him. 'Stage directions, you said?'

'Yes!' Ephialtes said. 'Now, I *know* the bounty stipulates that you and the girl Annabeth should be kept alive if possible, but, honestly, the girl is already doomed, so I hope you don't mind if we deviate from the plan.'

Percy's mouth tasted like bad nymph water. 'Already doomed. You don't mean she's –'

'Dead?' the giant asked. 'No. Not yet. But don't worry! We've got your other friends locked up, you see.'

Piper made a strangled sound. 'Leo? Hazel and Frank?'

'Those are the ones,' Ephialtes agreed. 'So we can use *them* for the sacrifice. We can let the Athena girl die, which will please Her Ladyship. And we can use you three for the show! Gaia will be a bit disappointed, but, really, this is a win-win. Your deaths will be *much* more entertaining.'

Jason snarled. 'You want entertaining? I'll give you entertaining.'

Piper stepped forward. Somehow she managed a sweet smile. 'I've got a better idea,' she told the giants. 'Why don't you let us go? That would be an incredible twist. Wonderful entertainment value, and it would prove to the world how cool you are.'

Nico stirred. Otis looked down at him. His snaky feet flicked their tongues at Nico's head.

'Plus!' Piper said quickly. 'Plus, we could do some dance moves as we're escaping. Perhaps a ballet number!'

Otis forgot all about Nico. He lumbered over and wagged his finger at Ephialtes. 'You see? That's what I was telling you! It would be incredible!'

For a second, Percy thought Piper was going to pull it off. Otis looked at his brother imploringly. Ephialtes tugged at his chin as if considering the idea.

At last he shook his head. 'No . . . no, I'm afraid not. You see, my girl, I am the anti-Dionysus. I have a reputation to uphold. Dionysus thinks he knows parties? He's wrong! His revels are tame compared to what I can do. That old stunt we pulled, for instance, when we piled up mountains to reach Olympus –'

'I told you that would never work,' Otis muttered.

'And the time my brother covered himself with meat and ran through an obstacle course of drakons –'

'You said Hephaestus-TV would show it during prime time,' Otis said. 'No one even *saw* me.'

'Well, this spectacle will be *even better*,' Ephialtes promised. 'The Romans always wanted bread and circuses – food and entertainment! As we destroy their city, I will offer them both. Behold, a sample!'

Something dropped from the ceiling and landed at Percy's feet: a loaf of sandwich bread in a white plastic wrapper with red and yellow dots.

Percy picked it up. 'Wonder bread?'

'Magnificent, isn't it?' Ephialtes's eyes danced with crazy excitement. 'You can keep that loaf. I plan on distributing millions to the people of Rome as I obliterate them.'

'Wonder bread is good,' Otis admitted. 'Though the Romans should dance for it.'

Percy glanced over at Nico, who was just starting to move. Percy wanted him to be at least conscious enough to crawl out of the way when the fighting started. And Percy needed more information from the giants about Annabeth and where his other friends were being kept.

'Maybe,' Percy ventured, 'you should bring our other friends here. You know, spectacular deaths . . . the more the merrier, right?'

'Hmm.' Ephialtes fiddled with a button on his Hawaiian shirt. 'No. It's really too late to change the choreography. But never fear. The circuses will be marvellous! Ah . . . not the *modern* sort of circus, mind you. That would require clowns, and I hate clowns.'

'Everyone hates clowns,' Otis said. 'Even other clowns hate clowns.'

'Exactly,' his brother agreed. 'But we have much better entertainment planned! The three of you will die in agony, up above, where all the gods and mortals can watch. But that's just the opening ceremony! In the old days, games went on for days or weeks. Our spectacle – the destruction of Rome – will go on for one full month until Gaia awakens.'

'Wait,' Jason said. 'One month, and Gaia wakes up?'

Ephialtes waved away the question. 'Yes, yes. Something about August first being the best date to destroy all humanity. Not important! In her infinite wisdom, the Earth Mother has agreed that Rome can be destroyed first, slowly and spectacularly. It's only fitting!'

'So . . .' Percy couldn't believe he was talking about the end of the world with a loaf of Wonder bread in his hand. 'You're Gaia's warm-up act.'

Ephialtes's face darkened. 'This is no warm-up, demigod! We'll release wild animals and monsters into the streets. Our special-effects department will produce fires and earthquakes.

Sinkholes and volcanoes will appear randomly out of nowhere! Ghosts will run rampant.'

'The ghost thing won't work,' Otis said. 'Our focus groups say it won't pull ratings.'

'Doubters!' Ephialtes said. 'This hypogeum can make anything work!'

Ephialtes stormed over to a big table covered with a sheet. He pulled the sheet away, revealing a collection of levers and knobs almost as complicated-looking as Leo's control panel on the *Argo II*.

'This button?' Ephialtes said. 'This one will eject a dozen rabid wolves into the Forum. And this one will summon automaton gladiators to battle tourists at the Trevi Fountain. This one will cause the Tiber to flood its banks so we can re-enact a naval battle right in the Piazza Navona! Percy Jackson, you should appreciate that, as a son of Poseidon!'

'Uh . . . I still think the *letting us go* idea is better,' Percy said.

'He's right,' Piper tried again. 'Otherwise we get into this whole confrontation thing. We fight you. You fight us. We wreck your plans. You know, we've defeated a lot of giants lately. I'd hate for things to get out of control.'

Ephialtes nodded thoughtfully. 'You're right.'

Piper blinked. 'I am?'

'We can't let things get out of control,' the giant agreed. 'Everything has to be timed perfectly. But don't worry. I've choreographed your deaths. You'll *love* it.'

Nico started to crawl away, groaning. Percy wanted him

to move faster and to groan less. He considered throwing his Wonder bread at him.

Jason switched his sword hand. 'And if we refuse to cooperate with your spectacle?'

'Well, you can't kill us.' Ephialtes laughed, as if the idea was ridiculous. 'You have no gods with you, and that's the only way you could hope to triumph. So, really, it would be much more sensible to die painfully. Sorry, but the show must go on.'

This giant was even worse than that sea god Phorcys back in Atlanta, Percy realized. Ephialtes wasn't so much the anti-Dionysus. He was Dionysus gone crazy on steroids. Sure, Dionysus was the god of revelry and out-of-control parties. But Ephialtes was all about riot and ruin for pleasure.

Percy looked at his friends. 'I'm getting tired of this guy's shirt.'

'Combat time?' Piper grabbed her horn of plenty.

'I hate Wonder bread,' Jason said.

Together, they charged.

XLVI

PERCY

THINGS WENT WRONG IMMEDIATELY. The giants vanished in twin puffs of smoke. They reappeared halfway across the room, each in a different spot. Percy sprinted towards Ephialtes, but slots in the floor opened under his feet and metal walls shot up on either side, separating him from his friends.

The walls started closing in on him like the sides of a vice grip. Percy jumped up and grabbed the bottom of the hydra's cage. He caught a brief glimpse of Piper leaping across a hopscotch pattern of fiery pits, making her way towards Nico, who was dazed and weaponless and being stalked by a pair of leopards.

Meanwhile Jason charged at Otis, who pulled his spear and heaved a great sigh, as if he would much rather dance *Swan Lake* than kill another demigod.

Percy registered all this in a split second, but there wasn't much he could do about it. The hydra snapped at his hands.

He swung and dropped, landing in a grove of painted plywood trees that sprang up from nowhere. The trees changed positions as he tried to run through them, so he slashed down the whole forest with Riptide.

'Wonderful!' Ephialtes cried. He stood at his control panel about sixty feet to Percy's left. 'We'll consider this a dress rehearsal. Shall I unleash the hydra onto the Spanish Steps now?'

He pulled a lever, and Percy glanced behind him. The cage he had just been hanging from was now rising towards a hatch in the ceiling. In three seconds it would be gone. If Percy attacked the giant, the hydra would ravage the city.

Cursing, he threw Riptide like a boomerang. The sword wasn't designed for that, but the Celestial bronze blade sliced through the chains suspending the hydra. The cage tumbled sideways. The door broke open, and the monster spilled out – right in front of Percy.

'Oh, you *are* a spoilsport, Jackson!' Ephialtes called. 'Very well. Battle it here, if you must, but your death won't be nearly as good without the cheering crowds.'

Percy stepped forward to confront the monster – then realized he'd just thrown his weapon away. A bit of bad planning on his part.

He rolled to one side as all eight hydra heads spat acid, turning the floor where he'd been standing into a steaming crater of melted stone. Percy really hated hydras. It was almost a good thing that he'd lost his sword, since his gut instinct would've been to slash at the heads, and a hydra simply grew two new ones for each one it lost.

The last time he'd faced a hydra, he'd been saved by a battleship with bronze cannons that blasted the monster to pieces. That strategy couldn't help him now . . . or could it?

The hydra lashed out. Percy ducked behind a giant hamster wheel and scanned the room, looking for the boxes he'd seen in his dream. He remembered something about rocket launchers.

At the dais, Piper stood guard over Nico as the leopards advanced. She aimed her cornucopia and shot a pot roast over the cats' heads. It must have smelled pretty good, because the leopards raced after it.

About eighty feet to Piper's right, Jason battled Otis, sword against spear. Otis had lost his diamond tiara and looked angry about it. He probably could have impaled Jason several times, but the giant insisted on doing a pirouette with every attack, which slowed him down.

Meanwhile Ephialtes laughed as he pushed buttons on his control board, cranking the conveyor belts into high gear and opening random animal cages.

The hydra charged around the hamster wheel. Percy swung behind a column, grabbed a garbage bag full of Wonder bread and threw it at the monster. The hydra spat acid, which was a mistake. The bag and wrappers dissolved in midair. The Wonder bread absorbed the acid like fire extinguisher foam and splattered against the hydra, covering it in a sticky, steaming layer of high-calorie poisonous goo.

As the monster reeled, shaking its heads and blinking Wonder acid out of its eyes, Percy looked around desperately. He didn't see the rocket-launcher boxes, but tucked against the back wall was a strange contraption like an artist's easel, fitted with rows of missile launchers. Percy spotted a bazooka, a grenade launcher, a giant Roman candle and a dozen other wicked-looking weapons. They all seemed to be wired together, pointing in the same direction and connected to a single bronze lever on the side. At the top of the easel, spelled in carnations, were the words: HAPPY DESTRUCTION, ROME!

Percy bolted towards the device. The hydra hissed and charged after him.

'I know!' Ephialtes cried out happily. 'We can start with explosions along the Via Labicana! We can't keep our audience waiting forever.'

Percy scrambled behind the easel and turned it towards Ephialtes. He didn't have Leo's skill with machines, but he knew how to aim a weapon.

The hydra barrelled towards him, blocking his view of the giant. Percy hoped this contraption would have enough firepower to take down two targets at once. He tugged at the lever. It didn't budge.

All eight hydra heads loomed over him, ready to melt him into a pool of sludge. He tugged the lever again. This time the easel shook and the weapons began to hiss.

'Duck and cover!' Percy yelled, hoping his friends got the message.

Percy leaped to one side as the easel fired. The sound was like a fiesta in the middle of an exploding gunpowder factory. The hydra vaporized instantly. Unfortunately, the recoil knocked the easel sideways and sent more projectiles shooting all over the room. A chunk of ceiling collapsed and crushed a waterwheel. More cages snapped off their chains, unleashing two zebras and a pack of hyenas. A grenade exploded over Ephialtes's head, but it only blasted him off his feet. The control board didn't even look damaged.

Across the room, sandbags rained down around Piper and Nico. Piper tried to pull Nico to safety, but one of the bags caught her shoulder and knocked her down.

'Piper!' Jason cried. He ran towards her, completely forgetting about Otis, who aimed his spear at Jason's back.

'Look out!' Percy yelled.

Jason had fast reflexes. As Otis threw, Jason rolled. The point sailed over him and Jason flicked his hand, summoning a gust of wind that changed the spear's direction. It flew across the room and skewered Ephialtes through his side just as he was getting to his feet.

'Otis!' Ephialtes stumbled away from his control board, clutching the spear as he began to crumble into monster dust. 'Will you *please* stop killing me!'

'Not my fault!'

Otis had barely finished speaking when Percy's missile-launching contraption spat out one last sphere of Roman candle fire. The fiery pink ball of death (naturally it had to be pink) hit the ceiling above Otis and exploded in a beautiful shower of light. Colourful sparks pirouetted gracefully around the giant. Then a ten-foot section of roof collapsed and crushed him flat.

Jason ran to Piper's side. She yelped when he touched her arm. Her shoulder looked unnaturally bent, but she muttered,

'Fine. I'm fine.' Next to her, Nico sat up, looking around him in bewilderment as if just realizing he'd missed a battle.

Sadly, the giants weren't finished. Ephialtes was already re-forming, his head and shoulders rising from the mound of dust. He tugged his arms free and glowered at Percy.

Across the room, the pile of rubble shifted, and Otis busted out. His head was slightly caved in. All the firecrackers in his hair had popped, and his braids were smoking. His leotard was in tatters, which was just about the only way it could've looked *less* attractive on him.

'Percy!' Jason shouted. 'The controls!'

Percy unfroze. He found Riptide in his pocket again, uncapped his sword and lunged for the switchboard. He slashed his blade across the top, decapitating the controls in a shower of bronze sparks.

'No!' Ephialtes wailed. 'You've ruined the spectacle!'

Percy turned too slowly. Ephialtes swung his spear like a bat and smacked him across the chest. He fell to his knees, the pain turning his stomach to lava.

Jason ran to his side, but Otis lumbered after him. Percy managed to rise and found himself shoulder to shoulder with Jason. Over by the dais, Piper was still on the floor, unable to get up. Nico was barely conscious.

The giants were healing, getting stronger by the minute. Percy was not.

Ephialtes smiled apologetically. 'Tired, Percy Jackson? As I said, you cannot kill us. So I guess we're at an impasse. Oh, wait . . . no we're not! Because we can kill you!'

'That,' Otis grumbled, picking up his fallen spear, 'is the first sensible thing you've said all day, brother.'

The giants pointed their weapons, ready to turn Percy and Jason into a demigod-kebab.

'We won't give up,' Jason growled. 'We'll cut you into pieces like Jupiter did to Saturn.'

'That's right,' Percy said. 'You're both dead. I don't care if we have a god on our side or not.'

'Well, that's a shame,' said a new voice.

To his right, another platform lowered from the ceiling. Leaning casually on a pinecone-topped staff was a man in a purple camp shirt, khaki shorts and sandals with white socks. He raised his broad-brimmed hat, and purple fire flickered in his eyes. 'I'd hate to think I made a special trip for nothing.'

XLVII

PERCY

PERCY HAD NEVER THOUGHT OF MR D as a calming influence, but suddenly everything got quiet. The machines ground to a halt. The wild animals stopped growling.

The two leopards paced over – still licking their lips from Piper's pot roast – and butted their heads affectionately against the god's legs. Mr D scratched their ears.

'Really, Ephialtes,' he chided. 'Killing demigods is one thing. But using leopards for your spectacle? That's over the line.'

The giant made a squeaking sound. 'This – this is impossible. D-D–'

'It's Bacchus, actually, my old friend,' said the god. 'And of course it's possible. Someone told me there was a party going on.'

He looked the same as he had in Kansas, but Percy still couldn't get over the differences between Bacchus and his old not-so-much-of-a-friend Mr D.

Bacchus was meaner and leaner, with less of a potbelly. He had longer hair, more spring in his step and a lot more anger in his eyes. He even managed to make a pinecone on a stick look intimidating.

Ephialtes's spear quivered. 'You – you gods are doomed! Be gone, in the name of Gaia!'

'Hmm.' Bacchus sounded unimpressed. He strolled through the ruined props, platforms and special effects.

'Tacky.' He waved his hand at a painted wooden gladiator, then turned to a machine that looked like an oversized rolling pin studded with knives. 'Cheap. Boring. And this . . .' He inspected the rocket-launching contraption, which was still smoking. 'Tacky, cheap *and* boring. Honestly, Ephialtes. You have no sense of style.'

'STYLE?' The giant's face flushed. 'I have *mountains* of style. I *define* style. I – I –'

'My brother *oozes* style,' Otis suggested.

'Thank you!' Ephialtes cried.

Bacchus stepped forward, and the giants stumbled back. 'Have you two got shorter?' asked the god.

'Oh, that's low,' Ephialtes growled. 'I'm quite tall enough to destroy you, Bacchus! You gods, always hiding behind your mortal heroes, trusting the fate of Olympus to the likes of *these*.'

He sneered at Percy.

Jason hefted his sword. 'Lord Bacchus, are we going to kill these giants or what?'

'Well, I certainly hope so,' Bacchus said. 'Please, carry on.'

Percy stared at him. 'Didn't you come here to help?'

Bacchus shrugged. 'Oh, I appreciated the sacrifice at sea. A whole ship full of Diet Coke. Very nice. Although I would've preferred Diet Pepsi.'

'And six million in gold and jewels,' Percy muttered.

'Yes,' Bacchus said, 'although with demigod parties of five or more the gratuity is included, so that wasn't necessary.'

'What?'

'Never mind,' Bacchus said. 'At any rate, you got my attention. I'm here. Now I need to see if you're worthy of my help. Go ahead. Battle. If I'm impressed, I'll jump in for the grand finale.'

'We speared one,' Percy said. 'Dropped the roof on the other. What do you consider impressive?'

'Ah, a good question . . .' Bacchus tapped his thyrsus. Then he smiled in a way that made Percy think, *Uh-oh.* 'Perhaps you need inspiration! The stage hasn't been properly set. You call this a spectacle, Ephialtes? Let me show you how it's done.'

The god dissolved into purple mist. Piper and Nico disappeared.

'Pipes!' Jason yelled. 'Bacchus, where did you –?'

The entire floor rumbled and began to rise. The ceiling opened in a series of panels. Sunlight poured in. The air shimmered like a mirage, and Percy heard the roar of a crowd above him.

The hypogeum ascended through a forest of weathered stone columns, into the middle of a ruined coliseum.

Percy's heart did a somersault. This wasn't just any coliseum. It was *the* Colosseum. The giants' special-effects machines had gone into overtime, laying planks across ruined support beams so the arena had a proper floor again. The bleachers repaired themselves until they were gleaming white. A giant red-and-gold canopy extended overhead to provide shade from the afternoon sun. The emperor's box was draped with silk, flanked by banners and golden eagles. The roar of applause came from thousands of shimmering purple ghosts, the Lares of Rome brought back for an encore performance.

Vents opened in the floor and sprayed sand across the arena. Huge props sprang up – garage-size mountains of plaster, stone columns and (for some reason) life-size plastic barnyard animals. A small lake appeared to one side. Ditches crisscrossed the arena floor in case anyone was in the mood for trench warfare. Percy and Jason stood together facing the twin giants.

'This is a proper show!' boomed the voice of Bacchus. He sat in the emperor's box wearing purple robes and golden laurels. At his left sat Nico and Piper, her shoulder being tended by a nymph in a nurse's uniform. At Bacchus's right crouched a satyr, offering up Doritos and grapes. The god raised a can of Diet Pepsi and the crowd went respectfully quiet.

Percy glared up at him. 'You're just going to *sit* there?'

'The demigod is right!' Ephialtes bellowed. 'Fight us yourself, coward! Um, without the demigods.'

Bacchus smiled lazily. 'Juno says she's assembled a worthy crew of demigods. Show me. Entertain me, heroes of Olympus. Give me a reason to do more. Being a god has its privileges.'

He popped his soda-can top, and the crowd cheered.

XLVIII

PERCY

PERCY HAD FOUGHT MANY BATTLES. He'd even fought in a couple of arenas, but nothing like this. In the huge Colosseum, with thousands of cheering ghosts, the god Bacchus staring down at him, and the two twelve-foot giants looming over him, Percy felt as small and insignificant as a bug. He also felt *very* angry.

Fighting giants was one thing. Bacchus making it into a game was something else.

Percy remembered what Luke Castellan had told him years ago, when Percy had come back from his very first quest: *Didn't you realize how useless it all is? All the heroics – being pawns of the Olympians?*

Percy was almost the same age now as Luke had been then. He could understand how Luke became so spiteful. In the past five years, Percy had been a pawn too many times. The Olympians seemed to take turns using him for their schemes.

Maybe the gods were better than the Titans, or the giants, or Gaia, but that didn't make them good or wise. It didn't make Percy like this stupid arena battle.

Unfortunately, he didn't have much choice. If he were going to save his friends, he had to beat these giants. He had to survive and find Annabeth.

Ephialtes and Otis made his decision easier by attacking. Together, the giants picked up a fake mountain as big as Percy's New York apartment and hurled it at the demigods.

Percy and Jason bolted. They dived together into the nearest trench and the mountain shattered above them, spraying them with plaster shrapnel. It wasn't deadly, but it stung like crazy.

The crowd jeered and shouted for blood. '*Fight! Fight!*'

'I'll take Otis again?' Jason called over the noise. 'Or do you want him this time?'

Percy tried to think. Dividing was the natural course – fighting the giants one on one, but that hadn't worked so well last time. It dawned on him that they needed a different strategy.

This whole trip, Percy had felt responsible for leading and protecting his friends. He was sure Jason felt the same way. They'd worked in small groups, hoping that would be safer. They'd fought as individuals, each demigod doing what he or she did best. But Hera had made them a team of seven for a reason. The few times Percy and Jason had worked together – summoning the storm at Fort Sumter, helping the *Argo II* escape the Pillars of Hercules, even filling the nymphaeum – Percy had felt more confident, better able to figure out problems, as if he'd been a Cyclops his whole life and suddenly woken up with two eyes.

'We attack together,' he said. 'Otis first, because he's weaker. Take him out quickly and move to Ephialtes. Bronze and gold together – maybe that'll keep them from re-forming a little longer.'

Jason smiled dryly, like he'd just found out he would die in an embarrassing way.

'Why not?' he agreed. 'But Ephialtes isn't going to stand there and wait while we kill his brother. Unless –'

'Good wind today,' Percy offered. 'And there're some water pipes running under the arena.'

Jason understood immediately. He laughed, and Percy felt a spark of friendship. This guy thought the same way he did about a lot of things.

'On three?' Jason said.

'Why wait?'

They charged out of the trench. As Percy suspected, the twins had lifted another plaster mountain and were waiting for a clear shot. The giants raised it above their heads, preparing to throw, and Percy caused a water pipe to burst at their feet, shaking the floor. Jason sent a blast of wind against Ephialtes's chest. The purple-haired giant toppled backwards and Otis lost his grip on the mountain, which promptly collapsed on top of his brother. Only Ephialtes's snake feet stuck out, darting their heads around, as if wondering where the rest of their body had gone.

The crowd roared with approval, but Percy suspected Ephialtes was only stunned. They had a few seconds at best.

'Hey, Otis!' he shouted. '*The Nutcracker* bites!'

'Ahhhhh!' Otis snatched up his spear and threw, but he was too angry to aim straight. Jason deflected it over Percy's head and into the lake.

The demigods backed towards the water, shouting insults about ballet – which was kind of a challenge, as Percy didn't know much about it.

Otis barrelled towards them empty-handed, before apparently realizing that a) he was empty-handed, and b) charging towards a large body of water to fight a son of Poseidon was maybe not a good idea.

Too late, he tried to stop. The demigods rolled to either side, and Jason summoned the wind, using the giant's own momentum to shove him into the water. As Otis struggled to rise, Percy and Jason attacked as one. They launched themselves at the giant and brought their blades down on Otis's head.

The poor guy didn't even have a chance to pirouette. He exploded into powder on the lake's surface like a huge packet of drink mix.

Percy churned the lake into a whirlpool. Otis's essence tried to re-form, but as his head appeared from the water Jason called lightning and blasted him to dust again.

So far so good, but they couldn't keep Otis down forever. Percy was already tired from his fight underground. His gut still ached from getting smacked with a spear shaft. He could feel his strength waning, and they still had another giant to deal with.

As if on cue, the plaster mountain exploded behind them. Ephialtes rose, bellowing with anger.

Percy and Jason waited as he lumbered towards them, his spear in hand. Apparently, getting flattened under a plaster mountain had only energized him. His eyes danced with murderous light. The afternoon sun glinted in his coin-braided hair. Even his snake feet looked angry, baring their fangs and hissing.

Jason called down another lightning strike, but Ephialtes caught it on his spear and deflected the blast, melting a life-size plastic cow. He slammed a stone column out of his way like a stack of building blocks.

Percy tried to keep the lake churning. He didn't want Otis rising to join this fight, but as Ephialtes closed the last few feet, Percy had to switch focus.

Jason and he met the giant's charge. They lunged around Ephialtes, stabbing and slashing in a blur of gold and bronze, but the giant parried every strike.

'I will not yield!' Ephialtes roared. 'You may have ruined my spectacle, but Gaia will still destroy your world!'

Percy lashed out, slicing the giant's spear in half. Ephialtes wasn't even fazed. The giant swept low with the blunt end and knocked Percy off his feet. Percy landed hard on his sword arm, and Riptide clattered out of his grip.

Jason tried to take advantage. He stepped inside the giant's guard and stabbed at his chest, but somehow Ephialtes parried the strike. He sliced the tip of his spear down Jason's chest, ripping his purple shirt. Jason stumbled, looking at the thin line of blood down his sternum. Ephialtes kicked him backwards.

Up in the emperor's box, Piper cried out, but her voice was drowned in the roar of the crowd. Bacchus looked on with an amused smile, munching from a bag of Doritos.

Ephialtes towered over Percy and Jason, both halves of his broken spear poised over their heads. Percy's sword arm was numb. Jason's *gladius* had skittered across the arena floor. Their plan had failed.

Percy glanced up at Bacchus, deciding what final curse he would hurl at the useless wine god, when he saw a shape in the sky above the Colosseum – a large dark oval descending rapidly.

From the lake, Otis yelled, trying to warn his brother, but his half-dissolved face could only manage: 'Uh-umh-moooo!'

'Don't worry, brother!' Ephialtes said, his eyes still fixed on the demigods. 'I will make them suffer!'

The *Argo II* turned in the sky, presenting its port side, and green fire blazed from the ballista.

'Actually,' Percy said. 'Look behind you.'

He and Jason rolled away as Ephialtes turned and bellowed in disbelief.

Percy dropped into a trench just as the explosion rocked the Colosseum.

When he climbed out again, the *Argo II* was coming in for a landing. Jason poked his head out from behind his improvised bomb shelter of a plastic horse. Ephialtes lay charred and groaning on the arena floor, the sand around him seared into a halo of glass by the heat of the Greek fire. Otis was floundering in the lake, trying to re-form, but from the arms down he looked like a puddle of burnt oatmeal.

Percy staggered over to Jason and clapped him on the shoulder. The ghostly crowd gave them a standing ovation as the *Argo II* extended its landing gear and settled on the arena floor. Leo stood at the helm, Hazel and Frank grinning at his side. Coach Hedge danced around the firing platform, pumping his fist in the air and yelling, 'That's what I'm talking about!'

Percy turned to the emperor's box. 'Well?' he yelled at Bacchus. 'Was that entertaining enough for you, you wine-breathed little –'

'No need for that.' Suddenly the god was standing right next to him in the arena. He brushed Dorito dust off his purple robes. 'I have decided you are worthy partners for this combat.'

'Partners?' Jason growled. 'You did nothing!'

Bacchus walked to the edge of the lake. The water instantly drained, leaving an Otis-headed pile of mush. Bacchus picked his way to the bottom and looked up at the crowd. He raised his thyrsus.

The crowd jeered and hollered and pointed their thumbs down. Percy had never been sure whether that meant *live* or *die*. He'd heard it both ways.

Bacchus chose the more entertaining option. He smacked Otis's head with his pinecone staff, and the giant pile of Otismeal disintegrated completely.

The crowd went wild. Bacchus climbed out of the lake and

strutted over to Ephialtes, who was still lying spread-eagled, overcooked and smoking.

Again, Bacchus raised his thyrsus.

'DO IT!' the crowd roared.

'DON'T DO IT!' Ephialtes wailed.

Bacchus tapped the giant on the nose, and Ephialtes crumbled to ashes.

The ghosts cheered and threw spectral confetti as Bacchus strode around the stadium with his arms raised triumphantly, exulting in the worship. He grinned at the demigods. '*That*, my friends, is a show! And of *course* I did something. I killed two giants!'

As Percy's friends disembarked from the ship, the crowd of ghosts shimmered and disappeared. Piper and Nico struggled down from the emperor's box as the Colosseum's magical renovations began to turn into mist. The arena floor remained solid, but otherwise the stadium looked as if it hadn't hosted a good giant killing for aeons.

'Well,' Bacchus said. 'That was fun. You have my permission to continue your voyage.'

'Your *permission*?' Percy snarled.

'Yes.' Bacchus raised an eyebrow. 'Although *your* voyage may be a little harder than you expect, son of Neptune.'

'Poseidon,' Percy corrected him automatically. 'What do you mean about *my* voyage?'

'You might try the parking lot behind the Emmanuel Building,' Bacchus said. 'Best place to break through. Now, goodbye, my friends. And, ah, good luck with that other little matter.'

The god vaporized in a cloud of mist that smelled faintly of grape juice. Jason ran to meet Piper and Nico.

Coach Hedge trotted up to Percy, with Hazel, Frank and Leo close behind. 'Was that Dionysus?' Hedge asked. 'I love that guy!'

'You're alive!' Percy said to the others. 'The giants said you were captured. What happened?'

Leo shrugged. 'Oh, just another brilliant plan by Leo Valdez. You'd be amazed what you can do with an Archimedes sphere, a girl who can sense stuff underground and a weasel.'

'I was the weasel,' Frank said glumly.

'Basically,' Leo explained, 'I activated a hydraulic screw with the Archimedes device – which is going to be *awesome* once I install it in the ship, by the way. Hazel sensed the easiest path to drill to the surface. We made a tunnel big enough for a weasel, and Frank climbed up with a simple transmitter that I slapped together. After that, it was just a matter of hacking into Coach Hedge's favourite satellite channels and telling him to bring the ship around to rescue us. After he got us, finding you was easy, thanks to that godly light show at the Colosseum.'

Percy understood about ten percent of Leo's story, but he decided it was enough since he had a more pressing question. 'Where's Annabeth?'

Leo winced. 'Yeah, about that . . . she's still in trouble, we think. Hurt, broken leg, maybe – at least according to this vision Gaia showed us. Rescuing her is our next stop.'

Two seconds before, Percy had been ready to collapse. Now another surge of adrenalin coursed through his body. He wanted to strangle Leo and demand why the *Argo II* hadn't sailed off to rescue Annabeth first, but he thought that might sound a little ungrateful.

'Tell me about the vision,' he said. 'Tell me everything.'

The floor shook. The wooden planks began to disappear, spilling sand into the pits of the hypogeum below.

'Let's talk on board,' Hazel suggested. 'We'd better take off while we still can.'

They sailed out of the Colosseum and veered south over the rooftops of Rome.

All around the Piazza del Colosseo, traffic had come to a standstill. A crowd of mortals had gathered, probably wondering about the strange lights and sounds that had come from the ruins. As far as Percy could see, none of the giants' spectacular plans for destruction had come off successfully. The city looked the same as before. No one seemed to notice the huge Greek trireme rising into the sky.

The demigods gathered around the helm. Jason bandaged Piper's sprained shoulder while Hazel sat at the stern, feeding Nico ambrosia. The son of Hades could barely lift his head. His voice was so quiet Hazel had to lean in whenever he spoke.

Frank and Leo recounted what had happened in the room with the Archimedes spheres and the visions Gaia had showed them in the bronze mirror. They quickly decided that their best lead for finding Annabeth was the cryptic advice Bacchus had provided: the Emmanuel Building, whatever that was. Frank started typing at the helm's computer while

Leo tapped furiously at his controls, muttering, 'Emmanuel Building. Emmanuel Building.' Coach Hedge tried to help by wrestling with an upside-down street map of Rome.

Percy knelt next to Jason and Piper. 'How's the shoulder?'

Piper smiled. 'It'll heal. Both of you did great.'

Jason elbowed Percy. 'Not a bad team, you and me.'

'Better than jousting in a Kansas cornfield,' Percy agreed.

'There it is!' Leo cried, pointing to his monitor. 'Frank, you're amazing! I'm setting course.'

Frank hunched his shoulders. 'I just read the name off the screen. Some Chinese tourist marked it on Google Maps.'

Leo grinned at the others. 'He reads Chinese.'

'Just a tiny bit,' Frank said.

'How cool is that?'

'Guys,' Hazel broke in. 'I hate to interrupt your admiration session, but you should hear this.'

She helped Nico to his feet. He'd always been pale, but now his skin looked like powdered milk. His dark sunken eyes reminded Percy of photos he'd seen of liberated prisoners-of-war, which Percy guessed Nico basically was.

'Thank you,' Nico rasped. His eyes darted nervously around the group. 'I'd given up hope.'

The past week or so, Percy had imagined a lot of scathing things he might say to Nico when they met again, but the guy looked so frail and sad that Percy couldn't muster much anger.

'You knew about the two camps all along,' Percy said. 'You could have told me who I was the first day I arrived at Camp Jupiter, but you didn't.'

Nico slumped against the helm. 'Percy, I'm sorry. I

discovered Camp Jupiter last year. My dad led me there, though I wasn't sure why. He told me the gods had kept the camps separate for centuries and that I couldn't tell anyone. The time wasn't right. But he said it would be important for me to know . . .' He doubled over in a fit of coughing.

Hazel held his shoulders until he could stand again.

'I – I thought Dad meant because of Hazel,' Nico continued. 'I'd need a safe place to take her. But now . . . I think he wanted me to know about both camps so I'd understand how important your quest was, and so I'd search for the Doors of Death.'

The air turned electric – literally, as Jason started throwing off sparks.

'Did you find the doors?' Percy asked.

Nico nodded. 'I was a fool. I thought I could go anywhere in the Underworld, but I walked right into Gaia's trap. I might as well have tried running from a black hole.'

'Um . . .' Frank chewed his lip. 'What kind of black hole are you talking about?'

Nico started to speak, but whatever he needed to say must have been too terrifying. He turned to Hazel.

She put her hand on her brother's arm. 'Nico told me that the Doors of Death have two sides – one in the mortal world, one in the Underworld. The *mortal* side of the portal is in Greece. It's heavily guarded by Gaia's forces. That's where they brought Nico back into the upper world. Then they transported him to Rome.'

Piper must've been nervous, because her cornucopia spat out a cheeseburger. 'Where exactly in Greece is this doorway?'

Nico took a rattling breath. 'The House of Hades. It's an underground temple in Epirus. I can mark it on a map, but – but the mortal side of the portal isn't the problem. In the Underworld, the Doors of Death are in . . . in . . .'

A cold pair of hands did the itsy-bitsy spider down Percy's back.

A black hole. An inescapable part of the Underworld where even Nico di Angelo couldn't go. Why hadn't Percy thought of this before? He'd been to the very edge of that place. He still had nightmares about it.

'Tartarus,' he guessed. 'The deepest part of the Underworld.'

Nico nodded. 'They pulled me into the pit, Percy. The things I saw down there . . .' His voice broke.

Hazel pursed her lips. 'No mortal has ever been to Tartarus,' she explained. 'At least, no one has ever gone in and returned alive. It's the maximum-security prison of Hades, where the old Titans and the other enemies of the gods are bound. It's where all monsters go when they die on the earth. It's . . . well, no one knows exactly what it's like.'

Her eyes drifted to her brother. The rest of her thought didn't need to be spoken: *No one except Nico.*

Hazel handed him his black sword.

Nico leaned on it like it was an old man's cane. 'Now I understand why Hades hasn't been able to close the doors,' he said. 'Even the gods don't go into Tartarus. Even the god of death, Thanatos himself, wouldn't go near that place.'

Leo glanced over from the wheel. 'So let me guess. We'll have to go there.'

Nico shook his head. 'It's impossible. I'm the son of Hades, and even I barely survived. Gaia's forces overwhelmed me instantly. They're so powerful down there . . . no demigod would stand a chance. I almost went insane.'

Nico's eyes looked like shattered glass. Percy wondered sadly if something inside him had broken permanently.

'Then we'll sail for Epirus,' Percy said. 'We'll just close the gates on this side.'

'I wish it were that easy,' Nico said. 'The doors would have to be controlled on both sides to be closed. It's like a double seal. Maybe, just maybe, all seven of you working together could defeat Gaia's forces on the mortal side, at the House of Hades. But unless you had a team fighting simultaneously on the Tartarus side, a team powerful enough to defeat a legion of monsters in their home territory –'

'There has to be a way,' Jason said.

Nobody volunteered any brilliant ideas.

Percy thought his stomach was sinking. Then he realized the entire ship was descending towards a big building like a palace.

Annabeth. Nico's news was so horrible Percy had momentarily forgotten she was still in danger, which made him feel incredibly guilty.

'We'll figure out the Tartarus problem later,' he said. 'Is that the Emmanuel Building?'

Leo nodded. 'Bacchus said something about the parking lot at the back? Well, there it is. What now?'

Percy remembered his dream of the dark chamber, the evil buzzing voice of the monster called Her Ladyship. He remembered how shaken Annabeth had looked when she'd come back from Fort Sumter after her encounter with the spiders. Percy had begun to suspect what might be down in that shrine . . . literally, the mother of all spiders. If he was right, and Annabeth had been trapped down there alone with that creature for hours, her leg broken . . . At this point, he didn't care if her quest was supposed to be solo or not.

'We have to get her out,' he said.

'Well, yeah,' Leo agreed. 'But, uh . . .'

He looked like he wanted to say, *What if we're too late?*

Wisely, he changed tack. 'There's a parking lot in the way.'

Percy looked at Coach Hedge. 'Bacchus said something about *breaking through*. Coach, you still have ammo for those ballistae?'

The satyr grinned like a wild goat. 'I thought you'd never ask.'

XLIX

ANNABETH

ANNABETH HAD REACHED HER TERROR LIMIT.

She'd been assaulted by chauvinist ghosts. She'd broken her ankle. She'd been chased across a chasm by an army of spiders. Now, in severe pain, with her ankle wrapped in boards and bubble wrap, and carrying no weapon except her dagger, she faced Arachne – a monstrous half-spider who wanted to kill her and make a commemorative tapestry about it.

In the last few hours, Annabeth had shivered, sweated, whimpered and blinked back so many tears that her body simply gave up on being scared. Her mind said something like, *Okay, sorry. I can't be any more terrified than I already am.*

So instead Annabeth started to think.

The monstrous creature picked her way down from the top of the web-covered statue. She moved from strand to strand, hissing with pleasure, her four eyes glittering in the dark. Either she was not in a hurry, or she was slow.

Annabeth hoped she was slow.

Not that it mattered. Annabeth was in no condition to run, and she didn't like her chances in combat. Arachne probably weighed several hundred pounds. Those barbed legs were perfect for capturing and killing prey. Besides, Arachne probably had other horrible powers – a poisonous bite, or web-slinging abilities like an Ancient Greek Spider-Man.

No. Combat was not the answer.

That left trickery and brains.

In the old legends, Arachne had got into trouble because of pride. She'd bragged about her tapestries being better than Athena's, which had led to Mount Olympus's first reality TV punishment programme: *So You Think You Can Weave Better Than a Goddess?* Arachne had lost in a big way.

Annabeth knew something about being prideful. It was *her* fatal flaw as well. She often had to remind herself that she couldn't do everything alone. She wasn't *always* the best person for every job. Sometimes she got tunnel vision and forgot about what other people needed, even Percy. And she could get easily distracted talking about her favourite projects.

But could she use that weakness against the spider? Maybe if she stalled for time . . . though she wasn't sure how stalling would help. Her friends wouldn't be able to reach her, even if they knew where to go. The cavalry would not be coming. Still, stalling was better than dying.

She tried to keep her expression calm, which wasn't easy with a broken ankle. She limped towards the nearest tapestry – a cityscape of Ancient Rome.

'Marvellous,' she said. 'Tell me about this tapestry.'

Arachne's lips curled over her mandibles. 'Why do you care? You're about to die.'

'Well, yes,' Annabeth said. 'But the way you captured the light is amazing. Did you use real golden thread for the sunbeams?'

The weaving truly was stunning. Annabeth didn't have to pretend to be impressed.

Arachne allowed herself a smug smile. 'No, child. Not gold. I blended the colours, contrasting bright yellow with darker hues. That's what gives it a three-dimensional effect.'

'Beautiful.' Annabeth's mind split into two different levels: one carrying on the conversation, the other madly grasping for a scheme to survive. Nothing came to her. Arachne had been beaten only once – by Athena herself, and that had taken godly magic and incredible skill in a weaving contest.

'So . . .' she said. 'Did you see this scene yourself?'

Arachne hissed, her mouth foaming in a not-very-attractive way. 'You are trying to delay your death. It won't work.'

'No, no,' Annabeth insisted. 'It just seems a shame that these beautiful tapestries can't be seen by everyone. They belong in a museum, or . . .'

'Or what?' Arachne asked.

A crazy idea sprang fully formed from Annabeth's mind, like her mom jumping out of Zeus's noggin. But could she make it work?

'Nothing.' She sighed wistfully. 'It's a silly thought. Too bad.'

Arachne scuttled down the statue until she was perched atop the goddess's shield. Even from that distance, Annabeth could smell the spider's stink, like an entire bakery full of pastries left to go bad for a month.

'What?' the spider pressed. 'What silly thought?'

Annabeth had to force herself not to back away. Broken ankle or no, every nerve in her body pulsed with fear, telling her to get away from the huge spider hovering over her.

'Oh . . . it's just that I was put in charge of redesigning Mount Olympus,' she said. 'You know, after the Titan War. I've completed most of the work, but we need a lot of quality public art. The throne room of the gods, for instance . . . I was thinking your work would be perfect to display there. The Olympians could finally see how talented you are. As I said, it was a silly thought.'

Arachne's hairy abdomen quivered. Her four eyes glimmered as if she had a separate thought behind each and was trying to weave them into a coherent web.

'You're redesigning Mount Olympus,' she said. 'My work . . . in the throne room.'

'Well, other places, too,' Annabeth said. 'The main pavilion could use several of these. That one with the Greek landscape – the Nine Muses would love that. And I'm sure the other gods would be fighting over your work as well. They'd compete to have your tapestries in their palaces. I guess, aside from Athena, none of the gods has ever seen what you can do?'

Arachne snapped her mandibles. 'Hardly. In the old days, Athena tore up all my best work. My tapestries depicted the gods in rather unflattering ways, you see. Your mother didn't appreciate that.'

'Rather hypocritical,' Annabeth said, 'since the gods make

fun of each other all the time. I think the trick would be to pit one god against another. Ares, for instance, would *love* a tapestry making fun of my mother. He's always resented Athena.'

Arachne's head tilted at an unnatural angle. 'You would work against your own mother?'

'I'm just telling you what Ares would like,' Annabeth said. 'And Zeus would love something that made fun of Poseidon. Oh, I'm sure if the Olympians saw your work they'd realize how amazing you are, and I'd have to broker a bidding war. As for working against my mother, why shouldn't I? She sent me here to die, didn't she? The last time I saw her in New York, she basically disowned me.'

Annabeth told her the story. She shared her bitterness and sorrow, and it must have sounded genuine. The spider did not pounce.

'This is Athena's nature,' Arachne hissed. 'She casts aside even her own daughter. The goddess would never allow my tapestries to be shown in the palaces of the gods. She was always jealous of me.'

'But imagine if you could get your revenge at long last.'

'By killing you!'

'I suppose.' Annabeth scratched her head. 'Or . . . by letting me be your agent. I could get your work into Mount Olympus. I could arrange an exhibition for the other gods. By the time my mother found out, it would be too late. The Olympians would finally *see* that your work is better.'

'Then you admit it!' Arachne cried. 'A daughter of Athena admits I am better! Oh, this is sweet to my ears.'

'But a lot of good it does you,' Annabeth pointed out. 'If I die down here, you go on living in the dark. Gaia destroys the gods, and they never realize you were the better weaver.'

The spider hissed.

Annabeth was afraid her mother might suddenly appear and curse her with some terrible affliction. The first lesson every child of Athena learned: Mom was the best at everything, and you should never, *ever* suggest otherwise.

But nothing bad happened. Maybe Athena understood that Annabeth was only saying these things to save her own life. Or maybe Athena was in such in bad shape, split between her Greek and Roman personalities, that she wasn't even paying attention.

'This will not do,' Arachne grumbled. 'I cannot allow it.'

'Well . . .' Annabeth shifted, trying to keep her weight off her throbbing ankle. A new crack appeared in the floor, and she hobbled back.

'Careful!' Arachne snapped. 'The foundations of this shrine have been eaten away over the centuries!'

Annabeth's heartbeat faltered. 'Eaten away?'

'You have no idea how much hatred boils beneath us,' the spider said. 'The spiteful thoughts of *so* many monsters trying to reach the Athena Parthenos and destroy it. My webbing is the only thing holding the room together, girl! One false step, and you'll fall all the way to Tartarus – and, believe me, unlike the Doors of Death, this would be a one-way trip, a very hard fall! I will *not* have you dying before you tell me your plan for my artwork.'

Annabeth's mouth tasted like rust. *All the way to Tartarus?*

She tried to stay focused, but it wasn't easy as she listened to the floor creak and crack, spilling rubble into the void below.

'Right, the plan,' Annabeth said. 'Um . . . as I said, I'd *love* to take your tapestries to Olympus and hang them everywhere. You could rub Athena's nose in your craftsmanship for all eternity. But the only way I could do that . . . No. It's too difficult. You might as well go ahead and kill me.'

'No!' Arachne cried. 'That is unacceptable. It no longer brings me any pleasure to contemplate. I must have my work on Mount Olympus! What must I do?'

Annabeth shook her head. 'Sorry, I shouldn't have said anything. Just push me into Tartarus or something.'

'I refuse!'

'Don't be ridiculous. Kill me.'

'I do not take orders from you! Tell me what I must do! Or . . . or –'

'Or you'll kill me?'

'Yes! No!' The spider pressed her front legs against her head. 'I *must* show my work on Mount Olympus.'

Annabeth tried to contain her excitement. Her plan might actually work . . . but she still had to convince Arachne to do something impossible. She remembered some good advice Frank Zhang had given her: *Keep it simple.*

'I suppose I could pull a few strings,' she conceded.

'I excel at pulling strings!' said Arachne. 'I'm a spider!'

'Yes, but to get your work shown on Mount Olympus, we'd need a proper audition. I'd have to pitch the idea, submit a proposal, put together a portfolio. Hmm . . . do you have any headshots?'

'Headshots?'

'Glossy black-and-white . . . Oh, never mind. The audition piece is the most important thing. These tapestries are excellent. But the gods would require something *really* special – something that shows off your talent in the extreme.'

Arachne snarled. 'Are you suggesting that these are not my best work? Are you challenging me to a contest?'

'Oh, no!' Annabeth laughed. 'Against me? Gosh, no. You are *much* too good. It would only be a contest against *yourself,* to see if you really have what it takes to show your work on Mount Olympus.'

'Of course I do!'

'Well, I certainly think so. But the audition, you know . . . it's a formality. I'm afraid it would be very difficult. Are you sure you don't just want to kill me?'

'Stop saying that!' Arachne screeched. 'What must I make?'

'I'll show you.' Annabeth unslung her backpack. She took out Daedalus's laptop and opened it. The delta logo glowed in the dark.

'What is that?' Arachne asked. 'Some sort of loom?'

'In a way,' Annabeth said. 'It's for weaving ideas. It holds a diagram of the artwork you would build.'

Her fingers trembled on the keyboard. Arachne lowered herself to peer directly over Annabeth's shoulder. Annabeth couldn't help thinking how easily those needlelike teeth could sink into her neck.

She opened her 3-D imaging program. Her last design was

still up – the key to Annabeth's plan, inspired by the most unlikely muse ever: Frank Zhang.

Annabeth did some quick calculations. She increased the dimensions of the model, then showed Arachne how it could be created – strands of material woven into strips, then braided into a long cylinder.

The golden light from the screen illuminated the spider's face. 'You want me to make that? But this is nothing! So small and simple!'

'The actual size would be much bigger,' Annabeth cautioned. 'You see these measurements? Naturally it must be large enough to impress the gods. It may look simple, but the structure has incredible properties. Your spider silk would be the perfect material – soft and flexible, yet strong as steel.'

'I see . . .' Arachne frowned. 'But this isn't even a tapestry.'

'That's why it's a challenge. It's outside your comfort zone. A piece like this – an abstract sculpture – is what the gods are looking for. It would stand in the entry hall of the Olympian throne room for every visitor to see. You would be famous forever!'

Arachne made a discontented hum in her throat. Annabeth could tell she wasn't going for the idea. Her hands started to feel cold and sweaty.

'This would take a great deal of web,' the spider complained. 'More than I could make in a year.'

Annabeth had been hoping for that. She'd calculated the mass and size accordingly. 'You'd need to unravel the statue,' she said. 'Reuse the silk.'

Arachne seemed about to object, but Annabeth waved at the Athena Parthenos like it was nothing. 'What's more important – covering that old statue or proving your artwork is the best? Of course, you'd have to be incredibly careful. You'd need to leave enough webbing to hold the room together. And if you think it's too difficult –'

'I didn't say that!'

'Okay. It's just . . . Athena said that creating this braided structure would be impossible for any weaver, even her. So if you don't think you can –'

'Athena said that?'

'Well, yeah.'

'Ridiculous! I can do it!'

'Great! But you'd need to start right away, before the Olympians choose another artist for their installations.'

Arachne growled. 'If you are tricking me, girl –'

'You'll have me right here as a hostage,' Annabeth reminded her. 'It's not like I can go anywhere. Once this sculpture is complete, you'll agree that it's the most amazing piece you've ever done. If not, I will gladly die.'

Arachne hesitated. Her barbed legs were so close she could've impaled Annabeth with a quick swipe.

'Fine,' the spider said. 'One last challenge – against myself!'

Arachne climbed her web and began to unravel the Athena Parthenos.

L

ANNABETH

ANNABETH LOST TRACK OF TIME.

She could feel the ambrosia she'd eaten earlier starting to repair her leg, but it still hurt so badly that the pain throbbed right up to her neck. All along the walls, small spiders scuttled in the darkness, as if awaiting their mistress's orders. Thousands of them rustled behind the tapestries, making the woven scenes move like wind.

Annabeth sat on the crumbling floor and tried to preserve her strength. While Arachne wasn't watching, she attempted to get some sort of signal on Daedalus's laptop to contact her friends, but of course she had no luck. That left her nothing to do but watch in amazement and horror as Arachne worked, her eight legs moving with hypnotic speed, slowly unravelling the silk strands around the statue.

With its golden clothes and its luminous ivory face, the Athena Parthenos was even scarier than Arachne. It gazed down sternly as if to say, *Bring me tasty snacks or else.* Annabeth could imagine being an Ancient Greek, walking into the Parthenon and seeing this massive goddess with her shield, spear and python, her free hand holding out Nike, the winged spirit of victory. It would've been enough to put a kink in the *chiton* of any mortal.

More than that, the statue radiated power. As Athena was unwrapped, the air around her grew warmer. Her ivory skin glowed with life. All across the room, the smaller spiders became agitated and began retreating back into the hallway.

Annabeth guessed that Arachne's webs had somehow masked and dampened the statue's magic. Now that it was free, the Athena Parthenos filled the chamber with magical energy. Centuries of mortal prayers and burnt offerings had been made in its presence. It was infused with the power of Athena.

Arachne didn't seem to notice. She kept muttering to herself, counting out yards of silk and calculating the number of strands her project would require. Whenever she hesitated, Annabeth called out encouragement and reminded her how wonderful her tapestries would look on Mount Olympus.

The statue grew so warm and bright that Annabeth could see more details of the shrine – the Roman masonry that had probably once been gleaming white, the dark bones of Arachne's past victims and meals hanging in the web, and the massive cables of silk that connected the floor to the ceiling. Annabeth now saw just how fragile the marble tiles were under her feet. They were covered in a fine layer of webbing, like mesh holding together a shattered mirror. Whenever the Athena Parthenos shifted even slightly, more cracks spread and widened along the floor. In some places, there were holes as big as manhole covers. Annabeth almost wished it were dark again. Even if her plan succeeded and she defeated Arachne, she wasn't sure how she could make it out of this chamber alive.

'So much silk,' Arachne muttered. 'I could make twenty tapestries –'

'Keep going!' Annabeth called up. 'You're doing a wonderful job.'

The spider kept working. After what seemed like forever, a mountain of glistening silk was piled at the feet of the statue. The walls of the chamber were still covered in webs. The support cables holding the room together hadn't been disturbed. But the Athena Parthenos was free.

Please wake up, Annabeth begged the statue. *Mother, help me.*

Nothing happened, but the cracks seemed to be spreading across the floor more rapidly. According to Arachne, the malicious thoughts of monsters had eaten away at the shrine's foundations for centuries. If that were true, now that it was free the Athena Parthenos might be attracting even more attention from the monsters in Tartarus.

'The design,' Annabeth said. 'You should hurry.'

She lifted the computer screen for Arachne to see, but the spider snapped, 'I've memorized it, child. I have an artist's eye for detail.'

'Of course you do. But we should hurry.'

'Why?'

'Well . . . so we can introduce your work to the world!'

'Hmm. Very well.'

Arachne began to weave. It was slow work, turning silk strands into long strips of cloth. The chamber rumbled. The cracks at Annabeth's feet became wider.

If Arachne noticed, she didn't seem to care. Annabeth considered trying to push the spider into the pit somehow, but she dismissed the idea. There wasn't a big enough hole and, besides, if the floor gave way, Arachne could probably hang from her silk and escape, while Annabeth and the ancient statue would tumble into Tartarus.

Slowly, Arachne finished the long strips of silk and braided them together. Her skill was flawless. Annabeth couldn't help being impressed. She felt another flicker of doubt about her own mother. What if Arachne *were* a better weaver than Athena?

But Arachne's skill wasn't the point. She had been punished for being prideful and rude. No matter how amazing you were, you couldn't go around insulting the gods. The Olympians were a reminder that there was *always* someone better than you, so you shouldn't get a big head. Still . . . being turned into a monstrous immortal spider seemed like a pretty harsh punishment for bragging.

Arachne worked more quickly, bringing the strands together. Soon, the structure was done. At the feet of the statue lay a braided cylinder of silk strips, five feet in diameter and ten feet long. The surface glistened like abalone shell, but it didn't seem beautiful to Annabeth. It was just functional: a trap. It would only be beautiful if it worked.

Arachne turned to her with a hungry smile. 'Done! Now,

my reward! Prove to me that you can deliver on your promises.'

Annabeth studied the trap. She frowned and walked around it, inspecting the weaving from every angle. Then, careful of her bad ankle, she got down on hands and knees and crawled inside. She'd done the measurements in her head. If she'd got them wrong, her plan was doomed. But she slipped through the silken tunnel without touching the sides. The webbing was sticky, but not impossibly so. She crawled out of the other end and shook her head.

'There's a flaw,' she said.

'What?!' Arachne cried. 'Impossible! I followed your instructions –'

'Inside,' Annabeth said. 'Crawl in and see for yourself. It's right in the middle – a flaw in the weaving.'

Arachne foamed at the mouth. Annabeth was afraid she'd pushed too hard, and the spider would snap her up. She'd be just another set of bones in the cobwebs.

Instead, Arachne stamped her eight legs petulantly. 'I do *not* make mistakes.'

'Oh, it's small,' Annabeth said. 'You can probably fix it. But I don't want to show the gods anything but your best work. Look, go inside and check. If you can fix it, then we'll show it to the Olympians. You'll be the most famous artist of all time. They'll probably fire the Nine Muses and hire you to oversee all the arts. The goddess Arachne . . . yes, I wouldn't be surprised.'

'The goddess . . .' Arachne's breathing turned shallow. 'Yes, yes. I will fix this flaw.'

She poked her head into the tunnel. 'Where is it?'

'Right in the middle,' Annabeth urged. 'Go ahead. It might be a bit snug for you.'

'I'm fine!' she snapped, and wriggled in.

As Annabeth had hoped, the spider's abdomen fitted, but only barely. As she pushed her way in, the braided strips of silk expanded to accommodate her. Arachne got all the way up to her spinnerets.

'I see no flaw!' she announced.

'Really?' Annabeth asked. 'Well, that's odd. Come out and I'll take another look.'

Moment of truth. Arachne wriggled, trying to back up. The woven tunnel contracted around her and held her fast. She tried to wriggle forward, but the trap was already stuck to her abdomen. She couldn't get through that way either. Annabeth had been afraid the spider's barbed legs might puncture the silk, but Arachne's legs were pressed so tightly against her body she could barely move them.

'What – what is this?' she called. 'I am stuck!'

'Ah,' Annabeth said. 'I forgot to tell you. This piece of art is called Chinese Handcuffs. At least, it's a larger variation on that idea. I call it Chinese Spidercuffs.'

'Treachery!' Arachne thrashed and rolled and squirmed, but the trap held her tight.

'It was a matter of survival,' Annabeth corrected. 'You were going to kill me either way, whether I helped you or not, yes?'

'Well, of course! You're a child of Athena.' The trap went still. 'I mean . . . no, of course not! I respect my promises.'

'Uh-huh.' Annabeth stepped back as the braided cylinder

began to thrash again. 'Normally these traps are made from woven bamboo, but spider silk is even better. It will hold you fast, and it's much too strong to break – even for you.'

'Gahhhh!' Arachne rolled and wriggled, but Annabeth moved out of the way. Even with her broken ankle, she could manage to avoid a giant silk finger trap.

'I will destroy you!' Arachne promised. 'I mean . . . no, I'll be very nice to you if you let me out.'

'I'd save my energy if I were you.' Annabeth took a deep breath, relaxing for the first time in hours. 'I'm going to call my friends.'

'You – you're going to call them about my artwork?' Arachne asked hopefully.

Annabeth scanned the room. There had to be a way to send an Iris-message to the *Argo II*. She had some water left in her bottle, but how to create enough light and mist to make a rainbow in a dark cavern?

Arachne began to roll around again. 'You're calling your friends to kill me!' she shrieked. 'I will *not* die! Not like this!'

'Calm down,' Annabeth said. 'We'll let you live. We just want the statue.'

'The statue?'

'Yes.' Annabeth should've left it at that, but her fear was turning to anger and resentment. 'The artwork that I'll display most prominently on Mount Olympus? It won't be yours. The Athena Parthenos belongs there – right in the central park of the gods.'

'No! No, that's horrible!'

'Oh, it won't happen right away,' Annabeth said. 'First

we'll take the statue with us to Greece. A prophecy told us it has the power to help defeat the giants. After that . . . well, we can't simply restore it to the Parthenon. That would raise too many questions. It'll be safer in Mount Olympus. It will unite the children of Athena and bring peace to the Romans and Greeks. Thanks for keeping it safe all these centuries. You've done Athena a great service.'

Arachne screamed and flailed. A strand of silk shot from the monster's spinnerets and attached itself to a tapestry on the far wall. Arachne contracted her abdomen and blindly ripped away the weaving. She continued to roll, shooting silk randomly, pulling over braziers of magic fire and ripping tiles out of the floor. The chamber shook. Tapestries began to burn.

'Stop that!' Annabeth tried to hobble out of the way of the spider's silk. 'You'll bring down the whole cavern and kill us both!'

'Better than seeing you win!' Arachne cried. 'My children! Help me!'

Oh, great. Annabeth had hoped the statue's magic aura would keep away the little spiders, but Arachne continued shrieking, imploring them to help. Annabeth considered killing the spider woman to shut her up. It would be easy to use her knife now. But she hesitated to kill any monster when it was so helpless, even Arachne. Besides, if she stabbed through the braided silk, the trap might unravel. It was possible Arachne could break free before Annabeth could finish her off.

All these thoughts came too late. Spiders began swarming into the chamber. The statue of Athena glowed brighter. The spiders clearly didn't want to approach, but they edged forward as if gathering their courage. Their mother was screaming for help. Eventually they would pour in, overwhelming Annabeth.

'Arachne, stop it!' she yelled. 'I'll –'

Somehow Arachne twisted in her prison, pointing her abdomen towards the sound of Annabeth's voice. A strand of silk hit her in the chest like a heavyweight's glove.

Annabeth fell, her leg flaring with pain. She slashed wildly at the webbing with her dagger as Arachne pulled her towards her snapping spinnerets.

Annabeth managed to cut the strand and crawl away, but the little spiders were closing around her.

She realized her best efforts had not been enough. She wouldn't make it out of here. Arachne's children would kill her at the feet of her mother's statue.

Percy, she thought, *I'm sorry*.

At that moment, the chamber groaned and the cavern ceiling exploded in a blast of fiery light.

ANNABETH

ANNABETH HAD SEEN SOME STRANGE THINGS BEFORE, but she'd never seen it rain cars.

As the roof of the cavern collapsed, sunlight blinded her. She got the briefest glimpse of the *Argo II* hovering above. It must have used its ballistae to blast a hole straight through the ground.

Chunks of tarmac as big as garage doors tumbled down, along with six or seven Italian cars. One would've crushed the Athena Parthenos, but the statue's glowing aura acted like a force field, and the car bounced off. Unfortunately, it fell straight towards Annabeth.

She jumped to one side, twisting her bad foot. A wave of agony almost made her pass out, but she flipped on her back in time to see a bright red Fiat 500 slam into Arachne's silk trap, punching through the cavern floor and disappearing with the Chinese Spidercuffs.

As Arachne fell, she screamed like a freight train on a

collision course, but her wailing rapidly faded. All around Annabeth, more chunks of debris slammed through the floor, riddling it with holes.

The Athena Parthenos remained undamaged, though the marble under its pedestal was a starburst of fractures. Annabeth was covered in cobwebs. Strands of leftover spider silk trailed from her arms and legs like the strings of a marionette, but somehow, amazingly, none of the debris had hit her. She wanted to believe that the statue had protected her, though she suspected it might've been nothing but luck.

The army of spiders had disappeared. Either they had fled back into the darkness, or they'd fallen into the chasm. As daylight flooded the cavern, Arachne's tapestries along the walls crumbled to dust, which Annabeth could hardly bear to watch – especially the tapestry depicting her and Percy.

But none of that mattered when she heard Percy's voice from above: 'Annabeth!'

'Here!' she sobbed.

All the terror seemed to leave her in one massive yelp. As the *Argo II* descended, she saw Percy leaning over the rail. His smile was better than any tapestry she'd ever seen.

The room kept shaking, but Annabeth managed to stand. The floor at her feet seemed stable for the moment. Her backpack was missing, along with Daedalus's laptop. Her bronze knife, which she'd had since she was seven, was also gone – probably fallen into the pit. But Annabeth didn't care. She was alive.

She edged closer to the gaping hole made by the Fiat 500. Jagged rock walls plunged into the darkness as far as

Annabeth could see. A few small ledges jutted out here and there, but Annabeth saw nothing on them – just strands of spider silk dripping over the sides like Christmas tinsel.

Annabeth wondered if Arachne had told the truth about the chasm. Had the spider fallen all the way to Tartarus? She tried to feel satisfied with that idea, but it made her sad. Arachne *had* made some beautiful things. She'd already suffered for aeons. Now her last tapestries had crumbled. After all that, falling into Tartarus seemed like too harsh an end.

Annabeth was dimly aware of the *Argo II* hovering to a stop about forty feet from the floor. It lowered a rope ladder, but Annabeth stood in a daze, staring into the darkness. Then suddenly Percy was next to her, lacing his fingers in hers.

He turned her gently away from the pit and wrapped his arms around her. She buried her face in his chest and broke down in tears.

'It's okay,' he said. 'We're together.'

He didn't say *you're okay*, or *we're alive*. After all they'd been through over the last year, he knew the most important thing was that they were together. She loved him for saying that.

Their friends gathered around them. Nico di Angelo was there, but Annabeth's thoughts were so fuzzy this didn't seem surprising to her. It seemed only right that he would be with them.

'Your leg.' Piper knelt next to her and examined the bubble-wrap cast. 'Oh, Annabeth, what *happened*?'

She started to explain. Talking was difficult, but, as she went along, her words came more easily. Percy didn't let go of her hand, which also made her feel more confident. When she finished, her friends' faces were slack with amazement.

'Gods of Olympus,' Jason said. 'You did all that alone. With a broken ankle.'

'Well . . . *some* of it with a broken ankle.'

Percy grinned. 'You made Arachne weave her own trap? I knew you were good, but Holy Hera – Annabeth, you *did* it. Generations of Athena kids tried and failed. You found the Athena Parthenos!'

Everyone gazed at the statue.

'What do we do with her?' Frank asked. 'She's huge.'

'We'll have to take her with us to Greece,' Annabeth said. 'The statue is powerful. Something about it will help us stop the giants.'

'*Giants' bane stands gold and pale*,' Hazel quoted. '*Won with pain from a woven jail.*' She looked at Annabeth with admiration. 'It was Arachne's jail. You tricked her into weaving it.'

With a *lot* of pain, Annabeth thought.

Leo raised his hands. He made a finger picture frame around the Athena Parthenos like he was taking measurements. 'Well, it might take some rearranging, but I think we can fit her through the bay doors in the stable. If she sticks out of the end, I might have to wrap a flag around her feet or something.'

Annabeth shuddered. She imagined the Athena Parthenos jutting from their trireme with a sign across her pedestal that read: WIDE LOAD.

Then she thought about the other lines of the prophecy:

The twins snuff out the angel's breath, who holds the keys to endless death.

'What about you guys?' she asked. 'What happened with the giants?'

Percy told her about rescuing Nico, the appearance of Bacchus and the fight with the twins in the Colosseum. Nico didn't say much. The poor guy looked like he'd been wandering through a wasteland for six weeks. Percy explained what Nico had found out about the Doors of Death and how they had to be closed on both sides. Even with sunlight streaming in from above, Percy's news made the cavern seem dark again.

'So the mortal side is in Epirus,' she said. 'At least that's somewhere we can reach.'

Nico grimaced. 'But the other side is the problem. Tartarus.'

The word seemed to echo through the chamber. The pit behind them exhaled a cold blast of air. That's when Annabeth knew with certainty. The chasm *did* go straight to the Underworld.

Percy must have felt it, too. He guided her a little further from the edge. Her arms and legs trailed spider silk like a bridal train. She wished she had her dagger to cut that junk off. She almost asked Percy to do the honours with Riptide, but, before she could, he said, 'Bacchus mentioned something about *my* voyage being harder than I expected. Not sure why –'

The chamber groaned. The Athena Parthenos tilted to one side. Its head caught on one of Arachne's support cables, but the marble foundation under the pedestal was crumbling.

Nausea swelled in Annabeth's chest. If the statue fell into the chasm, all her work would be for nothing. Their quest would fail.

'Secure it!' Annabeth cried.

Her friends understood immediately.

'Zhang!' Leo cried. 'Get me to the helm, quick! The coach is up there alone.'

Frank transformed into a giant eagle, and the two of them soared towards the ship.

Jason wrapped his arm around Piper. He turned to Percy. 'Back for you guys in a sec.' He summoned the wind and shot into the air.

'This floor won't last!' Hazel warned. 'The rest of us should get to the ladder.'

Plumes of dust and cobwebs blasted from holes in the floor. The spider's silk support cables trembled like massive guitar strings and began to snap. Hazel lunged for the bottom of the rope ladder and gestured for Nico to follow, but Nico was in no condition to sprint.

Percy gripped Annabeth's hand tighter. 'It'll be fine,' he muttered.

Looking up, she saw grappling lines shoot from the *Argo II* and wrap around the statue. One lassoed Athena's neck like a noose. Leo shouted orders from the helm as Jason and Frank flew frantically from line to line, trying to secure them.

Nico had just reached the ladder when a sharp pain shot up Annabeth's bad leg. She gasped and stumbled.

'What is it?' Percy asked.

She tried to stagger towards the ladder. Why was she

moving backwards instead? Her legs swept out from under her and she fell on her face.

'Her ankle!' Hazel shouted from the ladder. 'Cut it! Cut it!'

Annabeth's mind was woolly from the pain. Cut her ankle?

Apparently Percy didn't realize what Hazel meant either. Then something yanked Annabeth backwards and dragged her towards the pit. Percy lunged. He grabbed her arm, but the momentum carried him along as well.

'Help them!' Hazel yelled.

Annabeth glimpsed Nico hobbling in their direction, Hazel trying to disentangle her cavalry sword from the rope ladder. Their other friends were still focused on the statue, and Hazel's cry was lost in the general shouting and the rumbling of the cavern.

Annabeth sobbed as she hit the edge of the pit. Her legs went over the side. Too late, she realized what was happening: she was tangled in the spider silk. She should have cut it away immediately. She had thought it was just loose line, but with the entire floor covered in cobwebs, she hadn't noticed that one of the strands was wrapped around her foot – and the other end went straight into the pit. It was attached to something heavy down in the darkness, something that was pulling her in.

'No,' Percy muttered, light dawning in his eyes. 'My sword . . .'

But he couldn't reach Riptide without letting go of Annabeth's arm, and Annabeth's strength was gone. She slipped over the edge. Percy fell with her.

Her body slammed into something. She must have blacked out briefly from the pain. When she could see again, she realized that she'd fallen partway into the pit and was dangling over the void. Percy had managed to grab a ledge about fifteen feet below the top of the chasm. He was holding on with one hand, gripping Annabeth's wrist with the other, but the pull on her leg was much too strong.

No escape, said a voice in the darkness below. *I go to Tartarus, and you will come, too.*

Annabeth wasn't sure if she actually heard Arachne's voice or if it was just in her mind.

The pit shook. Percy was the only thing keeping her from falling. He was barely holding on to a ledge the size of a bookshelf.

Nico leaned over the edge of the chasm, thrusting out his hand, but he was much too far away to help. Hazel was yelling for the others, but even if they heard her over all the chaos they'd never make it in time.

Annabeth's leg felt like it was pulling free of her body. Pain washed everything in red. The force of the Underworld tugged at her like dark gravity. She didn't have the strength to fight. She knew she was too far down to be saved.

'Percy, let me go,' she croaked. 'You can't pull me up.'

His face was white with effort. She could see in his eyes that he knew it was hopeless.

'Never,' he said. He looked up at Nico, fifteen feet above. 'The other side, Nico! We'll see you there. Understand?'

Nico's eyes widened. 'But –'

'Lead them there!' Percy shouted. 'Promise me!'

'I – I will.'

Below them, the voice laughed in the darkness. *Sacrifices. Beautiful sacrifices to wake the goddess.*

Percy tightened his grip on Annabeth's wrist. His face was gaunt, scraped and bloody, his hair dusted with cobwebs, but when he locked eyes with her she thought he had never looked more handsome.

'We're staying together,' he promised. 'You're not getting away from me. Never again.'

Only then did she understand what would happen. *A one-way trip. A very hard fall.*

'As long as we're together,' she said.

She heard Nico and Hazel still screaming for help. She saw the sunlight far, far above – maybe the last sunlight she would ever see.

Then Percy let go of his tiny ledge, and together, holding hands, he and Annabeth fell into the endless darkness.

LEO

LEO WAS STILL IN SHOCK.

Everything had happened so quickly. They had secured grappling lines to the Athena Parthenos just as the floor gave way and the final columns of webbing snapped. Jason and Frank dived down to save the others, but they'd only found Nico and Hazel hanging from the rope ladder. Percy and Annabeth were gone. The pit to Tartarus had been buried under several tons of debris. Leo pulled the *Argo II* out of the cavern seconds before the entire place imploded, taking the rest of the parking lot with it.

The *Argo II* was now parked on a hill overlooking the city. Jason, Hazel and Frank had returned to the scene of the catastrophe, hoping to dig through the rubble and find a way to save Percy and Annabeth, but they'd come back demoralized. The cavern was simply gone. The scene was swarming with police and rescue workers. No mortals had been hurt, but the Italians would be scratching their heads for months, wondering how a massive sinkhole had opened right in the middle of a parking lot and swallowed a dozen perfectly good cars.

Dazed with grief, Leo and the others carefully loaded the Athena Parthenos into the hold, using the ship's hydraulic winches with an assist from Frank Zhang, part-time elephant. The statue just fitted, though what they were going to do with it, Leo had no idea.

Coach Hedge was too miserable to help. He kept pacing the deck with tears in his eyes, pulling at his goatee and slapping the side of his head, muttering, 'I should have saved them! I should have blown up more stuff!'

Finally Leo told him to go belowdecks and secure everything for departure. He wasn't doing any good beating himself up.

The six demigods gathered on the quarterdeck and gazed at the distant column of dust still rising from the site of the implosion.

Leo rested his hand on the Archimedes sphere, which now sat on the helm, ready to be installed. He should have been excited. It was the biggest discovery of his life – even bigger than Bunker 9. If he could decipher Archimedes's scrolls, he could do amazing things. He hardly dared to hope, but he might even be able to build a new control disk for a certain dragon friend of his.

Still, the price had been too high.

He could almost hear Nemesis laughing. *I told you we could do business, Leo Valdez.*

He had opened the fortune cookie. He'd got the access code for the sphere and saved Frank and Hazel. But the sacrifice had been Percy and Annabeth. Leo was sure of it.

'It's my fault,' he said miserably.

The others stared at him. Only Hazel seemed to understand. She'd been with him at the Great Salt Lake.

'No,' she insisted. 'No, this is *Gaia's* fault. It had nothing to do with you.'

Leo wanted to believe that, but he couldn't. They'd started this voyage with Leo messing up, firing on New Rome. They'd ended in old Rome with Leo breaking a cookie and paying a price much worse than an eye.

'Leo, listen to me.' Hazel gripped his hand. 'I won't allow you to take the blame. I couldn't bear that after – after Sammy . . .'

She choked up, but Leo knew what she meant. His *bisabuelo* had blamed himself for Hazel's disappearance. Sammy had lived a good life, but he'd gone to his grave believing that he'd spent a cursed diamond and doomed the girl he loved.

Leo didn't want to make Hazel miserable all over again, but this was different. *True success requires sacrifice.* Leo had chosen to break that cookie. Percy and Annabeth had fallen into Tartarus. That couldn't be a coincidence.

Nico di Angelo shuffled over, leaning on his black sword. 'Leo, they're not dead. If they were, I could feel it.'

'How can you be sure?' Leo asked. 'If that pit really led to . . . you know . . . how could you sense them so far away?'

Nico and Hazel shared a look, maybe comparing notes on

their Hades/Pluto death radar. Leo shivered. Hazel had never seemed like a child of the Underworld to him, but Nico di Angelo – that guy was creepy.

'We can't be one hundred percent sure,' Hazel admitted. 'But I think Nico is right. Percy and Annabeth are still alive . . . at least, so far.'

Jason pounded his fist against the rail. 'I should've been *paying attention*. I could have flown down and saved them.'

'Me, too,' Frank moaned. The big dude looked on the verge of tears.

Piper put her hand on Jason's back. 'It's not your fault, either of you. You were trying to save the statue.'

'She's right,' Nico said. 'Even if the pit hadn't been buried, you couldn't have flown into it without being pulled down. I'm the only one who has actually been into Tartarus. It's impossible to describe how powerful that place is. Once you get close, it sucks you in. I never stood a chance.'

Frank sniffled. 'Then Percy and Annabeth don't stand a chance either?'

Nico twisted his silver skull ring. 'Percy is the most powerful demigod I've ever met. No offence to you guys, but it's true. If anybody can survive, he will, especially if he's got Annabeth at his side. They're going to find a way through Tartarus.'

Jason turned. 'To the Doors of Death, you mean. But you told us it's guarded by Gaia's most powerful forces. How could two demigods possibly –?'

'I don't know,' Nico admitted. 'But Percy told me to lead you guys to Epirus, to the mortal side of the doorway. He's planning on meeting us there. If we can survive the House of Hades, fight our way through Gaia's forces, then maybe we can work together with Percy and Annabeth and seal the Doors of Death from both sides.'

'And get Percy and Annabeth back safely?' Leo asked.

'Maybe.'

Leo didn't like the way Nico said that, as if he wasn't sharing all his doubts. Besides, Leo knew something about locks and doors. If the Doors of Death needed to be sealed from both sides, how could they do that unless someone stayed in the Underworld, trapped?

Nico took a deep breath. 'I don't know how they'll manage it, but Percy and Annabeth will find a way. They'll journey through Tartarus and find the Doors of Death. When they do, we have to be ready.'

'It won't be easy,' Hazel said. 'Gaia will throw everything she's got at us to keep us from reaching Epirus.'

'What else is new?' Jason sighed.

Piper nodded. 'We've got no choice. We have to seal the Doors of Death before we can stop the giants from raising Gaia. Otherwise her armies will never die. And we've got to hurry. The Romans are in New York. Soon, they'll be marching on Camp Half-Blood.'

'We've got one month at best,' Jason added. 'Ephialtes said Gaia would awaken in exactly one month.'

Leo straightened. 'We can do it.'

Everyone stared at him.

'The Archimedes sphere can upgrade the ship,' he said, hoping he was right. 'I'm going to study those ancient scrolls we got. There's got to be all kinds of new weapons I can make.

We're going to hit Gaia's armies with a whole new arsenal of hurt.'

At the prow of the ship, Festus creaked his jaw and blew fire defiantly.

Jason managed a smile. He clapped Leo on the shoulder.

'Sounds like a plan, Admiral. You want to set the course?'

They kidded him, calling him Admiral, but for once Leo accepted the title. This was his ship. He hadn't come this far to be stopped.

They would find this House of Hades. They'd take the Doors of Death. And by the gods, if Leo had to design a grabber arm long enough to snatch Percy and Annabeth out of Tartarus, then that's what he would do.

Nemesis wanted him to wreak vengeance on Gaia? Leo would be happy to oblige. He was going to make Gaia sorry she had ever messed with Leo Valdez.

'Yeah.' He took one last look at the cityscape of Rome, turning blood-red in the sunset. 'Festus, raise the sails. We've got some friends to save.'

Glossary

AΘE   alpha, theta, epsilon. In Greek it stands for *of the Athenians*, or *the children of Athena*.

Achelous   a *potamus*, or river god

Alcyoneus   the eldest of the giants born to Gaia, destined to fight Pluto

Amazons   a nation of all-female warriors

Aphrodite   the Greek goddess of love and beauty. She was married to Hephaestus, but she loved Ares, the god of war. Roman form: Venus

Arachne   a weaver who claimed to have skills superior to Athena's. This angered the goddess, who destroyed Arachne's tapestry and loom. Arachne hung herself, and Athena brought her back to life as a spider.

Archimedes   a Greek mathematician, physicist, engineer, inventor and astronomer who lived between 287 and 212 BCE and is regarded as one of the leading scientists in classical antiquity

Ares   the Greek god of war; the son of Zeus and Hera, and half brother to Athena. Roman form: Mars

argentum   silver

Argo II   the fantastical ship built by Leo, which can both sail and fly and has Festus's bronze dragon head as its figurehead. The ship was named after the *Argo*, the vessel used by a band of Greek heroes who accompanied Jason on his quest to find the Golden Fleece.

Athena   the Greek goddess of wisdom. Roman form: Minerva

Athena Parthenos   a giant statue of Athena: the most famous Greek statue of all time

augury   a sign of something coming, an omen; the practice of divining the future

aurum   gold

Bacchus   the Roman god of wine and revelry. Greek form: Dionysus

ballista (ballistae, pl.)   a Roman missile siege weapon that launched a large projectile at a distant target (*see also* **scorpion ballista**)

Bellona   a Roman goddess of war

Camp Half-Blood   the training ground for Greek demigods, located on Long Island, New York

Camp Jupiter   the training ground for Roman demigods, located between the Oakland Hills and the Berkeley Hills, in California

Celestial bronze   a rare metal deadly to monsters

centaur   a race of creatures that is half human, half horse

centurion   an officer of the Roman army

Ceres the Roman goddess of agriculture. Greek form: Demeter

charmspeak a blessing bestowed by Aphrodite on her children that enables them to persuade others with their voice

chiton a Greek garment; a sleeveless piece of linen or wool secured at the shoulders by brooches and at the waist by a belt

Chrysaor the brother of Pegasus, the son of Poseidon and Medusa; known as 'the Gold Sword'

Circe a Greek sorceress. In ancient times, she turned Odysseus's crew into swine.

Colosseum an elliptical amphitheatre in the centre of Rome, Italy. Capable of seating 50,000 spectators, the Colosseum was used for gladiatorial contests and public spectacles such as mock sea battles, animal hunts, executions, re-enactments of famous battles and dramas.

cornucopia a large horn-shaped container overflowing with edibles or wealth in some form. The cornucopia was created when Heracles (Roman: Hercules) wrestled with the river god Achelous and wrenched off one of his horns.

Cyclops a member of a primordial race of giants (**Cyclopes**, pl.), each with a single eye in the middle of his or her forehead

Daedalus in Greek mythology, a skilled craftsman who created the Labyrinth on Crete in which the Minotaur (part man, part bull) was kept

Deianira Heracles's second wife. She was of such striking beauty that both Heracles and Achelous wanted to marry her and there was a contest to win her hand. The centaur Nessus tricked her into killing Heracles by dipping his tunic in what she thought was a love potion but was actually Nessus's poisonous blood.

Demeter   the Greek goddess of agriculture, a daughter of the Titans Rhea and Kronos. Roman form: Ceres

denarius   (**denarii**, pl.) the most common coin in the Roman currency system

Dionysus   the Greek god of wine and revelry, a son of Zeus. Roman form: Bacchus

Doors of Death   doors to a well-hidden passageway that when open allow souls to travel from the Underworld to the world of mortals

drachma   the silver coin of Ancient Greece

drakon   gigantic serpent

eidolon   possessing spirit

Ephialtes and Otis   twin giants, sons of Gaia

Epirus   a region presently in northwestern Greece and southern Albania

Eurystheus   a grandson of Perseus, who, through the favour of Hera, inherited the kingship of Mycenae, which Zeus had intended for Heracles

faun   a Roman forest god, part goat and part man. Greek form: satyr

Fortuna   the Roman goddess of fortune and good luck. Greek form: Tyche

Forum, Roman   the centre of Ancient Rome. The Roman Forum was a plaza where Romans conducted business, trials and religious activities.

Gaia the Greek earth goddess; mother of Titans, giants, Cyclopes and other monsters. Roman form: Terra

gladius a short sword

Gorgons three monstrous sisters who have hair of living, venomous snakes. The most famous, Medusa, had eyes that turned the beholder to stone.

greaves shin armour

Greek fire an incendiary weapon used in naval battles because it can continue burning in water

Hades the Greek god of death and riches. Roman form: Pluto

Hadrian a Roman Emperor who ruled from 117 to 138 CE. He is best known for building Hadrian's Wall, which marked the northern limit of Roman Britain. In Rome, he rebuilt the Pantheon and constructed the Temple of Venus and Roma.

Hagno a nymph who is said to have brought up Zeus. On Mount Lycaeus in Arcadia there was a well sacred to and named after her.

harpy a winged female creature that snatches things

Hebe the goddess of youth; the daughter of Zeus and Hera, and married to Heracles. Roman form: Juventas

Hephaestus the Greek god of fire and crafts and of blacksmiths; the son of Zeus and Hera, and married to Aphrodite. Roman form: Vulcan

Hera the Greek goddess of marriage; Zeus's wife and sister. Roman form: Juno

Heracles the Greek equivalent of Hercules; the son of Zeus and Alcmene; the strongest of all mortals

Hercules   the Roman equivalent of Heracles; the son of Jupiter and Alcmene, who was born with great strength

hippocampi   creatures that from the waist up have the body of a horse and from the waist down have silvery fish bodies, with glistening scales and rainbow tail fins. They were used to draw Poseidon's chariot, and sea foam was created by their movement.

hippodrome   a Greek stadium for horse racing and chariot racing

House of Hades   an underground temple in Epirus, Greece, dedicated to Hades and Persephone, sometimes called a necromanteion, or 'oracle of death'. Ancient Greeks believed it marked one entrance to the Underworld, and pilgrims would go there to commune with the dead.

hypogeum   the area under a coliseum that housed set pieces and machinery used for special effects

ichthyocentaur   a fish-centaur described as having the forefeet of a horse, a human torso and head, and a fish tail. It is sometimes shown with a pair of lobster-claw horns.

Imperial gold   a rare metal deadly to monsters, consecrated at the Pantheon; its existence was a closely guarded secret of the emperors

Invidia   the Roman goddess of revenge. Greek form: Nemesis

Iris   the Greek rainbow goddess and a messenger of the gods; the daughter of Thaumas and Electra. Roman form: Iris

Juno   the Roman goddess of women, marriage and fertility;

sister and wife of Jupiter; mother of Mars. Greek form: Hera

Jupiter   the Roman king of the gods; also called Jupiter Optimus Maximus (the best and the greatest). Greek form: Zeus

Juventas   the Roman goddess of youth. Greek form: Hebe

Kalends of July   the first day of July, which was sacred to Juno

karpoi   grain spirits

Katoptris   Piper's dagger, once owned by Helen of Troy. The word means 'looking glass'.

Keto   the Greek goddess of sea monsters and large sea creatures, such as whales and sharks. She is the daughter of Gaia and the sister-wife of Phorcys, god of the dangers of the sea.

Khione   the Greek goddess of snow; daughter of Boreas

Kronos   the Greek god of agriculture, the son of Uranus and Gaia and the father of Zeus. Roman form: Saturn

Lar   a house god, ancestral spirit of Rome (**Lares**, pl.)

Lupa   the sacred Roman she-wolf that nursed the foundling twins Romulus and Remus

Marcus Agrippa   a Roman statesman and general, defence minister to Octavian and responsible for most of his military victories. He commissioned the Pantheon as a temple to all the gods of Ancient Rome.

Mare Nostrum   Latin for *Our Sea*; a Roman name for the Mediterranean Sea

Mars   the Roman god of war; also called Mars Ultor. Patron of the empire; divine father of Romulus and Remus. Greek form: Ares

Minerva   the Roman goddess of wisdom. Greek form: Athena

Minotaur   a monster with the head of a bull on the body of a man

Mist   a magic force that disguises things from mortals

Mithras   Originally a Persian god of the sun, Mithras was worshipped by Roman warriors as a guardian of arms and a patron of soldiers.

muskeg   bog

Narcissus   a Greek hunter who was renowned for his beauty. He was exceptionally proud and disdained those who loved him. Nemesis saw this and attracted Narcissus to a pool where he saw his reflection in the water and fell in love with it. Unable to leave the beauty of his reflection, Narcissus died.

Nemesis   the Greek goddess of revenge. Roman form: Invidia

Neptune   the Roman god of the sea. Greek form: Poseidon

Nereids   fifty female sea spirits; patrons of sailors and fishermen and caretakers of the sea's bounty

Nessus   a crafty centaur who tricked Deianira into killing Heracles

New Rome   a community near Camp Jupiter where demigods can live together in peace, without interference from mortals or monsters

Nike   the Greek goddess of strength, speed and victory. Roman form: Victoria

nymph   a female nature deity who animates nature

nymphaeum   a shrine to nymphs

Pantheon   a building in Rome, Italy, commissioned by Marcus Agrippa as a temple to all the gods of Ancient Rome, and rebuilt by Emperor Hadrian in about 126 CE

pater   Latin for *father*; also the name of an Ancient Roman god of the Underworld, later subsumed by Pluto

pauldron   a piece of plate armour for the shoulder and the upper part of the arm

Pegasus   a winged divine horse in Greek mythology; sired by Poseidon in his role as horse-god, and foaled by the Gorgon Medusa; the brother of Chrysaor

Persephone   the Greek queen of the Underworld; wife of Hades; daughter of Zeus and Demeter. Roman form: Proserpine

Phorcys   a primordial god of the dangers of the sea in Greek mythology; son of Gaia; brother-husband of Keto

Piazza Navona   a city square in Rome, built on the site of the Stadium of Domitian, where Ancient Romans watched competitive games

Pluto   the Roman god of death and riches. Greek form: Hades

Polybotes   the giant son of Gaia, the Earth Mother

Pomerian Line   the boundary around New Rome and, in ancient times, the city limits of Rome

Porphyrion   the king of the Giants in Greek and Roman mythology

Poseidon   the Greek god of the sea; son of the Titans Kronos

and Rhea, and brother of Zeus and Hades. Roman form:
Neptune

praetor   an elected Roman magistrate and commander of
the army

Proserpine   Roman queen of the Underworld. Greek form:
Persephone

Rhea Silvia   a priestess and mother of the twins Romulus
and Remus, who founded Rome

Riptide   the name of Percy Jackson's sword (*Anaklusmos* in
Greek)

Romulus and Remus   the twin sons of Mars and the priestess Rhea Silvia. They were thrown into the River Tiber
by their human father, Amulius, and rescued and raised
by a she-wolf. Upon reaching adulthood, they founded
Rome.

Saturn   the Roman god of agriculture; the son of Uranus
and Gaia, and the father of Jupiter. Greek form: Kronos

satyr   a Greek forest god, part goat and part man. Roman
equivalent: faun

scorpion ballista   a Roman missile siege weapon that
launched a large projectile at a distant target

Senatus Populusque Romanus (SPQR)   meaning 'The Senate
and People of Rome', refers to the government of the
Roman Republic and is used as an official emblem of
Rome

skolopendra   a gargantuan Greek sea monster with hairy
nostrils, a flat crayfish-like tail and rows of webbed feet
lining its flanks

Stymphalian birds   in Greek mythology, man-eating birds with bronze beaks and sharp metallic feathers they could launch at their victims; sacred to Ares, the god of war

Sybilline Books   a collection of prophecies in rhyme written in Greek. Tarquinius Superbus, a king of Rome, bought them from a prophetess named Sibyl and consulted them in times of great danger.

Tartarus   husband of Gaia; spirit of the abyss; father of the giants

telkhines   mysterious sea demons and smiths native to the islands of Kaos and Rhodes; children of Thalassa and Pontus; they had flippers instead of hands, and dogs' heads, and were known as fish children

Terminus   the Roman god of boundaries and landmarks

Terra   the Roman goddess of the Earth. Greek form: Gaia

Thanatos   the Greek god of death. Roman form: Letus

thyrsus   Bacchus's weapon, a staff topped by a pinecone and twined with ivy

Tiber River   the third-longest river in Italy. Rome was founded on its banks. In Ancient Rome, executed criminals were thrown into the river.

Tiberius   was Roman Emperor from 14 CE to 37 CE. He was one of Rome's greatest generals, but he came to be remembered as a reclusive and sombre ruler who never really wanted to be emperor.

Titans   a race of powerful Greek deities, descendants of Gaia and Uranus, who ruled during the Golden Age and were overthrown by a race of younger gods, the Olympians

Trevi Fountain   a fountain in the Trevi district in Rome. Standing more than eighty-five feet high and sixty-five feet wide, it is the largest Baroque fountain in the city and one of the most famous fountains in the world.

trireme   an Ancient Greek or Roman warship, having three tiers of oars on each side

Tyche   the Greek goddess of good luck; daughter of Hermes and Aphrodite. Roman form: Fortuna

Venus   the Roman goddess of love and beauty. She was married to Vulcan, but she loved Mars, the god of war. Greek form: Aphrodite

Vestal Virgins   Roman priestesses of Vesta, goddess of the hearth. The Vestals were free of the usual social obligations to marry and bear children and took a vow of chastity in order to devote themselves to the study and observance of ritual.

Via Labicana   an ancient road of Italy, leading east-southeast from Rome

Via Principalis   the main street in a Roman camp or fort

Victoria   the Roman goddess of strength, speed and victory. Greek form: Nike

Vulcan   the Roman god of fire and crafts and of blacksmiths; the son of Jupiter and Juno, and married to Venus. Greek form: Hephaestus

Wolf House   a ruined mansion, originally commissioned by Jack London near Sonoma, California, where Percy Jackson was trained as a Roman demigod by Lupa

Zeus   Greek god of the sky and king of the gods. Roman form: Jupiter

Find out what happens next!

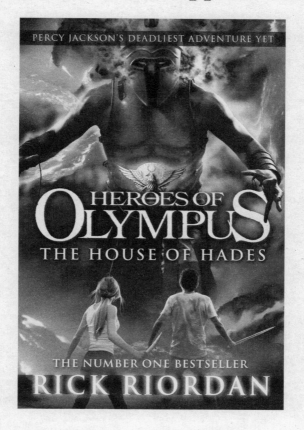

Turn over to read the
thrilling first chapter of

THE HOUSE OF HADES

I

HAZEL

DURING THE THIRD ATTACK, Hazel almost ate a boulder. She was peering into the fog, wondering how it could be so difficult to fly across one stupid mountain range, when the ship's alarm bells sounded.

'Hard to port!' Nico yelled from the foremast of the flying ship.

Back at the helm, Leo yanked the wheel. The *Argo II* veered left, its aerial oars slashing through the clouds like rows of knives.

Hazel made the mistake of looking over the rail. A dark, spherical shape hurtled towards her. She thought, *Why is the moon coming at us?* Then she yelped and hit the deck. The huge rock passed so close overhead it blew her hair out of her face.

CRACK!

The foremast collapsed – sail, spars and Nico all crashing to the deck. The boulder, roughly the size of a pickup truck, tumbled off into the fog like it had important business elsewhere.

'Nico!' Hazel scrambled over to him as Leo brought the ship level.

'I'm fine,' Nico muttered, kicking folds of canvas off his legs.

She helped him up, and they stumbled to the bow. Hazel peeked over more carefully this time. The clouds parted just long enough to reveal the top of the mountain below them: a spearhead of black rock jutting from mossy green slopes. Standing at the summit was a mountain god – one of the *numina montanum*, Jason had called them. Or *ourae*, in Greek. Whatever you called them, they were nasty.

Like the others they had faced, this one wore a simple white tunic over skin as rough and dark as basalt. He was about twenty feet tall and extremely muscular, with a flowing white beard, scraggly hair and a wild look in his eyes, like a crazy hermit. He bellowed something Hazel didn't understand, but it obviously wasn't welcoming. With his bare hands, he prised another chunk of rock from his mountain and began shaping it into a ball.

The scene disappeared in the fog, but when the mountain god bellowed again other *numina* answered in the distance, their voices echoing through the valleys.

'Stupid rock gods!' Leo yelled from the helm. 'That's the *third* time I've had to replace that mast! You think they grow on trees?'

Nico frowned. 'Masts *are* from trees.'

'That's not the point!' Leo snatched up one of his controls, rigged from a Nintendo Wii stick, and spun it in a circle. A few feet away, a trapdoor opened in the deck. A Celestial-bronze cannon rose. Hazel just had time to cover her ears before it discharged into the sky, spraying a dozen metal spheres that trailed green fire. The spheres grew spikes in midair, like helicopter blades, and hurtled away into the fog.

A moment later, a series of explosions crackled across the mountains, followed by the outraged roars of mountain gods.

'Ha!' Leo yelled.

Unfortunately, Hazel guessed, judging from their last two encounters, Leo's newest weapon had only annoyed the *numina*.

Another boulder whistled through the air off to their starboard side.

Nico yelled, 'Get us out of here!'

Leo muttered some unflattering comments about *numina*, but he turned the wheel. The engines hummed. Magical rigging lashed itself tight, and the ship tacked to port. The *Argo II* picked up speed, retreating north-west, as they'd been doing for the past two days.

Hazel didn't relax until they were out of the mountains. The fog cleared. Below them, morning sunlight illuminated the Italian countryside – rolling green hills and golden fields not too different from those in northern California. Hazel could almost imagine she was sailing home to Camp Jupiter.

The thought weighed on her chest. Camp Jupiter had only been her home for nine months, since Nico had brought her back from the Underworld. But she missed it more than her birthplace of New Orleans, and *definitely* more than Alaska, where she'd died back in 1942.

She missed her bunk in the Fifth Cohort barracks. She missed dinners in the mess hall, with wind spirits whisking platters through the air and legionnaires joking about the war games. She wanted to wander the streets of New Rome, holding hands with Frank Zhang. She wanted to experience just being a regular girl for once, with an actual sweet, caring boyfriend.

Most of all, she wanted to feel safe. She was tired of being scared and worried all the time.

She stood on the quarterdeck as Nico picked mast splinters out of his arms and Leo punched buttons on the ship's console.

'Well, *that* was sucktastic,' Leo said. 'Should I wake the others?'

Hazel was tempted to say yes, but the other crew members had taken the night shift and had earned their rest. They were exhausted from defending the ship. Every few hours, it seemed, some Roman monster had decided the *Argo II* looked like a tasty treat.

A few weeks ago, Hazel wouldn't have believed that anyone could sleep through a *numina* attack, but now she imagined her friends were still snoring away belowdecks. Whenever *she* got a chance to crash, she slept like a coma patient.

'They need rest,' she said. 'We'll have to figure out another way on our own.'

'Huh.' Leo scowled at his monitor. In his tattered work shirt and grease-splattered jeans, he looked like he'd just lost a wrestling match with a locomotive.

Ever since their friends Percy and Annabeth had fallen into Tartarus, Leo had been working almost non-stop. He'd been acting angrier and even more driven than usual.

Hazel worried about him. But part of her was relieved by the change. Whenever Leo smiled and joked, he looked *too* much like Sammy, his great-grandfather ... Hazel's first boyfriend back in 1942.

Ugh, why did her life have to be so complicated?

'Another way,' Leo muttered. 'Do you see one?'

On his monitor glowed a map of Italy. The Apennine Mountains ran down the middle of the boot-shaped country. A green dot for the *Argo II* blinked on the western side of the range, a few hundred miles north of Rome. Their path should have been simple. They needed to get to a place called Epirus in Greece and find an old temple called the House of Hades (or Pluto, as the Romans called him; or as Hazel liked to think of him: the World's Worst Absent Father).

To reach Epirus, all they had to do was go straight east – over the Apennines and across the Adriatic Sea. But it hadn't worked out that way. Each time they tried to cross the spine of Italy, the mountain gods attacked.

For the past two days they'd skirted north, hoping to find a safe pass, with no luck. The *numina montanum* were sons of Gaia, Hazel's least favourite goddess. That made them *very* determined enemies. The *Argo II* couldn't fly high enough to avoid their attacks and, even with all its defences, the ship couldn't make it across the range without being smashed to pieces.

'It's our fault,' Hazel said. 'Nico's and mine. The *numina* can sense us.'

She glanced at her half-brother. Since they'd rescued him from the giants, he'd started to regain his strength, but he was still painfully thin. His black shirt and jeans hung off his skeletal frame. Long, dark hair framed his sunken eyes. His olive complexion had turned a sickly greenish-white, like the colour of tree sap.

In human years, he was barely fourteen, just a year older than Hazel, but that didn't tell the whole story. Like Hazel, Nico di Angelo was a demigod from another era. He radiated a kind of *old* energy – a melancholy that came from knowing he didn't belong in the modern world.

Hazel hadn't known him very long, but she understood, even shared his sadness. The children of Hades (Pluto – whichever) rarely had happy lives. And, judging from what Nico had told her the night before, their biggest challenge was yet to come when they reached the House of Hades – a challenge he'd implored her to keep secret from the others.

Nico gripped the hilt of his Stygian iron sword. 'Earth spirits don't like children of the Underworld. That's true. We get under their skin – *literally*. But I think the *numina* could sense this ship anyway. We're carrying the Athena Parthenos. That thing is like a magical beacon.'

Hazel shivered, thinking of the massive statue that took up most of the hold. They'd sacrificed so much, saving it from the cavern under Rome, but they had no idea what to do with it. So far the only thing it seemed to be good for was alerting more monsters to their presence.

Leo traced his finger down the map of Italy. 'So crossing the mountains is out. Thing is they go a long way in either direction.'

'We could go by sea,' Hazel suggested. 'Sail around the southern tip of Italy.'

'That's a long way,' Nico said. 'Plus, we don't have . . .' His voice cracked. 'You know . . . our sea expert, Percy.'

The name hung in the air like an impending storm.

Percy Jackson, son of Poseidon . . . probably the demigod Hazel admired most. He'd saved her life so many times on their quest to Alaska, but when he had needed Hazel's help in Rome she'd failed him. She'd watched, powerless, as he and Annabeth had plunged into that pit . . .

Hazel took a deep breath. Percy and Annabeth were still alive. She knew that in her heart. She could *still* help them if she could get to the House of Hades, if she could survive the challenge Nico had warned her about . . .

'What about continuing north?' she asked. 'There *has* to be a break in the mountains, or something.'

Leo fiddled with the bronze Archimedes sphere that he'd installed on the console – his newest and most dangerous toy. Every time Hazel looked at the thing, her mouth went dry. She worried that Leo would turn the wrong combination on the sphere and accidentally eject them all from the deck, or blow up the ship, or turn the *Argo II* into a giant toaster.

Fortunately, they got lucky. The sphere grew a camera lens and projected a 3-D image of the Apennine Mountains above the console.

'I dunno.' Leo examined the hologram. 'I don't see any good passes to the north. But I like that idea better than backtracking south. I'm done with Rome.'

No one argued with that. Rome had not been a good experience.

'Whatever we do,' Nico said, 'we have to hurry. Every day that Annabeth and Percy are in Tartarus . . .'

He didn't need to finish. They had to hope Percy and Annabeth could survive long enough to find the Tartarus side of the Doors of Death. Then, assuming the *Argo II* could reach the House of Hades, they *might* be able to open the doors on the mortal side, save their friends and seal the entrance, stopping Gaia's forces from being reincarnated in the mortal world, over and over.

Yes . . . nothing could go wrong with *that* plan.

Nico scowled at the Italian countryside below them. 'Maybe we *should* wake the others. This decision affects us all.'

'No,' Hazel said. 'We can find a solution.'

She wasn't sure why she felt so strongly about it, but since leaving Rome the crew had started to lose its cohesion. They'd been learning to work as a team. Then *bam* . . . their two most important members had fallen into Tartarus. Percy had been their backbone. He'd given them confidence as they sailed across the Atlantic and into the Mediterranean. As for Annabeth – she'd been the de facto leader of the quest. She'd recovered the Athena Parthenos single-handedly. She was the smartest of the seven, the one with the answers.

If Hazel woke up the rest of the crew every time they had

a problem, they'd just start arguing again, feeling more and more hopeless.

She had to make Percy and Annabeth proud of her. She had to take the initiative. She couldn't believe her only role in this quest would be what Nico had warned her about – removing the obstacle waiting for them in the House of Hades. She pushed the thought aside.

'We need some creative thinking,' she said. 'Another way to cross those mountains, or a way to hide ourselves from the *numina*.'

Nico sighed. 'If I was on my own, I could shadow-travel. But that won't work for an entire ship. And, honestly, I'm not sure I have the strength to even transport *myself* any more.'

'I could maybe rig some kind of camouflage,' Leo said, 'like a smoke screen to hide us in the clouds.' He didn't sound very enthusiastic.

Hazel stared down at the rolling farmland, thinking about what lay beneath it – the realm of her father, lord of the Underworld. She'd only met Pluto once, and she hadn't even realized who he was. She certainly had never expected help from him – not when she was alive the first time, not during her time as a spirit in the Underworld, not since Nico had brought her back to the world of the living.

Her dad's servant Thanatos, god of death, had suggested that Pluto might be doing Hazel a favour by ignoring her. After all, she wasn't supposed to be alive. If Pluto took notice of her, he might have to return her to the land of the dead.

Which meant calling on Pluto would be a very bad idea. And yet . . .

Please, Dad, she found herself praying. *I have to find a way to your temple in Greece – the House of Hades. If you're down there, show me what to do.*

At the edge of the horizon, a flicker of movement caught her eye – something small and beige racing across the fields at incredible speed, leaving a vapour trail like a plane's.

Hazel couldn't believe it. She didn't dare hope, but it *had* to be . . . 'Arion.'

'What?' Nico asked.

Leo let out a happy whoop as the dust cloud got closer. 'It's her horse, man! You missed that whole part. We haven't seen him since Kansas!'

Hazel laughed – the first time she'd laughed in days. It felt so good to see her old friend.

About a mile to the north, the small beige dot circled a hill and stopped at the summit. He was difficult to make out, but when the horse reared and whinnied the sound carried all the way to the *Argo II*. Hazel had no doubt – it was Arion.

'We have to meet him,' she said. 'He's here to help.'

'Yeah, okay.' Leo scratched his head. 'But, uh, we talked about not landing the ship on the ground any more, remember? You know, with Gaia wanting to destroy us, and all.'

'Just get me close, and I'll use the rope ladder.' Hazel's heart was pounding. 'I think Arion wants to tell me something.'

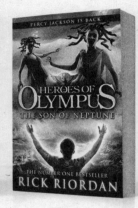

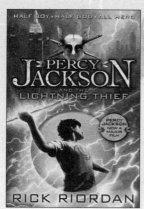

FROM

THE MYTH MASTER
RICK RIORDAN

PERCY JACKSON FOUGHT GREEK GODS.
NOW THE GODS OF EGYPT ARE WAKING IN
THE MODERN WORLD. . .

www.rickriordanmythmaster.co.uk